T0267613

ADAM CESARE

CLOWN IN A CORNFIELD

3

The CHURCH of FRENDO

HARPER TEEN

An Imprint of HarperCollinsPublishers

ALSO BY
ADAM CESARE

Clown in a Cornfield
Clown in a Cornfield 2: Frendo Lives

Library of Congress Control Number: 2023948480
ISBN 978-0-06-332501-2

Typography Jenna Stempel-Lobell
24 25 26 27 28 LBC 5 4 3 2 1
First Edition

For MQ. And Jen, again.

PROLOGUE

SOMEWHERE OUTSIDE TALLAHASSEE, FLORIDA

I haven't done anything to deserve this!

That was the final thought through Charlie Rome's mind before losing consciousness in the Waffle House parking lot.

Several hours later, a less coherent version of that same thought—"Nothing! Did nothing!"—were the first words Charlie sputtered upon waking.

If there was anyone to hear him, they didn't answer.

Charlie shivered in the dark, felt around to discover that his left wrist was chained to a length of pipe.

The floor was cold under him. And the pipe must have been leaking, because the back of his jeans was wet. He tried to stand but couldn't, there was an algae slickness under his heel. The leak must've been going for a while.

He jangled his wrist. There wasn't enough slack in the chain to let him stand anyway.

"Hello?" he asked into the dark, and then, louder: "Help!"

That was all Charlie could manage; his head throbbed, and the reverb of his own voice against tile made the pain even worse.

He wondered how long he'd been here. There were no windows in this place, just a faint line of green/blue light straight ahead, probably the gap under a door. To either side of that door . . . how the fuck did he know? He couldn't see anything but the line, the rest of the room an abyss.

It had been two or three a.m. when he'd been walking to his car. He wondered how much time he'd spent unconscious, if it was daytime by now.

Never mind time or light, Charlie's head was killing him. It was hard to tell how much of his headache was from the hit and how much was the pre–Waffle House drinking he'd been doing down at the Corner Pocket.

Fuck, Charlie thought.

This was why he hated drinking alone. This was why he should've kept more than one friend. Alone, there was nobody with you to help, nobody but the bartender to keep a count, nobody to . . .

He tried to remember how he'd gotten here. Where here even was.

Did he owe money?

Yes, of course he owed money. More than usual. Recent events had cleaned him out. But he didn't think the cable company would've jumped to kidnapping after final notice and shutting off his HBO.

I haven't done anything to deserve this.

Why had he been thinking that?

It was because, while fumbling for his keys, in the window glare he'd seen someone.

But *who* had he seen creeping up behind h—

There was a noise.

In the blackness to the right side of the door, someone sighed.

Charlie wasn't alone in here.

There was someone standing in that corner.

He stared.

His eyes didn't adjust, but he kept staring.

No image resolved itself out of the blackness.

There were no additional noises. But he knew what he'd heard.

He *knew* there was someone there, his eyes working to see something, any shape in the gloom.

Click.

The sudden flash of white light was worse than the hit in the parking lot. Worse than the hangover. Worse than anything.

Charlie Rome clenched his eyelids closed, squeezing out

tears, his vision swimming pink and splotchy with his own blood vessels.

The first thing he noticed as the pain subsided was now the *front* of his jeans was wet.

And when he could finally open his eyes, to see who was in this cold, wet room with him? He wished he hadn't.

Frendo the Clown stood in the corner.

Not the full costume.

Just the mask.

A female figure wearing a Frendo mask, a grease-stained tank top, and holding behind her a . . .

Eeeeeeeeeeeeeeeee.

The screech of metal against tile caused Charlie to spasm in pain, his left wrist pinching as he tried to cover his ears but the chain stopping his hand short.

Frendo moved to the center of the room.

She stood above a drain in the tile.

The sound had been a pair of bolt cutters, blades down, dragged across the floor behind her. The tool's handles were several feet long, tall enough they came to the woman's waist.

"Where is he?" Frendo asked. The person behind the mask didn't growl, didn't menace him with the bolt cutters. She was almost calm about it.

"W-where's w-who?" He didn't need to exaggerate the tremor in his voice. He was scared shitless.

And he *hadn't done anything to deserve this.*

"Your buddy," Frendo said.

Charlie looked up at her, confused. *Trying* to look confused. If she was able to read the confusion on his face, that he had *no idea* what she was talking about, then she would let him go. Right?

"The buddy you went on a road trip with last October," she said.

Oh, Charlie thought.

And beyond the dark eyeholes of the mask, she must have seen him thinking it.

Because Charlie *did* know who she meant.

Frendo lifted one hand, could have been reading from a note she had there, could have been messing with him. "Guy I'm looking for. His legal name is Benjamin Koontz. And his internet alias is . . ." She paused, humor in her voice.

Clownstick, Charlie thought, goose bumps breaking out on his arms. *Clownstick oh fuck oh fuck I told Ben not to get into this shit.*

"Clownstick69," she said.

"Who?" Charlie asked. "What are you talking about?"

But it was no use. Charlie wasn't a great actor under the best of conditions, had never talked his way out of a ticket in his life. And she'd already seen the expression on his face.

He looked beyond her, toward the door, and started to scream: "Help! Help!"

The young woman in the mask ignored him.

5

"Are you right- or left-handed?" she asked.

"What?"

She swung the bolt cutters around, a short screech, the muscles in her arms flexing.

"I said," she started, then made a frustrated groan and yanked at the heavy cutters, the tip skittering forward, digging at the grout one tile away from Charlie's knees. "Goddamn," she said. "Can't breathe."

Frendo pulled away the mask and there she was:

Quinn Maybrook.

She looked different from the pictures he'd seen.

But when you took those images from the news a couple years ago, where she was looking younger and healthier, had longer hair, and combined them with the last few months of blurry security cam and cell phone footage? This was her all right.

"I don't know how you guys walk around in these things," she said. "Never mind run. Can't see. Can't talk."

It was her, Quinn Maybrook. She was the vision Charlie had seen swimming up behind him in the reflection of his car window.

The split second of realization that'd put him on the defensive. Why he'd needed to yell out that he'd done nothing wrong. He'd just been along for the ride. What was he going to do, let his only friend in the world drive thirteen hours by himself? No, not with Ben's suspended license.

And the money. Not that Charlie had much to give, but the guy needed it. Acted like he was going to die without it. . . .

"One more time, Chuck. Where is Benjamin Koontz?"

"I don't know! At his house? I can give you the address. He lives—"

"Come on. I don't have time for this. He's not at his house. Or I should say, he's not at his *sister's* house. His wife and sister aren't there either. Kids haven't been to school. So either tell me where I can find him or choose. Right or left?"

"Right or—"

"What hand do you use more?"

"North!"

"Are you okay? Are you concussed? Your *north* hand?"

"Ben left town. He took his family and he went up north."

"We're in the southernmost state, Chuck, you're going to have to do better than that if you're planning on piano lessons anytime in the future."

Was she joking with him? Was this all a *joke* to her? What was happening? His head hurt so bad and he wasn't supposed to be here. He hadn't even done anything. Truly! When things started getting crowded, when there were gunshots and bonfires in the streets of that town, Charlie had stayed in the car! He only got out of the driver's seat like one time in the entire state of Missouri, and that was to take a piss! And the money, it was—

Eeeeee.

She adjusted the cutters again, getting both hands into position on the textured grips. The head and joints were rusty, but the blades themselves gleamed, the edges clean and sharp as polished silver.

"If you're not going to choose, we'll start small. The pinkie on your left hand."

She had to step on the back of Charlie's hand to get him to uncurl his fist.

Even if the girl was bluffing, even if she didn't *use* the bolt cutters on him, he felt something pop, knew some bone or ligament in his hand was now broken.

The pain was immense. Pain that snowballed with the confusion and the light and the tacky cool wetness on the back of his head.

"It's not fair," Charlie said. He didn't mean to snivel, but he did.

There was a pause, the blades of the bolt cutters pinching.

"Do you know how many kids I've known who thought the same thing? How few of them are going to get to grow up?" Quinn Maybrook asked, no more humor in her voice.

The blades were still open. He wriggled, cutting into the flesh between his pinkie and ring finger, shaving off the hair below the knuckle.

"I don't know where he is," Charlie said. "I'm telling you the truth. I was with him in Kettle Springs, for the riot, but

I didn't participate. I don't even follow this shit. I think it's terrible what happened to you and your friends."

"I appreciate that," Quinn Maybrook said, then tensed up, ready to cut his finger off.

"Wait! Wait!" Charlie screamed. She stopped, listened.

"I don't know *where* he is, but I know that he left. He asked for money, said he only needed a little more to cover the move for five people. When I asked him, 'Move to where?' he told me it was safer that I didn't know. That I could be hurt, if I knew where he was staying. That I could be killed, if I told. That *they* kill people."

Quinn Maybrook paused, seemed to consider this. Then she looked back down at him.

"But Charlie, haven't you heard?" she said. "*I* kill people." Then she cut off his finger.

ONE

KETTLE SPRINGS

God walked Tabitha Werther to school.

She could feel his presence. He was a warmth that took the chill out of the moist air on the long walk through dead fields and pitted roads.

He was an inner strength that—

Thwack!

The sound of split firewood echoed over the rise. The noise was coming from the small collection of rooftops ahead.

Someone in the town center was swinging an ax.

It was a strange time to be chopping firewood, odd in both the hour of the day and time in the season.

One more instance of strangeness to add to her town, beset by settlers, unquiet for this last year. A year of change and transformation.

As Tabitha approached the schoolhouse, the sound grew louder and the dirt road under her feet grew softer.

Thwack.

The soles of Tabitha's shoes started to sink into the loam. Started to, but God lifted her up.

Her faith kept her aloft, gave her strength to pull against the suck.

He was an escort at her arm and she was able to stand tall even as the buckles of her shoes began to strain.

The sensation, his presence, was difficult to describe. God walked with Tabitha and did not. He was also elsewhere. He was yards, chains, full acres away. At this same moment, he was watching over their livestock. In the larder, keeping cream from curdling. Helping a clumsy mason regain his balance atop a ladder. He was up in the sky, guiding the sunbeams into the earth.

God was in every corner of the newly incorporated township of Kettle Springs.

She turned, now standing in the doorway of the schoolhouse. She tilted her head, looking up at the church.

Whitewash siding that'd never seemed less white.

It wasn't just the overcast day or her imagination: the outer walls of the church were green with algae and brown with mud fleck.

All that prosperity promised by the Pastor and the church had never looked shabbier, not while Tabitha had been alive.

The steeple tilted slightly, always seeming to hold you in its shadow.

Tabitha wasn't sure God was—

Thwack.

Tabitha flinched.

Inside the door, her schoolmates tittered.

She ignored them.

She didn't know them. She had not grown up with them. Not that the children, all younger than Tabitha, were *grown*.

It took strength, patience, not to scowl at the children. She reminded herself that they couldn't help it, that they lacked her grace because their parents hadn't raised them to know God.

At least not the God who'd walked Tabitha to school.

Tabitha took her seat on the bench beside Hannah Trent.

Kind, considerate, quiet Hannah Trent. A new arrival, but nothing like their classmates.

The little girl nodded a greeting.

A few moments later, Mrs. Hill began the day's lesson.

Tabitha found it difficult to—

Thwack.

Tabitha watched out the schoolhouse window as the man swung the axe.

She didn't know much about Isaiah Dunne. She didn't know his history or from where he'd traveled to be here with them.

But watching Isaiah, she knew one thing: wherever he was from, he *hadn't* been a woodworker.

His stance was wrong and his aim was scattershot. She watched him swing and her own calluses from splitting firewood itched.

Isaiah Dunne was going to injure himself.

Thwack.

He was able to compensate for his poor form with powerful strokes. He was a big man. Unnaturally big, with muscles in his neck as big around as Tabitha's arms. He stood a head taller than Tabitha's father and was probably five stone heavier.

The lumber he was chopping wasn't firewood. The finished pieces were too long. The material was slab wood with most of its bark intact, nothing you would use to build a house. Tabitha wasn't sure of the project's end goal, but she could guess that the Pastor himself had set Isaiah on the task. The giant man was working enthusiastically. Fervently.

Watching him, his corded muscles, the bulge of his forearms, Tabitha was reminded of a story.

Several stories, now that she thought about it. There were often woodsmen in the stories her father told. Back when he told bedtime stories. Back when he said anything at all, except for repeating what the Pastor had said last Sunday in—

"Werther. Tabitha Werther. Are you listening, girl?"

Mrs. Hill asked. "The word is to you."

Oh dear.

The word. And what had the word been?

Tabitha could ask the teacher to repeat what she'd said while Tabitha had been daydreaming, but that would only give Mrs. Hill a reason to be spiteful. Not that their new schoolteacher tended to need a reason.

Tabitha looked around the schoolhouse.

Her classmates grinned at her.

Hannah Trent was the only one of Tabitha's schoolmates who would be willing to help, the only one of these strange, new children to show Tabitha kindness and friendship.

Tabitha could see in Hannah's eyes that the young girl was *willing* to help. Not that she could. Hannah couldn't speak and Mrs. Hill was staring too intently in their direction for the girl to mouth the word.

Instead, Hannah gave a sad look, then a regretful raise of her brows.

Tabitha sighed.

"May I hear the word again, ma'am?"

Mrs. Hill smiled softly, deciding Tabitha's fate, then said: "You may. It's a word for you, girl. Dissent."

Tabitha stood, the wooden bench groaning in the quiet of the classroom.

Beside her, Hannah made a loud swallowing sound. The girl was anxious.

Outside, Isaiah Dunne completed another downward swing.

Thwack.

There was no need for Hannah to be uneasy. Yes, this was a difficult word, but Tabitha knew it.

At fifteen, Tabitha was the oldest student in the room. Mrs. Hill had been in charge of the schoolhouse for four months now, and Tabitha was used to playing this game, the woman always giving her difficult words.

It was okay. God was with Tabitha. Whispering to her. And even if he weren't, Tabitha *knew* difficult words.

She had been a prodigious reader, before.

Before the arrival of the Pastor.

Before Kettle Springs *was* Kettle Springs.

"Descent," Tabitha said, then spelled: "D-e-s-c-e-n-t. Descent, that is the word."

Mrs. Hill frowned.

Tabitha felt a small twinge of pride, to see she'd bested the teacher.

The pride wasn't God's doing, but she didn't apologize to him.

Thwack.

"Incorrect."

There was a group intake of breath and the children around Tabitha began to snicker. Hateful little goblins.

Tabitha felt herself getting flush, knowing she shouldn't

argue with Mrs. Hill, but also knowing that she hadn't misspoken, that she'd spelled the word properly.

"Incorrect? Ma'am, I—"

"Talk back. You talk back too much, Tabitha Werther. And you have an overabundance of confidence. You *should* have asked to hear the word used in context, because the word I asked you to spell was—"

There was the chime of a bell.

Not the school bell, small and tinny.

The *big* bell.

The church bell, ringing loud enough to shake the frame of the schoolhouse.

The church bell was sounding on a Wednesday, during a lesson.

The children began to trade smiles and whispers.

They were hellions, all of them except Hannah. And Hannah would likely have been a hellion, too, if she spoke, or if her family had arrived in town a month or two earlier so there'd been time for the other children to view her as one of their own.

The change in the town had begun as a small thing, a little over a year ago.

A deal had been struck between the town's church elders and the Pastor, not yet *the* Pastor but *a* pastor, from the West. The Pastor, well coffered and generous, would pay for various civic improvements around the town, offer failing farms loans on favorable terms, and in exchange all he asked was that the town expand. That new people, *his* people, could move in and live among them. At first these new settlers had coexisted with the town's old residents. They prayed in their own places, in their own way. Then, starting around seven months ago, there had been an influx of new settlers, many of them with children, and they'd quickly outnumbered the faces Tabitha had grown up knowing, the men and women she'd sat beside during Sunday service. Outnumbered and then replaced.

Until finally the Pastor had moved into the church building. Changed it to reflect his strange faith. Chased the old God into—

Outside the window, Isaiah Dunne had ceased working, stowed his axe, and was reaching into his back pocket.

Under the desk Tabitha felt Hannah Trent's hand find hers and then squeeze. The little girl was afraid. The other children were not.

Settlers were *still* arriving, sometimes in groups, sometimes alone, very few had children. Hannah's family had arrived a month ago, a few days before the caravan that'd brought Isaiah Dunne.

The Trents lived one plot of land over from Tabitha's family, on the western border of the Werthers' field. It was where Ruth Miller used to live.

"Calm down now. Calm down," Mrs. Hill said, trying to regain control of the students excited to have class interrupted by the big bell.

Tabitha missed Ruth so much.

Ruth, headstrong and brash, who would have spelled even more difficult words for Mrs. Hill. And who Mrs. Hill would have liked even less than Tabitha.

Tabitha had befriended Hannah, and the quiet girl was good company. But she was too young to be any kind of replacement for Ruth.

Still, Tabitha held the girl's hand under the desk, tried to reassure her without words.

A girl of fifteen years couldn't be anything more than a role model for a nine-year-old. A big-sisterly friend, not a feminine confidante or best and true friend. But it was good to have *a* friend.

Especially as the church bell continued to chime.

"Silence! This is not how we behave," Mrs. Hill said. "We know what the bell means. Town meeting. Single file. Girls behind Elizabeth, boys to Samuel."

Hannah was looking up at Tabitha. The girl had big, frightened eyes like a yearling.

"It's okay," Tabitha said, even though she was becoming less and less sure things were okay with each passing Sunday that her parents went to services without her. They had resisted joining the Pastor's services, stayed home for a number of Sundays in the weeks after the old sermons had ended. But eventually the pressure became too much. They'd been attending for five weeks now without Tabitha. She gave excuses not to attend, faked sick, studied the gospel at home. But she knew that one day soon her father would insist.

Every Sunday her parents came back . . . different, less patient, less kind, all for having listened to the Pastor and taken the host.

The students formed two lines, shortest to tallest. Tabitha was nearly as tall as Mrs. Hill, meaning she was the last of the girls.

The day had gotten colder, more overcast, and God's warmth could no longer stop Tabitha from shivering. She readjusted her bonnet, wishing she and the rest of the girls were allowed their old woolen caps. But, no: woolen caps were immodest, or untraditional, or unfeminine—whatever word the Pastor had used when he'd decided on the dress code after installing their new teacher.

The church bells had stopped ringing by the time they reached the thoroughfare. The duckboard that led from the school to the center of town was narrow and missing segments. Noah Blevins lost a shoe to the mud, and Mrs. Hill needed to stop and help the young child replace it onto his foot.

There did not use to be this much mud. Even in the wettest of seasons.

Under the steeple of the church, the Pastor was waiting.

He stood on the bottom step of the church. Not raised above the gathered townspeople, not noticeably, but also not standing in the mud.

The children didn't snicker now, didn't whisper; they fanned out from their lines and stood at silent attention while the Pastor waited for the last of the townspeople, those who didn't live far enough afield that they'd need to saddle horses to join this surprise meeting.

"Thank you. Thank you for heeding the call. For joining me here," the Pastor said, ceremonial hood obscuring his face, his eyes and chin concealed. "Now that we're all gathered . . ."

He raised his arms.

He had a soft voice, but he spoke with enough slowness, clarity, and force that it was easy to hear him.

"I am . . . I am ecstatic today, brothers and sisters."

Tabitha listened to the man's words and tried to see him the way the eyes all around her, some already rheumy with tears, seemed to hear him. The way her parents, once critical of the man and his theology, had come to hear him.

"We have had struggles. Of course. But what do struggles do? They fortify us. Strengthen us."

Some townspeople nodded, some just stared. Some seemed as though they could hear the words, some just the intonation of the voice.

Tabitha would admit, it was a nice voice.

It could soothe her if she'd let it. How many more Sundays could she feign illness? No, she resolved, she would attend this man's services. She would give him a chance. She would listen to his voice, and she would make herself *find* God in it.

The voice, if not the face, because the Pastor had stopped letting them see his face.

She would listen to this man's ideology, delivered with that voice, and let herself sink into it.

Like her parents had. Her mother and father had been holdouts, the last of the town's original population that had clung to the old ways. The last who hadn't moved away or been accused of—

"And when we are strengthened we become a community of plenty," the Pastor continued. "It's happening even now. We've all seen the latest shipments I've brought from the West, have we not? Fine tools, to fix our irrigation troubles. High-yield seeds that I've no doubt, this time, will sprout."

Yes. If Tabitha used her reason, thought about his words, she could tell that the things the Pastor was saying were lies. Empty promises that she'd heard before. But she could abandon reason. And if that was too difficult? She would pretend. She could continue to read the true scriptures in secret. It didn't mean she had to abandon God, she just had to—

"But when we have plenty, what does that attract?" the Pastor asked, his voice changing, no longer soothing.

The crowd shifted, some faces uneasy, some oblivious.

"Not a rhetorical question, flock. What happens to a

home of plenty when there are holes in the foundation?"

None of the gathered parishioners answered.

"Pests! Pests are attracted to our paradise of plenty."

He waved.

"Constable, bring forth the apostate."

From around the side of the church, the direction of the town's lone jail cell, marched a naked man, his hands bound in front of him. The man was older than Tabitha but younger than most of the fathers and grown-adult brothers of Kettle Springs.

He may have been an apostate, but he was nobody Tabitha knew. Which was good. He was an outsider, not someone Tabitha had grown up with who'd managed to offend the church. Not that there were any familiar faces left.

When the naked man raised his head, Tabitha could see that one eye was swollen shut. And that the other had gone wide, frantic, to see the townspeople gathered here in front of the church steps.

Many of the gathered townspeople had been called in from working their fields, mud coating their arms up to their elbows. Vacant stares and blank expressions on their faces. The blankest of them almost asleep with their eyes open.

"Please, help me. He's insane—"

"Walk *silently*," the Constable said, kicking the man behind one of his knees, sending him sprawling.

Nobody moved to help the man. In fact, the crowd

stepped back when he fell forward. As if being an apostate were a pox that they could catch.

"There are members of our congregation," the Pastor said, "who *still* seem to think that I am speaking in metaphor."

The Pastor paused, but there was no chorus of "Amen" and nods, as there would have been at a happier meeting.

"The world on all sides of us is hostile. *His* world—" He pointed down at the naked man, who'd stopped trying to get up after the Constable had kicked out his knees for a second time. "—would love nothing more than to take away your sons and daughters."

The Pastor gestured to the children of the schoolhouse, and Tabitha got a chill, noticing how his pointing hand seemed to linger on her.

"Please, I'll do whatever you want. I'll leave and—" The Constable silenced the man by kicking him in the side of the head, boot to naked ear.

"This"—the Pastor nodded at the crying man—"is *not* an apostate."

That elicited a reaction from the crowd, whispers of, "No, it must be," traded between Mrs. Hill and some new settler's wife.

"Not *only* an apostate," the Pastor continued. "He's a herald of things to come. A herald of the Adversary."

Tabitha scanned the faces of the town, looking for her

23

parents, hoping that they'd ignored the bell and had kept working. But, no. They were there, shoulder to shoulder, and Tabitha was sad when she saw them.

Her mother and father were nodding along to the Pastor's words. They agreed that, yes, of course, this naked, mewling man was a herald. Whatever that meant.

"The Adversary is not sin. The Adversary is not a concept. The Adversary is flesh and blood, as real as the host you take on Sundays. And it is on the way here, to your town. To *our* town. What will we do when it arrives? I know, brothers and sisters, that you've sacrificed so much, struggled to bring us to the cusp of plenty. But do you have a little more to give? Or will you sit quietly? Will you allow the Adversary to take me from you? To kill me because they hate me? To make me a martyr? Or will you take up arms and protect me? We need to protect our way of life! To protect our children!"

The Pastor paused, hand up to silence the shouts and whispers of, "We'll fight!" "We'll give," that had begun.

"I believe you, that most of you will. But I speak now to those of you who are *not* prepared to fight." He looked at Tabitha. Or at least she assumed he did, could feel the pressure of his shadowed eyes on her under his hood. "For those of you, I want to know: Are you prepared for the hell that awaits?"

The townspeople didn't voice an answer.

Tabitha heard the crowd split, stepping aside to make

way for their answer to walk up to the naked man.

Isaiah Dunne held his axe in front of him.

He had his mask pulled down over his chin, the thin burlap bunched over his mouth. A red nose stitched into the lye-bleached fabric.

Isaiah Dunne was not Isaiah Dunne anymore, not in this moment.

He was the clown.

"I can't protect you." The Pastor spoke from the stairs. "Not alone. We, all of us, need *him*."

"Wait, don't—" the apostate said, his one good eye pleading with the man in the simple cloth clown mask, hands up to try to deflect the swing.

Thwack.

The first chop took half the young man's left hand and cleaved off the right at the wrist, disembodied flesh slapping the wood of the church steps.

No, Isaiah was no woodsman, but he was very strong.

The second chop muffled the screams.

And on the third chop the man's head rolled free, the blood trail dark in the shadow of the church steeple.

The people of Kettle Springs, all except little Hannah, the mute girl, said, "Amen."

No, Tabitha thought.

God was not in that church.

TWO

KETTLE SPRINGS

Book bans at the high school library, city budget reports due, there was even the unresolved matter of the walking dead at the funeral home. . . .

Glenn Maybrook wasn't letting any of it bother him.

No. Not Glenn. Not the *new* Glenn Maybrook.

Hydrated and unbothered. That was Mayor Maybrook.

Last year, he'd entered his first term as mayor an anxious person. Someone who dreaded social interaction, but also didn't like being alone with his thoughts. A man who could never get his words right, but *constantly* found himself in positions where he talked too much.

The near-death experience of being attacked with a box cutter last Halloween had quieted him down.

And not only because of the nerve damage he'd sustained

to his face and throat.

But the nerve damage helped.

Months of recovery and PT had fostered a well of calmness inside Glenn that he never thought he'd possess. Having a razor run across his throat had a way of making zoning laws and parking complaints seem less important.

Multiple times in his life, especially after Samantha's death, Glenn had attempted to learn mindfulness and meditation techniques. Even if the "attempts" didn't get much further than installing an app on his phone.

But losing a third of the blood in his body had given him the time to try again.

It took a lot of patience, relearning how to chew and swallow. Patience he'd needed to *stay* mayor after he'd initially decided to quit.

He couldn't give up on this town. He—

He checked his watch. . . .

With all this personal growth, Glenn Maybrook had *almost* enough patience to deal with a long line at the post office.

Almost.

There was only one overworked postal worker in the small office and a line of five other patrons, each with a package or two under their arm. Glenn didn't know every constituent's name, but he knew the woman behind the desk. Her name was Gloria. Glenn liked her, she was a nice older woman who always called him "sweetie" and never asked him personal questions during their small talk.

But as much as he liked her, Gloria was by far the slowest of the post office's three employees.

This'd take all day.

But that was fine, Glenn told himself.

What did the mayor have to hurry to? Any problem he solved today would be instantaneously replaced by five more.

Glenn would wait in this line. Calmly. He would collect the mail he'd allowed to accrue in his PO box. The mailbox at home was full of hate and/or junk mail. He threw everything that arrived to the address on Marshall Lane into the garbage, unread. The PO box was where—

"Media mail, girl. I would like to send it *media* mail. What's so hard to understand about that?" Del Ryan said to Gloria, loud enough to break Glenn out of his thoughts.

Oh boy. Here we go.

"Girl?!" Gloria said. "Del, I'm the same age as you. And I *watched* you pack this box. It doesn't qualify for media mail."

"There's media in it, ain't there?"

"Yeah, I saw the town almanacs and the yearbooks. But I also saw a bunch of other items you crammed in," she said, tapping her long, manicured nails on the box Del had placed on the scale in front of her. "You're paying for first class, Del, I'm sorry."

The owner of Ryan's Thrift scrunched up his gray

stubble, looked like he was trying to think of something mean to say, but Gloria didn't let him get it out.

"And don't make me regret all the favors I've done you, Del. You're a business, selling the town's knickknacks on eBay. You shouldn't qualify for media mail *ever*."

"And why not!"

"Because media mail's supposed to be an *educational* rate, Del. You aren't educating. You're profiteering."

Ouch. Glenn cringed. That was probably a little extreme. Del Ryan wasn't one of the bad guys, and Gloria likely knew that. The old man had stood up to the crowd of outsiders who'd invaded the town seven months ago and gotten his windows broken out and his store wrecked in the process.

Or had it been eight months now? Time flew.

"Profiteering!"

Del turned back, pointed right at Glenn.

Uh-oh.

"Are you hearing this, Mayor? Can't you do something?" he asked.

"Do something?" Glenn asked, but he wasn't sure the words came out.

"Yes! The post office is a government operation, is it not?"

Glenn cleared his throat before speaking again. Even still, his words were a hushed croak: "The, uh, *federal* government, Mr. Ryan."

"What'd he say?" Del turned back to the postal worker

and asked. "His voice is all fucked up. Can't understand anything the little twerp says anymore."

"*I* said," Gloria began, "leave that poor man alone and pay what you owe so I can move this line along." To punctuate, the woman put her hand down on the counter. Hard.

Around Glenn, the other people waiting in line muttered words of agreement.

Del grumbled and reached for his wallet, paid his non–media mail postage, and left.

Glenn was one spot away from the front of the line when his shirt pocket began to buzz.

His phone was ringing.

The call was probably Jerri, wondering where he was. When she wasn't at school or the movie theater, the girl had become a kind of assistant since . . .

Glenn readjusted his glasses, stared down at the phone.

The call was coming from an unknown number.

These were the moments where the old Glenn, nervous and bothered, fluttered to the surface on a wave of gooseflesh.

But it was never *her* calling.

Or at least, it hadn't been for months.

And maybe that was his fault. Maybe he'd searched for her a little too hard, forced her to abandon her phone.

But it was never her.

It's always spam.

And even as he told himself that, Glenn Maybrook left his spot in line and retraced his path through the stanchions.

This happened all the time. His heart rate spiking, rushing to a quiet place to pick up, and then an automated message informing him that "we've been trying to get in touch with you about your car's extended warranty."

It is never. Her.

But still he pushed out the door into the cool spring Missouri air.

Hope in his chest.

Hope and anxiety.

"Hello," he said. The word sounded like a cough.

There was no answer.

But no prerecorded message, either. There was no background bustle of a crowded call center, the telemarketer's headset momentarily away from their face, never expecting anyone to actually pick up.

On the other end of the line there was a gentle wind, a wind that could have been breathing, and slight static.

Maybe it was her.

"Hello?" Glenn said again, his voice clearer. Closer to what he used to sound like. A voice that she'd be able to recognize as his.

After a pause, she said two words:

"Hey, Dad."

The world around him blurred, Main Street, Kettle

Springs, awash with tears.

"Oh God, Quinn . . ." There was so much Glenn wanted to say. So much he'd rehearsed, but his throat closed to a rasp and wouldn't let him say any of it. "Please. Please come home."

Quinn, please stop what you're doing. It's not too late for us to explain this. There are lawyers who've offered to help. I love you so much. I want you home.

And then there were the questions. The things he wanted desperately to know, but knew not to ask, because they might scare her off:

How haven't you been caught? Are your friends helping you do this? Is Cole sending you money? This is insane, you're going to be killed.

Quinn interrupted his coughing fit.

"Dad, please listen. There's no time to talk, not on your cell phone. I love you, but it's important you stop coughing and listen."

He closed his mouth, tried to refocus his breathing, and was able to get himself under control.

She waited a beat before speaking again, taking time to make sure he was listening.

"They're going to say I killed someone."

Glenn kept breathing, not sure what to do.

Then he asked:

"Did you?"

But the line was already dead.

THREE

SUMTER COUNTY, ALABAMA

"Christ, give me strength," Johnny D muttered, and pushed his braids off his neck.

He needed a break from all the chatter and the hiss of bottle tops. A moment away from these dumbasses.

So he decided he'd work on the car.

"Yo, ye're a liar."

"Yeah. Full of shit."

Johnny listened to them argue as he moved over to the tools arrayed on the lawn.

"No, man. I swear," Trevor said. "Swear to God. On my mother. On everything I got."

Trevor and Johnny D's mother was dead. And their dads were in two different states, neither within visiting distance of Alabama.

The house was theirs, all the brothers owned, outside of the cars. Two bedrooms and a bathroom where if the toilet tank ever had a lid, Johnny had never seen it.

So when Trevor swore on his mother, then everything he had, he wasn't swearing on much.

But Johnny stayed quiet.

"It's science," Trevor said to his friends.

"Oh yeah?" Weez asked, the boy's interest piqued. "You're saying if a girl drinks Diet Mountain Dew then she can't get pregnant?"

"Not like, if she drinks it right after," Trevor explained. "It's not plan B. I'm saying she *can't* get pregnant if she drinks it regularly. It's something in the dye. One of the colors they use. It builds up in the reproductive system. Blocks hormones and shit."

Johnny had turned seventeen in February, and the week before, Trevor had helped him prepare the paperwork so that he could drop out of school on his birthday.

It'd seemed like a good idea at the time. But it took only a few months of "the good life" of seeing what Trevor and his friends got up to when he'd been at school, the stupid shit they talked about, and Johnny was ready to be back in Algebra 1.

"Man," Bobby said. "Diet Mountain Dew is my brand. Guess I'll never be getting pregnant."

"Doing the world a favor," Trevor said, the three of them

giggling and then lapsing into a moment of blessed quiet while they sipped their drinks, Bobby spitting into his dip cup.

The topics of conversation only got worse later in the day. And it was getting late, spring heat cooling into the stagnant sweat of late afternoon. Trevor's phone had already run through their normal four-hour classic ICP playlist and was now serving random tracks from Twiztid and MC Breed out of the Bluetooth speaker propped on the cooler.

Johnny turned his head, used the creeper to roll under the car. The mechanic's seat glided on well-oiled bearings, sleek and comfortable. The equipment was new and expensive. Johnny and Trevor had stolen it from a Love's Travel Stop.

A lot of people would have said the creeper was nicer than the car.

Johnny's car was a 1999 Ford Mustang. Not the GT or the Cobra, but the base model. A car that'd been widely considered a piece of shit in 1999, before all the mileage and the primer-over-rust paint job and before the passenger seat had lost all its foam and upholstery.

It was *his* car, though. Johnny had traded for it on Facebook Marketplace for two hundred bucks and a pallet of Coors Light. He didn't ask the former owner what'd happened to the passenger seat. And the former owner didn't ask where a teenager had gotten the beer.

The Mustang *looked* like a trash heap, but Johnny liked it that way. Meant that anyone he pulled alongside wouldn't know about the improvements he'd been making, slowly and surely, parts begged, borrowed, and stolen. Mostly stolen.

There was muscle in the Mustang, under the Hatchet Man decals Johnny had been collecting since sixth grade.

But even with all that aftermarket power, the car's transmission had been making a noise and Johnny needed to—

In the direction of the guys and their cooler, there was the loud clink of glass on glass.

"Bitch!"

Then there was the pitter-pat of foam hitting gravel.

Johnny eased the creeper back. He didn't need to look over at Trevor and his friends to know what had happened. Trevor had gotten too relaxed, let his guard down, and had the mouth of his beer tapped.

"You're buying next time, Bobby, if you think food waste is so funny."

"Food waste. Please. Shut up and drink that head, before I rat your clown ass out."

Ooof. Johnny thought Trevor wasn't going to like that.

Instead of staying quiet, Weez laughed.

Weez was too much of a coward to start shit, but he'd definitely laugh and pile on, given the opportunity.

"Here he is," Weez said, "I found one of 'em! Look, it's Frendo. Give him a concussion, teen girl."

The friends were all Juggalos, Johnny, too, but only

Trevor wore his family pride on his face.

Johnny's half-brother had clown makeup tattooed under his eyes and on his nose and a big stitched smile inked across his mouth.

Contrary to what the nation's concerned grandmas liked to warn, Trevor's tattoos had never stopped him from holding down a job. Or at least hadn't until clowns had become national news. Now even the road crew was reluctant to have Trevor, but Johnny's brother was a good worker so they kept him on night shifts.

"That shit's not funny," Trevor said. "Haven't you seen the news? She's *killing* folks now."

"Yeah. Chopping 'em up!" Weez said, chopping the air above his beer with the side of his hand.

"Not funny, man. That could be me next! I can't help the way I look."

"Or your internet search history," Bobby added.

Ooooooooo.

That was one joke too many out of Bobby.

Johnny knew what had to be coming next and he peeked out from under the Mustang to watch.

Trevor took a half step, leaned down, and slapped Bobby across the chin and neck.

Not hard, only the bottom three fingers of his right hand connecting, but the impact still staggered Bobby so that dip spit rolled down his shirt.

Bobby squealed, then looked like he might hit back, but Trevor shouted him down.

"We're even," Trevor said, pointing at Bobby. "Don't do it again. Don't say one more fucking extra word."

The friends joked and argued, all gave each other shit, but when things got serious there was a pretty firm pecking order.

Trevor was at the top.

And Trevor didn't like anyone bringing up his flirtation with that Frendo stuff. It wasn't ever serious. Mostly sharing YouTube videos with their friends, starting conversations at parties with, "Hey, I've just got questions about what went down in Missouri."

One day, with Johnny's help, Weez and Bobby had gotten Trevor high, locked the door, and told him to cut it out. A kind of dope-smoke intervention.

Luckily, that was before all the shit went down on Halloween, or else Trevor might have been there in Kettle Springs.

The siblings had never talked about it after that day spent watching the news, but Johnny thought Trevor was ashamed. Ashamed that he'd almost joined up, almost enlisted in an ideology that was so . . . so fucking lame, honestly.

Trevor was even more ashamed when, in the days after Halloween, Violent J and Shaggy 2 Dope had put out an official statement. Trevor's heroes, the Insane Clown Posse themselves, had said that what had happened on Halloween was not cool. Not what family was about. That any Juggalo who supported those wack-ass ideas, their crews should be shunning them. "Excommunicado" was the word J had used.

On top of that shame, in this last twenty-four hours, hearing the news that Quinn Maybrook had snipped some dude's fingers off, tortured him, then beheaded him with a hacksaw, Trevor was scared.

The girl had graduated to murder. A murder in a bordering state. And if she had a hit list, like the news said she did, Trevor was worried he might be on it.

With the excitement in the front yard over, Johnny rolled back and felt around in his toolbox. He didn't find the socket extension he needed, but fished into the side pockets of his black cargo pants and there it was.

He worked for a few minutes until the car arrived.

"What's all this now?" Johnny heard Trevor say. There was the crash of an empty bottle tossed into a garbage bag, followed by the crunch of tires on gravel.

Someone had opened the gate and was rolling up the long, overgrown driveway out front of their house.

"Private property," Trevor shouted at the approaching car. "Turn around."

"Hey, Trev, you got a 'No Solicitation' sign?" Weez asked Trevor, not shouting.

"What?"

"You can get one at the Ace. Three bucks. You put it on your front post. Stops all the salesmen and Jehovah's Witnesses."

"Weez?"

"Yes."

"Thank you."

"Anytime."

The sound of tires crept forward. Whoever was visiting, it didn't sound like they were turning their car around.

Who was it?

The cops, maybe?

No. The brothers hadn't done anything illegal. Not recently.

And Trevor didn't like cops, but he wasn't stupid enough to *yell* at cops to get off his property.

Johnny was curious who was here, but not curious enough to roll himself out from under the Mustang and get involved. Using his heels, he wheeled the creeper around so he could lie back in the shadow of the car and watch the driveway while he worked.

Coming up the drive was a black Lincoln Town Car. Mid-2000s, maybe 2010s. Which meant whoever was inside, they definitely weren't the cops. The county's unmarked cop cars were all junkers.

The Lincoln was the kind of car you saw leading funeral processions, but rarely just driving on the highway.

There seemed to be something written on the sides of the car. Johnny could see glimpses of gold lettering, but the angle was wrong, with the car coming down the drive toward him head-on.

The car rolled to a stop.

Two guys in button-down shirts exited the vehicle, their motions nearly synchronized.

No, the gold glimmer wasn't a trick of the light. The car belonged to a business or something. Johnny could see a few letters as both front doors opened.

Alt— he strained to read.

But then he took a closer look at the guys who'd gotten out.

No, they weren't guys. They were two *boys*. Closer in age to Johnny than they were to Trevor and his friends.

Weez had chanced into being correct, telling Trevor how to get rid of Jehovah's Witnesses.

Kind of.

The boys wore crisp white shirts and black dress pants. They could be Mormon missionaries. Except Johnny had never seen Mormon missionaries missing their black ties and name tags.

"Nope. Nah nah nah. We're all good," Trevor said.

The boys lifted their hands. Either *We don't want any trouble* or *We come in peace*, but Bobby got in their faces before they could speak.

"Git back in your car!" Bobby yelled, then moved his cup up to his lip, scraping up the last of the spit with the plastic edge.

"Please. Gentlemen. Good afternoon. Don't send us away yet," the lead boy, the one who'd been driving, said.

"You haven't even heard who we are or why we're here," the other added. "Hear us out."

Listening to them speak, Johnny realized these weren't teenagers. The lead kid was in his early twenties. But Johnny still reserved the right to think of the two of them as boys. Look how they were dressed.

"Hear you out? I know enough by looking at you," Trevor said. He pointed back toward the house, motioning beyond the building. "We go to the Baptist church up in the 'ville. We're not looking to change religions. Thank you, now please get off my property."

"Your property?" the second boy asked.

Johnny couldn't see the second boy's face.

Weez had moved and was blocking his view.

Johnny watched Weez sneak a beer out of the cooler and into his back pocket, presumably saving it for later.

"This is *your* property?" the lead boy asked again.

It was and it wasn't. When Johnny turned eighteen, it would be *his* property, too. The brothers would share.

"Yes," Trevor said.

The boy in the dress shirt squinted, scrutinizing Trevor's

face. Johnny was surprised to see that the kid wasn't scared of Trevor's tattoos. Most normies they met, especially the religious types, were warned off talking to Trevor at the mere sight of the inked smile.

"So you don't have any parents here? No adults we might talk to?"

"Adults?" Trevor said, offended. "Youngblood, I am *thirty* years old." Not true, he was twenty-eight. "I probably got kids I don't know about as old as you," he continued. "Now get in your car and go."

But the two boys dressed like missionaries didn't move.

Instead, they shared a look, the hood of the Town Car between them.

"There's no one else here," the one said.

"I heard. That's good," said the other. "That'll make things much easier."

"What are you two fuckheads doing?" Trevor said. "Just give us a brochure and go, before we stomp your ass."

"Uhhh, Trev?" Weez said. "I don't know I'm gonna stomp religious kids. Feel like you go to hell for that or something."

The lead boy held up his hand, two fingers extended, the *eyes on me* motion that Johnny remembered the teachers doing in elementary school.

"Did he just call you Trev?" the boy asked. "As in Trevor R. Dale?"

"Yes, who's asking?"

"You're who we came to meet," the second boy said, then looked over to the other and nodded.

Johnny had taken his eyes off the lead boy.

Johnny hadn't seen him produce the pistol.

"You'll never see the glory of heaven," the lead boy said. "Not with all that shit on your face."

"Wait—" Trevor started.

The *sound* of the gunshot tore through the warm afternoon and set every bird in the yard off their perches and into the air.

The *bullet* tore through Trevor's head, leaving an exit wound in the back of his skull like the breaking of a terra-cotta pot.

Trevor, whose dad had been so much worse than Johnny's dad. Trevor, who never got along with their mom. Trevor, who'd stuck around for so many years just to take care of Johnny because he'd been too young to take care of himself.

Trevor, who'd taught Johnny how to burn CDs like they had back in the day.

Trevor, Johnny's whiteboy half-brother with the clown face tattoos . . .

Trevor was dead.

Johnny's jaw strained, his mouth open so wide it hurt.

But if Johnny was trying to scream, no sound was coming out.

In the end, that was for the best.

"Fuck! What are you doing, why did you—"

The second boy closed the distance to Bobby and before Bobby could finish his questions began stabbing him in the neck.

As with the gun, Johnny had no idea where the blade had come from. Had it been up the missionary boy's sleeve? Collapsed and spring-loaded like a magician's wand?

Bobby's feet began to tip to the side; the boy tried to grip his neck to keep the blood in, but his arms and legs went limp before he hit the ground.

This time, with sense and reality slamming into him, Johnny knew he was going to scream. He put both hands over his mouth, laced his fingers, and squeezed to muffle the sound.

Johnny's hands stank of sump oil and tasted bitter against his lips.

But what did it matter if he screamed? It wasn't like he was invisible. They were going to see him, curled up here under the car. All they had to do was look. They'd see the jack, see the creeper, and if they bent their knees a little, they'd catch the glint of Johnny's beat-up sneakers, the ones he'd patched with glossy electrical tape.

And when the two boys in white shirts saw him, they'd kill him.

Johnny looked out onto the yard and driveway, hands trembling over his mouth.

The boy with the gun and the boy with the knife began to circle Toby "Weez" Pargin.

"Look, I don't know what Trev and Bobby did to you, but," Weez said, his words pleading, "I was *not* involved. Like, I don't even know *why* you killed them. Or *who* you are. Which means you've got no reason to kill *me*, right?"

The boys looked at each other and smiled, keeping their footsteps even and synchronized as they moved around Weez.

That was how sharks hunted bigger prey. They circled.

"No," the one boy said.

"No *reason*," the other finished.

The boy with the gun reached the weapon out, pressed it against the back of Weez's left knee, and pulled the trigger.

With the gun's caliber and proximity, it was like an amputation. The hinge of Weez's knee broke back as he fell over onto his face.

Moaning, Weez tried to raise himself. His arms shook and he fell back on his stomach, a push-up he was too exhausted, in too much pain, to complete.

As Weez lay there, his eyes found Johnny's under the car.

Please, Johnny thought. *Please, Weez. I can't help you. You're already done. Don't point. Don't even look at me. Don't let them know I'm here.*

The guy they all called Weez could see Johnny curled in the shadow of the Mustang. Johnny with his knees against his chest and his hands over his mouth. But Weez didn't wave at him and cry out for help.

No. Whether it was bravery or shock, Weez didn't give Johnny away.

They stared into each other's eyes, Johnny bearing witness as the boy with the knife began to cut Weez's scalp away from his skull.

It took Weez minutes to bleed out. But Johnny never broke their gaze.

When the boys were finished, the pair returned to their car and opened the trunk.

Their white shirts were spattered and streaked with blood, and each helped the other undo the buttons of their cuffs so they could strip.

Bare chested, the boy who'd shot Trevor produced a package of baby wipes, then a black garbage bag. They put their shirts and undershirts inside the bag, then wiped their hands and necks.

Clean, they took two fresh button-down shirts from the trunk.

Once they were dressed, their shirttails tucked in, the two teenagers-who-weren't-teenagers got into their car and drove away.

But not before Johnny was able to read the two words written on the side of the Town Car in gold vinyl decals:

Alton Ministries.

It took Johnny D Lawson fifteen minutes to figure out what he should do next, time he'd mostly spent throwing up.

By then the sun had gone amber, and he was getting cold huddling under the car, so he crawled out into the sunlight.

After he'd finally dry heaved enough to stop, it took him a few more deadened, foggy minutes to remember the number for 911.

Then he stood among the bodies and waited.

It took longer than he would have liked.

When a car finally did pull out front of the house Johnny wanted to own with his brother, it wasn't the cops.

And it wasn't the missionary kids back to finish the job.

It was someone worse.

FOUR

KETTLE SPRINGS

Tabitha Werther woke before dawn.

She always woke before dawn, but today was different.

This morning every aspect of the chores she needed to finish before school felt more difficult.

She felt heavy.

Weighted down with mud and fear.

She remembered the way the apostate's skull had split. How he'd kept screaming for much longer than she would have imagined a person could, with no lower jaw.

But she didn't fear violent death as much as she feared the look she'd seen on her neighbors' faces. The look on her parents' faces. What that look meant about what they were becoming, now that they'd joined the new faith.

She prayed for a short moment after dressing for the day.

Talking to God helped.

Somewhat.

But there was too much work to talk long.

It had rained last night and the night before, and the moisture clung to the earth in thick clouds of mist that hovered a foot or two above the dirt.

The first of her morning tasks finished, Tabitha left the root cellar, moving toward the barn.

It was difficult to see in the gray-green fog, and she hadn't realized the barn doors had been pushed open until she groped in the darkness and felt the clasp, swinging free.

"Misery me," Tabitha said, though not loud enough to be heard by anyone in the house. Her mother was awake, plucking a chicken, and her father hadn't ever gone to bed. He had work to continue around the farm, but she guessed he wouldn't be doing it today. This morning he'd been sitting at the family table, a taper burning and a book of hymns open. He had been in that same position, unmoving and unspeaking, all night. In the small hours, Tabitha had needed to creep past him, staying at the edge of the candlelight, crossing through the common room in order to use the backhouse, her father an angry statue.

Now, in the barn, Tabitha lit the lantern and located the pail, but—as she feared—Nellie's stall was empty.

The cow was loose again.

She adjusted the knob to a wide glow, hoisted the

lantern, and pushed out into the predawn gloom to find the creature.

Tabitha was a fraction of the cow's weight and *she* was having trouble navigating the mud. In a bid for freedom, to wander the fields and visit their neighbors, the stupid animal was going to break all four of her legs.

She looked down, following Nellie's deep and uneven hoof tracks.

It was later in the season than they'd typically plant their corn crop. To safeguard their seed stock, only half of the Werther acreage had been sown. "The rains are too heavy," her father had said a few weeks ago, when his melancholia hadn't been quite as strong, when he could form whole, coherent sentences. "Watch. The newcomers who plant now. They will have nothing but rot and wasted work when nothing lives to harvest."

Newcomers.

That was one word for them.

Tabitha stepped wide, trying to avoid the neat, wet mounds where her father's planter shoe had turned up the soil. Nellie wasn't choosing her footing as carefully. The cow headed west, trampling a mostly straight line under which no seed would germinate with the soil so compacted.

As Tabitha trudged after, the cow still not in sight, the sky began to lighten. The coming sunrise wasn't helping the search. The warmth of the sun heated the ground and thickened the mist until even the lantern, a foot from Tabitha's face, became a hazy, indistinct orange ball.

But even without being able to see, Tabitha found it easy to tell when she'd crossed over into the next farm.

The air here smelled different.

This was the land Ruth's family tended.

No, Tabitha corrected herself, *not Ruth's family. Not the Millers. Not anymore.*

Hannah lived here now. This was the Trents' farm.

Kind, wordless Hannah Trent, the little girl Tabitha enjoyed sharing a schoolhouse desk with, but who couldn't compare to the friend that Ruth had been. Ruth was clever. Ruth was brave. Ruth would have been able to give Tabitha advice about how she could convince her parents to leave Kettle Springs, this long after they'd made the decision to stay. Ruth would have known how they could escape.

The entire Miller family had been clever. Clever enough to move away. They were the first to see the Pastor's offer for what it was, and the first to say so, before they left.

The Millers hadn't been the only family to leave, hardly. The last decade had been difficult, the town nearly a ghost town as it was, before the arrival of the Pastor. And the trial of the first apostates had whittled the population down even further.

But the Millers had left well before then, when leaving was an option.

Ruth's family had lit out for St. Genevieve before the first death.

As much as Tabitha envied the Millers, she flushed with anger when she thought about how Ruth hadn't even said goodbye. She'd left her here alone and—

Tabitha tripped over something in the fog, but recovered before she could fall forward into the mud.

The Trents, Hannah's family, weren't so much tending this land as *abusing* it.

Mr. Trent—a man who drank—had ignored her father's advice and planted his corn crop too early, shortly after the family arrived a month ago.

The seedlings, never thinned once sprouted, had drowned and died, as her father warned they would.

That was the smell around her. The stench of death and failure. The decay caused by a man too pigheaded to take guidance from someone who knew the land better.

Hannah's family needed to hurry up and mulch so they could start planting again, if they were going to grow anything this season. Regardless of what the Pastor said, it was likely too late to get new seeds in the ground. No matter how "high the yield" whoever sold them to him had claimed.

Outsiders, Tabitha thought. Not newcomers or settlers or any of the kinder terms. They were outsiders. They could not integrate into their society, even if they wanted to. The arrogance and presumption of them. It was dangerous for Tabitha to show her anger. There was nobody to talk with about how she felt, and it was a risk to even allow herself to feel her anger, but she *was* angry. Angry at the outsiders, angry at the Pastor, angry at his executioner clown, angry at the tongues of the townspeople outstretched on Sundays to—

There was a crunch.

A few yards up ahead, the sound came again, like fresh vegetation snapping.

But there was no fresh vegetation in this field, just putrid roots and wilted stalks.

So what was making the sound?

Tabitha thought of the whacks that'd been haunting her since yesterday afternoon. The axe-head that had split flesh more confidently than it'd split wood.

A shape appeared in the white fog ahead of her. The largeness and suddenness of it unnerved her.

It was as if the Pastor had heard Tabitha's thoughts, had sent the wide shoulders of Isaiah Dunne to strike her down.

The dark gray shape approached and Tabitha shivered to see it, felt dwarfed by its mass.

And then the bell rang.

Not the big bell.

Or the school bell.

Or any of the other terrible bells in her life.

But Nellie's bell. The one the animal wore around her neck on a length of twine.

Out of the gloom, the creature's huge head and black eyes pressed forward into the lantern light and licked the back of Tabitha's hand.

"Stop, Nel," Tabitha said, laughing despite the cold of the creature's nose and the muddy slickness of her tongue. It felt good and safe to laugh, to realize that she'd startled herself with dark thoughts, that God's gentlest creature was with Tabitha now, in this field.

There was hope in that realization. A light in the darkness.

Nellie continued nuzzling Tabitha, the animal snorting warm flecks of mucus onto her hands and wrists.

Nellie pressed the flat, fuzzy part of her forehead against Tabitha, the animal requesting a scratch.

The cow might have left the barn searching for adventure, but she was now glad to see her mistress.

"Yes, because you are past due for milking, silly," Tabitha said, using her free hand to pull at the hem of her frock, trying to stop the cow from nibbling the fabric.

She used the same hand to pat the animal on the head, begin to scratch, and then realized . . . blood.

There was blood in Nellie's fur and blood coating Tabitha's hand.

Tabitha jumped back, felt her heels squelch into the mud.

There was blood rimming Nellie's mouth.

Tabitha's first thought was that the cow had cut herself on

a piece of farm equipment while stumbling through the fog. But that couldn't be right. The blood streaking the cow's fur and slimed between Tabitha's fingers was *old* blood. It was coppery and thick, but still too red to be confused with mud.

The fog around them had begun to lift. Not entirely, but enough that Tabitha could see the ground beneath her feet.

Nellie's bell tinged as the animal, apparently losing interest in their reunion, went back to rooting in the dirt.

The cow was crunching on the soft tubers of failed crop. Tabitha had to stop her, she'd make herself sick. Minding beasts was like this, they'd eat anything, with no regard for whether it would make them—

"Go home," Tabitha said firmly, then swatted Nellie's ear.

The cow ignored her and kept chewing.

Tabitha crossed around to the side of the animal, set her lantern down, and began to push on Nellie's rump.

"Home. Get back home."

The cow listened and began heading back east. Tabitha, still pushing, lost her footing. She landed with one knee in the soft loam and shot out an elbow to try to keep her chin out of the muck.

It didn't work.

Her body began to sink into the cool mud.

She sighed and grunted as something wet dribbled down her cheek.

Now, on top of the milking that would make her late for school, Tabitha had to change her clothes and do the wash.

She sniffed.

The smell was worse down here, in the mud.

And it wasn't the smell of *plant* death.

Tabitha pushed to a seated position and then scrambled back, her skirts getting caught up in her knees and the muddy toes of her shoes, her wet, heavy clothes feeling like a prison, shackles holding her to the ground, hemming her in with with with . . .

A body.

A dead body.

No.

That was too many hands. Waxen skin with red and white gouges where rats and field mice had picked spots of the fingers down to bone.

It wasn't *a* body. It was multiple bodies, uncovered by the rain and then stumbled upon by the Werther family cow.

Tabitha screamed, then stood back, took in the scene, and began to cry. The mist had cleared and her eyes had adjusted so that she could see the three graves.

The body in the center was unlike the other two.

It was a smaller body with a pallid gray face.

A clever face.

Ruth's family hadn't left Kettle Springs after all.

FIVE

In Quinn Maybrook's dreams, Arthur Hill was there.

Outside her dreams, Arthur Hill was there.

The dead man lived in her psyche.

Skulked around her, hiding himself behind every corner, every turn in the road.

Which was a macabre way of living, but it was made even stranger by the fact that . . . she'd seen Arthur Hill only twice and talked to him what, once?

She couldn't even remember what he looked like. Not really. When she tried to recall his appearance, the general structure of his facial features as they'd stared each other down across the Baypen factory floor, she couldn't.

True, she had a clearer memory of how he'd looked a year later, on Halloween. But then he'd been filth flecked and skinny, with several broken bones in his face.

When Quinn thought of Cole's dad, the only image she was able to conjure was the black-and-white headshot news outlets used when they talked about him. Would CNN have replaced that photo with a mug shot if the man had ever been captured? Maybe. But maybe not. He had been very rich.

Even without remembering what he looked like, Arthur Hill was with her.

And he had been since she'd read the news that his body had disappeared.

After his death outside the municipal building, during the riot, law enforcement had transferred the body to the county coroner, who'd held on to it for a long while, as cases were being closed and forensics compared, until the decision had been made to send it back to the funeral home in Kettle Springs, where it would be prepared for burial.

The burial was a compromise between Cole and his extended family.

No press. No ceremony. Simple headstone.

But the burial, however stripped down, hadn't happened.

Quinn told herself that stealing the body was someone's idea of a prank.

Just a ghoulish prank.

Probably.

What other explanation could there be?

It wasn't like Arthur Hill had come back to life.

Quinn wasn't living *that* kind of horror story.

Was she?

Cole, Rust, and Quinn had all watched Arthur Hill take that arrow to the neck. He died, smelling like shit, with everybody in the gathered crowd wearing a clown mask, but not one of them aware the man whose death they were cheering was their leader.

But still, the funeral home *misplacing* the corpse had changed things.

Her quest for revenge had become routine by that point, her bloody knuckles scabbing over in the same ways, again and again. Fewer people on her list seemed to know *why* they were getting their asses beaten.

Then Arthur Hill's body disappeared. And hearing that had *done* something to the people she was after. Given them hope.

Or that's what it'd done to the ones she *could* find, the ones who hadn't gone off the grid themselves, disappeared just like Arthur Hill.

"I'm out there. You know that, right?" said a gruff voice from the passenger's seat beside her.

"Go away," Quinn said. But did she really say it out loud? Was any of this real? Or was she dreaming?

When Arthur Hill appeared to Quinn, he was always wearing the mask.

But never the pom-pom coveralls.

She turned to him.

The old man was shirtless, the hair on his chest mostly gray and curly. Y incision where the coroner had cut him open puckered at the edges, stitched together with thick black thread like shoelaces.

She didn't sleep much these days. Either in her prepaid motel room beds or in the reclined driver's seats of her various getaway cars.

But she didn't need to be asleep for Arthur Hill to visit. She was at the point where she dreamed while driving. White-line fever was a real thing, it turned out, the blacktop and double yellows of the highway becoming a kind of hypnotist's watch.

Arthur Hill didn't acknowledge her, just kept talking. "Yes. I'm out here traveling the open road," he said. "Like you."

She checked her mirrors, tried to watch the road, then checked her mirrors again when she realized she could see him in the glare of the windshield.

She didn't want to see him and his suppurating wounds oozing formaldehyde.

"It's fine," he said, something wrong in his dead throat. Like the arrow and autopsy had changed his voice, made it hard to speak. "You don't need to look at me, Quinn. But, from what I've been hearing . . ."

She wanted to scream at him. But she didn't, just kept her eyes forward, focusing on the textured synthetic leather of the steering wheel.

"I'm not the only *maniac* on the loose."

Quinn's head dipped, the wheel jolted, and she snapped awake, regaining control of the car before she could careen into a guardrail.

Sometimes she was awake when she saw him.

Sometimes not.

Quinn's fingertips tingled with adrenaline and her heart beat so hard it gave her a headache.

Cole's dad was no longer in the seat beside her, having dissolved back into her subconscious.

This car was a mess. It had a weird smell. The floor and seats were covered in fast-food containers from a burger chain called Krystal. A month ago, Quinn hadn't even *heard* of Krystal, but since crossing into Georgia she saw locations everywhere.

She hated stolen cars.

New cars couldn't be started without the key fob. And if there was a way to disable the onboard computer's GPS, Quinn didn't possess the technical know-how.

So she didn't steal new cars. She'd be caught.

It had to be old cars, but cars like this one she was driving . . . when you stole those, it meant you were stealing from a person who really *needed* their car.

The only cars she *enjoyed* stealing were the cars of the people she attacked. But those she didn't keep too long or cross state lines in.

Which meant she wouldn't have driven Charles Rome's car out of the state of Florida, even if she could've.

But she couldn't, once she'd heard that Charles Rome was dead.

No, Charlie Rome's car was a mobile crime scene. A clue that could get her caught for a crime the cops would *actually* care about.

So, along some wetlands back road, she'd laid a brick down on the accelerator and driven Charlie's car into the water under a canopy of cypress trees.

But Charlie, haven't you heard? I *kill people.*

Why had Quinn said that to him? He was already terrified and chained to a pipe. Well, to scare him some more, of course. Get him talking.

Besides, it had become an accepted fact on the Frendo message boards in the last few weeks, long before it'd become national news yesterday, that Quinn Maybrook was a murderer.

The people who'd disappeared, the rioters and shitposters who'd staged an armed takeover of a town in Missouri? The clowns believed Quinn Maybrook was killing them. It was a story that had germinated into a full-blown conspiracy inside a group of people who were *already* conspiracy theorists.

It went like this: The users of these boards believed the mainstream media was covering for Quinn, downplaying the number and severity of her attacks.

To pull this off, of course, there had to be collusion between the media and the cops. But that made sense, they reasoned, because the cops *wanted* Quinn to keep going. She was cleaning up undesirables.

God. If only that part about the cops wanting Quinn to succeed were true.

If only Quinn weren't on the run. If only she could stop using burner phones that couldn't install apps. If only she could call her dad with FaceTime again, like she had in the early days of this trip, before it had gotten too risky. If only she could walk into a place without changing her glasses. Or without restyling her hair. Or without wearing a hat. Or *during* the daytime.

Quinn never really liked malls, but right now all she wanted was to go to a mall food court. She wanted to let the sun hit her face from beneath skylights while she ate free teriyaki chicken samples and breathed deep, enjoying the buttery air from the pretzel place.

But she wouldn't have risked capture to do that, back when her plan had been to beat up 150 people. And she certainly couldn't do that now. . . .

Yes. She wanted to beat up 150 people. She wanted to break their bones. But she had rules, procedures to ensure she never mistakenly killed one. She never hit them over the head or caused substantial blood loss. She never . . .

Killing them was too far.

She wanted them to pay. But they didn't deserve to die.

The message boards were wrong. Law enforcement *was* looking for her. State and federal. In the early weeks she marveled at every day she wasn't caught, crossing state lines to commit dozens of cases of premeditated aggravated assault.

But her approach had been working and she *hadn't* killed anyone.

So the cops weren't looking *that* hard.

And after a few weeks the news had grown bored of Quinn Maybrook. "Two-Time Mass-Killing Survivor Breaks Man's Ankles" couldn't compete as a headline. Not once it'd gone stale, when those same news outlets had wars and murders and prescription weight-loss injections to run stories about.

Quinn hadn't killed anyone.

Not on this trip.

She'd *killed* people before setting out on the road, true. Plenty of people. But those had all been self-defense. And it wasn't like she'd grown a taste for it. All that killing haunted her. *Actually* haunted her, as Arthur Hill could attest.

These clowns, these bastards who'd come into her town, had gathered to watch her and her friends die . . . they just needed a lesson. Even if learning meant they needed to walk into an emergency room carrying their little finger packed in ice.

"I didn't kill him," Quinn said out loud, to nobody.

She'd been thinking the same thing on a loop, since leaving Florida and for the last few hours of Alabama driving.

She hadn't killed Charlie Rome!

She hadn't killed him. . . .

Right?

She'd been imagining things, sure, visits from an undead man in a clown mask, but she hadn't snapped and . . .

No. She remembered what had happened. After cutting off Charlie Rome's finger, she'd handed him the cooler. Even taken time to explain to him where she was leaving him in relation to the closest hospital.

She'd exchanged Charlie's car with the Nissan she'd taken off the guy in Tampa.

Yes, the last time Quinn had seen Charlie Rome his head was attached to his body and he had a ride to the ER.

"I've done nothing to deserve this!" Charlie had screamed in his chloroform sleep.

And he hadn't.

Quinn was sorry it'd ended up this way.

But she couldn't wallow in his death. She had to pay more attention than ever, be better at this than she had been.

Because she was close.

Whoever had beheaded Charlie, they'd done it *because* she was getting close.

She consulted the map.

Speaking of getting close, this was her turnoff.

She followed signs for Birmingham.

Charlie told her his buddy had gone north, so she was headed north. With a slight detour to check off a few more names from her list.

The names were all small fries. One or two that she might not even bother with, might quietly show up at their jobs or homes and check that they were still there. She needed to know who on her list was disappeared like Charlie's friend Clownstick69 and who had stayed around.

Clownstick69, Benjamin Koontz, had been an odd case. Not only was Koontz missing, but he'd taken his whole family with him. That wasn't the odd part. The disappeared sometimes took their families. But Koontz's adult sister, a woman who didn't fit the profile at all, seemed to have emptied her bank accounts and fled, too. She was a grade school teacher.

Grade school teachers were not, typically, the type of people Quinn found herself beating with tire irons.

And the money. The money borrowed, the money withdrawn. She wished she'd stayed in better contact with Cole, there was probably something he could do to find where it'd gone, with routing numbers or pay stubs. Something financial and technical a rich kid might know about.

Quinn drove for two more hours, even though it should have taken half as long to arrive at her destination. But there were speed traps on the highway, cops waiting, so she chose to wend along the back roads.

She pressed the old paper map against the steering wheel, tracing lines with her finger and longing for Google Maps. Or Waze. Hell, she'd settle for MapQuest.

Or, maybe she didn't want a phone that could run apps.

Maybe she didn't want her road atlases, either.

Maybe what she needed was to stop all this. Return to Kettle Springs and let her dad—and Cole's lawyers—do their thing.

She'd done enough.

She no longer received any catharsis from their screams.

She should give up and go home. . . .

But . . .

Nah.

Quinn had only a single semester of freshman psych, but she'd been there long enough to learn what she was feeling now was called "the sunk-cost fallacy."

She was in too deep. Had invested too much of herself to stop now. Of her original 150 names—a list that had expanded and contracted as she researched—only about 20 remained.

But it wasn't those 20 keeping her going.

She couldn't stop until she knew where the missing ones had gone.

And maybe the next person on her list could give her a clue.

Not that it was likely. The next guy was Trevor Dale. A twenty-something with mean-looking face tattoos, but nothing but petty crimes on his record. Not that active in the Frendo community and enough of an upstanding citizen to have legal custody of his younger brother.

It was a long shot that Dale knew anything, but at least this'd be an easy one. Two guys, one of them younger than Quinn. No wife, no parents, no jobs. In Quinn's experience, people like this were the type of target where you could pull right into their driveway and—

Oh shit!

The kid seemed to materialize a few yards in front of her, the orange of the evening sun turning his body into a dark flicker in the glare.

Quinn hit the brakes, the fryer-oil-scented car turning into a skid.

The gravel under the tires turned into projectiles, pelting the kid in his face, arms, and legs.

But he made no attempt to jump out of the way of the car.

He had a dazed look, kept his hands above his head, trying to wave her down.

The left side of the bumper came to a stop inches from the boy's knees.

If Quinn had been going any faster—or braked a half second later—she would have *actually* killed somebody this week.

There was a loud pop from beneath the dashboard and suddenly it wasn't the old fast-food containers making the interior of the car stink. The ozone puff of an electrical short steamed through the A/C vents and burned Quinn's nostrils.

She felt bad. Worse than she had, somehow. Even if the cops returned this car to the original owner, it wouldn't run. And she doubted whoever she'd stolen from had kept good insurance. She hated that, the fact that she'd hurt this stranger, damaged their life and livelihood.

The kid was banging on her window.

"Yo, help me, please help me," the boy said. Quinn pushed him back with the door, lifting herself out of the car.

The boy was pointing toward the ramshackle single-story house with a porch swing and an ugly black muscle car parked out front.

At first glance she thought the car was up on blocks. But it wasn't, just raised on a jack.

Quinn had become so used to sizing up cars, searching for her next ride, that it took her a moment to realize the boy wasn't pointing toward the car.

He was pointing at the three corpses in the driveway.

Quinn followed the boy for a few steps, the scene resolving itself.

It wasn't a gas leak or an auto accident that'd killed these guys.

They'd been dismantled.

The one closest to the car had died screaming, with half the skin covering his head peeled away.

"Oh God," the boy said while Quinn tried to assess the situation.

She flicked her eyes up to make sure the kid wasn't carrying a weapon.

He wasn't.

There was no way he was the killer.

He was wearing black cargo shorts and a black T-shirt, and while neither would have shown stains well, she could still see that he didn't have a speck of blood on his hands and arms.

The boy's mouth hung open as he leaned away from her and stepped back. His eyes were wide, like *he* was the one prone to waking nightmares, like *he* was the one seeing ghosts.

Quinn looked to the nearest body, ignoring the large entry wound and instead inspecting the guy's tattooed face.

Permanent clown makeup.

This body was Trevor Dale.

She looked up at the scared kid, unable to hide the anger

and frustration in her eyes. She wasn't angry at Trevor Dale, but at the fact she was being toyed with. Someone had known she was coming here and had beaten her to these guys, possibly by a matter of minutes.

"Oh God, you're her," the kid said, blinking.

He took a step back, then again, starting to stumble.

She chanced a look at the bodies again.

The two who weren't Dale were older, couldn't be the younger brother.

"Listen," Quinn said, trying to put a soothing tone in her voice and failing, "I'm not going to hurt you."

Was that a lie? She had no idea how to calm people anymore.

And then even after all he'd seen, his brother killed, the horrors in the driveway, Quinn could tell that the soft-faced teenager with patchy facial hair and tight-knit braids was *afraid* of her.

"You need to tell me what happened here," she said. "And *when* did it—"

Before she could get her last question out, she heard the first police siren.

Fuck.

"Did you call the cops?" Quinn screamed at the boy.

"Yeah." The kid shrank back, put his hands up. "Please don't hurt me."

Quinn ran a hand through her short hair, then headed

back to the car. Inside, she upended fast-food containers as she stuffed her maps and road atlases into the duffel she kept behind the driver's seat.

Clothes, her masks, an envelope of cash, and a few weapons: the bag contained all she owned and was all she needed to transfer between cars.

"That looks like a shitbox, but does it run?" Quinn asked.

"What?" The kid squinted back at her, confused and sweating.

The sirens were getting louder, engines roaring under the wail. The noise made it hard to concentrate, but she thought back to her notes, tried to remember the name of Trevor Dale's brother.

What had it been? It was something regular. A common first name with a different last name, not Dale.

"John?" she said, a quick squint of recognition from him. "Johnny?" she corrected.

"Yeah. Johnny D. That's me. How do you know—"

That Quinn knew his name didn't seem to put him at ease. If anything, he looked even more ready to accept that she was the devil incarnate.

"Johnny. You need to listen to me—"

"Johnny D," he corrected, sounding addled.

"Johnny D," she said, trying to stay calm but her patience fraying as the police sirens approached. "Does that car run?"

She pointed at it, and when he still didn't turn to look,

she placed a hand on his shoulder and squeezed. His flesh was solid and damp under a black T-shirt. A T-shirt with holes in the armpits.

"The Mustang?" he asked, his voice dreamy.

"Yes. Does the Mustang run, Johnny D?"

The boy's eyes focused and the skin of his face seemed to dry in a chill. His expression changed, the softness of his face seeming to tighten into something closer to handsomeness and confidence.

It was like she'd turned some kind of switch, hit a nerve that caused Johnny D to forget his dead brother for a moment, to forget his mortal terror and focus on his car:

"Of course the Mustang runs," he said. "I rebuilt it myself."

SIX

KETTLE SPRINGS

Tabitha stayed with Ruth's body until the sun burned away the last of the mist.

She wept.

She prayed.

She remembered what it had been like to spend time with Ruth. How good it had been to have a friend. Someone to talk to about something other than scripture.

It wasn't only Ruth she mourned. She remembered how Mr. and Mrs. Miller, buried on either side of Ruth, had been kind and fair parents.

Mrs. Miller's fingertips had been chewed away by Nellie.

The general form of Ruth's face was still there, paler than it should be, but there. Ruth could have been alive, until you spotted the maggots wriggling around her ears and nose, displacing the thin skin under her lower lip.

No, this wasn't Ruth anymore.

Any spirit, any soul, was in the kingdom of heaven.

This body at Tabitha's feet was meat that hadn't been properly larded and had spoiled during the winter.

When there were no more tears, Tabitha wondered what came next.

She could push the soil back over the bodies, pretend she was never here, but that felt wrong.

It felt like a sin, to leave them. They weren't apostate. Not by any definition of the word. They were innocents. A family of grace and charity.

And they'd clearly been killed. Buried in a shallow, unmarked grave.

Why, then, hadn't Tabitha screamed, run to the nearest home—the Trent farmhouse—and pounded on the door, crying, "Murder! Murder! Murder!"?

It would be so easy. She could see the lights of the farmhouse from here.

She wasn't yelling because that wouldn't be smart.

Someone had *put* this family out here. Someone in their town had killed the Millers and planted them in their own field.

Ruth's family hadn't fled town under cover of darkness.

Ruth hadn't left without saying goodbye.

"They will be missed." Tabitha remembered the Pastor's

words at a town meeting called to introduce a batch of settlers.

The church had lied.

Even if he hadn't *intended* to lie, even if he hadn't known about the bodies, the Pastor had helped the murderer spread the fiction among the congregation that the Millers had moved to St. Genevieve.

Which meant that she couldn't trust—

Tabitha looked across the field, to the farmhouse, and ducked low.

In the leftmost first-floor window of the Trent farmhouse, the curtains billowed.

Could they see her out here? How sharp was Hannah's vision? How sharp was her father's, when he wasn't drinking and ignoring farming advice?

This close to the ground, to the Millers, she could smell their deaths. The miasma that clung above the bodies was so thick she could almost feel it in her mouth, pushing against the back of her throat.

Tabitha put her head up, looked to the horizon, tried to focus on something else so she wouldn't be sick.

The house.

Tabitha had been a guest inside that house only a few days ago. How had she not been suspicious before? She remembered how the Millers had taken no furniture with them to St. Genevieve. How Hannah's room now was arranged the same as Ruth's room had been.

Hannah. That the girl didn't speak made Tabitha feel safe, that she could tell her anything. But what could she do now, if Tabitha told her about Ruth? How could Hannah possibly help?

But if Tabitha couldn't tell Hannah, who *could* Tabitha talk to?

Who in Kettle Springs she could trust?

Tabitha's mother placed the lid over the chicken pot, then spoke:

"Lies, girl."

Some part of her knew this was a mistake, trying to confide in her mother.

But she was streaked with the slime of dead flesh and rotted corn crop. During the town's transition, then more recently, during her parents' seduction to the Pastor's way of thinking, Tabitha had allowed herself to hope that her mother wasn't truly gone, that she'd come back to her daughter if there came a time where Tabitha really needed her.

If Tabitha needed her as much as she did now.

"It—they—" Tabitha stuttered, couldn't stop the tremble shaking her chin.

"How many times have you been warned?" Her mother took a long blink, then swallowed and continued, finding her words after an apparent bout of nausea: "Warned about telling lies and stories?"

Many times. But none that she could remember before this year. Before Kettle Springs was *this* Kettle Springs. Before the Hills and the Dunnes and the Blevinses had reincorporated the town.

Her mother spoke to herself, muttering: "She won't go to church, sick, she says. Now murder, she cries. We'll see how sick . . . lies . . ."

She trailed off, biting her nails. It was a nervous habit her mother had started only recently.

There'd been a time where Tabitha's parents had loved to hear her stories. There'd been a time they'd stayed up by the fire, listening, when they'd all taken turns telling tales, Father the most skillful storyteller of them all.

Once upon a time . . .

This wasn't once upon a time. This was now. And now her mother's eyes had that hollow look that they did.

Tabitha clenched every muscle in her neck and shoulders, trying to get her tremble under control. She had to make her understand.

"It is not lies!" Tabitha said. She'd never raised her voice to her mother.

Silence.

Tabitha flicked her eyes to the window, worried that if she shouted loud enough, her father would come in from the fields.

When she looked back, her mother was clicking her jaw side to side.

But maybe that meant she was listening. Tabitha spread her fingers and lifted her hands, showing the blood and the dirt on her skin and dress.

"Look, Mother, blood! The Millers have been killed. I can *take* you to their bodies."

More silence, her mother's eyes wobbling, as if the woman were reading invisible words in the air and making no sense of them.

"Do you think they were apostates, Mother? If they were, why no trial?"

"Stop it," her mother said, her voice a whisper.

Tabitha could feel the warning, the hairs on her own neck rising, begging her not to continue down this path.

But she couldn't stop now:

"If Ruth Miller and Justine Miller and Uri Miller were heathens who deserved to die, then why no trial and why no ceremony?"

"S-s-stop it. You dare to—"

If Father was going to hear her, let him. She continued screaming.

"Answer me, Mother: Why was there no execution in the town square? Why weren't they burned, or strung up? Why didn't the clown knock their heads off!?"

Her mother's hand slapped onto the countertop, flour

and grist flying into the air.

"Stop it! Story too ghastly! Stop." Her mother's tone was emotional, pleading, missing words, but the emotion never reached those eyes.

"It is not a *story*. It's true, Mother. You know it is."

Those eyes. Glassy and dry at the same time. Like marbles.

Those eyes locking into place, coming to a decision.

"Then we inform the Constable," her mother said.

This wasn't the victory Tabitha had been hoping for, a return of her mother's maternal instincts.

It was a threat. Everyone feared the Constable. And with good reason. Tabitha's mother was threatening her.

The Constable? The man who could tie a noose fast enough he needn't pause to ash his cigarette?

Yes. That was who Mother was threatening her with.

What now? How could Tabitha proceed? How could she *survive* the decisions she'd made in the last half hour?

There was only one way.

"Yes, ma'am," Tabitha said. "We need to tell him."

Was that surprise flitting across her mother's dulled expression?

Tabitha was committed now. Whatever happened next, let it happen, she would not betray the memory of Ruth by backing down. "We *must* tell him. We must then do our best to tell the whole town what's happened, that the Millers

81

never made it to St. Genevieve. There needs to be an inquiry and our neighbors must be warned that there is an assassin among us. Possibly more than one."

As impassive as her mother's face had become since taking the host, the woman seemed to think about this. She checked the chicken again. Yes, there was still a chicken in the pot. She'd made a mistake and her daughter had called her bluff.

"Your father will call on him. Tomorrow when he's in town."

Tabitha swallowed. No. She couldn't allow time for them, whoever they were, to hide the bodies, to cover things up.

She had to be brave, for Ruth.

"The chicken can simmer, Mother. I'll walk you. We can go now."

The town's jail cell hadn't been used for an overnight stay in months.

There were no jailable crimes anymore. The people of Kettle Springs either behaved or they were apostates. And apostates didn't need a bed or a privy bucket. They didn't get a last meal.

The Constable didn't lock the cell behind Tabitha, just pushed the door closed until the jamb gave a light clang.

She rarely saw the man from this close up. The Constable kept strange facial hair, shaved in places her father never would have, long in others he'd never keep it, tobacco stains in the gray at the corners of his mouth. There used to be a stricture about mustaches. And all the smokers she'd known, before, had used pipes.

But things in town had changed. Obviously.

The Constable wore the sign of the clown over his breast pocket, and a cross hung from his collar.

"Wait here. I . . ." He blinked, seemed to remember where he was. "I'll be in the next room with your mother," he said.

If he wasn't turning the key, Tabitha wasn't being locked up. Not officially. But that didn't make her heart beat any quieter in her chest.

Tabitha's gaze settled on the key's iron curve.

The Constable seemed to read her thoughts.

Or maybe leaving the key was a test. Mind games.

"Don't be thinking of running out of here," he said. "This isn't schoolhouse trouble you're in, and there won't be schoolhouse punishments."

Tabitha nodded and the man left.

She felt tears begin to well in the corners of her eyes.

She'd made a terrible mistake.

How could a girl choosing to trust her mother be such folly? How could it lead to sitting on a termite-eaten bench in a jail cell?

It was all because of *him*. All because of what he'd told them, what he'd promised, and what the settlers had believed. They'd . . . infected her parents with their belief.

What kind of man of God did this?

Not a man of *her* God, that was for certain and true.

Outside, Tabitha could hear the thwack of Isaiah Dunne chopping wood.

A day later and he was still at it.

The sound entered through the cell's small window, echoing against the brick.

Tabitha and her mother had passed Isaiah Dunne's worksite on the way into town. The structure Dunne had been tasked with building was beginning to take shape. It had a foundation, at least, an assemblage of lumber that looked to Tabitha like a row of sharp teeth, but that couldn't be right.

"Good morning, Tabitha," the Pastor said, startling her.

He stood against the bars to her cell, having entered the room from a passage Tabitha hadn't noticed. If anyone else in town had been prone to such theatrical entrances, the Pastor would have had them killed as a suspected witch or warlock.

"Good morning," she said, hugging her arms to herself, the cold and damp in the cell suddenly noticeable, nearly overwhelming.

The Pastor knocked a finger against the bars to her cell. "Is this really better than Mrs. Hill's lessons?"

"I . . ." Tabitha was confused.

"Seems like a long way to go to skip class, is what I mean."

Oh . . . He was joking. Tabitha wasn't sure what to say to the jest. So she said nothing.

"I hear you've had a frightening day, child," the Pastor said, becoming serious.

Thwack. The sound of Isaiah's chopping was becoming more unsettling by the moment.

"Or," the Pastor said, "I hear you've had a frightening morning. But don't worry. The bell hasn't yet chimed noon. Plenty of time for the sun to shine and the fearsomeness to abate."

He was changing his speech to match his tone. He was performing for her, like she'd seen him do with his followers, like she'd seen him change himself to better communicate with her parents.

Tabitha stood from the bench.

"Yes," she said, unsure how to respond. "It's been very frightening."

It was Thursday, not Sunday, but the Pastor was wearing his full vestments. He also had his hood pulled up to obscure his face. Was it raining outside? No, it hadn't been. The point of the hood made him seem taller, under the low ceilings.

"But I've heard that you *enjoy* things that are frightening."

"Sir?"

"Father, please."

She recoiled at the word. He wasn't her father. That wasn't what they'd called the last leader of the church. It wasn't their way.

"I mean to say that," the Pastor continued, "I've heard from your mother that you enjoy fantastical stories." He stepped forward and took hold of the iron key, turning it to lock the door with a *clunk*, then unlocking the mechanism, then opening the door inward. "That you like frightening stories."

Tabitha stepped away from the door, feeling the cool stones of the cell wall against her back.

"I enjoy stories of faith persevering and the glory of God," she said.

The Pastor acted like he hadn't heard.

She tried to look him in the face but found it difficult. The skin of his cheeks and chin didn't move correctly.

This wasn't the way he'd been when he'd first arrived to town. Back then, when he'd exchanged money and supplies for safe haven for him and his people, he'd been perfumed and overgroomed, his teeth square and too white.

Both looks, shiny and happy as he had been, or enrobed and earthy as he stood before her now, were facades. Neither was the real man, if there had ever been a real man in there. They were masks.

"I used to enjoy stories as well, when I was a boy," the Pastor continued. "But it's dangerous. You can lose yourself to lies and fiction. I almost did. I began to think the story I was telling was more important than the lesson I was imparting. And there were children listening."

"I know," Tabitha said. Then she added, *"Father."* She didn't mean the word to sound like it did, but if the Pastor noticed her disrespect, he didn't react.

Thwack.

He didn't react to much, under that hood. His face was impassive in the shadows of the cell.

"Sit with me," he said.

She did. How could she refuse?

There was barely space for both of them on the bench.

"Stories are childish things," he said. "You'll be a woman soon, Tabitha."

Even over the linen of her dress, the shock of his hand touching her knee was like ice. Under the hood, she could feel his eyes.

"I must ask, you look well enough to me, why are you suddenly too ill to join the congregation on Sundays?"

"I . . . I plan to attend with my family soon. I only . . ."

He removed his hand from her knee, waved it, changed the subject.

"If the Constable follows you and your mother back to home, if he went through your things, he wouldn't find any contraband, would he?"

"Contraband?" she asked. Thinking of all the *contraband*

she used to enjoy. The books had become too dangerous to keep, after the town's second apostate—not a hapless outsider, but a neighbor who'd fallen under inquiry—had been found.

"Surely you know what I mean. You don't keep *secular* literature, do you, Tabitha?"

"No. Of course not."

"Then holy books, maybe? But the wrong kind of holy."

Thwack.

"The wrong kind?"

He replaced his hand. Squeezed.

"Is there an echo in here, Tabitha?" His voice was playful. "Let me be clearer: If the Constable and your mother pulled up the floorboards, would they find journals of heathen prayers? Would they find jewelry of bones and woven grasses? Would they find the materials and talismans of witchcraft?"

The cool traveled from the palm of the Pastor's hand, up Tabitha's knee, and spread through her entire body until she was sure the shivers would shake her off the edge of the seat.

She tried to find the glare of his eyes under that hood, beyond his mask, then said:

"No, Father. I would never."

The Pastor waited for a long time, the dark hole of his hood turned back toward her.

This close, she could smell him.

He smelled like dried flowers and incense.

88

A ghost of the old perfumes and scented body lotions? Perhaps.

But there was another smell, under those.

"Good," the Pastor said. "I believe you. I didn't *think* we'd find anything like that. But I wanted to make sure. Always easiest to simply ask."

She slumped. Why was he doing this? Why was he torturing her? His tone of voice, it was so . . . informal? Unmannered. Playful.

"You know Kettle Springs only works, that it can only be called a community, if we adhere to traditions. Especially the young people of the town. You are our future. You have to watch and learn and help us pass on these traditions so the town can endure. The mask that Isaiah wears? It's our message to the future. It's our culture. It always has been."

Tabitha nodded. She couldn't bring herself to speak, could no longer tell the man what he wanted to hear. Because he was lying.

It had not *always* been this way.

"This was a good talk," he said, giving Tabitha's knee one final pat and then standing. "I'm feeling justified in my decision."

He put his back to her, ducked low so that his hood cleared the cell doorway.

"Your decision, s— Father?" Tabitha asked.

"Yes," he said, turning to face her, leaving the cell door

open behind him. "You're free to go."

The relief must have been apparent on her face, in her posture, because somewhere behind those lips that barely moved, the Pastor clicked his tongue.

Thwack.

"That's not all. You're the town's oldest child, yes?"

"Yes."

"Not for long. On Sunday you'll take the host."

"I—"

"You won't be ill *this* Sunday, child. I promise. I will pray for fortitude and health. I've indulged your reluctance long enough. Your hesitancy to attend services is beginning to look like apostasy. You will join us, join your parents."

A pause.

Today was Thursday.

"Don't look so glum, girl. This is a blessing." And he left the room with a swirl of his cloaks and collars.

As terrified as Tabitha was by that proclamation, she couldn't focus on what it meant. Because she recognized that smell, the one that lingered on the Pastor's clothes, seemed to puff out under his hood as he spoke.

She'd smelled that same scent just this morning.

Rot. Putrefaction. Death.

The Pastor was rotting. Under his cloaks the man was a corpse, just like Ruth and her parents.

SEVEN

INTERSTATE 65, THIRTY MILES OUTSIDE NASHVILLE, TENNESSEE

Johnny D's fingers hurt from bracing himself between the Mustang's window and doorframe. Back in 1998, the designers at Ford decided that next year's model didn't need grab handles. Great choice.

It wasn't only Johnny's fingers, the rest of him was in pain, too.

His ass hurt from sitting in the foam-free passenger seat, its springs digging into his backside.

His stomach ached from hunger since his last meal, at ten this morning, had been a single microwaved Eggo waffle.

His neck hurt from where Quinn Maybrook had punched him in the throat.

And his back hurt from where he'd hit the ground after.

The punch might have been his fault, though.

He shouldn't have tried to run when they'd stopped for gas.

Not because he didn't want to escape. But he'd misjudged how many witnesses were around and how far away they were from the gas pumps.

Johnny was a lot of things, but he wasn't much of a runner.

Trees and mile markers swished by in the headlights.

He sat silent, listening to the rattle of the transmission. That sound was what he'd been trying to fix when he'd rolled under the car and watched as Weez, Bobby, and his brother . . .

He tried to push the thought away, but it was too late, he was already thinking about Trevor. The memory was a mental image, isolated and played on a loop. He watched the burst-balloon effect of Trevor's skull popping open, then time reversing and the wound resealing and popping again.

Quinn took the Mustang into a corner and Johnny turned away from her, tried not to let her see him clenching his eyes and shaking his head so the image would go away.

It was strange . . . he wasn't sad about Trevor. Or he wasn't sad *yet*. He loved his brother—half-brother, but he almost never said the half part. He loved Trevor more than he'd loved their mother. *Way* more than he'd loved his dad, if love was even the word for what they had in that strained relationship.

But Johnny couldn't be sad, couldn't even be mad, all he could feel when he thought about Trevor was a disoriented shock, the pop of the pistol and Trevor's hair and brain splashing the gravel.

The sadness would come, though, he knew it would. He needed time to get used to a world without Trevor's doofy fucking smile. It was a kind smile. Which, admittedly, was hard to see behind the tattoo.

Process. That was the word one of his social workers would use.

Johnny needed time to *process*.

He had plenty of other things to focus on right now. So maybe it was good that overwhelming grief wasn't one of them.

Was Quinn Maybrook taking him to a second location to cut his head off? It seemed unlikely, but she'd already hit him once and that shit hurt, so he didn't want to attempt escape again until he was sure his situation was life or death.

He looked over at her, trying to be smooth about it and using the side mirror.

If this were a concert? Sure. Or somebody's backyard? Yeah, he'd down a beer and take his chances talking to the girl in the reflection. It might even make her hotter, if somebody at the party whispered to him, "Yo, that girl merc'd a bunch of people."

But context was everything.

So right now, Quinn Maybrook was a threat. Not a cute older girl with a dirty face who knew how to drive the Mustang better than he did.

Yes, better than he did. Which wasn't easy to admit, but it was true. And Johnny may have been seventeen, only recently receiving his full license, but the way his brother raised him, on the back roads *where* he'd raised him, Johnny had been driving since he was twelve.

It felt weird, not just Maybrook's skill behind the wheel, but for someone else to be driving the Mustang at all.

It was like Johnny was a ghost, an impartial observer in his own life, watching while his only belonging of any consequence was being driven out of state.

He wished he could take his mind off it. But by doing what?

Usually, if he were a passenger in a car, he would be scrolling on his phone.

But his phone was long gone.

As soon as they'd had a moment to slow down, when there were no more sirens behind them, Quinn Maybrook had asked Johnny to hand over his Samsung.

He'd watched her type "Alton Ministries" into the cracked screen and mark something on her old-ass, spiral-bound *Rand McNally Road Atlas*.

Then she'd tossed his phone off a bridge, into a creek.

You don't notice how much you rely on something

important until it's gone.

Which, Johnny knew, could mean the phone or Trevor.

"Nice night," she said, breaking the silence. "No clouds."

It was the first time Quinn Maybrook had spoken in an hour.

Her tone was different from what it had been. Before now, everything she'd said in the car had been barked one- or two-word commands. And this was a comment about . . . the weather?

"Yeah. Guess so," he said.

"Have you been to Tennessee before?"

Was she really trying to make small talk? This was the first question she'd posed to Johnny since asking him to describe the killers. *Demanding* that he describe his brother's killers in as great a detail as he could, then asking him to do it again, to make sure he didn't contradict himself.

It was horrible.

"Yeah, uh, couple times. I went to Dollywood once."

He'd gone with his brother. But he didn't say that.

She nodded and lapsed back into quiet.

When he'd told her about the missionary kids, she hadn't asked any follow-up questions. But she did express surprise they hadn't been wearing Frendo masks. He hadn't even thought of that, until she'd said it. It should have been obvious that the Murder Mormons and a national celebrity arriving to the same location, moments apart, were related to each other, but it hadn't been obvious to Johnny. Maybe that was a symptom of shock.

It was weird to think, but the second those two boys had rolled onto their property, even before they'd gotten their weapons out, Johnny D and Trevor had become entangled in current events.

And once those weapons had been used? They were a news item.

They were true crime. Johnny Lawson and Trevor Dale were names that'd be spoken on *The Last Podcast on the Left*. And not as a brief news update on "Side Stories." They were in a multipart episode like the hosts had given to Dahmer or Manson or Columbine. Real-meal prime-time shit. Three hours minimum, even without all the commercials for mattresses and home security systems.

A few minutes went by with no further discussion. Their route was bending east, away from Nashville, threading through the middle of the state. That made sense, that she'd avoid the bigger cities.

"Why do you like them, Johnny?" she asked after a while.

"Johnny D, please. Use the D in there."

It was something he didn't usually insist on. He was fine going by Johnny in most settings. Except with teachers or cops or anyone else he didn't want to hear calling him by his father's name.

To her credit, she didn't ask him to explain.

"Johnny *D*," she said, correcting herself. "Why do you like them?"

She motioned to the bobbleheads he'd hot glue–gunned to the dash.

Violent J and Shaggy 2 Dope, bopping along in the shadows, bumping to the whistle of wind through the Mustang's grille.

Johnny thought about this girl's relationship with clowns and wondered if he should lie, say that this had been Trevor's car.

Was it just Frendo? Or would *any* clown trip Quinn Maybrook's murder reflex?

He searched back in his memory, tried to remember if he'd already referred to the Mustang as his car. He wasn't sure. He probably had.

Then he looked down at his hands and arms. He didn't have nearly as much visible ink as Trevor. But they'd been to the same parties and Johnny'd been just as drunk and bored those nights when Bobby's ex-girlfriend got the gun out. There were hatchets tattooed between the knuckles of both his pointer fingers, a jack-in-the-box peeking out from his shirtsleeve, and the Great Milenko on the other side, facing the car door where Quinn couldn't see.

Yeah. She already knew about his relationship to the Dark Carnival.

"It's not a trap," Quinn said. "I don't care that you're a

Juggalo. I'm just making conversation."

"Oh," Johnny said.

He thought for a moment.

Ah, fine, they should get into it, if they were going to be driving for however long. If she was planning on hurting him anyway, what did it matter?

He'd had this conversation, or a version of it, a few times.

"Do you know their music?" he asked. Then, before she could respond: "Or do you just know the jokes they like to make about us on *Saturday Night Live* or whatever?"

"Can't say I watch much *Saturday Night Live*."

"Oh yeah. I forgot. You're on the run."

"Well, that and I'm not like forty-five years old."

"Yo, what's wrong with—" He stopped himself. She was goading him. *Stick to one argument at a time*, he thought. "Never mind that. Do you know their music?"

"Can't say I do."

Johnny paused, tried to think of how he'd phrased his defense of ICP on previous occasions. Not that he needed to defend himself. It was okay for people to like what they liked and fuck the haters, but . . . he needed her to know it was deeper than that with him and ICP.

"I like them because their music is good. That's part of it. It's fun. It's different. Look at their stuff from the nineties. Nobody sounded like that."

"Fair. I'll have to check them—"

"Don't."

Quinn blinked, raised her eyebrows. She was out of practice talking to people, he could tell, and she certainly wasn't used to them talking back.

"Fuck out of here with patronizing me and telling me you'll have to give them a try. We don't need you, and I know you're not going to."

"Also fair," she said, and smiled.

He wasn't sure if it was a *nice* smile.

So he cleared his throat and continued.

"I like them because my brother liked them, and it was something we could like together."

Quinn checked the rearview. There was nothing back there, just dotted lines tinted red from their taillights. No matter the context, he got the feeling she was always checking behind her.

"And they don't take anything too seriously. And they're all about family, even if you hate your family or it's fucked up, ICP can be your family."

"That's . . ." She paused. "Actually, very sweet."

He nodded, then added:

"That and I like songs about people getting dismembered."

Quinn laughed.

"Or, I *did*, I guess the jury's out on whether I'll keep liking that. After what I just saw. It was—"

Fuck. He felt a sob catch.

He didn't mean to get all serious and shit. So he shut his mouth and turned away in his seat again.

In the mirror he watched her nod, like she understood.

He wondered if she was going to let him live when this was all over. An hour ago, he would have said his odds were fifty-fifty, but now he thought it was eighty-twenty she might let him walk.

That was an improvement.

They didn't talk for the next hour or two. It was hard to tell time, with no phone and the digital clock in the Mustang blinking 12:00.

Whatever time it was, the next they spoke they had arrived at the strip mall and soon after that everything was going wrong.

There hadn't been a police chase as they sped away from Johnny's house. They weren't pursued. No cops had spotted them speeding around the dirt road that led away from the property.

Yes, Quinn had torn down the dirt road behind the property with haste. It had *sounded* like they were being surrounded.

But once they'd hit pavement it was apparent that none of those sirens were following, just echoing out through the hills of Alabama.

But that realization hadn't made Quinn decelerate.

When she was in a new car, it had become custom to open the engine and see what she was working with.

During the not-chase, Johnny Lawson groaned and gritted his teeth, one moment seemingly worried she was going to lose control, exhilarated at the speed the next.

If the kid thought they were in an action movie, who was she to ruin the illusion?

Those kinds of stories were fun.

She could let him live in one for a while.

Eventually she slowed down to the speed limit, eyes watching the side of the road for the noses of patrol cars among the trees.

The Mustang recked. Not of burger grease like the last car, instead it smelled like that type of incense that potheads liked to burn. She always thought that smell was less to cover up the odor of pot, more to indicate that the person burning it was, in fact, a pothead.

Under the scent of incense, Quinn could smell—and see—that the floor mats were spotted with spilled automotive lubricant. Combine that with the fact that the car had been hoisted up on a jack when she'd first seen it, and it was obvious she was driving a work in progress.

That could be an issue.

But the car seemed sturdy. It didn't seem like the wheels were about to fly off or the engine drop out at the next pothole . . . but that slight rattle over the right wheel well concerned her.

Johnny—sorry, Johnny *D*—shifted in his seat. If they were keeping this car for any length of time, they'd have to get him a travel pillow to sit on. He did not look comfortable.

There was no reason for her to keep him miserable.

He wasn't a bad kid, just had an attitude, iffy taste in music, and shitty luck.

She was sorry about his half-brother.

She was also sorry about the throat punch, but couldn't say that.

The sun had just set as they approached the cashier window together, so everything had that dim blue of twilight. Quinn with a hat on, brim pulled down, Johnny instructed to pay for twenty bucks' worth of regular with the cash she'd given him. Then, before she could even get the nozzle inserted to start filling, he'd made a break for the diesel pumps, waving to the truckers parked that way for help, yelling that he was being kidnapped.

Quinn had been angrier with herself than Johnny.

But he was the one who'd gotten punched.

It'd been an overreaction. The truckers wouldn't have done anything. There was one thing Quinn had learned in the last few months: truckers had selective vision. If something shady looked like it was none of their business . . . they *weren't* looking.

And a young woman kidnapping a teen boy who out-weighed her by thirty or forty pounds? Yeah, right. Sounded unlikely.

"Is that five oh one or five oh seven?" Quinn asked, fold-ing the map over, angling it under the ceiling light to show Johnny where she'd scribbled the address. "What do you think that says?"

She knew what it said—and it didn't matter, both of those addresses would be on the same side of the road—but why not try to involve Johnny D? He'd been sitting in the passenger seat for hours, thinking about his dead brother.

That kind of thing, Quinn knew . . . it could drive you insane.

"Try having a dead daughter," Arthur Hill said from the back seat of the Mustang.

She ignored him.

Johnny D finished studying the address and said:

"It says that you got some fucked-up handwriting."

Ha. She liked that.

"And you're squinting at my handwriting like you should maybe go see the eye doctor."

"Sorry, I guess I forgot to grab my readers when we were leaving."

She turned into the parking lot.

The night was full dark, clouds over the stars and moon, and only half of the lot's lampposts had working bulbs.

It was around eleven p.m. and the only open business in the shopping center was a Food Lion. There were fifteen or twenty cars out front of the grocery store, then five more vehicles scattered across the other half of the lot.

Were these cars abandoned? Did they belong to Food Lion employees?

Or were people sleeping in these cars?

Quinn had gotten an education on stuff like this over the last few months. Each town had a whisper network that'd let you know where it was okay to sleep in your car, where the local cops or corporate security wouldn't accost you.

She parked as close as she could to their destination and as far as possible from the next closest vehicle, in case there was someone awake in the nearest car to witness what came next.

"Hand me my bag," she said, keeping her eyes focused out the window, scanning the darkened storefronts.

These businesses weren't closed for the day . . . they were closed for good.

There was a "For Lease" sign in the window of a defunct hobby store. The insignia for a children's clothing store was partially scraped off the glass with a razor blade, off-model cartoon characters smiling underneath.

Standing between those two abandoned shops was an empty, double-sized storefront: 507.

The address and suite number she'd found when she'd used Johnny's phone to search for Alton Ministries.

Retail couldn't thrive in this corner of Tennessee. And apparently neither could a small church.

Johnny, springs squeaking under him, had the bag lifted up from behind Quinn's seat.

Metal clinked against metal inside the duffel.

He began to hand the bag over, then pulled back.

"Wait," he said. "What's in here?"

He didn't wait for her to answer, unzipping and pulling the top open.

They'd shared some chummy exchanges and it hadn't taken Johnny long to get bold. To get overly comfortable with her.

That boldness annoyed her, but she respected his bravery.

Maybe she should hit him again, bring back some of that mortal terror she'd seen in his eyes when they'd first met.

On top of the duffel was a change of clothes, and under that . . . well, she couldn't see, but judging from the shock on his face, she guessed it was her masks.

Johnny D Lawson pulled a stack of twelve plastic Frendo the Clown masks from the bag.

"What the fuck?" Johnny said, confusion on his face. "Did you, like, switch teams or something?"

She didn't carry a phone. She packed no computer, no toiletries, and no weapons she couldn't dump at a moment's notice.

On this journey, Quinn had distanced herself from the

concept of personal property.

Except the masks.

The masks were the only thing in the bag she couldn't lose.

"Like are you evil Quinn Maybrook now?" Johnny D asked, waving the stack around.

Only five of the masks had elastic straps in wearable condition, and two were damaged to the point they wouldn't be worth what you paid to ship them, if you tried to sell them online.

"No," she said, snatching the masks away from him and peeling off the top two. "Here, put one on."

"I'm good, thanks."

"Put it on. In case there's cameras. I can't leave you out here, so you're coming in with me."

"That's a shame," he said. "Because I'm definitely not wearing one of—"

She lowered her voice to a growl, began enunciating: "Do you think I'm asking? Put . . . it . . ." She didn't even get to "on" before the beads at the ends of Johnny's braids were clicking, elastic pulled taut over the back of his head.

She still scared him. Good.

"It smells funny," he said, voice nasal, nose squished against plastic. "Someone didn't die in this one, right?"

"No. Nobody died in any of them. I'm keeping them as evidence," she said. "Not all of the people I hunt have them.

Most don't. Originals are rare and hard to come by. So when I find someone who's got one, I take it."

"Gotcha, baby-girl. Gotcha," Johnny said. Then he pulled up the mask to show her he was smiling. "So trophies, you mean, not evidence."

She scowled at him, waited for his smile to become pleading. *Please don't punch me again.*

Then she smiled back.

She felt around inside the bag, not wanting to use the car's overhead light and make them more visible to the rest of the lot.

After a moment she removed her hand and was holding the rip hammer.

She could feel Johnny D recoil at the sight of it, losing his bravado for a second.

"Yeah. Maybe you're right," she said, trying to sound crazy. Or what she thought crazy might sound like, as someone who regularly saw visions of her friend's dead father. "Maybe they are trophies, baby-girl."

Johnny D swallowed hard.

Quinn was pretty sure he wouldn't be calling her "baby-girl" again.

The rip hammer had two long, sharp claws on the back and a textured steel face on the head, like a small meat tenderizer. It was a tool meant for demolition. She hadn't seen what it'd do to flesh and bone yet, but she could guess.

"For protection," she said, pointing at the storefronts, "if there's anyone in there."

She missed her combat baton. But the baton had been lost a lot of weapons ago. And she couldn't get attached to any of them.

Johnny looked out the windshield, at the building where the hard plastic sign for "Alton Ministries" had been turned around in its frame so that the words were hazy and backward.

He turned back to her. She'd found the flashlight, then covered the bulb with the fabric of her shirt and checked that it worked. It did.

"Do I get one of those?"

"No. I don't need you taking a swing at me with a flashlight. You wouldn't knock me out. You'd just piss me off."

His eyes flickered behind the mask, going from the hammer, to the flashlight, back to Quinn's face. Then he nodded.

"You know what? I've thought about it. I can be down with it," Johnny D said.

"Down with it?"

"Yeah. This whole thing. I can be, like, your accomplice. I can help you."

"Thanks?"

"What I mean is you can feel comfortable letting me hold a flashlight. I'm not going to try and hit you with it. I promise that I'm not going to try and run away again, okay?"

Quinn placed the flashlight behind her on the seat, put her hand back in the bag, and said: "Sure, here."

She pulled out the same empty hand, only this time she was flipping Johnny the bird.

He laughed. "Ha. Like you say, fair. That's fair, baby-g—" She scowled again and he stopped himself from saying the whole word. "But I mean it. This is badass, what you're doing. Nazi-hunting behavior. Real Mossad in South America in the 1960s shit."

She readied herself to pull her mask down, but didn't, not yet. She wanted him to see on her face that she was impressed with what he'd said.

"What? Don't underestimate Juggalos."

"I won't."

"I've watched plenty of History Channel."

She let her expression fall back to its natural, unimpressed state.

"Which means I also know a lot about ghosts." He waved out at the cobwebbed corpses of dead businesses. "If we turn out to need any knowledge like that in this Silent Hill–looking ass place."

"Thanks, but I think we'll be good."

She hoped.

The specter of Arthur Hill laid his dead hand on her shoulder, Quinn feeling the cool weight of it. Reminding her that there *were* ghosts present.

Shivering, she pulled down her mask and opened the car door.

"By the way, they don't like it when you compare them to Nazis," Quinn said as they approached the curb.

"I bet they don't. But if the shiny red nose fits," Johnny D said.

She let him finish his last joke, then shushed him as he started to say something else as they advanced on the door.

The time for camaraderie was done. Quinn wasn't going to risk her life because it felt nice to spend a few moments talking with another human being.

Especially since Johnny D's friendliness could all be a ploy to get her to drop her guard so he could escape. She couldn't have him going to the cops, not yet, not if he had any inkling of where she was headed. They would investigate here, then she'd make a decision where she was dropping him off.

After a moment inspecting the door to the strip mall church, Quinn applied two small raps with the clawed side of the hammer. A large chunk of glass fell away, and she used the tool's exposed steel neck to knock away the pieces left in the doorframe.

She then ducked low, crawling under the door's push handle, glass crunching under her shoes.

Behind her, there was the sound of *no* crunching.

She turned back.

Johnny was standing there, looking down at his shoes.

"Yo. I'm serious, are these—" Johnny asked, but his voice was too loud.

"Come on," she hissed, shushing him.

Johnny reached inside the door.

"Duh, why don't you just . . ."

And before she could stop him, he turned the lock, pushing the doorframe open so he didn't have to crouch.

"Don't!"

He froze, maybe putting it together, maybe just worried the tone of her voice meant he was about to be punched again.

"It's probably alarmed, dipshit!"

"Oh."

They waited for a sound, but no sound came.

But just because there wasn't an alarm they could *hear* didn't mean there wasn't one.

The security company might have turned a blind eye to people sleeping in the lot, but they almost certainly had trip alarms on the doors. Even if the empty stores had nothing worth stealing . . . security had to deter squatters.

Which meant Quinn and Johnny were now on the clock.

"Sorry—"

She shushed him. "Quiet. I need to look. Stay close. Don't touch anything."

Behind her, at the doorway, Johnny started to speak again. "What about—"

She whipped back, and he blinked against the glare of her flashlight.

"Silence."

He nodded. Johnny fucking up, then seeing him standing there in a Frendo mask: it may not have been fair, but these were things that eroded the empathy Quinn had begun to feel for the boy during the ride.

But that was hypocritical, wasn't it?

She was wearing the same thing.

Quinn turned back into the building, moved the flashlight beam to scan her surroundings. There was nothing helpful in this large front room, nothing *apparently* helpful. It was an empty expanse of carpeted floor with indentations where the furniture used to sit. She tried to picture what this space had looked like before. There had likely been a welcome desk in that corner, possibly a bank of file cabinets behind it, and above them, where wires now dangled and brackets hung loose, TVs that played informational videos.

But that wasn't the entirety of the space. A wheeled movable partition was blocking off most of the big room. Behind that, there might be offices they could scour for any leftover paperwork or literature.

All they needed was one clue, one tiny clue to who the guys were who'd killed Johnny's brother. Because they had to be the same guys who'd killed Charlie Rome and framed Quinn for murder, right? Had to be.

"Come on," Quinn said, pulling Johnny closer. She couldn't move any farther into the building and let him out of her sight. He'd run if she gave him the chance. She was sure he'd run.

So best to keep him in front of her.

Let Johnny D be the one to explore the unknown corners of this big, empty, quiet space.

Probably empty.

Yes, just because the door had been locked didn't mean there weren't already squatters in here with them.

Quinn felt her muscles tense, her grip tightening on both the hammer and the flashlight.

Then she thought about the people sleeping in their cars.

No. Squatters weren't her enemy. They wouldn't hurt her, and she shouldn't be tensing up to hurt them. They were just poor, tired people. The faces she'd been seeing all across this country.

"Go," Quinn said, pushing the hammer flat against Johnny's back, forcing him around the lip of the partition.

He stepped over and out of sight. He could see what she couldn't.

"Anything?"

Silence. Had he glimpsed an exit? Was he about to make a run for it?

"Johnny. Johnny *D*, do you see anything?"

There was a beat, then:

"Uh. Yeah. There's a Tony Robbins motherfucker back here."

"What?"

She peered around the corner, angled the flashlight to where Johnny was looking, and . . .

He was right.

There was someone standing there.

The man was too tall. With too many teeth that were too white.

Quinn knew what Johnny meant. He didn't look like Tony Robbins, exactly, he was too young, for one thing. But the cardboard cutout of the man *did* look like he was trying to sell her something in a self-help kind of way.

There was a light layer of dust on the man's face, but other than that, the promotional standee was in great shape. The man was dressed in an off-white linen suit reminiscent of biblical times dress and surfer hemp. He had his arms slightly outstretched, palms up.

There were a dozen or so folding chairs in semicircle rows around the cardboard holy man. But there was room for way more than a dozen chairs in this low-ceilinged auditorium. It was as if the chairs had begun to be packed away, but the ministry had lost its lease halfway through and the custodians had just decided to leave the remaining chairs where they lay.

There were words printed between the man's hands. Stacked, one on top of the other, the words read:

Loyalty
Solidarity
Praise
Family
Tradition

And then there was a half inch of space, and the attribution:

—Jason Alton

"Not much of a quote," Johnny said, poking the man in his cardboard chest. "That's not even a full sentence, guy."

Quinn pointed up at Jason Alton's face.

"I take it this isn't either of the kids you saw?"

"No. Way too old. I don't think they even attended church here. Maybe the car was stolen, because . . ."

"Because what?"

Johnny waved his hand; she couldn't see his face, but from his body language she could tell he was having a problem finding the right words.

"Well, they weren't *like* this."

They should discuss this later.

There was no time, she told herself.

But Quinn was intrigued, had to know what he meant.

"Meaning?"

"They were dressed religious, but not *this* kind of religion. This kind of religious . . ."

He trailed off, flicked at something that, in the low light, Quinn had mistaken for a flower or patch over the heart of Alton's suit.

It wasn't either, it was a QR code with the words "Fund *His* Revolution" written below.

"Fund my ass. My grandmother used to send money to guys with that same smile and even worse suits. No. The missionary-looking guys who killed Trevor weren't like this guy, they were—"

He stopped talking, the eyeholes of his mask tilting up to look above and behind Quinn.

For a dizzy, exhausted moment Quinn thought he was able to see Arthur Hill, standing behind her, fetid chest cut open and stitched closed with black wire.

But then she turned to follow his gaze.

There was yellow light sweeping over the top of the partition, hitting the tiles of the drop ceiling.

Headlights.

Damn. The door had been rigged with a silent alarm.

"How'd they get here so quick, we—"

Quinn shushed him, then clicked off her flashlight.

There was no indication yet that it *was* security. But if it was, the guards could have been parked in the same lot or could have been circling the block, splitting their time

116

watching one of the developer's other buildings.

If they *were* security guards.

The alarm could just as easily connect to a call center operator who contacted the police.

Quinn chilled at the thought. Police would be so much worse than security.

Behind the partition and beyond the waiting room, there were hushed voices at the door.

"Yeah, I see it, be quiet," a man's voice said.

There were at least two of them.

Quinn raised the hammer, turned her head to watch Johnny's posture grow tense. She hated how little peripheral vision she had in the mask. It was amazing the clowns had been able to kill anyone wearing these fucking things.

"We know you're still in there," the voice outside yelled in. Quinn allowed herself to feel slight relief that they weren't coming in immediately, were at least announcing themselves. "Come out quickly, quietly, and without violence, and no charges will be pressed."

Are you cops or security guards? Quinn wondered. They needed to announce if they were police, didn't they? They needed to. To let her know the degree of problem this was turning into. Whether it all ended here, in a dusty strip mall auditorium, standing in the shadow of a cardboard evangelist.

"He means," a second, reedier voice corrected, "no charges will be pressed *after* you pay for the window."

"Yes, after you pay for the window."

From their voices, Quinn was imagining two cartoon dogs. One big and muscular but soft-spoken, the other tiny but scrappier. But maybe that was a shitty analogy. Quinn's imagination was doing weird things these days, she'd admit that.

Quinn made sure Johnny D was meeting her eyes, then put a finger up to the lips of her clown mask. She couldn't read the boy's expression, but the shuffle of his feet on the carpet looked twitchy, like he was about to march out with his hands above his head and give them both up.

Are you cops or security guards? Quinn wondered again.

One she could handle, not the other.

Then the first voice, the calmer, lower voice, gave an answer:

"We are private security. But we are legally obligated to warn you that if a private security officer meets all licensing requirements of the Tennessee Private Protective Services Act, then they are legally permitted to carry a firearm."

There was a pause.

"Which we certainly fuckin' are," the second guy added.

Okay. Quinn swallowed, tried to assess.

The men outside were in some ways worse than cops.

They were fake cops with real guns.

Johnny started to make a whining sound behind his mask.

Quinn shook her head no. And she meant it.

None of that shit.

Not today.

They weren't cops.

This wasn't how this ended.

She pushed the flashlight into Johnny D's hand to free up one of her own and whispered: "Don't hit me with it."

Then she grabbed him by the back of his shirt and walked him the thirty or forty feet to the far end of the partition, so that they were both facing a blank white wall.

This was a risk. A big risk. They could try running to the back of the auditorium. There was a pretty good chance this place had a back door that led to a service alley behind the strip mall, but even under the best of circumstances that would leave them with no car.

There was nowhere to hide in here and Quinn had forced them into a corner, even farther from the exit.

So this had to work.

They were going to have only thirty seconds, maybe a minute, before the armed security guards got tired of waiting and came in.

"Okay," Quinn yelled, "we're coming out. Please don't shoot us."

Johnny started to turn, but she held him in place and shook her head. That was a lie. They weren't going out that way.

Then Quinn turned the rip hammer around, claw facing the wall, and swung as hard as she could.

She let her follow-through become a long *scraaaatch* as the sharp claws of the hammer tore away chunks of plaster.

Then she sidestepped, moving a few inches to the right before striking out with the hammer again.

Yes. It was working.

The wall had no concrete. No pipes. No crossbeams. Just drywall.

She would be able to turn this wall into a door.

Finally, something had gone right today.

Under her mask, Quinn smiled. Then she swung again, this time with the hammer's head, making a hole the size of a bowling ball.

"Hey, we hear you. Stop what you're doing! Leave the copper in the walls," one guard yelled, overlapping with his friend:

"We're coming in, assholes."

"Help me dig!" Quinn whisper-yelled to Johnny, who was standing and watching, holding her unignited flashlight.

He snapped out of his stupor and began to help, knocking away bits of wall with the end of the flashlight.

Sheetrock crumbs tinged off Quinn's mask, dust entering her nostrils.

A few more clawing whacks and they were through both layers of drywall and into the next store. She heard the crunch of glass underfoot as the security guards, one of them, at least, made good on their threat and came in after them.

But it was okay. They were through the wall and into the neighboring business.

The defunct children's clothing store had tiled floors and their footfalls echoed around them. With no flashlight to see by, Quinn was colliding with obstacles in the dark.

"Oh God oh God I hate this shit yo," Johnny cried as they worked their way through empty clothing racks.

Quinn could see what he meant. Headless mannequin children seemed to reach out as they passed bare displays.

Quinn chanced a look back toward the hole in the wall. There was a white LED flashlight beam cutting through the swirls of drywall dust.

"Fuckin' A, Harry! They took out a wall! One store over! They're getting away," the one guard, not-Harry, shrieked.

Hell yeah, they were getting away, Quinn thought as she unlocked the front door to the children's clothing store and ushered Johnny outside.

She sprinted to the Mustang, fumbling with the unfamiliar key ring. She certainly wasn't looking for the clown-faced bottle opener, the word "family" tattooed on the clown's lower lip.

She found the key and they jumped inside, Johnny D a little slower, taking care not to skewer himself on the springs jutting up from his seat.

"I can't believe that worked," Johnny said as Quinn pushed the key into the ignition and turned over the engine. "My brother and I, we've done a shitload of trespassing, but never once did we—"

The engine roared, the headlights flashed, and there in the doorway to Alton Ministries was a large man squeezed into a black flak jacket with two yellow "Security" patches over the breast pockets.

Harry.

The security guard was squatted down into a firing position and had a handgun leveled. He moved the barrel of the gun between Quinn's and Johnny's faces in quick, jumpy jerks.

Shit.

"Step out of the vehicle!" the man yelled.

"Welp," Johnny D said, "guess this is—"

Quinn waited until the gun was pointed at Johnny, then dropped her hand to the gearshift, pulling the car into reverse and slamming down on the ignition while turning the wheel sharply left.

They were yanked backward, Quinn's seat belt barely able to hold her against the sudden forces.

Johnny's seat belt couldn't hold him because Johnny had never engaged his seat belt.

The boy's face bounced off the dashboard, the plastic of his mask cracking.

Quinn winced.

There went one of her trophies.

Burning tire rubber, hot and acrid and smoky, filled the air.

Quinn slammed into drive and kept her foot on the pedal, pushing them both back into their seats, the nose of the car rising, fighting gravity, their wheels vaguely pointed back to the highway.

Security guards, Quinn thought.

Pssshhh.

She knew that guy wouldn't shoot.

Then there was a pop like a distant firework and a puff of white fluff floated into her vision.

The bullet had whizzed through the trunk and out the back seat.

Holy shit, Harry was a good shot.

There was another pop, accompanied by another ping of metal against metal. Quinn just needed to keep accelerating; every foot they made it away from the strip mall meant they were a smaller target.

Harry stopped firing and Quinn decelerated just enough to turn the wheel without rolling.

They'd made it.

Only once they were on the highway did she notice that Johnny was doubled over in his seat.

Oh god.

Had he been hit? Had Quinn gotten another person killed?

She remembered the sound the second shot had made. Then she imagined the bullet tinging through the trunk, the ricochet sending it first into the headrest, then into the back of Johnny D's skull.

With that mental image, the roiling in Quinn's stomach was immediate and violent.

How many lives would she take, directly or indirectly, before she stopped?

Quinn removed one hand from the wheel to pull her mask off, then reached over and pulled Johnny's cracked mask free from his face.

"Johnny. Johnny, are you okay?" she asked, shaking him.

Wait.

Was he . . . crying?

Crying was good, it meant he was still alive, it—

The boy sat up straight, rubbing his face, moist with breathlessness.

"Deee," he said, wheezing. "Call me Johnny D, baby."

No. He wasn't crying. Johnny D Lawson was laughing.

"I'm okay, but . . ." He pointed to the dash. "Violent J didn't make it."

One of the Insane Clown Posse figures had been hit, his plastic head blown off so only the stub of his neck remained.

"Miracles," Johnny said to himself, then kept cackling,

trying and failing to catch his breath.

Maybe they *were* in an action movie. This was the kind of break under pressure that happened in action movies.

"You're laughing? We almost died," Quinn started. "I'm sorry I got you into this. I'm sorry. I'm so sorry."

"No, it's not that," Johnny said, pulling something from the waistband of his jeans. Crumpled papers and sweaty envelopes. He splayed the papers against the dash.

"What I was trying to say before, when you were shushing me," he said, opening up one of the envelopes to show her. "There was a bunch of mail wedged under the front door. We didn't even have to go in! You want to know where this Alton guy lives? These are all bills. Charges and shit with a corporate credit card. And there's a billing address listed on all of them. Same place in Pennsylvania."

Huh. How had she missed that?

It didn't matter.

"North," Quinn said, smiling, remembering what Charles Rome had told her. He hadn't been specific, but he hadn't been lying, either.

Pennsylvania was certainly north of here.

And so, they drove.

EIGHT

KETTLE SPRINGS

"God's in everything," Tabitha said. She was sitting with Hannah. They had a basket of linens set between them, separated into two stacks. Patchwork for each of their families. "That's what I believe."

Hannah, of course, said nothing in response.

The mute girl didn't even look up.

Hannah wasn't being rude. She was concentrating on the sock in her lap. Tabitha could see that the girl's needle was trembling.

Hannah had arrived in Kettle Springs without any skills. But that was okay, she was a young child, and Tabitha liked teaching. Over the last few weeks—every day but Sunday, since Hannah attended church with her parents—Tabitha had trained Hannah. Together they had gotten her proficient at the kind of field and housework Tabitha had been doing for years.

Proficient, but not fast.

In the old days, with her unhurried nature, Hannah would have been chastised for sloth.

But the town had new sins now and sloth wasn't one of them.

Finished with her stitch, Hannah looked up and tilted her head, the motion that Tabitha had taken to mean *I'm listening, go on.*

Tabitha tried to remember what she'd been saying. It wasn't easy. Her mind was distracted. Mrs. Hill had been especially cruel today. As had the other students. And there was that sound bouncing over the horizon, and—

"God's in everything," Tabitha made herself continue. "Don't mistake me. My faith is not shaken. The light of the Lord lives inside my breast. Which is exactly what I mean. It lives everywhere and in every one of his creations. All creatures great and small. Not just in . . ."

She trailed off.

From here, seated on the bench beside the barn, they couldn't see any hint of the town square. Except the very top of the church spire.

The church reminded her of the bell, the long keening tone it held after ringing.

No. That wasn't correct.

She wasn't hearing the bell.

It was Friday, not Sunday. There was no reason for the bell to sound. Noon had struck hours ago and nobody was being executed today that she knew of.

But there *was* a noise in her ears, making it difficult to articulate her point.

It was a buzz, a trill that vibrated Tabitha's inner ear. The days were getting warmer, so she reasoned that it must be cicadas, digging their way out of their yearslong hibernation.

But it wasn't cicadas, she knew that.

It was a different sound, alien and dangerous, growing louder.

Living as they did, Tabitha needed to convince herself she didn't see a lot of the things she saw.

That she didn't hear a lot of the things she heard.

That was how you survived. It was why Tabitha's parents had stayed when others had left. You ignored some aspects of the life, then embraced what you could of what remained.

Compromise.

A compromised reality.

And this sound was just another example, something else to be ignored, reasoned away, blocked out.

Tabitha finished her own sock, then moved to patch the hem on one of her mother's dresses. At this rate, Tabitha would be mucking Nellie's stall before Hannah had finished a single item of her own patchwork.

"What I mean is not, is not . . . ," Tabitha stuttered. It took tremendous effort to talk over the buzzing sound and she felt her eyes beginning to water. It was an almost physical strain, to try to block out such an insistent noise. "Not in buildings. God doesn't live in buildings, no matter how sacred. Is what I'm trying to say."

She was fixating on the church. What could lie inside. Why she thought God wasn't there. What it was about the building that made her parents act so differently since changing their faith. Since compromising.

The girls continued working in a silence that wasn't silence, Hannah looking to the horizon, beyond their parents' fields, over the crest of the hills to the south.

The younger girl could hear the buzz as well.

Of course she could.

She couldn't speak, but she could hear perfectly well.

But they weren't going to acknowledge it. Weren't going to speculate what the sound could be.

They weren't even going to move inside.

Not when Tabitha was so filled with worry about what was going to happen to her on Sunday.

In two days, she would join the church as an adult. After their first mass, after a midday rest from the "exhaustion of praise," Tabitha's mother had returned home and told her about it. Told her it wasn't so bad, then described the changes to the church, both the service and the building.

The congregation would rise from the pews, she would step to the end of the line with her parents, kneel against the chancel rail, open her mouth, and . . .

All of this was new. Every part of the process, almost every physical aspect of the church itself.

A year ago, months ago even, they hadn't had pews, they'd had benches. The church hadn't had a chancel rail because they hadn't taken communion. But it wasn't the strangeness of these structural changes that haunted her now.

She thought of the smell that wafted out of the church and into the thoroughfare. Warm and tangy. Like orange peels discovered in some forgotten corner of the pantry a week too late. How that same smell was on Mother's and Father's tongues when they returned home.

"What do you think the host tastes like?" Tabitha asked.

Hannah frowned.

Well, at least she'd gotten their minds off the buzzing sound.

They were both thinking about the host ceremony now. How it made their parents act. Each Sunday, chewing and swallowing, their eyes a little duller.

You'll be a woman soon, Tabitha.

The memory of the Pastor's words was like cold mud, slipping down the small of Tabitha's back and chilling her.

What do you think the host tastes like?

It wasn't a question idly asked. She wanted Hannah to answer, even if the girl had to act one out for her by playing a game of charades.

"Do you think it intoxicates?" Tabitha asked.

Hannah flinched.

Tabitha should have chosen her words more carefully. "Intoxicates" had special meaning to the daughter of the town drunk.

Taking the host week after week wasn't the only thing making Hannah's father worse. The adults of the town took the host every Sunday. Mr. Trent drank every day.

Drinking was another sin that, in this new order the Pastor was building in Kettle Springs, seemed to go unremarked and unpunished. Many of the settlers drank. But none more than Hannah's father.

Even Isaiah Dunne drank. She'd seen him just this week, after the execution, crouched beside the general store, sipping from a flask of grain alcohol, trying to stop his big hands from shaking.

But that same hour, Mr. Trent had drunk so much he was unaware he'd even attended an execution.

The buzzing in the distance became louder, more insistent, but Tabitha tried to ignore it.

Not that there'd been a written law against alcohol previously, but if Hannah's father had been around before the incorporation, Tabitha thought the town would have shunned him. They would have invoked Meidung to try to—

To the south, the buzz crescendoed in a bang.

After a half second's delay, a flock of land fowl took flight, the birds roused from pecking at the rot in the Trent family field.

There was no further buzzing.

The sound had ended.

Tabitha felt her shoulders unclench.

It was over now. It was blessedly over. Whatever the sound was it'd—

But, no.

Tabitha could see out of the corner of her eye, beyond the edge of her bonnet, that Hannah was looking up at her. There was a question on the little girl's face.

There could be no pretending anymore.

Cicadas didn't explode.

"What do you think it is?" Tabitha asked.

Hannah shrugged. Was she ready to ignore the sound? That was good. That's what you needed to do in Kettle Springs. You needed to put aside your curiosity.

Which was a sad realization to have. Maybe Tabitha *was* ready to join the adults of the village.

No. They wouldn't investigate the sound, but Tabitha could keep that innocence and wonder alive for Hannah.

So she smiled, crept her fingers along the bench toward the younger girl, and said: "It could be . . . monsters!"

Hannah shook her head and scooted away from Tabitha's fingers. It was a denial of the joke, denial of the sound, denial of reality.

It was a silly thing for Tabitha to have done, to affect the voice she would use to tease Hannah about ghosts and the bogeyman.

Because they both could guess what had made that sound, and it was worse than monsters.

That buzzing sound was . . . not of Kettle Springs.

"Hannah, don't be that way, there's nothing to fear if we—"

The girl kept shaking her head while she stood, pointed toward the Trent farmhouse, and began to pack away her stack of laundry.

Hannah was going home.

"No, wait. Don't leave me," Tabitha said.

But Hannah didn't wait, she closed her sewing kit atop the laundry and began marching back toward the former home of Ruth Miller.

Tabitha followed after and grabbed the little girl by the wrist.

"Don't be ridiculous, we didn't see anything," Tabitha said. "That sound could have been a mile away!"

This felt *wrong*. To have her fingers around the tiny

wrist, so tight that she could feel the birdlike thrum of the girl's heartbeat. She was restraining Hannah in a way her parents or their teacher might.

Hannah didn't speak, but she did growl. For a second, she'd allowed herself to go wild and mean, like their classmates at the schoolhouse. It was a growl that told Tabitha: *I'm not joking. Let go of me.*

Would Hannah bite her?

All animals would bite if left no other option—

"Hey!"

The voice didn't belong to Tabitha, and it certainly wasn't Hannah's.

It was a male voice, coming from the direction of the bang.

Both girls turned their heads slowly, reluctant to see who the stranger calling to them might be.

And as they did, they saw it was actually *two* strangers.

The strangers walked toward them, crossing from one field into the other, on a course to join them under the shadow of the barn but still a long way off.

Two strangers and a motorcycle.

It was a man and a woman, and they were dressed in secular clothing.

Apostates.

Between them, the pair walked a white-and-red motorbike, steam rising from its now quiet engine.

They were still a few dozen yards away, but approaching fast.

Beside Tabitha, Hannah made an apprehensive squeal, then started to run.

But Tabitha still had the little girl by her wrist. Hannah wriggled to escape, dropping her laundry into the mud.

Tabitha looked down at the wrist, saw she was causing the girl pain, and thought: *She's right. We should be running*.

Then her feet were also moving, ready to leave the laundry where it lay.

"Kids, wait! Can you help us?" the man called out.

"Don't, Seth. Can't you see you're scaring them?"

It was odd to see apostates with their clothes on.

Recently, having run out of neighbors to accuse, put on trial, and *find* to be apostates, the town saw apostates only once they'd been stripped. Outsiders, trespassers undeterred by the signs. Men and women made anonymous by their nudity, interchangeable because they were all screaming for their lives.

Tabitha glanced back.

These two still had their clothes. They still had their dignity and individuality.

Tabitha and Hannah could do what they'd been told to do: report outsiders to the Constable.

Or.

Or they could do the unthinkable.

They could *warn* these people.

They were at the southern tip of the village, the Werther and Trent farms set at a remove from the rest of the population. There was a very real possibility that nobody else in Kettle Springs had heard the engine backfire.

Tabitha and Hannah were about to reach the corner of the barn when Tabitha released the girl's wrist and stopped running.

Hannah slowed, then stopped herself.

"We can save them, Hannah," Tabitha said.

Hannah wrinkled her brow in confusion.

"You don't have to help me," Tabitha continued, her voice low. "But you can't tell anyone." She paused, repeated: "You *cannot* tell anyone."

The confusion stayed on Hannah's face, joined quickly by concern, the girl's thin eyebrows meeting, an expression that made her look older than her nine years.

There was no time to explain further. Hannah would have to stay and watch what Tabitha was about to do.

They were in this together now.

Tabitha turned, then she extended a finger and began shushing the couple.

The man didn't get any quieter.

"It's okay. It's okay," he said. "We're not hurt or anything. It's just engine trouble."

He was wearing jeans, a black hooded sweatshirt,

unzipped in the spring heat, and a T-shirt advertising a movie, television show, or rock band that Tabitha had never heard of, back when she'd been *allowed* to hear about such things.

The woman was wearing jeans and a machine-knit sweater. She was holding a helmet, bright purple with glitter inlays, and as she spoke, she moved the helmet over her stomach: "We weren't speeding. I took a tumble but I'm okay, it—"

"Please be quiet," Tabitha hissed. "You're on private property, you need to be quiet."

"Yeah. We saw the signs, but we . . . well . . ." The man looked at his wife, smiling.

Tabitha hadn't seen anyone smile like that in months.

But right now, she needed the man to shut up.

"Do you have a phone we can borrow, hon?" the woman asked Tabitha. At least the woman was keeping her voice low.

"Ours are back at our van." The man patted his jeans pocket. "I've cracked a lot of screens riding with a phone in my—"

"No phone. Please, you don't seem to understand me. You must leave right now."

Tabitha grabbed the handlebars of the motorbike, halting the couple's progress. They both let go. It was a small bike, but the machine was still heavy. Tabitha wasn't strong enough to flip the wheel around and point the bike in the opposite direction like she wanted to.

"Wait, shit, please. It's a rental," the man said. "We'll leave. We can get off your property. But we need to call Triple-A."

Then the woman asked: "Do you mean you don't have a cell phone on you or that you and your parents have no phones at all?"

"No phones," Tabitha said, giving up on pushing the motorcycle. The tires had thick pads of mud caked into their treads.

There would be tracks, once she chased them off she would need to find a way to cover them.

"Fuck. Are you Amish?" the man asked.

The woman hit the man with a slap against the back of his neck. "Seth, don't swear in front of the kids," she said.

Kids. Tabitha looked beside her.

Hannah hadn't run home. The girl stood a few steps behind them, her eyes wide.

That was good. Hannah wasn't running to tell her parents or into town to alert the Constable.

"Sorry," Seth said, directing his apology to Hannah.

Seth. That was a biblical name. Tabitha had known a few Seths in her life.

There'd been a Seth in Kettle Springs as recently as two months ago.

He was dead now.

"Then is there a—"

"We are not Amish," Tabitha said. "This is a private community and private property." She was repeating what she'd been told to say, what they'd all been taught to say if they ever came face-to-face with an apostate.

Hannah whined. Tabitha looked to her, and the girl pointed to the woman's helmet.

Yes, Tabitha saw it now. There was something strange about the motorcycle helmet the woman had shifted to keep crooked under her arm. And the way she was positioning it, making sure to keep parts of it uncovered. It had an eye. A black glass eye mounted to a square at the top.

"Is that on?" Tabitha asked.

"What?" The woman blinked.

"The camera," Tabitha said.

"Look," Seth said, stepping in front of his wife. "We clearly started on the wrong foot. I'm Seth, and this is my fiancée, Lizzie. Whatever you and your parents have going on here, we're not spying on your community. Honest."

Fiancée. Not wife. It was a small thing, but it reminded Tabitha that in the outside world there weren't only husbands and wives, mothers and fathers, brothers and sisters.

The woman, Lizzie, readjusted her grip on the helmet.

"It *is* on, but look, I'm turning it off," she said. "Because I can tell how anxious it's making you."

"That's not making me anxious," Tabitha said, frustrated, nearing her breaking point, the tears about to flow. "You not listening to me is making me anxious. You need to leave. Right now. You need to push your motorcycle over the horizon before—"

"It's a dirt bike," Seth said, interrupting.

Tabitha stared at him for a moment, hating him, hating herself for wanting to save him.

And then there was the clatter.

The sound of a screen door slamming shut.

Tabitha's mother—or her father, but more likely her mother—had just left the main house.

The four of them were being blocked from view by the barn. But only just.

There would be no way that Seth and Lizzie would be able to make it back across the field and out of sight.

And there would be no shooing them away.

There was now no easy way to handle this that involved something as simple as brushing away tire treads and swearing Hannah to secrecy.

Tabitha was crying. She could taste her tears, the salt stinging the chapped corners of her lips.

"Seth, Lizzie," Tabitha whispered. If her father or mother was headed this way, Tabitha would need to start screaming for help, that there were apostates invading the farm.

But she wasn't going to condemn these people until the last possible moment.

She would try to do the right thing.

Try to do what God was telling her to do.

Save them.

"You are both going to be killed if you don't do exactly as I say," Tabitha said, pushing all the seriousness and finality she could into the words.

"Ki—" Seth started to speak, but Lizzie stopped him with a sharp chop of her hand.

The woman had a child's name, but obviously Lizzie was the sensible one in their relationship.

Good. That was good. One of them believed her.

And one believer was all Tabitha needed to get the two apostates to follow her into the barn and hide.

NINE

ILLINOIS

"Murray. Soon-Ja Murray. Step forward."

The COs didn't typically read given names when taking roll or requesting a prisoner.

But they *always* read Vivian Murray's given name.

And she knew why. They all knew why.

Not a lot of Soon-Jas in here.

Her name was something to single her out for, a difference to ridicule. Never mind that "Soon-Ja" had been going by Vivian since her early twenties, two husbands ago. She'd never done the paperwork to have her first name legally changed, though, and Soon-Ja Murray was the name on Vivian's intake papers.

But they could taunt her all they wanted. They could ask Vivian Murray questions about what it was like.

To kill her daughter.

How'd that work, sending your daughter, your own daughter, to die? What did it feel like?

You were at home, crying? Bullshit. I heard that your alibi's weak. That you were the one out in that field. That you cut Janet's head off yourself. That you were swinging that circular saw. That true?

They could ask all they liked.

They could be as terrible as they wanted.

They wouldn't provoke Vivian into talking.

Not a word.

And she hadn't been in Tillerson's field, by the way.

She really had been home crying, all that night. Crying about what Alec had convinced her to go along with.

But Vivian never spoke up to defend herself.

There was no point.

She'd been instructed not to speak. It was the last thing Vivian's lawyer had told her, after bail had been set, an unpayable sum, and she was headed back to a facility:

"Don't say anything. Not to guards, not to cellmates. You shouldn't even make phone calls. Anything you tell them or anything they overhear can be used against you. We'll get a trial date soon and get you out of there, but in the meantime: not a word."

In some ways it was difficult, living this code of silence.

Before Alec and for *most* of their marriage, Vivian Murray

had been outgoing, opinionated. If she wasn't the warmest or most maternal of the moms at Kettle Springs PTA meetings or elementary school recitals and concerts, she was the mom the other moms were most entertained by. Before the darker times—the trouble with the dead Hill girl, Janet and her friends' behavior spiraling out of control—Vivian Murray had been a well-liked member of her boring community. She'd been funny—at least funny in a mean way. And the midwesterners around her, even if they gasped at Vivian's "coastal directness," they enjoyed listening to her.

So Vivian Murray was good at talking. Liked to do it.

But she was also great at following directions. You couldn't be a beauty queen without being able to. Pageants required exactitude. This many degrees of a head tilt, this many steps on the catwalk until you turn. This many calories in your diet. Green starter before a starch, never after. This much makeup, applied in exactly this way, to look good under this *specific* stage's lighting rig.

In pageants you followed a coach's instructions, held rigidly to your prep, met and then *exceeded* expectations, or you lost.

And so it was easy for Vivian to follow her lawyer's instructions. She hadn't said anything. Not a single word beyond yes or no answers for the COs, in over two years now.

Yes. Two years.

They'd gotten close to a trial. Last September and

October the media heat had died down and her lawyer had begun calling more often, preparing to go to court.

But then Halloween delayed things, sprouting fresh headlines to bias potential jurors.

So a trial date *still* hadn't been set.

And Vivian had stayed silent.

Sometimes late at night she'd whisper into her pillow, making up a piece of nonsense gossip to tell, just to make sure she was still *able* to speak.

"Murray . . ." The correctional officer said her name again. "I said step *forward*, Soon-Ja."

What?

She already had. Vivian was out of her cell and standing against the second-floor railing. The woman calling her name knew she'd stepped forward. They were making eye contact.

"Turn and keep stepping, Murray," the woman said. The CO had a side part. It was a severe hairstyle for a severe woman. "March down those stairs, to me."

There was a chorus of "Oooooooooooo" from the other inmates, each standing at attention outside their own cell doors. "Quiet!" another CO yelled. The second woman, big, with a perm, stood at the end of the gangway with Vivian and her fellow inmates.

"Soon-Ja's in trouble!" Vivian's neighbor, a woman who'd killed her husband—allegedly—cackled into her hand.

The CO with the perm banged her forearm shell against the railing. The sound shut everyone up.

Vivian did as she was told and walked down to the ground floor. She didn't look at anyone she passed, as they mumbled what they thought of her, loud enough to be heard but not loud enough for the CO with the perm to start handing out punishments.

She stopped behind the dotted line that divided lockup from the gate-point door.

The CO with the side part waved a carbon copy in her face.

She could have learned the guards' names. Their last names were embroidered above their shirt pockets. But Vivian preferred to think of them as hairstyles.

Vivian grunted, unsure if she should be taking the paper.

Vivian had seen documents printed on that same onion paper before.

They never indicated anything good was about to happen.

That shade of pink meant transfer, right?

Vivian Murray had spent time in three different correctional facilities, along with the holding cells and courthouses from the early days and weeks of her ordeal.

Most of the time, since she had no view from her window but barbed wire, sometimes a spot of grass, it was difficult to even know what state she was in.

This was Illinois. Where next?

"Soon-Ja. It's your lucky day," the officer said, projecting her voice for their gathered audience, the women all waiting to be escorted to the caf. "You're on your way out of here."

"Tell me it's to death row," an inmate shouted. There was laughter. Then another added:

"Bitch!"

Ignoring them, the CO looked into Vivian's eyes. She had too much product in her hair, might have made the part with a straightedge, and no discernible skin-care treatment beyond bar soap. The guard smiled and said three words Vivian hadn't been expecting to hear:

"You made bail."

Oh.

How?

Not speaking, Vivian followed the CO to a processing room.

The clothes she'd worn to report for booking over two years ago were returned to her. Vivian Murray had entered jail in the same slim black dress she'd worn to Janet's funeral. Inappropriate? Maybe. But she had no other outfits that could be called modest and solemn, and since there'd been photographers at intake . . .

Vivian stared at the dress, not saying anything.

"Well. Get changed."

Vivian pursed her lips, almost spoke. But no. She wasn't

out yet. She didn't understand what was happening, but she was still in custody and couldn't allow herself to speak. Not yet.

"You can't keep those." The guard motioned to the jeans and sweatshirt. "They're property of the state."

Vivian changed in front of the CO.

And when she couldn't reach far enough behind her back, the other woman helped with the zipper.

The black dress still fit but was too large in the hips and breast.

The shoes didn't fit at all. Must have been the sodium in the prison food.

But her white trainers were also property of the state. So Vivian made them work, her toes jammed in, cramped.

She was given no further information about who had paid her bail, why, or what the next steps would be, with regard to probation limitations or when she would need to report back to court.

They might have told her if she asked, but she was not going to ask. She was not going to say anything.

The CO with the side part was joined by another officer with a ponytail, the braid tucked under the collar of her shirt so an inmate couldn't grab it, and the two of them walked Vivian out into the Illinois sun.

"Good luck," Side Part said. "State'll be in contact with your guarantor."

My what? Vivian wanted to ask. But, of course, didn't.

Then the guards retreated back inside the fence and Vivian was left next to an abandoned road, the gate closing behind her with a loud robotic *beeeep*.

The sun was out and there was no shade. In less than thirty seconds, standing bewildered, Vivian Murray was covered in a light layer of sweat. The zipper of her dress itched.

This . . .

Could she speak?

Could she scream and cry and show all the emotion and rage she'd been holding inside for nearly thre—

No.

You made bail.

How? Who? It wasn't possible. And wouldn't her lawyer have called?

No. There was some kind of mistake.

Or.

Or this was some elaborate joke.

Or *prank*.

Maybe Cole Hill had arranged this, paid her bail just so she could have a few moments of freedom on this side of the yard, only for the gate to reopen and guards to usher her back inside once he rescinded payment.

Vivian looked over to her left. A hundred paces down the fence, there was a pay phone. It must be there so released inmates could call a cab or a relative to pick them up.

A cab? And she'd pay for it with what? Alec's assets were frozen, and she doubted the forty dollars cash she'd entered prison with would be enough to get her back to Missouri.

Relatives? Her husband was dead. Her daughter was dead. Her parents were dead. Not from violent deaths like the other two, but from heart disease.

There was no one to call.

But then a car appeared.

And two young men in white shirts got out of the car. The two of them argued for a moment, she couldn't hear what they hissed at each other, but it seemed like they were arguing about something small and stupid: which one of them would get to open the back door for her.

Then they crossed the distance to her and one of them said:

"Mrs. Murray, I'm Taylor and this is Colby. We were hired to bring you to the settlement of New Kettle Springs."

Vivian blinked at the two boys, at the yawning back door of the car, the leather seats, and spoke:

"You were hired . . . to . . ." She coughed. It was a pleasant sensation, like she was clearing an obstruction that'd been silencing her for years. "You're here to bring me where?"

"Home, ma'am. We're here to bring you home."

TEN

FIFTEEN MILES TO THE KENTUCKY–WEST VIRGINIA BORDER

It was hard to tell if the library's internet connection was bad or if the Alton Ministries–related videos on YouTube were just shitty and low-quality.

Probably a little bit of both.

Quinn didn't devote much time to any one video but skipped around to sample a bunch.

A few were short commercials for the church, with higher production values, but the majority were hour-long sermons, filmed years before their upload dates, on a mix of camcorders and phones.

Many of the older sermons had watermarks, like they'd been ripped from other sites and then uploaded by third parties. She didn't recognize any of the watermarks; the insignias included crosses and cursive fonts and generally looked . . . churchy.

Only one or two of the videos had over a hundred views, their comment sections were mostly ghost towns, and it didn't take Quinn long to get the gist of Jason Alton's general message.

"We need to get back to the Word," Jason Alton intoned on the video Quinn was currently watching with one earphone in, "back to a simpler time."

And the main way to do that, of course, was with cash, check, or credit card.

Maybe Quinn was being cynical; she was watching only short snippets of each video, after all. But she didn't think she was.

Not that she had much to compare the preacher to.

Neither of her parents had been particularly religious, and Quinn had never felt the pull to explore faith for herself, so she hadn't spent much time in church or synagogue.

Growing up in Philly, she'd been to Beth Israel for a few holidays. And had attended a handful of Baptist funerals to support school friends when their grandparents had died. There'd been funerals in Kettle Springs, many. But she'd mourned in her own ways, away from the press, and hadn't gone to any church services or burials.

Those institutions had seemed fine, for those who believed, and far less focused on money and donations than Alton seemed to be.

So, no, Quinn didn't think she was being cynical. It seemed pretty obvious to her that this guy was a con artist.

But then even though the underlying message of the videos never really changed . . . Jason Alton himself clearly did.

In the video she was watching, dated 2019, he looked more or less like he had as a cardboard cutout, even if he was wearing a darker, more traditional suit.

But in each of the earlier videos, he seemed to have different styles, like he was constantly reinventing himself. It reminded Quinn of her own time on the road, how she'd needed to change herself to keep from being recognized.

In some videos Jason Alton was wearing an all-white suit with ruffled shirts. Jewelry, as varied and incongruous as pinkie rings and pulka necklaces, appeared and disappeared. In some videos he was dressed casually, jeans and a T-shirt, accented by a cordless microphone headset. He'd had a bigger audience then and had been speaking on a different stage from the strip mall ministry they'd searched. In the oldest video she could find, Alton was barely twenty years old and wore rolled shirtsleeves, and his hair had frosted tips. In that old video, it looked more like he was speaking at a professional sporting event than a church, the crowd was so vast.

"What a tool," Johnny D said, leaning over from his own computer monitor.

Quinn had kept him close, which was the right decision,

even if she didn't think he was going to attempt to escape again. Twice now she'd caught him trying to disable the browser's locks against explicit websites.

"Yeah," Quinn agreed. "A tool."

She checked around them.

The library was a single large room, but they weren't completely out in the open. Bookshelves and desks formed alcoves and blind spots in the space. The room smelled like moldering books and acrylic carpet. The library wasn't crowded, but they also weren't alone. There were pods of teenagers, some with binders and laptops out in front of them, presumably working on group projects for school, some alone or in pairs, dozing or watching their phones with the sound low.

The library would be closing soon, but thanks to daylight savings, it was still light outside. Long vertical blinds in need of dusting cut the glare through the windows.

Normally Quinn wouldn't be in a public, well-lighted place like this. But they needed the info, and when you didn't have a phone, where else could you get online but the library?

She opened a new tab, letting Jason Alton continue to speak, the cadence of his words of praise almost musical. He was good at the devotional stuff, enough to balance out how desperate he seemed in his pleas for cash. Into the new search box, she typed an address from her notebook.

A Kentucky address.

Yes, they would get to Pennsylvania. Eventually. Soon.

But that didn't mean she was going to ignore the high-value target they would pass along the way.

Using Google Street View, she tried to map as many paths as she could to and from the Dozer household. Or "household," as the address was located inside an RV campsite.

It was always risky, this kind of research, since it left digital footprints, but it was better than walking into a dangerous situation unprepared.

Quinn took her time, using her avatar to walk as many of the digital back roads of the campsite as she could via Street View, then switching to a Google Image search to look up the married couple one last time.

She was being more thorough in her research than she normally would.

Partly because these two might be tough, but also because . . . well, she wasn't looking forward to what came next, *after* the Dozers.

But before whatever came next, however final it was, Quinn and Johnny needed a new car.

She'd brought the subject up once already, while they were leaving Tennessee. But Johnny had flipped out. The boy didn't want to abandon his beloved Mustang.

She'd tried intimidation. But this was an area where he wouldn't be pushed. Johnny D showed a lot of spine. The car clearly meant a lot to him.

But they couldn't keep it.

It was too recognizable, and Quinn had already broken her own rule, crossing one state line with it. She didn't want to break it again by crossing another, into Virginia, and then another, into Pennsylvania.

It was a miracle they hadn't been pulled over already. Johnny used a mixture of chewing gum and shoe polish to patch the bullet holes in the trunk and fender, but that would only hold up for so long.

Really, she also didn't *need* Johnny anymore. She could let him go. But . . .

No.

He knew their ultimate destination, and that was . . . that was too much information to trust him with.

Yes. That was it.

In her ear, the quality of the audio had changed. A new voice, not Alton, was introducing Alton to a round of weak applause.

At some point while she'd been staring at pictures of the Dozers, over in the YouTube tab her video had ended and a new one had begun autoplaying.

"Brothers and sisters, during today's sermon I'm going to pose a question. I always ask questions. I ask you to ask questions. But today you're going to find my question shocking. A question you might even call out of character, since we preach nonviolence and tolerance here in this house."

Quinn couldn't help it. She was intrigued. He might have been a con artist, but you had to have a certain way, a charisma, if you were going to get even the most gullible parishioners to open their wallets.

Quinn leaned forward.

"What if," Alton said, "what if they're right?"

She listened while staring at pictures of the married couple, but before Alton could continue, he was interrupted. An advertisement for Allstate insurance, the audio on the commercial much higher than the video itself, began to blare in her ear.

Quinn navigated back to the video and muted the ad.

As the video resumed, volume still muted, she could see that this version of Jason Alton was dressed like he had been in the cardboard cutout, the linen suit a little shabbier than it had been when he'd posed for the photo. This sermon was being presented in the strip mall ministry Johnny D and Quinn had visited. So more recent, 2020 maybe.

That's when she saw it:

The comment section on *this* video wasn't empty.

"Come on, people, DONATE!" the pinned comment read. There was a tiny link, font blue and clickable, beside it.

The pinned comment had many likes and replies.

She expanded the thread and started to read. The replies were phrases like "Praise be!" and "He's exactly right!" and "We've got to help these people get their lives back!"

alternating with the clapping hand emojis and the praise hands emojis and the prayer hand emojis.

And not every single one, but maybe every third comment . . .

The clown emoji.

Quinn scrolled back up to the top comment and clicked the link.

A new page began to load, the library's internet connection seeming to stutter and churn with effort.

The assets on the browser window's dark gray background filled in a piece at a time.

First the text.

Resettle Kettle Springs.

Quinn's blood ran cold.

She had to warn Dad.

Or did she? Was this an old website? Was "resettle" referring to what had happened at Halloween?

The page continued to load.

A round red button appeared:

Donate to the Freedom Fund.

Then the final image on the page:

Jason Alton's face, a transparent play symbol over his

upper lip. This was the thumbnail to a video. A video not hosted by YouTube but embedded into this fundraiser page with some other media player.

No. This wasn't an old site.

It couldn't have been, because Jason Alton's hair was much longer than it had been in the most recent YouTube uploads. That kind of growth took time.

It wasn't just the hair on his head; for the first time in his career he was keeping facial hair.

He looked like a hippie.

Or, maybe not, but a wholesome version of a hippie. A clean hippie.

He was still wearing the linen jacket. But the collar had gone even shaggier and—it was hard to tell, since she was seeing him only from a little below the shoulders up—it didn't seem like he was wearing a shirt.

He was . . . sexy?

Jason Alton had found a look that worked for him. Or at least worked for Quinn, in the abstract way she could tell that someone was attractive while not *being* attracted to them.

Before Quinn could click the thumbnail to start this newest video playing, a shadow spread over the computer bank.

Oh.

Quinn straightened her back. She didn't think she was

jumpy enough to give herself away, but she was still disturbed that someone had been able to get this close without her noticing.

She must have been exhausted.

"I can't believe it," a female voice said behind her. Quinn didn't turn, but she could sense the girl entering her personal space. "You're her!"

"Oh fuck," Johnny said, not attempting to keep his voice library quiet.

Quinn shot a hand over to Johnny's arm and dug her nails in.

He needed to stay cool. They were not caught yet. This was *not* a cop.

Quinn and Johnny turned away from the bank of computers to face the teen girl standing above them.

The girl had blond hair that had been dyed green weeks and months ago, the roots growing out and the color fading.

"I'm who?" Quinn asked, trying to look casual as she pulled her earbud free.

The girl smiled, peeled a fleck of black nail polish off one thumbnail. The girl was nervous, but happy.

"Oh, you know who you are," she said. "And I know. Sorry. I just needed to see you close up."

Quinn looked around. The librarian at the help desk was in the same spot as when they'd come in, not looking in this direction. Quinn scanned the rest of the room, having chosen the computer on the end of the row, with the best view of the library's front doors.

Was this teenager here with anyone?

"I'm not sure I know what you mean," Quinn said, turning back to her workstation, closing windows as she spoke, clearing search histories, then pointing to her bag.

Johnny understood, handed her the duffel.

He was getting better. More comfortable interpreting what Quinn meant and acting fast.

"Oh, I getcha," the girl said, giving Quinn a slight smile, then winking. "I'm not going to blow up your spot or anything. I just want you to know that there's a lot of us out there, we really love what you're doing."

Was this a trap? Quinn had been recognized before. Had spent a whole year having it happen, before she cut her hair off. But if it had happened recently, it'd been askance looks in rest-stop bathrooms and cupped hands whispering to ears in diners, after hours.

And she'd never stayed in a place long enough to see what those people who'd recognized her were planning to do next.

But this girl had gotten within arm's length.

This girl had Quinn cornered.

"I'm not going to tell anyone," the girl said, looking back at an empty circular table, indicating where she'd been sitting alone and watching them. No, she wasn't here with friends.

"I don't know who you think I am," Quinn said, "but we were just leaving."

"Sure, Quinn. But . . ."

The girl slid a ballpoint pen and an Arby's receipt onto the desk, stopping at the library computer's frayed and stained mouse pad.

"Can I have your autograph?"

Quinn's stomach hurt, thinking about signing an autograph. But whatever made the least amount of noise and drew the least attention. It was probably best to keep this girl happy.

Quinn sighed, took up the pen, and made an unidentifiable squiggle that wasn't her signature.

Then she and Johnny stood.

The girl smiled and gripped the receipt to her chest, but hadn't stepped back to let Quinn pass.

This close, Quinn could see the girl's stained teeth.

She watched those teeth, chapped lips peeling back, as the girl smirked and said:

"I'm so glad you started killing these fuckers."

Quinn and Johnny left the library.

This was too much.

She needed to get out.

She needed to find out where all the disappeared were going.

"Resettle Kettle Springs," Arthur Hill said in her ear.

She shivered, willed him to disappear, to leave her alone. To go be dead again for a while.

"Hey, you okay?" Johnny asked, his voice kind.

But Quinn didn't need kind right now, so she shrugged him away.

She needed—

They needed to hurry on to find the Dozers.

The Mustang's engine clicked, cooling after the drive.

Johnny was quiet. He sat on the edge of his ludicrously uncomfortable seat, letting what Quinn had just said sink in.

"Pro wrestlers? Are we kidding right now?" he finally asked.

This was crazy, but he had said he was in, right? That he'd help her? Yeah. He did. Johnny wasn't going to back out of that.

He had the passenger door cracked, one foot down on the dirt outside.

Quinn was standing on the other side, stopping him from pushing the door open all the way.

"Gabriel and Cheryl Dozer," Quinn said. "And I wouldn't say *pro* wrestlers. They do shows at the VFW and down card matches when the larger local promotion needs them."

"'Down card.' You a fan of this stuff?"

"It's called *research*."

Everything about this girl confused Johnny. Confused

and compelled him. It had been over twenty-four hours on the road, with only a few hours of fitful, nightmare-filled sleep for Johnny, but Quinn Maybrook had already grown too relaxed around him.

Today there had been plenty of opportunities for him to slip away. Or for him to start yelling, "Kidnapping! Help!" But . . .

He no longer *wanted* to escape.

He wanted to see where she was leading him. Where this quest she was on ended. And not just because he had nothing to go home to. But because he thought that her revenge and his revenge, they overlapped now. He wanted to see what she'd do to those little starched-shirt freaks. He wanted to help her do it.

"I'm after Gabriel Dozer. Specifically. He shot someone last October. One of the haunted house staffers who'd helped me retake the town. Someone who'd trusted me. . . ."

"Shot like killed or shot, like, just *shot*?" Johnny asked.

"*Just* shot?" she said, shaking her head. "She survived. But I still want to . . ." She trailed off. Johnny had annoyed her. He was always doing that, always annoying people into giving up rather than continue talking with him. He wanted to get better with that, especially around girls. Exhausting. That was the word some of the classier girls had used to describe him. Johnny was exhausting.

"Look, I'm sorry. It was brave, what you did with those

kids," he said. "How you led them into battle." He'd read about that, how she'd recruited a bunch of high schoolers to go up against dudes with guns. Was Johnny like them? Was he one of her followers now? Someone for her to lead into battle?

"The guy wrestles under the name Jacksaw," Quinn continued, ignoring the apology and compliment.

"Wait. So his first name *isn't* Jack and his real last name is *Dozer*? And he wrestles as *Jacksaw*? Why not Bull—"

"Can we stop? I have to go." He'd done it again, annoyed her.

Johnny looked around. They were parked on the side of the road, in what could have been deep woods until you remembered all the tents and RVs you passed on the way in. There was maybe fifty yards of land separating each campground. Which was nice. More secluded than any of the places Trevor's dad or Johnny's dad had ever taken them camping. There was privacy, but not so your neighbor could throw a party or fire a gun without you knowing. Pine needles carpeted the trail ahead, string lights and campfires twinkled through the branches. They were a few hours past dusk, so it was, what . . . ten or eleven? It was so weird, not having a phone to know the time anymore.

"Wait," Johnny said, taking a moment to decode what she'd just said. "*You* have to go? I'm coming too."

"Give me your hand," Quinn said, taking something out of her back pocket.

"What?"

"Hand. Now."

Oh, she wasn't going to—

"No. Wait. Take me with you. You're going to need me."

"No. I won't. They probably aren't even home. RV's dark."

"But I can help," he said.

"Oh, I'm sure you could. But you could also fuck up royally. Or run."

"Look. If I was going to run I'd already have—"

She grabbed his arm while he was busy gesticulating and held it in place against the passenger door's window frame.

Zzzzip.

The zip tie was tight enough he wouldn't be getting his thumb through, but not tight enough she'd cut off his circulation.

Johnny didn't know why, but he found something encouraging in that. That she was willing to minimize his discomfort.

"You said there's two of them! Two pro wrestlers! Why can't I help?"

"Johnny. How many fights have you been in?"

"Plenty."

"How many without your brother?"

Johnny hadn't been expecting that question, the sharpness of it, and didn't have a smartass answer for it.

How could she know that? They hadn't talked *that* much.

How could she know that Johnny D was the brother who started fights and Trevor the one who finished them?

"Yo . . . ," he said.

She frowned.

"Please. Just stay here, keep a lookout, and honk if there's an emergency."

He didn't have the strength to answer her. Suddenly he was so tired. Maybe he'd still be able to sleep with his hand above his head like this.

Yeah. That was it. He'd try to sleep while Quinn Maybrook did the fighting for both of them.

Like Trevor used to.

Not for the first time since beginning her revenge project, Quinn Maybrook wished she had a gun.

Which sucked. Because she hated guns. Hated all that she'd had to *do* with them, all she'd needed to *learn* about them to stay alive.

The brass knuckles pulled at her jacket pocket. They were heavy, but they didn't feel like enough as she knocked on the Winnebago door.

The pictures she'd found of the Dozers were publicity shots taken fifteen or twenty years ago, judging by the hairstyles. The two of them were huge. Their veins throbbing like worms under their bronze skin. Spandex and baby oil glistening. A husband-and-wife tag team. She thought back on the photos, doubting that a small-caliber gun would kill these juiced-up superheroes. But at least a gun would give Quinn more than a fighting chance.

She knocked again. Listened, ready to give up, and then a sleepy woman's voice spoke from inside the mobile home:

"Coming!"

Quinn put her left hand in her jacket pocket, felt the metal, warm, but didn't slip her fingers into the grooves of the knuckles.

"Rent's paid and I have no—"

The door opened.

Quinn had to look down to meet the old woman's gaze.

"Oh. It's you," the woman said. She wore gray sweatpants and a sweatshirt that, while also gray, didn't match the pants.

The old woman recognized Quinn, but it took Quinn a moment to do the same.

Cheryl Dozer was a lot shorter than she'd been expecting. Shorter, smaller, and older. But the woman's golden-blond hair, gone mostly white, and her wide shoulders gave her away.

"You want me to come out or do you want to come in?" Cheryl Dozer asked Quinn from behind the screen door.

"Depends. Is your husband home?"

"He's dead."

Quinn tried to hide her surprise, keep her face impassive.

But that didn't seem true. There would have been an obituary. Or a Facebook post in some local wrestling fan group. And nothing like that had come up during her search in the library.

"Dead?" Quinn asked. Neither of them had moved, they were still talking through the screen door.

"Dead to me. Haven't seen him in weeks. He left a note saying he was sorry and that he'd paid off the campsite for the rest of the year."

Quinn nodded. Gabriel Dozer was one of the disappeared. And his wife *wasn't*.

"That was . . . nice of him?" Quinn said.

"Sure. And the rest of our shared bank account drained. Not closed, just empty. There was a twenty-dollar overdraft fee. Which I couldn't pay because he also took the cashbox we bring to shows." Cheryl Dozer cracked her neck, the sound like soft firecrackers. "So not *that* nice."

"I'm sorry," Quinn said to the old woman.

Old*er* woman.

It wasn't right to think of her as old. It was unkind, yes. But more than unkind, it was stupid. This was not an "old woman," this was someone with the capacity to be dangerous. And "old" wasn't even an apt descriptor. She was *weathered*, not old. Cheryl Dozer was likely younger than Glenn Maybrook. Somewhere between forty-five and fifty. Her leathered skin had been dried out by tanning beds, and if she wasn't as tall and imposing as she'd been in her publicity shots, that was probably because her joints and spine had compressed in the ring. The woman was short and withered because of years of ass kicking.

"So do you want to come in or do you want me to come out?" the wrestler asked. "If you're going to try and kill me, I'd rather outside, so I can defend myself without breaking anything in the camper." There was humor in the woman's voice. "If you want to talk beforehand . . . then come in because I need a Sanka."

Quinn looked down at the woman. She held her hands where Quinn could see them. Hands where the knuckles came to gnarled balls and the fingers met at unnatural angles.

Arthritis.

"Make your coffee," Quinn said, taking her hand out of her jacket pocket, off her weapon, and letting herself be led inside the dark RV.

The RV was roomier than Quinn had been expecting, its center corridor wider than two arm's lengths. To her left was an accordion door, half-open so Quinn could see there was no space to hide a male pro wrestler beside the bed, its sheets unmade. To the right, a kitchenette and beyond that the cab.

"Want a cup?" Cheryl asked, going to tiptoes to put a mug of water into the microwave.

Quinn declined.

There was a blank spot above their heads where the sun had discolored the wallpaper, an empty metal hook screwed into the wall.

The sun-bleached section was in the shape of a cross.

"Yeah. He took that too," Cheryl said. "It'd been his mother's. Ugly dime-store thing. Good riddance."

"Would you say he was religious?" Quinn asked.

"No. Not that way. The ring was his religion. Gabe had taken enough bumps in his career that he couldn't tell brushed iron from silver."

Quinn must have given a confused look.

"I mean he took the cross because he thought he could pawn it."

The microwave dinged and Cheryl motioned for Quinn to sit down at the table, booth and chair bolted into the wall of the RV.

"You know *I* didn't shoot anyone in your town, right?" Cheryl asked, stirring her decaffeinated coffee crystals into her water. "Or am I guilty by association?"

Quinn didn't answer, just listened to the sound of spoon against ceramic.

She'd learned a thing or two in all the interactions she'd had like this. If you let people talk, they'll give you more answers than if you'd asked. Especially if they thought you might attack them at any moment.

And the old woman was tough. But there was still a touch

of fear in her. She was just better at hiding it than most. It was probably a wrestler thing, being able to perform. What was it called? There was a term for that kind of performance, and at one point Quinn had known it. . . .

Ah yes.

Kayfabe.

Cheryl took two slow sips of her coffee before speaking again:

"I'd ask if you knew where Gabe is, but you wouldn't be here if you did, right? And you wouldn't have looked so surprised when I said he was dead."

Quinn shrugged.

Some things Quinn had gotten good at. Lying wasn't one of them.

"Yeah. Not going to be able to beat it out of you," Cheryl said, her laugh as dry and cracked as her skin.

"I thought I was the one looking for your husband," Quinn said.

"See that?" Cheryl asked, pointing a pinkie, the most articulated digit on that hand, to the large cardboard box behind the camper's driver seat.

"Looks like laundry," Quinn said.

"No. Worse. That's about eighty T-shirts with my husband's face on them. There's more in the basement. Starting at kids' sizes and going all the way up to three-X. Shirts nobody wants to buy, if there's no match beforehand."

Did . . . did RVs have basements?

"What I'm saying is," Cheryl continued, "I want to find him. I want to make him eat one hundred percent cotton. All of them."

She blew on her Sanka, took a sip, then the toughness in her expression faltered and she looked like a scared old woman again.

"Wrestlers don't live long," she said, a tear hitting her wrinkles, diffusing. "But we were supposed to do the rest of it together. Two weddings and a vow renewal. Bastard said that was how it was going to be, us taking hits with our walkers, and then he goes and disappears. . . ."

"I'm sorry," Quinn said.

There would be no violence tonight. Whatever blame Cheryl Dozer bore, whatever she'd helped her husband do, driving their home out to Missouri, picking up Gabriel's friends from the internet along the way like a clown-mask car pool, the woman sitting in front of Quinn had already paid that blame off.

Literally, if the guy had taken all her money.

Taken it to . . .

Quinn couldn't help herself. And the old woman was in tears, couldn't have been less threatening.

She had to ask.

"Would Gabriel know anyone in Pennsylvania? Maybe he'd have a place to stay up there. Was anyone you met last

Halloween from that area?" Quinn asked.

There was a pause. Quinn wished she hadn't said anything. Asking questions like a TV detective was unwise, because you gave more information than you got.

Cheryl's hand was off the mug and around Quinn's wrist in a flash. The flesh over those knuckles might have been twisted and calcified, but the muscles and ligaments underneath were strong, strong like steel.

"Is that where he is?" Cheryl asked, the puckered skin around her mouth going wide enough it looked ready to split.

Quinn tried to pull her hand back, but it wouldn't move.

Cheryl's voice went up an octave with each word: "I thought that might be it. But Pennsylvania's a big state. Do you know where in PA? Give me a town. A county even."

Quinn started pawing at her jacket pocket, reaching across her body and unable to get hold of the brass knuckles.

"I don't care that you got a *violent reputation*, girlie," Cheryl said. "I got one too. And I still take my vitamins."

The woman's sweatshirt seemed to undulate. There they were. There were the muscles, hidden by baggy clothes but tensed, ready to strike. Like Cheryl Dozer was built of snakes, coiled around each other, ready to burst.

Quinn looked around them, at the cabinets and shelves stocked with protein powder and pill bottles. The syringes and cotton balls by the sink. Then up at the light fixtures. Those exposed glass bulbs would hurt when Cheryl Dozer suplexed Quinn's body off the ceiling.

Quinn needed to reach the brass knuckles in her pocket. She needed to end this fight before it had a chance to start.

Then Cheryl's fingers unclenched, and Quinn was free.

"I'm sorry," the woman said.

"It . . . ," Quinn said, her breath hitching. "It's okay."

"That man drives me crazy. I forgot who you were for a second. What it'd mean for me if I started shit."

Quinn looked at her, allowing her puzzlement to show.

"I'm used to going into fights where I know the outcome," Cheryl said. "Easy to be confident when you know you're getting over."

Quinn nodded that she understood that term, waited until the old woman took another sip of coffee before standing.

"Thank you for your time," Quinn said.

There was nothing here to learn, so Quinn left, letting the screen door slam behind her and heading back to the Mustang.

She walked through the woods, not along the path.

Which meant Johnny D hadn't seen her approach from where he was sitting in the passenger's seat, his door open, his body half in and half out of the car. She knocked at the driver's-side window. Johnny flinched, dropped the Monster Energy Drink pop-top he'd been trying to saw through his zip tie with.

"It's not what it looks like," he said.

"I don't care," Quinn said.

She then walked to the trunk and retrieved her duffel.

Seated in the driver's seat, she began to search the bag for snips she'd use to cut him free.

"If you want to run, I'll cut you loose and you can go."

She waited for an answer. Johnny looked at his tethered arm, seemed to think about it. Then he pulled his legs inside and shut the passenger door, his arm still tied to the top of the window frame.

"Go where? I'm, like, invested in this shit, baby-girl." He smiled.

God, she hated that name. It was so demeaning, but he couldn't stop himself from using it. She doubted he even heard himself say it.

Was it a name he used with every girl? Or was it just for the ones he had crushes on?

She brushed the thought away and kept looking for the snips.

There were knives in the bag that would work, but she didn't want to cut him. She should get a tackle box or something, or a bag with more interior pockets, to stay organized.

"How were the wrestlers?" he asked.

She raised her head, looked over to him.

"Unimpressive. They didn't even do any flips or anything."

"You didn't, like . . ."

He used his free hand to mime sawing his own head off.

She couldn't help it, she laughed.

"No. Only the wife was there and . . ." She paused. How much did she want to let this kid into her life, into her mind?

He deserved to know. He was part of the team now.

"It was really weird," she continued. "For the first time in months, I felt bad for one of these people. She didn't—"

"Oh shit!" Johnny screamed, interrupting her.

He was pointing out the driver's-side window, into the woods.

Quinn wasn't able to turn in her seat quickly enough to see what was approaching, before impact.

Thud. Thud.

Two hits, shaking the car.

The Mustang began to rock, tires sliding sideways on gravel and pine needles.

Quinn blinked, her mind trying to make sense out of what she was seeing. It wasn't a car or truck that'd hit them, it was a person.

Cheryl Dozer had changed out of her sweats. The woman wore blue tights, the suspender straps bulging against her muscles, runner's pouch around her waist. She had a Frendo the Clown mask pulled down over her face, wild strands of her white-blond hair winding through the mask's eyeholes.

"Where is he, you crazy little bitch?!" the woman yelled,

punctuating the question with a smack against the driver's-side window. Her arthritic hands were like clubs or hammer heads.

When Cheryl couldn't break the glass with her palms, she reeled back and put an elbow into the same window.

Automotive glass slapped Quinn in the face, bounced off her clenched eyelids.

"The fuck!" Johnny D yelled. The boy was terrified.

Quinn was expecting the next hit to be gnarled hands wrapping around her jacket and pulling her out of the car, but instead Cheryl Dozer began hammering the hood and windshield with her fists, screaming as she did so.

"My car!" Johnny screamed.

Quinn felt for the bag, tried pushing it toward him.

"Cut yourself," Quinn said. She still had her eyes mashed closed. Her forehead was wet. She wasn't sure how bad she was bleeding, and if she opened her eyes, she might end up blood-blind.

"What?"

She threw the bag in his direction.

"Find something to cut yourself free," she said. A jewel of glass slid under her tongue and she felt blood, hot and thin, begin to pool behind her teeth.

Quinn squinted, testing her eyesight. She did so slowly, while wiping at her face and eyebrows.

It wasn't that bad. Not too much blood. She could see.

"Give me a weapon," she said, her hand out toward Johnny.

"Cut myself loose or give you a weapon, which is it because—"

The hammering on the hood was finished and, looking up, Quinn thought the worst might be over. That the woman had retreated.

But then the car groaned, began to slide.

They were being pushed off the side of the road.

Johnny looked out the passenger window, jumped in surprise to see Frendo's face pressed there.

Cheryl Dozer had both hands down under the passenger's-side door and was attempting to flip the Mustang onto its side.

Attempting and succeeding, the gravity inside the car beginning to shift sideways.

"I thought wrestling was fake!" Johnny yelled. "She's not gonna do it, right? She can't do it on her own."

Quinn didn't answer him, just began groping for her seat belt. Johnny looked back, tried to get his own seat belt engaged but couldn't get it past his zip-tied arm.

"No!" he said.

There was a weightless moment where Quinn watched the contents of the duffel bag spill out.

And then they were both crashing down against the ceiling of the car.

Johnny had broken a lot of bones in his life.

Well. *He* only broke some of them. His dad had broken the rest.

The wrist he'd had tied to the doorframe of the Mustang had already been broken. The smaller bone of the arm, the ulna? He'd broken that before.

And even with all the sound in the car, the twisting metal, the clatter of the Mustang's wheels bouncing up off their shocks, he *heard* the bone in his forearm pop. He *knew* it was the ulna.

The break had sounded exactly like it did when Johnny had been ten years old. When Dad had pulled his hand away from a hot plate, told him never to touch it. Which was a fine lesson to teach a kid, but not when you were three Steel Reserves into the day and didn't know your own strength.

"Oww," Johnny said. He tried to keep his arm straight so he wasn't rolling the broken bone around in there, but it hurt so fucking much.

He bit the inside of his cheek, then turned to check on Quinn.

"You okay? Anything—" But he was asking a girl who wasn't there.

Outside the car, there was the sound of boots on gravel. And then wheezing and grappling.

"Not that I *want* the bastard back," the wrestler lady's

voice said. "But you know what'd do it? If I killed the person in this world Gabe hates most."

Quinn didn't say anything in response. Just a choking sound that was kind of a "Gak!"

Johnny pulled his free hand out from under himself, his broken arm howling, then began to feel around for the tools that had spilled.

He felt the plastic nose and mouth of Frendo the Clown and recoiled. *Just one of Quinn's trophy masks*, he reminded himself.

His thumb scraped against the teeth of a hacksaw. No, that wouldn't work.

Then, bruised and bleeding, he reached out one more time and came back with his hand wrapped around the rubberized handles of the gardening snips.

Freedom.

"When you do an aerial move in wrestling, your opponent has to help you. They're collaborative. And if you do them on someone, and you *hurt* that person, it means that one or both of you screwed up. That you did the move wrong," Cheryl Dozer said in Quinn's ear.

The tension around Quinn's throat eased. Did the wrestler want her to breathe? Or want her to say something?

Quinn sucked in air, started to exhale, and then Cheryl shifted her weight and closed her airway back up.

"But then there are wrestlers called shooters," the woman continued. "And shooters don't do a lot of aerial moves. They train in the submission holds of *traditional* wrestling. Not pro wrestling."

It felt like Quinn's lungs were going to burst, like they were balloons under the knees of a very muscular woman.

"Most wrestlers hate getting in the ring with shooters. . . ." Black spots began to fill Quinn's vision, the shadows between the trees blotting out and the crickets going silent. "If a shooter's not causing pain, they're not doing it right."

She'd lost consciousness before, but never like this. Never because every nerve in her body sizzled with pain.

"Hey, Hulkamania!" Johnny's voice yelled, sounding like it was coming from three football fields away.

No, Quinn thought. He was so new to this. So bad at it. *Don't say something smart. Just fucking hit her if you're going to hit her.*

"Whooop whoop!" Johnny yelled.

There was a wet smack. Meat being tenderized or several eggs slapping down into the same pan at once.

The leathery muscles around Quinn's neck, the pointed bones curling up her back, shifted away and she could breathe.

Quinn rolled onto her side, finding it hard to get the coughing under control and tasting blood.

She had to get up. Whatever Johnny had done, it'd

probably just pissed the woman off. Cheryl Dozer could have been folding the boy in two right now, somewhere in the darkness of the woods.

But as Quinn rolled onto her back and sat up . . . no, Cheryl Dozer was down for the count.

And Johnny Lawson was standing over the woman, holding an adjustable wrench.

"Yo," he said, his face uneasy in the low light. "Do you think she's okay?"

Quinn looked down. Cheryl Dozer's eyes were open, spittle at the corners of her mouth, one of her booted toes tapping spasmodically in the dirt and pine needles.

No. The woman was not okay.

"Yes," Quinn said. "You knocked her unconscious."

Why burden the boy? Why make him feel the way Quinn felt every day, waking up?

Johnny seemed satisfied with her answer.

Quinn pulled herself to her feet, hands out, worried she might pass out.

Johnny didn't move to hold her or rub her back, instead he pointed back to the car.

"Oh my fucking God!" He turned to Quinn, suddenly looking younger than seventeen. "You think we can both flip it back? Maybe it still runs!"

She stared at him, her lungs burning. It was hard to tell where the joke began and ended with Johnny D.

Quinn collapsed back down onto her butt. She'd tried standing too soon and didn't have the strength.

"No . . . ," she said. "I think we're going to need another car."

Johnny was then crouched beside her, holding her cheek. "You're cut real bad."

It was a tender motion. But Quinn didn't need tenderness or sympathy. She needed a new car and the box of butterfly bandages that had been in the duffel.

"The neighbors had to have heard the screaming and the crash," she said. "You might ignore *some* of those sounds, if you're used to them. But not all of them at the same time."

Johnny nodded, then said: "Cops soon, then."

He sat beside her, shaking his head so his braids clicked together. It was a Juggalo version of Winnie-the-Pooh's *think think think* motion.

Then he pointed at Cheryl Dozer. Or at Cheryl Dozer's body.

"Did her house look like it'd run?"

ELEVEN

THE SETTLEMENT OF NEW KETTLE SPRINGS
Tabitha dug the pitchfork forward, then slung a load of hay over her shoulder.

Her hand slipped, then stung. Her movements were too hurried. She thought back to Isaiah Dunne chopping wood—how quickly she'd dismissed him as an amateur—and realized she was making the same mistakes. She would be tweezing splinters out from between her thumbs and forefingers for days.

Bugs and fodder dropped onto her bonnet, collected down in her collar, and itched at the back of her neck.

"Is there another way to do this?" Seth said, poking his head out from behind Nellie's stall. "I think I mentioned that's a rental."

He was pointing at his bike, mostly covered under a pile of hay, dry wheat straw that had to have been at least a year old, since nothing seemed to grow in Kettle Springs anymore.

"Babe," Lizzie said, not raising herself to the man's level, but reaching a hand up to his shoulder to pull him back down into their hiding spot. "Shut up."

Next to the couple in the stall, Nellie sniffed, then exhaled, then gave a small, agitated *moo*. The cow was a sweet creature, uncommonly docile, but the strangers in her pen were making her nervous.

Tabitha cooed, clicked her tongue in the way Nellie liked.

The cow would need to help Tabitha. She would watch over these two tonight. Seth and Lizzie were too big for the loft, and if Mother or Father came out to the barn for anything, it was unlikely they'd look in the stall.

Hannah was small enough for the loft, though. The child was above them now, keeping lookout. Tabitha could hear soft footsteps. She imagined the girl moving between the rafters, lifting up shingles to peek down at the house.

Yes, the girl didn't talk, but if someone approached, she could stomp her feet to warn them.

But Tabitha was feeling hopeful that they wouldn't be caught.

Ten minutes ago, they'd heard Mother leave the house.

Everyone had tensed, Tabitha had softly prayed, but

Mother didn't enter the barn. Her destination had been the coop. They listened as she'd caught a chicken, wrung the unlucky bird's neck, and gone back inside.

Mother would be cooking for the next hour, at least.

But if Tabitha didn't hurry and finish up here in the barn, she would be missed. There were tasks she needed to help with, cleaning the feathers, setting the table, et cetera.

They were having chicken for dinner twice in one week. A foolish extravagance.

Tabitha frowned. Her mother must not remember that she'd already killed a chicken this week.

The roost would be depleted by winter.

They'd need to leave Kettle Springs or . . .

Tabitha wondered if the threat of starvation could convince her parents to leave. Or if they'd be too far gone by that point, poisoned by their new religion. Her once vibrant parents depleted incrementally, dulled by stepping into that church week after week.

When was this going to end? When would things return to normal, to how they used to be? With the arrival of the Adversary? When one too many apostates went missing and the outside world took notice?

Tabitha grunted, pushing the tines into the dirt, bracing the pitchfork's handle against the barn wall.

Still not good enough.

She used her hands to smooth clumps of hay over the

uncovered sections of the motorbike. The "dirt" bike, as Seth had called it.

Tabitha whistled, and above them, she heard Hannah make her way to the ladder. The little girl descended from the loft and Tabitha approached the stall to talk with their apostates.

No, this hadn't been Hannah's idea. They were *her* pet apostates.

"I will come out in a few hours," Tabitha began. "I can't risk lighting a lantern, so you will have to listen for me in the dark. Then, together, we can uncover your bike and I can lead you to the edge of the field. Once there you will keep walking until you've reached the state road or the next town. Whichever comes first."

"What?" Seth said.

Tabitha thought her instructions had been very clear.

"I'm risking my life. This is the best I can do for you."

"Appreciate that. But we have to wait here for *hours*? It's cold. There's a cow and I'm probably allergic, I can feel my sinuses already and—"

Lizzie patted the man on his arm.

"Think of it as an adventure."

Seth looked over at the woman.

"Look. I'm all for adventure—" Then he indicated Tabitha and Hannah. "But I think we're being punked, hon."

"Seth—"

"No. Listen. Sure, they're dressed old-timey, but they're teenagers. This is their entertainment for the week, getting us to sleep out here with Bessie."

"Nellie," Tabitha corrected.

"See? Come on with this! An extremist religious cult that's going to strip us naked and kill us? That's just *Midsommar*."

Tabitha hadn't used the word "cult" when describing the situation to Seth and Lizzie, and she winced to hear the man say it.

"If it is a joke," Lizzie said, "think of it as something fun to vlog then, when it's all over."

"We're in Pennsylvania, babe! It's not the middle of nowhere. Not ye old fucking English countryside. The Sixers play here!"

Tabitha shushed him, then spoke:

"I don't know what any of that means, but listen to your wife. If Nellie starts to—"

Seth wasn't listening.

"She's not my wife," he whined. Then he smiled to Lizzie. "Not yet, babe."

"If Nellie gets agitated or starts pushing at the gate, redirect her. I'll be back once my house is asleep," Tabitha continued. Then she thought of her father, awake all of last night, reading scripture. "If I'm unable to for any reason, Hannah will come get you before dawn."

Tabitha looked over to Hannah. They hadn't discussed this. They hadn't discussed or planned *any* of this.

But the little girl nodded that she understood, that she'd be the alternate savior, if the couple needed.

"Great. First, it's a few hours, then it's overnight. This is a prank, Liz. We are sleeping in a barn, with a cow, because two teen girls are bored."

"She's nine," Tabitha said, pointing to Hannah. Then, to Seth: "Give me your hand."

"What?"

"Give me your hand, Mr. . . ."

"Just Seth."

"Seth. Please. Take my hand."

She remembered Isaiah Dunne again, and something she knew most apostates and settlers shared.

Seth reached over the side of the stall.

She dragged her hand against his, feeling the sharpness of her calluses catch across the folds of his palm.

He pulled back, mouth twisted into a sneer of disgust about what he'd felt against his own soft hands.

"I'm not pretending," Tabitha said.

It felt good to talk to someone from outside Kettle Springs. To drop the act of submissiveness. She'd spent so long just surviving, being quiet, ignoring the children in the schoolhouse, all of them the offspring of the settlers, as they needled her. Keeping as quiet as she could while the new teacher hated her, asked impossible questions. Whenever they were in town, supplicating herself before the eyes of the Pastor. Knowing that one day soon she'd no longer have a choice, that she'd be pulled into the doors of his church.

She'd stayed quiet through it all. But no more.

"I am fifteen years old," she began, "and I've done more work than you. More work than you will likely *ever* do, even if you live a hundred years. Which you won't if you don't listen to me."

Seth looked about to respond, but his fiancée squeezed his arm, stopping him.

"I promise, I do not jest. I do not prank. I don't have time. I do not have time because I am not idle. It's not how I was raised. My family has lived a traditional, simple life since coming to this country. An unbroken line we can draw back for two centuries."

She pointed to the dirt bike, the gleam of its chrome still visible if you stared at the hay long enough and moved your head side to side.

"You've been traveling the area. So I'm sure you've seen the neighboring towns and their stores. Their faith made into an economy."

"Amish."

"Yes. And Mennonite. Likely you took pictures of their horses and buggies. That's fine. But *we* are not a tourist attraction. They've chosen to compromise. They have easier lives because of how they've integrated with modernity. But we, in this town, fifty or so families, have never compromised, even as we felt the press of hardship until—"

"We get it. You're hard-core religious. Nuts."

If Isaiah Dunne were in this barn, if he'd let Tabitha borrow his axe, she'd have swung it.

"No. You *don't* get it. I'm describing the way we *were*. We are not that anymore. Something horrible has happened. An evil person has come here. He brought money and supplies, yes, to bargain with our desperate leaders, but he also brought with him a sickness. One that started in the secular world but has now infected mine. That clown and all it represents, it . . ."

Tabitha wasn't sure when during her speech the tears had started, but they were flowing freely now. She needed to pause to wipe her eyes.

"A clown sickness?" Lizzie said in a whisper.

"On my weaker days I have hated you for it, for what your world's done to mine. But when we saw you out in the field, I couldn't let you die. Because that is not what God teaches."

Seth looked to Lizzie, swallowed, then back to Nellie, then finally Tabitha again. Belief in his eyes.

"We appreciate that, uhhhh," Seth said. "This'll be fine. We'll nap here for a few hours until we can be on our way. The cow is . . . super cute."

Tabitha trembled, Hannah reached up and patted her on the shoulder.

"Good," Tabitha said.

The two girls left the barn to help their mothers make dinner.

Tabitha had never lied to her parents. She'd told stories, sure. All children tell their parents stories. And she hadn't stopped telling stories, when stories were banned. Over the last few months her stories had simply become . . . different. Since her parents had joined the church, Tabitha's stories—not *lies*—had been about how much she believed in the cause, that she just needed time to worship in her own way before joining the church proper, but that she believed in what Frendo and the Prophet Arthur Hill represented.

And that was fiction. But it wasn't a *lie*. More a performance.

Tonight there could be no equivocation:

Tabitha was lying. She was hiding the truth from her parents.

"Nellie's milked, hayed, and I double-checked the latch," she said.

Her mother only grunted in response.

Her father was already seated at the table, napkin tucked into the sweat stains around his shirt collar.

She started to quaver.

No. Dinner would be fine.

It would not be hard to lie to her parents, not these days. They'd become different people. The church had made them irrational, sometimes cruel, but they couldn't be called canny or suspicious.

Not with those eyes, black and watery, staring forward.

"It's meat tonight," her father said. Tabitha took her seat beside him. "So we will say the blessing for . . ."

He trailed off, distracted by a spot of dried food on the edge of his knife.

"Meat," her mother said, setting down the pot and joining them at the table. "You mean we'll say the blessing for meat."

"Yes," her father said, furrowing his brow in thought.

He took up Tabitha's hand, then her mother's hand, and squeezed both until the tips of their fingers were white.

Tabitha closed her eyes as he began reciting the prayer:

"Be present at our table, Lord. Be here and everywhere . . . everywhere . . ."

He paused again.

Tabitha peeked to her side. Her father wasn't distracted by his silverware again, but instead was crushing his eyes closed in frustration.

"What is the damn word?" he asked, not sounding like he wanted help. "This next word in the prayer rhymes with Lord. What *is* it?"

Her mother cleared her throat, then gave him the first syllable: "Ahhh . . ."

Tabitha felt her father's grip tighten as he continued:

"Adored! Be here and everywhere adored. These mercies bless and grant that we may feast in . . . feast in . . . feast in . . ."

Feast in fellowship with thee, Tabitha finished silently. *Amen. Amen. Amen!* She needed the prayer to end. She did not want to hear the addendum that her father would surely add.

"Feast in famine," her father said, getting the words wrong. He released her hand, but not before one final, painful squeeze. "Good for the gander. Who gives a damn anymore?" Then he crossed himself. "Frendo preserve us. Host of the martyr, fortify our faith. Protect our children. Keep them and all of us pure and good and simple. Amen."

Then he dove for the chicken, cracking bones with his fingers, peeling back the breast with dirty fingernails, taking most of the white meat onto his own plate.

"I'm working too hard these days. It makes my memory fail." He took a large bite of chicken, the grease and juices mingling with the thin runnels of anticipatory drool that had crept from the corners of his mouth. Then he looked over to Tabitha and smiled. "The girl's a woman on Sunday. No longer sick. No longer filled with excuses. She can lead prayers now. Add it to her chores, Mother."

"Yes, Father," her mother said.

Tabitha shivered, a reminder of her own problems making her temporarily forget the two apostates she had secreted in the barn.

There was no conversation, and the sounds of dinner were the tearing of chicken flesh and the occasional spoon against the serving bowl.

Tabitha ate a helping of carrots and a helping of greens, both from jars they'd preserved before the arrival of the Pastor, when they'd *had* food to preserve, and then reached for a chicken leg.

There was a light sear to the skin and she took a large bite.

Warm blood filled her mouth and she pulled the leg away.

The chicken was raw. Tabitha had a mouth full of raw and bleeding poultry flesh.

Her gorge rose.

Don't spit. Don't yell, she told herself.

She would be punished if she retched. And wasn't punishment more work? She couldn't have her mother escorting her out to the barn.

She looked over to her mother and saw that the woman had her own drumstick cleaned to the nub, pink flecks clinging to white bone.

After a few moments, Tabitha spit the pink glob into her napkin.

She moved her utensils but did not eat anything else for the rest of the meal.

After dinner, Tabitha cleaned and restocked the cabinets, then changed into her bedclothes.

Tabitha's body ached after a long day. Her bed, usually lumpen and uncomfortable, seemed soft and comforting tonight.

But she could not fall asleep.

This wasn't rest, she reminded herself, this was a performance. She was playacting at being asleep. She had to stay alert.

She could not *actually* fall asleep.

She would listen until her father's snores began, and once she'd counted thirty exhalations, she would sneak out into the barn.

She would point Seth and Lizzie in the right direction and wish them luck, watching as they disappeared into the night, returning back to their world of vlogs and movies and Sixers.

She *could not* fall asleep.

Her eyes searched the ceiling above her. As they did, she tried to picture the people who'd been responsible for raising the beams and spreading on the paste.

Others had likely helped, but it had been her

great-grandparents who'd built the home. Or was it her great-great-grandparents? She wasn't sure. It was hard to remember. And now there was nobody to ask. All their elderly neighbors were gone. Her father and mother would have known at one point, but now her father couldn't even remember the words to simple prayers.

Tabitha could not allow herself to fall asleep.

A few yards away, in the darkness of the house, she heard her mother's breathing, soft and shallow, asleep.

She did not hear her father. He was there, surely. There in the darkness, a wall dividing them. Breath even and silent and awake. It was a small home and sound carried.

There were small, encouraging signs that he would soon be asleep. She hadn't heard a match strike to light a taper. There was no glow of candlelight under her door to indicate he was seated at the table.

He was going to sleep tonight.

It would only be a few moments.

She just had to wait.

Her eyes fluttered.

Fluttered.

And closed.

They felt so good closed.

Resting. Not sleeping. Eyes simply resting.

But surely, even if Tabitha *did* fall asleep, she trusted Hannah to lead the apostates from the barn. Correct?

Mr. Trent slept much sounder than her own father. The alcohol saw to that.

Yes. Hannah was a child, but over this last month Tabitha had taught the girl well, provided a good example for her in both school- and housework. Tabitha knew Hannah to be trustworthy, a girl of her word.

A girl of no words.

But someone who would uphold an agreement.

And that was what they'd agreed.

If Tabitha could not leave her own house—if her father stayed awake all night again—then Hannah would get the apostates from the barn and send them on their way.

But no. It was too much to ask of the girl. She was only nine. She couldn't speak.

Tabitha just needed to . . .

She woke Saturday morning, hearing the first call of the rooster.

And, shortly after that, hearing the woman's scream.

TWELVE

COPY CITY, INTERSTATE 81, PENNSYLVANIA

Robert Chansley never went by Bob.

Bob was a guy with a beer gut who fished two weekends a month on a leased boat.

Bob might've owned a gun, but it was a janky hand-me-down from his father or grandfather. That gun didn't shoot right and Bob never cleaned it because Bob didn't like hunting.

Robert Chansley was *not* Bob Chansley.

Robert Chansley didn't have a man-cave, he had a home gym.

Robert Chansley owned several firearms, all sighted, oiled, and in pristine condition.

Beyond his physical fitness and combat readiness, Robert had mental fortitude. He had a set of ethics, a backbone, and was willing to die for his convictions.

He had several tattoos, but none of them were of band logos or video game characters. He was an *adult*, a student of history and philosophy, he was—

"Is this jammed or am I doing something wrong?" the woman standing at the copier asked.

"I'll be over to assist you in one moment, ma'am," Robert said.

The only thing Robert didn't like about himself, the only aspect of his life that felt like a *Bob* way of living, was his job.

Copy City was formerly a Kinko's, then a FedEx Kinko's, and was now Copy City, a privately owned copy and mail center. After twenty-five years in the business, Robert's boss had tired of keeping up the licensing and franchisee training and had become an independent store. It wasn't going well.

Robert Chansley had worked at Copy City since high school, though he sometimes slipped and thought of it as Kinko's.

Glamorous? No. But it was a living. A means to an end. His hourly wages were more than fair and, considering his seniority, better than he could do elsewhere since he had no formal education.

"No, everything seems correct," Robert said. "There's toner and I can see here that you've purchased fifteen dollars' worth of printer credit." Robert smiled at the woman. "Did you try . . ." He depressed the machine's large green button and listened to the Canon whir to life.

Warm, chemical-scented air wafted up as the woman's copies began to roll through the system.

"Oh dear," she said, patting his arm. She looked like she'd been crying. "I'm sorry. I'm so scattered, I . . ."

Robert looked down to see what the woman was copying.

It was a "Missing" poster for a small dog named Socks.

Studying the picture—bug eyes, pushed-in chin—Robert thought Socks looked like he deserved to be missing.

Robert loved dogs. But *real* dogs. Pure breeds. German shepherds or rottweilers or Dobermans.

Inbred genetic freaks like Socks . . . Robert hoped a hawk flew away with him.

"It's all right, ma'am," Robert said. "Glad I could help. Hope you find him. And please remember Copy City when you have happier business that needs doing."

The woman took her posters, deposited a small pile of used tissues from her purse onto the counter, and left.

Robert was alone in the store again.

He pushed the tissues into the garbage pail with an empty shipping tube and then took a project, an informational pamphlet about spotted lantern flies commissioned by the Parks Department, over to the Swingline and began cutting.

He lifted the arm of the paper cutter, squared the edges of the stack, and sliced down.

There were three pamphlet pages per sheet, so it took two cuts to separate them before folding. The Swingline was graded for a fifteen-page maximum, but the upper and lower blades were both dull and any more than five sheets at a time would result in ragged edges.

Robert made his cuts, muscle memory kicking in, his mind wandering.

The blade made him think of a deli slicer, and that mental image reminded him that he hadn't packed lunch today.

Which meant either Quiznos or Chipotle, both restaurants in the next lot down the parkway.

He considered the choice for a few minutes but hadn't arrived at a decision when the boys arrived at Copy City.

The Town Car glided close to the curb. Robert couldn't read the gold lettering on the side, through the blinds and signage at the front of the store, but he didn't need to. He knew that car.

And he knew what the boys were here for.

Robert moved down the counter, away from the Swingline, and typed in his code at the cash register. The drawer slid open. He scooped two fingers into the tray beside the pennies and grabbed the keys for the PO boxes.

The contents of Box 34 were lighter than usual, but that was expected. The boys had already been in this week, on Tuesday. They didn't usually come more than once or twice a month.

Robert pulled a rubber band around the envelopes. Most were addressed to Copy City, Box 34. Anonymous, plain. But a few were to Alton Ministries, with a few more addressed specifically to Jason Alton. The latter envelopes were thick with—Robert assumed—cash and had stamps with crosses or doves or little praying cartoon angels.

The bell dinged and Colby and Taylor entered the store. And they weren't alone.

There was a woman in sunglasses and a black dress with them.

A beautiful woman. Robert could see that, even though she wore no makeup under her sunglasses. The woman hugged her bare arms, clearly cold without a jacket, both overdressed and underdressed at the same time.

"Robert," Colby said, nodding. Then the younger man pointed toward the back room of Copy City.

Robert shook his head. No. His boss wasn't here. She was never here, just cashed the checks and paid the orders for paper and toner. But the boys were nothing if not careful and professional. They dealt in cash. They must have been aware how much they looked like altar boys.

Robert had underestimated them the first time they met, assuming the two baby-faced young men were children. He wouldn't make the same mistake again.

As was his habit, Taylor locked the front door and turned the "Open" sign around to "Closed."

Probably overkill, since the old woman looking for her lost dog had been Copy City's only customer today.

"New ink?" Colby asked. The question confused Robert for a second, he heard "ink" and thought toner, but then, as if to clarify, Colby pointed to the Celtic cross on Robert's forearm. The skin under the tattoo was pink and the whole expanse glistened with aftercare lotion.

"Yes."

Colby shrugged, an expression that seemed to say, *Different strokes for different folks,* but still somehow heavy with condescension and judgment.

Robert didn't know the exact dogma the two boys subscribed to, but he knew enough to guess there were no tattoos under their white dress shirts.

The woman in black seemed unsure what she should be doing. She stood by the door and spun a rack of bubble mailers, pretending to read the prices.

That dress. More than the woman—Asian, middle-aged, the curve of her face under the dark glasses ringing a distant bell—that *dress* seemed so familiar to Robert.

Not that he was the type of guy to notice things like that. Bob might have been, but Robert was not a fashionista.

"Who's—" Robert started to say, and Taylor waved two fingers.

"Don't concern yourself with her. We're in a hurry."

"A hurry?"

"Yes. Haven't you heard? She's on her way here," Colby said.

"She?"

Colby would have to be more specific. Robert was distracted, trying to place the woman who didn't look like she belonged in an ailing copy center in an ailing suburb of Harrisburg.

Robert had seen that dress, and that woman in it, on TV.

Where on TV? In what context?

"The A—" Colby started, then looked up at the security camera dome in the corner and snapped his fingers. It was empty. The camera inside had died five years ago and Robert's boss had never replaced it. What was there to steal? High-gloss card stock?

"It's off," Robert said.

"He means Quinn Maybrook," Taylor said. But Robert barely tracked that the boy had spoken, because as soon as he did, the woman flinched and backed into a display of poster tubes, knocking them over.

"Is she okay?" Robert asked.

Was this woman traveling with the boys under duress? Should Robert be rescuing her?

"You okay?" Robert said again, and for the first time the woman turned her sunglasses in his direction.

It was Vivian Murray.

One of the Founders was here.

One of the only *living* Founders.

In his store.

Wait. Wouldn't she be in jail? Had the boys—

"Did you hear what he said?" Colby asked, snapping Robert's attention back. The boy was so close now, and Robert didn't like that. He was coming around the side of the counter. The side meant for employees only. "We just told you that Quinn Maybrook is on her way here."

Robert looked at both boys, then down at the rubber-banded stack of letters.

They weren't here to collect church donations.

They had one of the Founders with them. Which meant they were bringing her back to their little camp.

Something big was happening.

Robert was their man on the outside. He was one of them. To a point. Not to the point he was playing dress-up, but . . . he was a facilitator, taking care that shipments were left where they were supposed to be, never where they weren't, and communicating with their friends at the PD when missing persons issues arose. He was sworn to secrecy and paid well enough that . . . well, he was able to afford that home gym.

He may have been sympathetic to the cause, believed in their freedoms, but he was an employee, just like the two boys were. Colby and Taylor were Alton's gofers. And sometimes his enforcers. . . .

"Wait. She's coming here like into the general area?" Robert asked. "Or here like *here*, the copy store?" He was trying to stay calm, to project a casual attitude, but it was difficult with the boys creeping up, getting closer.

"*Here* here," Colby said.

"She has the address," Taylor added.

Robert thought of the last few days of news. The loud stuff, on the TV, and the quiet stuff, police blotter highlights decoded and shared around online. Of the beheading. And the scalping. And how he didn't think that seemed like a Quinn Maybrook thing to do, at all. Even though he hated the girl.

How that seemed like a Colby and Taylor thing to do. . . .

"Ha," Robert said, trying to laugh but the sound coming out like a cough. "You two are joking with me. I *wish* Quinn Maybrook were coming here. She'd get a boot up her ass. Maybe a bullet too, if it came to that."

"No joke?" Taylor said, faking surprise. "You've got a gun on you?" he asked. The boy had his stomach pressed against the counter.

"What kind of gun?" Colby asked. "Can we see it?"

"No. Not at work." *Boss won't let me*, Robert thought, but didn't say that last part. That was a Bob thing to say, admitting his seventy-five-year-old absentee boss forbade him from protecting the business with a SIG Sauer P320.

He kept the gun in a portable gun safe in the trunk of his car.

He wanted it now.

"So you're unarmed and Quinn Maybrook is coming here?" Colby said, looking over Robert's left shoulder.

Robert turned his head, following the look. There was nothing there but an advertisement for Identi-Kit, a thumb-printing service that Copy City no longer offered.

Little bastard was playing "made you look" and . . .

When Robert turned back, Colby had advanced on him, brushing the keys of the cash register with the backs of his knuckles. There was a strange look in the boy's eyes. Humor in his smile but nothing in his eyes.

"What's this about? Step back." Robert put a hand on the boy's chest and pushed him back. But he had no leverage and the boy was planted, heavier than he looked, and didn't move. More than heavier, older than he looked, this close. It was in the quality of the skin around the eyes, the wrinkles. You didn't need alcohol and caffeine to do that, all you needed was an aversion to sunscreen.

"Yeah. I see her too," Taylor said. The boy grabbed Robert's right wrist in both hands and pulled him against the counter. "And she's got some kind of accomplice with her. A boy dressed all in black with dreadlocks or braids or something. Kid looks like trouble to me."

"Let go of me. You little fuckers get out of here. Get before I call the cops."

Vivian Murray made a whining sound, then sobbed. "What are you doing?" she asked. "Stop."

"Mrs. Murray!" Colby shouted. "You could have waited in the car. I'm sorry you have to see this."

"Maybe you can turn to face the corner?" Taylor added.

With a boy on either side, Robert didn't know where to look. He was being pulled backward now. It seemed like it took no exertion at all on their part.

This wasn't possible. Robert was bigger. He trained. They shouldn't be this strong.

Maybe they were built under those white shirts.

No. He thought of the efficiency with which they moved. The way they would end every interaction when they were here making a pickup with "God bless."

The power of faith.

Robert looked away from Taylor to see that the other boy had a knife out.

And before he could get his free hand up, the knife was pressed against his neck, stopped short there, the scratch of his stubble cutting against the blade.

"What do you want from me?"

"When Quinn Maybrook gets here, Alton needs you to give her a message. Can you do that?"

"Whatever you want! What's the message?"

Colby nodded to his partner.

There was the metal-on-metal *schooom* of the paper cutter's arm being raised.

No.

Taylor had dragged him back against the countertop, all the way to the wall of the store. To the Swingline Guillotine. It was a commercial-grade machine with a thirty-six-inch cutting surface.

"Oh, it's not that kind of message."

Scho— The sound of the Guillotine arm being lowered, but not all the way.

The cutting arm traveled through flesh and muscle but stopped at bone.

The pain was immense.

The cuts hurt, but where the skin of Robert's hand had *torn* was worse.

He'd emailed his boss twice about it, how she needed to order a set of replacement blades.

Vivian Murray was crying.

"It's okay," Taylor said. But not to Robert. He was trying to calm the woman.

"Mrs. Murray," Robert said, pleading through the pain, flecks of spit landing on his face. If these two couldn't be reasoned with, and they couldn't, then maybe he could reach the Founder. "Please. I believe in you. I believe in Frendo. I believe in America." He began to sit up, but Colby's knife pinned him in place, began to cut into his neck.

"You believe in all that, but you don't believe in *God*," Colby said.

What was this fucking lunatic talking about?

"I'm a deacon at my church!" Robert yelled, crying now.

He hadn't attended in a few months. But that wasn't a lie, Robert *was* a deacon.

"Then you know Leviticus," Colby said, then gave Taylor another nod.

"What?" Robert asked.

Taylor reeled back, raising the cutting arm, and lowered it again, bearing down with all his weight.

Schoooom.

The pressure let off Robert's forearm, Taylor releasing him.

Robert lifted his hand up to his face, saw that all four of his fingers had been severed, bone chips and lacerations where Taylor had needed to readjust and try again.

"You shall not make gashes in your flesh for the dead," Colby continued, taking the knife away from Robert's neck, pressing the point into his chest, around his heart and sternum, poking him repeatedly, punctuating his words: "Or incise any marks on yourselves."

What? It was hard to concentrate on anything but the *shick-shick-shick* rapid movement of the knife, getting progressively bloodier, pinpricks of spatter appearing on the boy's white shirt, like a star system.

"Your tattoos, Bob," Taylor said, explaining. "I don't think he likes your tattoos."

"Not B—" Robert started to correct the boy, but then felt his knees buckle. He was woozy. He began to crawl from around the counter. If he could make it to the window, claw at the partially closed blinds, maybe someone on the road would see him.

But he only made it halfway, to the foot of the copier.

"Mrs. Murray, please," Robert said, his mouth full of blood and spit, bubbling up from somewhere deep inside him, air from his lungs released into parts of his chest cavity where there wasn't supposed to be any air.

He held out his hand, the one with fingers. He waved it around into the encroaching dimness in front of his prone body. And, like a miracle, she held it. Her skin was soft.

She stroked his tattoo.

Robert had never met a celebrity before. And he'd certainly never met someone *more* than a celebrity.

A saint.

He watched tears begin to roll down from under her dark glasses.

Colby's and Taylor's footsteps echoed in the small shop, and they met above him.

"You have to step back now, Mrs. Murray."

No. Don't make her leave me, Robert thought.

Let me die like this, graced by her touch.

"You don't have to do this," Vivian Murray said.

But the two boys insisted, Taylor scooting the woman back from beside the copier.

"Actually, we do," Taylor said, his voice heavy with regret. He wasn't enjoying this, not like his friend. Or maybe he was, maybe his sympathy was a put-on for the woman.

Then there was something cold and solid pushed into Robert's mouth. He didn't have the strength to work it back out, too weak to move his tongue.

Colby took one side of the machine and Taylor took the other, the two strong boys beginning to rock the copier back and forth.

"Sorry about this, Bob," Colby said, then let go of his side.

Not Bob.

But he didn't have time or energy to turn the thought into words.

The boys pushed the copier down on top of him, the corner meeting his temple, caving in his skull.

THIRTEEN

A PULLOFF ON INTERSTATE 219, MARYLAND

The RV may have handled like a cinder block on wheels, but Quinn didn't know how she'd gone this long without regular access to a shower.

Well, she *knew* how. But it hadn't been pleasant.

The Dozers' home was a midsize RV, definitely not a deluxe model, but it *did* have a shower. A small one, with a separate water-heating unit that Quinn wasn't sure how to switch on at first.

She had to wash with her elbows tucked against her side, and she was taller than the showerhead, so she needed to crouch to rinse her hair.

Even with those caveats, every second of the experience was bliss.

As she stepped out of the shower and dressed in the

small bathroom, she wondered how much water was left in the tank and how often it needed to be refilled.

But, no, it was unlikely they were keeping the RV long enough for that to matter.

They were less than fifty miles from their destination, a mailbox in Pennsylvania.

And what then?

How many more legs did this journey have? How many more states? How many more showers?

"None," Arthur Hill said.

There was no room to stand behind her, and her knees pressed against the toilet lid as she pulled down her shirt.

She was hiding herself from him. He was *dead*, and still she didn't want him to see her.

Arthur Hill, who'd been taller than Quinn in life and was now even bigger, was crammed into the small shower beside her.

Quinn closed her eyes, the pleasant moisture of her shower becoming the dampness of decay.

She tried to will him away.

It didn't work.

"No more showers and no more states," he said.

He was too close, the room was too small, and there was a mirror in front of Quinn.

"But you know that, don't you? You're about to reach the end."

She had no choice but to open her eyes and look.

A centipede skittered from between the suppurating lips of Arthur Hill's Y-incision, crawled up his neck until it disappeared into the crack at the bottom of his mask.

"And you *want* it to be the end, Quinn. It's why you've been getting sloppy. You're impatient for it all to be over. You're rushing towards it and—"

His jaws snapped shut on the centipede. She listened to the mouth sounds as he chewed, the crunch like a mouthful of sunflower seeds, his mask moving slightly.

She waited for Arthur Hill to speak again, but he didn't, only chewed, swallowed, and stared.

Dead eyes watched her in the mirror.

The worst part was . . . he was right.

Partially, at least.

She *was* getting sloppy.

Crossing state lines in the Mustang, with its bullet holes and highly identifiable Insane Clown Posse bumper stickers. Leaving Cheryl Dozer's body where it lay. Driving a Winnebago through West Virginia, through a sliver of Maryland, and in a few miles about to cross into Pennsylvania.

She was *asking* for trouble, and it was a miracle they hadn't been pulled over yet.

Arthur Hill wasn't a ghost. He wasn't. What was standing in the room with her was just a part of her subconscious and—

"You sure about that?" he asked.

"Yes," she said.

Because he was just her, a scarred and broken corner of her psyche, what he was saying was true, a reflection of her own thoughts.

But was she really trying to end things *before* she reached Jason Alton's mailbox? Was she trying to sabotage her mission enough that she got caught? Safe in police custody before she reached the true, final end?

Being caught meant game over, sure. But it also meant seeing Dad again and sleeping in a bed and regular access to a shower. Even if it was a shower of the prison variety.

And if the end was finding out where all "the disappeared" had gone? She was stumbling into a collision course with a group of people who hated her, with only a teen boy she barely knew as backup, and then . . .

"Death," Arthur Hill said. "You've got a death wish, Quinn Maybrook. But death's not so bad. Don't I look happy?"

He smeared two oily fingers across the smile of his mask.

"Shut the fuck up!" Quinn said, turning from the mirror to scream at an empty shower, its walls still dripping.

Arthur Hill was gone.

And so was the stink of his dead flesh.

A smell that had been replaced with . . .

Barbecue?

Wait.

They had been alone in this rest stop when she'd gone into the shower. How was she smelling barbecue through the bathroom's small cracked wind—

Shit!

There was someone out there.

She undid the latch to the bathroom door and stumbled out into the rest of the RV. She looked to her right, into the bedroom, then left, into the kitchenette and cab.

Johnny was gone.

She hadn't zip-tied him, hadn't even threatened to do it.

He'd said he would stay, and she had *trusted* him to stay.

Following the scent of meat, she pushed out of the RV.

Johnny D was standing over a small charcoal grill, cooking four hot dogs. There was a plastic bag of buns, a bottle of ketchup, and a stubby squeeze bottle of mustard on the picnic table nearest him.

"Lunch!" he said, a smile on his face in the noon sun. He hadn't used the shower yet, Quinn hadn't volunteered it, but while she'd been inside, he'd changed his shirt. Gabriel "Jacksaw" Dozer's face was printed across Johnny's chest and the words "The Saw Is Family" ran across his belly. In front of the shirt, he held his broken wrist, splinted, no sling.

"Put it out. We've got to go," Quinn said. She barely got the words out without drooling, her mouth was watering so badly.

Johnny poked at the dogs, rolling them a quarter turn with the spatula he held in his unbroken hand.

"Why?" he asked. "You vegan?"

"You watched me eat KFC yesterday." It was true, before the Dozers they'd flipped a coin and Johnny D had won, his choice of whatever they saw on the next blue rest-stop sign.

"Oh yeah."

"Leave that and let's go."

"Again, I gotta ask: Why? Nobody's passed through here all morning, can't we sit and have lunch?"

She looked around. There were empty picnic tables, empty parking spots, and almost zero traffic on the main road. Since they'd pulled in, the most activity Quinn had seen was a truck or two, pulling in across the interstate to use the weigh station. They'd parked the RV here to check the maps and rewrap the splint on Johnny's wrist, but when nobody else had joined them, she'd decided to chance a shower.

"You rush too much, baby-girl. Gotta learn to relax. Gotta learn to appreciate when life's telling you to"—he used the end of the spatula to scoot the buns over to reveal the four beers, the remnants of a six-pack—"give yourself a present."

She thought of the ghost of Arthur Hill, how he said she was moving toward an ending. *Rushing* toward her ending, even.

Then she smelled the hot dogs, watched the beer sweat with condensation.

And then she thought of a term from English class, a vocabulary word from a poetry unit that felt like a lifetime ago:

Caesura.

It was when a line broke for a pause, helped you get more out of the poem, allowed for a moment of dramatic effect.

Or simply the poet offering a moment to catch your breath.

If they were reaching the end, she needed the pause.

"Sure," she said. "But no ketchup or I'll break your other wrist."

"Hot damn," Johnny said, banging the flat of the spatula down across the charcoal bricks, embers flying up. "I fuckin' love a scary girl."

They sat and ate, Quinn putting mustard on her dog, Johnny D putting the most ketchup she'd ever seen anyone use on his.

"Hydrate," Johnny said, popping the top on two cans at the same time. How he was able to do such a thing one-handed, Quinn had no clue. Practice, she guessed. An entire adolescence of opening a beer for yourself and a beer for your brother.

Quinn looked down. The mouth of the can brimmed with foam.

Watching the suds, she didn't think of the dead.

She thought of the living.

She thought of her friends, everyone she'd met in Kettle Springs, the people who'd stayed and rebuilt. Cole and Rust might have left, but Cole still owned half the town, flew in often. They hadn't given up, like she had. They hadn't gotten selfish and violent.

"Come on, don't make me drink alone," Johnny D said.

And Quinn picked up the can.

"To friends," she said.

"To family," Johnny D said back, his beer against hers, splashing them both.

Quinn took a sip, Johnny D gulped.

She looked at him. He didn't look back, stared off at the trees across the highway.

Maybe it was the alcohol on her tongue. Maybe it was the sensation of having clean skin, her hair drying in the sun.

But Quinn seemed to *see* Johnny D for the first time. With his relaxed posture on the park bench—not hunched on an uncomfortable passenger seat, not afraid for his life— he seemed to have . . . uncurled.

Arms and legs slicked with days of dried sweat, but not dirty in an off-putting way. The end of his shorts up past his knee, his thighs with less hair than the rest of him.

He looked . . . good.

Quinn took another sip and looked back toward the RV. To the bed.

Was it insane? Was this another symptom of her ongoing mental deterioration?

She didn't think so.

She'd been doing this so long, fighting to survive, surviving to fight. She hadn't gone through high school completely untouched, but there were things, milestones, she had been saving for college. Things she'd been wanting to do, in some abstract way, that never really linked up with specific desire for anybody. And then it had been too late. No time for romance. No time for—

Why not?

Why not with Johnny D—

Pssht!

He had finished his beer and was opening the next can.

"Slow down, we still need to—"

She stopped, not because she was at it again, giving orders, being a killjoy, but because there was the sound of tires on warming asphalt.

"What?" Johnny asked, taking a bite of hot dog.

The state trooper rolled into view. The cruiser drove past the RV, then past their picnic table, and past four of the five available parking spots . . .

And turned into the fifth spot, cutting the engine.

"Fuuuuuuck," Johnny D said, huffing the word out

around a mouthful of meat and bun.

"Don't speak. Just chew," Quinn said. "Silence."

For the longest time they sat and watched the trooper's car. It didn't seem like the man would ever leave the vehicle, until he finally did.

The trooper was big, muscular. The pleats in his uniform were so crisp they gave the illusion that his arms and legs came to geometric points instead of rounded flesh.

Quinn had known many cops in her life, some of them good—she felt the splash of Marta Lee's blood hitting her face—some of them bad—she heard the soft click of an Adam's apple collapsing. But none of them looked this much like the cartoon cliché of a lawman.

"Yo, it's the fuckin' Terminator," Johnny whispered, wet bun crumbs hitting Quinn's bare forearm.

Quinn looked over at the boy. He closed his mouth.

It took the trooper a while to cross the difference between where he'd parked and the picnic table, more time than it needed to because he didn't take the route in a straight line. The man stopped at one of the park's garbage cans, peering inside. Was that something he was here to do? Part of his duties, checking that the Highway Administration had changed the bags? Or was the big man trying to *look* nonchalant?

"Morning," the officer said, then checked his watch with

224

a quick downward flick of his arm. "Or, afternoon, I guess I should say."

"Morning," Quinn said.

She looked over at Johnny D.

She had demanded silence, but she hadn't meant a suspicious or rude kind of silence.

"Oh. Ah. Morning, Officer," he said.

"Smells good," the man said, taking off his sunglasses and putting them into his shirt pocket. The motion was effortless, like he practiced holster draws and replacements, but with his sunglasses.

"Sure is," Quinn said, holding up the remaining third of her hot dog.

There was no way out of this, if the man recognized Quinn. Or if he'd run the plates on the RV. Or any of the hundred ways they could be caught.

Quinn squirmed as the man approached, wondering if they should offer him a hot dog.

If the trooper did anything other than wish them a good day and get back in his car, then this was the end.

"But not the ending you wanted," Arthur Hill said into her ear, his rancid breath hot.

No. He was wrong. That fucker was wrong. All Quinn wanted was justice. All she wanted was to know where all the disappeared were going. Who was doing all this killing while pretending to be her.

She didn't have a "death wish." She wasn't wishing for the death of herself *or* anyone else. But death kept happening anyway.

The trooper reached their table and stopped, raising one boot to set it on the bench opposite Quinn and Johnny, resting his elbow on his knee. Casual.

"Feels a little early and you two look a little young for . . ." The trooper pointed at the beers.

It was easy to forget Quinn wasn't old enough to legally drink, since all four of her fake IDs could. The oldest of these alternate identities, Irene Montoya, was twenty-five. Cole said she needed one that old in case she ever needed to rent a car. And, no, Quinn hadn't been allowed to pick the names.

"I'm twenty-one. Last month, actually," Quinn said.

"Happy birthday." The trooper nodded.

"And Jackson is just keeping that warm for our dad," she said, swatting Johnny D's hand away from his second beer.

Johnny D looked over at her. Jackson? Our dad? She could hear his inner monologue and was very thankful that it was *staying* inner.

"Your dad?" the man asked, looking around.

"Yeah, uh, different mothers," Johnny said.

What the fuck. Silence. She'd said silence.

"But we both got the same nose," he continued, then

turned his head, his eyes wide, apologizing to her. "If you look from the side?"

"Dad's inside taking a shower, Officer," Quinn said. "Should I get him?"

The trooper seemed to consider her offer. He kept his elbow on his knee, taking in the empty picnic tables, the grass, the soft *whoosh-whoosh* of passing cars on the main road. Then he looked at Johnny's wrapped hand. Then back to the grill.

This is the end, Quinn thought. Not a blaze of glory but an anticlimax. A whimper and charcoal smoke. All because she'd showered. All because she'd let a boy with shitty tattoos convince her to stop and smell the hot dogs.

"Nahhhh," the trooper finally said, holding on to the word for longer than he needed. "No need to drag a man out of the shower. You two just make sure that garbage ends up in the trash bin."

Quinn didn't say anything, didn't think she could form words, just nodded.

"I mean it," the trooper said, standing up straight, readjusting his belt. "Not *next to* the bin, and not so much leftover food that raccoons tear up the bag. Okay? You two eat your crusts, just to be safe."

Was this for real?

"You got it, man," Johnny D said, stuffing the rest of the bun in his mouth.

The trooper grimaced. Quinn felt a record-scratch sound across her entire nervous system.

Johnny D swallowed down the gob of bread.

"Officer. Sorry. Not man. I meant to call you Officer."

The trooper smiled, saluted them both with finger guns, then returned to his car and drove away.

"Man?" Quinn asked once the car was no longer visible on the horizon.

"What do you want? I was lost in the abject fucking horror of you telling him we're siblings."

"Relax, little bro," she said.

"Ick. Gross me out."

She took that as a compliment.

They threw away their trash and continued on into Pennsylvania.

Once they had arrived at Copy City, they ignored the "Closed" sign and the shut blinds and kicked in the door.

Johnny D threw up his hot dogs and beer as soon as he saw what was waiting for them.

FOURTEEN

THE SETTLEMENT OF NEW KETTLE SPRINGS
Lizzie Santomero had been engaged to Seth Platz for five months. In that time Lizzie hadn't made one phone call, sent one email, researched one venue, or created a single log-in for a registry website.

They had no wedding date set.

She wanted to marry Seth. She really did.

But she wasn't going to be Elizabeth Platz.

Setting aside the antiquated idea of taking her husband's name and, in essence, becoming his property . . . she was not going to have a Z in both her names.

Three Zs in total, when she wrote her name out as Lizzie.

Seth didn't care, wanted her to keep Santomero if it made her happy.

Their moms, two very different women but both

traditional in their own ways, had a big problem with it, though.

It had become a whole thing.

Lizzie hadn't talked to her own mother in weeks.

So now, instead of picking out table settings, Lizzie had been on a work stoppage. She hadn't planned anything.

They were going to have to return to the negotiating table soon and figure out a compromise. Lizzie—Santomero or Platz—had about three or four months until she would be walking the aisle as a visibly pregnant bride.

Her head was against Seth's chest, the cow dozing at her feet, as she lay awake thinking about this problem.

Everything else aside, this was kind of nice.

Cute, even.

It was like a nativity play.

Romantic, in a fashion.

"You awake?" she asked.

No. He was not.

Seth was a mouth breather, and she could feel the breeze of his exhalation in her hair.

He'd put up such a stink about all of this. Had cast doubt on everything that spooky girl had said. And then he fell asleep, minutes after lying down, using his helmet like a pillow against the cold ground of the barn.

It was frustrating.

Lizzie wasn't sure what she thought about what the girl

had said. She didn't think the girl was kidding per se. But she didn't think they were in *mortal* danger, either. Seth had been right: this was the twenty-first century. They were an hour's drive from a Tanger outlet mall.

Teens exaggerated. They catastrophized. They felt things more deeply than adults. Lizzie was young enough, she remembered that part of her life.

And the girl, Tabitha, was within her rights to catastrophize.

Lizzie and Seth *were* trespassing. They'd even pushed down a length of fence to get the bike through.

So it made sense to sleep in this barn as penance, if they were going to be run out of town by some weirdo fundamentalists.

They weren't in a life-threatening emergency.

Still . . . the events of the day were enough to keep her awake.

It was fine. Lizzie'd had sleepless nights before. Before exams, before job interviews, before medium to large social events. If anything, this was training: she would have plenty more sleep deprivation and anxiety once little Eve or Jasper arrived.

She hadn't discussed baby names with Seth yet. But as of this week, Eve and Jasper were her top contenders.

She could try closing her eyes, but what was the use?

Her bottle of melatonin was back at the motel. She'd

worked her way up to 15 mg dissolvable tablets. She could rewatch their GoPro footage again, but it hadn't been that interesting. A lot of riding the dirt bike through flat fields and back roads, and the camera's battery charge was already in the red.

She burrowed the back of her head into Seth's chest and listened to the quiet of the country.

Farm life.

Quaint and quiet.

Peaceful.

If they were outside, they'd be able to see a lot of stars, without the light pollution of the city.

But they were in a barn and . . .

The stillness, no phone or TV or laptop to anesthetize her mind, made Lizzie want to claw the skin of her arms off.

How could the people who lived out here stand the silence?

Well, according to that girl Tabitha, they hadn't withstood it. They'd all gone crazy.

After about ten or so minutes of trying and failing to consider the stillness, fighting against her desire to fidget, the quiet was interrupted by a flock of geese flying overhead.

The birds honked through the night.

That must have meant dawn was coming soon, right? Geese weren't nocturnal, didn't take red-eye flights.

Or did they? She'd never given it much thought.

A minute or so after the geese passed, there were more noises. Closer noises.

There was the sigh of wood sliding against wood and the groan of iron hinges.

Lizzie lifted her head off Seth's chest to listen.

Must have been the wind.

Had to have been, because the world outside was so quiet that she would have heard footsteps approaching the barn.

There wasn't anyone out there.

Then there was a soft clatter, like the sound of the barn door being closed.

Lizzie parted her lips to say hello, to ask who's there.

But she didn't speak.

Because what if it *wasn't* Amish Wednesday Addams coming to guide them home? Or the little one? Because that was the contingency plan if Tabitha couldn't sneak out, right? If the night had gone this late into morning, then the little one would come. The nine-year-old.

Lizzie and Seth were in an urgent but definitely not life-threatening situation, and they were depending on . . . a nine-year-old girl.

The fear Lizzie hadn't been feeling was suddenly more pronounced.

Lizzie jostled Seth's shoulder. Softly—she didn't want him to wake up groggy and say something to reveal their hiding spot.

Nothing.

She jostled a little more and still Seth didn't wake. He kept mouth breathing, the paleness of his upper palate visible in the dark, uvula waving back at her.

Seth didn't wake, but the cow did.

The creature didn't stand, but it did shiver and then open one big eye, keeping its legs folded under itself. It looked . . . annoyed? Like it had gone to sleep and forgotten that the two strangers were here, inside its stall. Trespassing.

There was a little patch of fuzzed-up fur on the side of Nellie's face, sleep lines. Cows got sleep lines, wasn't that funny?

Shhhurrr-shurrr-clak.

It was a sound Lizzie couldn't place. Cloth shifting and then a soft click.

Whatever was out there, it grew closer, but she still didn't hear any footsteps.

How was that possible?

The ground in the barn was hard dirt, then floorboards in the far corner where a root cellar had been dug, and there was a thin layer of straw covering it all, but how could there be no—

In the direction of Lizzie's and Seth's feet, above the cow's head, a latch was lifted and the stall gate began to *creeeeeeeeak* open.

The cow looked up. The animal might have been able to

see someone in the darkness, but it was hard to tell.

"Seth, get up," Lizzie said, louder than she meant to.

He stirred with a sharp intake of breath, and she clamped her hand softly down over his mouth to stop him from speaking.

She looked up at the entrance to the stall and the gate . . . it had stopped moving, was open only a crack, maybe a foot, the Dutch door hanging loose in the air.

"What?" Seth asked.

She shooshed him, not vocally but with a trembling finger over her own mouth.

"There's someone in here," Lizzie whispered, so low there was no sound. Just her lips moving in darkness.

Outside the barn there was more light now than there had been ten minutes ago, thin blue predawn slashes coming through the slats in the wood around them.

Seth nodded to show he understood, sitting up straighter.

"Hello?" he said.

Lizzie shushed him.

"Why shush?" he asked, then turned to face the entrance to the stall. "Can we leave now?"

Then they saw it: the face.

Smiling at them.

No. It wasn't a face. Or: it was a face, but it was made out of fabric. A pillowcase or some other white linen, a mouth and a nose stitched in red so dark that the features looked black in the low light of the barn.

It was a clown face.

The lumpy smile hung in the partially open gate, two feet off the ground. Was it a puppet? A mask? Yes, probably a mask. If so, the face was so low to the ground that whoever was wearing the mask must have been seated on their haunches, their knees invisible in the shadows.

"Oh fuck," Seth said, shoes scrabbling against dirt to climb to his feet and crouch alongside her.

As they watched, the clown face went back around the corner of the stall and disappeared into the rest of the barn.

"What do we do?" Lizzie whispered.

He put his mouth to her ear, pulling at her arm to raise them both to their feet as he spoke.

"I still think it's a joke," he said. "But it's also scary as shit. Fuck the dirt bike. Let's run for it. If we put the buildings at our backs, we'll be going the direction we came in, we can—"

He stopped.

Noisily, the cow began to stand up.

The big creature was clumsy, its neck stretching out, bracing itself against the side of the stall as its hooves righted themselves, its joints cracking.

Once steady on its feet, the cow glanced at them, seeming unfazed by their panic, more interested in the open gate. It left them, using its head to push the stall gate open as wide as it could go. The flimsy dry wood swung back, clanging against the doorjamb, lock mechanism not catching, the stall door hanging loose.

Seth nodded at her.

"Let's go for it."

Then he took a step. A step Lizzie could *hear*. If there were people in here moving around, she would surely hear them, too. How had she not heard whoever was in the clown mask?

She followed him.

They stopped at the threshold to the stall.

"Want to go first?" he asked.

Lizzie narrowed her eyes at him.

"Fine," he said, then raised his voice: "Agatha or Mildred or whatever your name is. If you try to jump out to scare me, I will punch you. Don't try me. I'll punch a teen girl. I don't give a fuck." He pushed the gate open, not hard enough that it swung back, just far enough to step out. "Joke's over. I—"

Outside the barn, there was the call of a rooster.

Seth flinched, paused his progress.

Lizzie struggled to remember if she'd ever heard the *actual* call of an actual rooster. Yes, it was a cockadoodle-doo, like on TV or in a children's book, but in real life there was a desperate tone to the sound, like the animal was screaming, horrified by the fact that another morning had arrived.

The rooster went quiet, and Seth turned back to give Lizzie a look.

There was grit in his expression, his hand reached out for her.

They were going to run for it, and they were going to do it together. Seth could be a goofball sometimes. Most of the time. But she always *knew*, if an emergency ever did happen, that he'd be able to pull it together and be an adult.

She was glad she was marrying him.

Glad that he was going to be a dad.

He was going to be a good one.

They needed to set a date for the wedding.

As soon as they got out of this, she'd start making plans. Kiss and make up with both of their mothers.

Lizzie took Seth's hand and they started to run.

They'd made it two strides out of the stall and were still ten paces from the barn door that led outside when Seth fell forward, screaming, tumbling into the darkness.

"My leg my leg my fucking leg!"

Lizzie herself was unhurt, nothing had touched her, there'd been nothing to trip over, and she hadn't seen anything in the darkness, not shadows or the clown face or anything.

She reached down to touch the back of Seth's leg slightly above the heel where he was holding it and her hands came back wet.

She'd seen blood before, of course, but this was different. She'd never seen this much of it. The blood coated her hands like she was suddenly wearing gloves. It was thinner, less viscous than she would have thought, and very red, even in the gloom, like it was its own light source, phosphorescent. She put her hands back down, searched for the wound itself, trying to apply pressure to the long slash that'd cut through the back of Seth's pant leg.

"Don't touch it," Seth said, his eyes meeting hers, pleading, then he said something that was almost too mature and heroic to be Seth. "Lizzie, you've got to leave me and run. There's someone in here with a knife. Someone cut me."

She tried to make sense of the words and couldn't. It didn't sound like *her* Seth. There wasn't a trace of goofball in his voice. And a knife? Someone in here?

"I can't, I—"

And she finally heard footsteps. Then a slight shuffling, a displacing of hay.

Lizzie looked up from where she was crouched over her fiancé to see that it was only the cow.

Nellie was waiting by the barn's outer door, nuzzling the space.

The cow stood there, front hoof pawing at the ground like a dog begging to be let out.

The cow seemed wholly unconcerned that Seth was moaning in pain, bleeding profusely from a deep gouge in his leg.

Then the barn echoed with laughter, high and childish,

and the sound of hay crunching and sliding over itself.

Lizzie couldn't believe it.

Laughter.

Seth had been right. This *was* a prank.

A sick one.

"I'm not leaving you," Lizzie snapped at Seth. They'd been dating for a long time. Nearly ten years, since sophomore year of college. If she could tell an argument was brewing and she didn't have the energy for it, she would use this same tone of voice she was using right now. This tone cut things short. "I'm not going anywhere without you, so it'll be faster to try and stand. Can you put weight on it?"

Seth shook his head no, then stood anyway.

But he couldn't put *much* weight on it, because she felt the crush of him, most of the 220 pounds of him, leaned against her with an arm over her shoulders.

"Get the pitchfork," he said, motioning to where the girl Tabitha had left it.

"I can't carry it *and* you," she hissed back.

"For protection. And I can use it like a"—he started to tip over, and she had to brace him against the nearest wood beam—"like a cane."

This was unsustainable. They wouldn't be able to run like this. Maybe she should grab the pitchfork for him, even though she couldn't imagine how he'd "use it like a cane."

The laugh came again, a small giggle, originating from

a different corner of the barn now, rattling around in the rafters.

Lizzie looked up into the loft, expecting to see a figure in a clown mask ready to dive-bomb them from the ladder.

"You girls are in so much trouble," she said.

But there was no one up there, only an echoey copy of her own voice coming back to her.

"Look," Seth said, pointing in front of them, and Lizzie lowered her eyes.

There, standing between them and the barn door, was Seth's attacker.

All four feet of them.

If the mask was supposed to be Frendo the Clown, it looked nothing like the ones they'd seen on the news. The rough cloth mask was homemade. And it was too big, with eyeholes so far apart they were nearly on the side of the wearer's head. The mask had to be cinched with twine around the neck, the excess fabric spread out over their shoulders in a bib.

But less important than the mask was the gleam in the masked figure's hand.

It was a straight razor, the kind a man had to have surer hands than Seth to shave with. The blade and hilt glinted pearly and silver in the darkness, a line of red across the edge.

The clown laughed again.

This wasn't a little person. Or a ghost. Or a mutant with chameleon eyes on the sides of its head.

It was a child.

A *child* had used a straight razor to open Seth's leg wide enough the tendons were showing.

"Stop what you're doing," Lizzie said. She didn't have kids, but some of her friends did. What were you supposed to do, to stop bad or dangerous behavior, to snap children out of their little manias? "This is serious. You hurt him."

"Hurrrrr," the child said, not fully a word.

The child began to step toward them.

Beside the door, the cow snuffled. Nellie sounded agitated, not by the screaming and excitement, but because nobody was letting her out.

The child slashed the razor through the air, menacing Lizzie and Seth.

The clown-child swung again, laughing, the shimmer of the blade catching one of the slashes of dim sunlight entering the barn, the glare like a jewel.

The rooster crowed a second time.

The cow huffed one final annoyed sound.

And as the child passed the back side of the cow, the creature raised its backward-jointed hind leg and kicked.

Nellie's hoof connected with a tiny chest.

The small clown went flying, arms and legs rag-dolling. The clown hit the ground, a clod of hay gathering against its mask as the child's head skidded to a stop.

It should have been a relief, that they'd been saved on the freak whim of a farm animal. But Lizzie felt no relief. Maybe it was the hormones she was sharing with little Eve or Jasper, but she let out a shocked gasp.

"Whoa! Good job, Bessie!" Seth said. He unwrapped his arm from over her shoulder, seeming to gain strength and coordination now that the threat was gone.

He hopped on one leg over to the prone child.

"Don't," Lizzie said, not sure what Seth was going to do but knowing it wasn't smart.

"It's a kid," Seth said, ignoring her, going to one knee so that he could lift the child by the arm, show that it—she? it was wearing a dark dress—was unconscious. "I told you. Bored. They're bored and they're fucked up." He bent down to poke a finger at the small, unconscious body. "Lawyers better not be against your family's religion, kiddo, because you're going to fucking need one."

Seth kept cursing at the tiny body, shaking the arm, then finally tugging the child's oversize mask free to reveal . . .

Hannah. That had been the nine-year-old's name.

Seth kept shaking her.

"Stop it, you're hurting her," Lizzie said.

As proud of Seth as she'd been when he'd taken charge, what he was doing now disgusted her.

"*I'm* hurting *her*?"

He was going to separate the kid's shoulder. Who was Lizzie marrying? You couldn't do that to someone else's kid, even if they had just . . .

And the girl's little body went from slack to rigid in an instant, Hannah whipping her free hand—and the razor—up. "Seth!"

But by the time Lizzie got the word out it was far too late.

The razor dug into the meat of Seth's eyebrow, splitting the skin there instantly. The blade was then dragged down, into the eye itself, halving the orb, jelly glistening. Seth let go of the girl's arm and the child's body began to drop, gravity helping her continue to cut a deep gouge in his cheek.

The child rolled into the dirt and then began to laugh. The sound was much different from the mischievous titter of before. The laugh was a wheezing that transformed into a pained cry as the little girl hugged her ribs.

Seth, his back to the barn door, pressed his hand to his ruined eye and screamed.

It became difficult to see for a moment, and Lizzie thought something had happened to her own vision, a kind of sympathy blindness.

But the temporary blindness was light flooding into the barn, an amber sunrise revealed as the barn door rolled open.

There were three figures there, silhouetted in the backlight, one of them amplifying the sun's glare by holding a lantern aloft.

"On your knees, heretic!" the man with the lantern yelled.

"Never mind that, take him, Isaiah," the man wearing a hood said.

A large man, muscles bulging on his arms and neck, moved to beside Seth and put a hand on his shoulder.

The big man was also wearing a fabric clown mask, but this one fit much better, was almost too small, hugging the contours of the muscular man's face.

"Who's there?" Seth asked, his voice a pathetic squeak, one hand pawing at the big man, the other trying to stop his face from unraveling, stanching the flow of blood and eye jelly.

Lizzie sobbed. Because she knew what came next. She'd glimpsed the ax, held behind the muscular man, dragged down at his side.

The man in the clown mask kicked Seth to the ground, pulled the ax up, and cleaved Seth's skull in half.

There was no time to react, no time to mourn, because the hooded man's finger was outstretched and pointing at her.

"There's no time for this now. The people can't be distracted by a trial. Not when our guest is set to arrive in a matter of hours. Kill her too."

Daddy didn't shave anymore.

Which meant Daddy didn't need the razor.

But he might still miss it.

Hannah wanted to tell them that. Tell them to give the razor back to Daddy.

She wanted to tell a lot of people a lot of things.

She hadn't talked since they'd arrived in town, though. First it had been because she was afraid. Because the other kids were mean. Because the new town had been strange.

But she'd been listening in church, listening in school, learning, but by the time she'd *wanted* to speak, she couldn't.

The words wouldn't come out.

And she knew why:

God was punishing her.

Daddy couldn't get anything to grow, and Mommy cried when she was supposed to be praying.

They'd come to this place for a second chance, taken Hannah out of school, taken her away from Grandma and Grandpop, and for what?

"They've squandered his gifts," was what the Pastor had said, Hannah on his knee.

Then he'd explained what squandered meant.

She was pretty sure she would have been able to speak now. Now that she'd done something good and right for the town.

The Lord and the sainted blood of Arthur Hill had unfixed her tongue. She could feel that he had.

But her chest hurt so bad.

The lady apostate screamed as Isaiah Dunne stalked after her, kicking hay out of his path as the woman tried to dig.

Lizzie would have been very bad at hide-and-seek.

Hannah rolled over, toward the door of the barn. Did they see her here? If she could call for the Pastor, then surely he would lay hands on her.

He had the power to heal her chest, she was sure of it.

Hannah tried to call, but no sound came out.

She could wave, if he'd only look over here.

But the Pastor wasn't looking this way. He was watching Mr. Dunne, the avatar of Frendo, chase the woman.

Tabitha was here now, at the door to the barn, behind the Pastor and the Constable. Her parents were with her. Boy, did the Werthers look angry with their daughter.

Tabitha was in trouble.

Tabitha.

Traitor bitch.

Over the last month Hannah had gone along with a lot, had listened to Tabitha share a lot of bad thoughts and bad ideas. And she'd told the Pastor about all of them, for two Sunday services now, using chalk and a small blackboard. He still wouldn't let Hannah try the host, though.

It had been a long walk into town last night, in the cold and dark, but Hannah had made it.

But there'd been no answer when she'd knocked on the church door. She wasn't sure what to do, wasn't sure she'd

247

be able to talk to anyone but the Pastor, so she'd left a note. Four words, spelled the best she could, and a map.

Then she'd gone home, gotten the mask she'd been practicing her stitching with, and taken Daddy's razor.

Her parents were asleep. And her parents couldn't be trusted, either. Drunk Daddy and sad Mommy. They were like Tabitha. Almost-apostates.

It didn't matter.

The Pastor was her daddy now, or close enough to it.

"Stop with the theatrics and finish her," the Pastor shouted at Isaiah.

The big man had Lizzie by the hair, was dragging her into the middle of the barn so they all could see.

"Just do it," the Constable agreed, nodding.

And Isaiah Dunne wasn't like Tabitha or Daddy. He wasn't weak and he didn't have bad thoughts or think he was smarter than everyone else.

He lifted his ax and aimed down at the woman's body.

"Please don't. Please God," Lizzie screamed, each please going squeaky every time Isaiah took a practice swing. "I'm going to have a baby. Please don't hurt my baby."

Isaiah pulled the ax up short.

There was silence and Hannah tried to breathe, but the breathing hurt and made her whine.

The Pastor crossed into the barn, knelt beside Lizzie.

"Don't lie," the Pastor said. "Are you with child?"

"Yes. Yes. Three months."

The Pastor snapped his fingers at the Constable.

"The jail. Now. Lock her up. But feed her. No violence. Kettle Springs needs the baby."

The woman was dragged away, still screaming.

"And you," the Pastor said, whirling on Tabitha.

Oh, good. A lashing.

But Hannah couldn't hear what was being said; her ears whooshed and popped like she had a bad head cold.

And when she looked back up, they were gone. The Pastor and everyone.

They'd left Hannah here.

Hannah, who'd given everything to them. They hadn't even seen her. Hadn't thanked her. Told her what a good job she'd done, taking care of these apostates.

Some time passed, and suddenly there was someone beside her in the hay.

"Hannah, oh Lord, Hannah," Tabitha said. The older girl took up her hand and stroked her hair.

Tabitha looked down at the razor. Then at the mask still dangling from Hannah's neck by its twine cinch.

"Why?" Tabitha asked. "Why, Hannah?"

Hannah spit in Tabitha's face.

It hurt a lot, doing that. And her spit was dark and gummy.

But that wasn't much of an explanation.

So she tried to talk.

"God told me to," she said.

The world got very dark, and Hannah Trent—a name the girl had been given only a month ago—died, unsure if she'd actually spoken the words or not.

FIFTEEN

COPY CITY

This was fucked up.

It was so fucked up.

Why wasn't Quinn throwing up, why was he the only one—

"Hurrrrrkkk!"

Johnny bent at the waist. His knees were weak and his stomach felt folded in two, but he couldn't go to his hands and knees or he'd fuck up his wrist.

And get puke on himself.

The carpet of the copy store wasn't absorbing the vomit at all. The solids bounced and the liquids beaded.

He was dry heaving now. The food was long gone.

"His brains!" were the first words Johnny was able to form. "They crushed his fucking head."

"They did," Quinn said. "Cut off a few fingers too."

How was she so fucking calm!?

Johnny stood straight, rubbed at his lower back. It was done. He was done.

There was cool air flowing into the store through the glass they'd broken out to enter. He tried to breathe through his mouth, to lessen the stink of the tangy, moist room. God, the smell. And it wasn't the puke. The half-digested hot dogs actually made the air in here *more* tolerable.

Johnny began to back away from the mess, get closer to the door.

"Don't step," Quinn said, her hand out at him. "Stand right there. We've got to clean that."

"Clean?" Johnny asked, swatting at a fly hard enough he almost fell. "You've lost it. Guy gets killed with a Xerox machine, you want to stick around and tidy up. We've gotta go. We've got to get out of here."

Quinn looked down, looking like she was choosing her footing so she didn't step in Johnny's vomit or the line of blood that had shot out of the guy's head and ended in a travel toothpaste tube's worth of soft tissue.

Quinn came within a few inches of Johnny and grabbed his arm.

His good arm. Not that his broken wrist hurt much anymore. He was rolling on four tablets of store-brand Tylenol. There had been stronger stuff in the RV, but the moment he'd reached for the percs, Quinn had taken them off the shelf and flushed them.

She said she'd known someone who'd died on that shit.

Didn't they all.

"Johnny," she started. "Johnny *D*," she corrected. "I know you're upset. It's a horrible thing to see. But look at the flies. This guy's been here since last night, at least. The cops aren't coming. Coworkers aren't coming. We have a minute. You need to listen to me. You need to trust me."

"I don't have to do shit, lady," he said. And winced, in case she was going to react violently to being called a "lady."

But instead, Quinn did something he wasn't expecting: she shushed him.

It wasn't a librarian shush, harsh and commanding.

It was the calm, warm shush that a mother used with a child. That someone used during a tragedy, to calm the bereaved when they were spiraling. The kind of shush bookended by whispers of "I know I know I know . . ."

And she was right to do it. Because Johnny *was* spiraling. All these miles and he'd kept it together, hadn't lost his fucking mind with grief over Trevor, over the life he used to have but now didn't.

He closed his eyes and focused on the rub of her hand on his arm, the sureness of it.

His breathing quieted.

Then she spoke:

"They knew you were under the car."

She said it quick, like pulling off a Band-Aid.

And his eyes shot open.

"What?"

"When they were killing your brother. Think about it. They're driving a car with the name of the church on the side. We find the church, then outside the door, not even inside, we find the address that leads us here. You weren't hiding from them. They let you live so you could tell me what you saw. So that they could lead me here."

"What?"

He was starting to understand what she was saying, but "what" was the only word that made sense.

The boys in the white shirts had known he was under the car? The terror he'd felt. The terror that'd bolted him in place so he could watch his friends die . . . Those two bastards had been counting on it?

"Listen. Their first kill, I was ahead of them. But only by a few minutes. They had to have been watching me as I picked up Charles Rome and did my thing."

Her "thing" had been torturing a guy.

Johnny felt like he was going to be sick again. But not really, because his stomach had no more left to give.

"For their second kill," she continued, "they arrived at your house less than an hour before me. They *know* who's on my list, or can guess well enough, and they were able to figure out where I was headed next—"

"Trevor," Johnny said.

"Yes, your brother and his friends."

"No. Not what I meant. His name wasn't Second Kill. His name was Trevor Dale. If we've got all the time in the world, then you have time to say his name out loud. Him and Toby Pargin. And Bobby . . . Bobby . . ."

Johnny couldn't remember Bobby's last name right now. But that wasn't the point.

Quinn squeezed his arm.

"*They* killed Trevor. Not me," she said. "And I'm sorry for that. But we're standing in a trap right now. And your DNA is all over the trap. I'm going into the back to find something with bleach in it. Then we're going to see what they left us."

Johnny's eyes went down to the man's crushed head, the ruptured flesh around his skull.

"What *else* they left us," she said.

Quinn stepped wide around the guy's splayed legs and moved to the back room of the store. A few moments later she returned with a bottle half-full of blue liquid.

"Best we can do," she said, working the spray trigger and layering blue foam on Johnny's vomit pile. She handed him the bottle. "Keep spritzing. I'm going to check the box."

He sprayed. He wasn't *trying* to inspect the contents of his stomach, but caught a flash of orange and was reminded of a few hours ago and the box of Cheez-Its he'd found in the RV.

When he looked up, Quinn was marching her fingers along a row of metal mailboxes, looking at the numbers etched into each.

"Don't you want, like, gloves and shit?" he asked. "If you're touching everything?"

"No. I'm leaving prints on purpose. We want them to think it's just me."

"Who's them?"

"Who's not? Cops, FBI. Keep spritzing."

"Yo, there's cameras," he said, pointing up to the black plastic bubble in the ceiling with the end of the spray bottle.

"No, there's not," she said without looking up from the boxes. "There's a computer monitor back there that's not plugged into anything."

Hmmm. Okay. Maybe she was pretty good at this.

"Here it is. The address on Alton's mail. Box thirty-four," she said, jiggling the door to show him it was locked. "No key."

"Welp. No key. Gotta go home, then."

She walked back over, took the spray bottle from him, wiped the handle with her shirt, then pressed her own fingers and thumb against the smooth plastic of the trigger.

When she was done, her fingerprints good and planted, she tossed the bottle into the corner.

"Oh, it's here," she said. "They left that key, no way they didn't."

Her eyes began to search the floor. After a few moments she crouched beside the overturned copy machine. She didn't even flinch, even though her face was less than a foot away from the dead man.

"Do you know who that is?" Johnny asked. She would be able to see his face from that angle.

"No. Nobody on my list. And look at the apron: this guy worked here," she said, then reached out and grabbed the dead man's arm.

"Poor bastard," Johnny said.

"I said he wasn't on my list. That doesn't mean he *shouldn't* have been on my list."

She extended the guy's bent elbow, one smooth motion, but it took obvious effort because Johnny saw the muscle definition in her arms pop.

The movement revealed the man's fresh Celtic cross tattoo. The tattoo was the last patch of pink skin on his whole body, the rest of him gone gray and ashy.

"That's how you're doing it, isn't it?" Johnny asked her. "That's how you're staying so calm about all this."

Quinn grunted. Now that she had the man's arm straight, she was unballing his fist, finger by finger.

"That's how you're able to stand it," Johnny said. "You mark them down as just another asshole from your list. My

257

brother was on that list. You tell yourself that this guy probably deserved it. That my—"

"Nobody deserves this," Quinn said. He didn't believe her. "And I'm not calm. I'm tired. I've seen a lot of bodies. His isn't the worst."

She had the hand all the way open now and was gazing down into the palm, disappointed.

"Key's not on a hook somewhere? Or in the cash register?"

She seemed annoyed by the questions.

"Register's open and empty. But you're welcome to go look as long as you don't track vomit between here and there."

He hated the way they were talking to each other. In the RV, they'd been getting somewhere, vibing together, escaping the madness by laughing and talking and—

Quinn pressed her face down into the carpet, peering under the overturned copier so that she was looking into the dead man's face.

The copy machine was being propped up off the carpet, wedged about a foot in the air by the man's partially collapsed skull. It was enough room, from the right angle, to take a picture for identification, if you were a crime scene photographer or someone else who might need to do something like that.

"These guys," Quinn said, tsking.

"What is it?"

Then she reached her arm into the space under the copier to touch the man's face.

There was the sound of wet flesh sliding, then the chatter of teeth clacking together as Quinn tugged her hand back.

"Ew," Johnny said.

Quinn held up a key ring with three small, circular locker keys. The nickel finish on the keys was slick with bloody saliva.

They'd sliced him up, dropped a copier on his head, then stuffed a set of keys in the guy's mouth.

Watching his step, Johnny followed her over to the box. Quinn wasn't avoiding anything, she just waded through blood spatter, leaving dark footprints behind her.

She inserted the key into the mailbox, turned, and hesitated before cracking the small metal door open.

He didn't like that hesitation.

"Yo, wait!" he yelled.

"Why?" Quinn asked.

He took a step back.

"What if it's, like, a bomb or something?"

She looked back at the dead man. Then over at the countertop, the fingers that'd rolled and left smudges beside the paper cutter. The lines and puddles of blood slashed and pooled over most of the surfaces of the shop's modest square footage.

"No. That's not how they're planning to do it," she said.

"They want to watch me die."

With that, she pulled open the mailbox.

Johnny flinched. Quinn didn't.

Inside the box, there was a single piece of paper, folded into quarters, with "Quinn Maybrook" written in the middle in old-timey cursive.

Quinn didn't wait. She didn't even wipe her hands, getting bloody fingerprints on the note.

She didn't open the letter toward Johnny to let him have a look, like they were equals in this adventure. But still, she had enough angled to him that he could see there was a map.

The map was hand drawn, with a scale at one corner and tiny trees sketched in between the roads for decoration.

"This is the last stop," Quinn said, her voice not sounding like she was speaking to Johnny, only that she was speaking. "This is the end."

He didn't like that. Didn't like *what* she was saying and liked *how* she was saying it even less.

"Let's go," she said. "I can drop you at the next diner."

"Drop me?"

"It's been fun," Quinn Maybrook said, her voice serious, "but we're done traveling together."

"First of all, fuck you with fun. Second, there's no way I'm—"

"I can give you a phone number. You'll call it and you'll tell the guy that picks up what's happened, the best you can.

If you're willing to relocate, he can give you a job. Or he can just wire you money, if you want to stay in your house."

"Money? What are you talking about? Quinn, I'm not leaving you."

"You should. You are. But I'll let you think about it on the way to the next diner."

He had to prove to her that he was all-in.

That he had to know how it ended.

Did he, like . . . kiss her? Or would she punch him in the throat again?

The moment passed as the wind changed and Johnny D caught a whiff of the dead guy again.

Maybe he wasn't in the mood for kissing.

"Wait. So if this was a trap," he said, indicating the room, "then that"—he pointed to the map in her hand—"is *definitely* a trap. You're just going to drive straight there, no preparation, no plan? You'd let them play you like that?"

Quinn smiled.

She was standing three paces from a dead body, maggot eggs being laid in its gray matter, and she was smiling.

The smile chilled him.

And turned him on a bit, which made him worry he was just as fucked up, just as damaged, by this road trip.

"Who said anything about going in unprepared?"

SIXTEEN

THE SETTLEMENT OF NEW KETTLE SPRINGS

At least Tabitha wasn't in the jailhouse.

There was too much to do, for an able-bodied villager to be locked up.

Or at least that was what the Pastor had decreed this morning, ringing the bell for ten straight minutes, calling a town meeting.

She thought that was *part* of the man's reasoning. But only part. There were a lot of preparations to be made for tonight, and because of that, it would be easier for him to hide the existence of Seth and Lizzie from the town.

Tabitha wondered where Seth's body had ended up. Whether they'd left him in the barn or if they'd walked out into the neighbor's field and dug a hole for him beside Ruth's family.

Likely the barn.

She remembered Isaiah Dunne dragging Lizzie by her hair, the woman's nose bloody and her chin scraped. Were she and the baby *really* being kept safe? That might have been something the Pastor had said for the benefit of Tabitha's parents. Mother and Father might not have been themselves, might have changed in so many fundamental ways, but the killing of the unborn . . .

"Your daughter has let apostates into our town." The Pastor's words from this morning came back to her. How he'd lectured her mother and father. "She's tried to ruin what we've cultivated here. If she *weren't* a child, she'd be executed. Luckily, she's still a child." He put a hand on Tabitha's shoulder. "For a few more hours."

Yes.

It was midday Saturday.

Tomorrow was Sunday.

She would be a woman soon.

Typically, at this same time on a Saturday, Tabitha would be finishing chores and allowed to take a couple hours of rest. For the last few weeks, her Saturday leisure time had been spent studying the gospel. The family Bible was the only book she was allowed to read anymore, but beyond that, it was nice to be reminded of the *real* Word of God, on the day before her father entered the church and returned home with the perverted word.

But this Saturday she was up on a ladder, hanging garland from the rainspout of the general store.

The garland was pastel ribbons she'd been instructed to weave into streamers and bunting. Kettle Springs couldn't make anything this vibrant or polished. The fabric was machine-made, bought at a crafts store and brought into town by the Pastor himself, only he and the boys in the white shirts allowed to open the town's fences, cross to the other side, and return. The Pastor boasted that their community was "self-sustaining." But it was not. Far from it.

Everything about the town was a lie.

And today they would celebrate that lie with a party.

Seven hours ago, she'd been holding the body of a dead little girl. Now, instead of being garbed in the black of mourning, Tabitha had streamers of pink, purple, and baby-blue ribbon tossed over her shoulder.

From this vantage above the general store, she could look down and see most of the town.

Party preparations were nearly concluded.

The duckboards had been pulled up. A few days without rain meant the clay of the town square was firm and dry enough to walk on.

Long tables constructed out of sawhorses and plywood lined the thoroughfare. Tablecloths had been laid over the chipboard, to hide the ugliness of the modern construction materials.

In the distance, Tabitha could hear the unmistakable sound of a lamb bleating before slaughter. And smell the smoke of cook pits being fired.

In the shadow of the church steeple, Isaiah Dunne directed several men. Notched logs were laid into place. The men were helping combine the sections of the large structure Dunne had been building this week.

The town had never known pageantry like this before it had been renamed Kettle Springs.

Tabitha and her family had observed holidays, of course. They celebrated Christmas quietly, by dining with family and neighbors. But they didn't decorate. Decoration was a secular idea.

It was silly, of course, to compare then to now. As if the absence of Christmas trees were a key difference.

Before last year, everyone in the village had been a strict pacifist. Pacifists didn't knock the heads off intruders and brainwash their children into becoming razor-blade-wielding murderers.

At this distance, it looked almost like the adults of the town were working together toward a common goal. From up here, you could almost forget about the algae-spotted blight of the church and the host ceremony, because from up here, the townspeople seemed competent and industrious.

As Tabitha descended the ladder, though, she saw her neighbors as they were. The worst of them staring off into space, swinging and missing with hammers, drooling down their chins and necks.

She saw now why the Pastor needed her. His inner circle—the Constable and Isaiah Dunne—might have been able to stand up straight, but who else in town could be trusted to climb a ladder?

Sure of foot, steady of mind, Tabitha had made quick work of the assignment.

It would be one more trip, up and down, and the last of the garland would be hung.

Tabitha lifted the ladder and walked it to the alley on the side of the building. From this spot, she'd be able to join the bunting of the general store to the length she'd strung from the old community building and jailhouse.

She stood on the bottom step, waiting for the ladder's feet to sink the inch or two into the soft earth before climbing.

"Where is she?" a voice said from behind her.

Tabitha could smell who it was before she turned to see him.

Hannah's father stood in the alley, not close enough to feel like a danger, but closer than he needed to be to have a friendly conversation.

Tabitha glanced out into the town square, to see if anyone was looking into the alley. They weren't.

"She's not in her bed," the man said. "Not out back playing by your family's barn . . ."

"Maybe she's—"

"No. I checked the school. She's not painting or making signs with other kids," Mr. Trent huffed. "So where is sch-eee?" The last word was slurred at the start, then bisected by a hiccup.

Mr. Trent was drunk. If you couldn't smell it rolling out of his pores, you could see it in how he stood, weaving for balance.

You could also see it in how he was dressed.

He had his woven cotton shirtsleeves rolled up to reveal his tattoos.

Like the pressed plywood and orange sawhorses hidden underneath the tablecloths, the tattoos were another example of the outside world pushing up from under the skin of Kettle Springs. The Pastor had fought so hard to immerse his flock in life "as it would have been before this country was founded."

But it'd been less than a year since the man had started buying property and moving his people in, and he couldn't sustain the illusion.

Not that he'd *ever* sustained the illusion. Like the Pastor's invented religion—everything about the town's historical basis and culture was inconsistent.

Tabitha didn't know much about the outside world that she hadn't gleaned from books, but even she knew that. The settlement of New Kettle Springs was based on an understanding of seventeenth-century life sourced from movies and television.

"Since we moved here the girl's been following you around, Tabitha," Mr. Trent said. "Now where is she? Where's Amber?"

"Amber," Tabitha said. Not a question.

She'd heard adults slip and refer to themselves and others by the wrong names a few times. And she knew the *real* names of most of the other students in the schoolhouse.

But she'd never known that Hannah's name had been Amber.

It was a pretty name.

Mr. Trent punched himself in the side of the head, sent his dark hair flying.

"Ah, I mean Hannah. Goddamn it. You know who I mean. Where is she?"

"I have no idea."

It made Tabitha uneasy. How readily she was willing to lie now.

"You're a shitty liar," the man said. "Where?"

"Mr. Trent, you're—"

Swearing. Blaspheming. Using abusive language. About to learn something that'll make you violent, if I have to tell you how I covered your little girl's body with hay.

"I'm drunk. Yes. But where's my kid?"

Tabitha didn't answer.

Mr. Trent—or whatever his name really was—leaned a shoulder against the general store's exterior wall and wiped at his eyes. Was he crying now or had he *been* crying?

"Shit. All week," he said, "I've been ready to leave." He hiccuped. "Working up the courage."

"You're leaving?" Tabitha asked.

"My wife and daughter don't deserve this. They deserve more than me."

He reached his hand into the waistband of his pants, and Tabitha felt herself begin to scream for help, but stopped at the last moment. He wasn't holding a weapon, only his flask. A clear plastic bottle with a black plastic cap. Mr. Trent had peeled off the label, but the bottle, like his tattoos, was still an item from the modern world.

He sipped.

"Amber. Hannah. Did she ever talk to you? Use her voice?"

Tabitha was so taken aback with how Mr. Trent had lapsed into past tense when talking about his daughter that she couldn't even begin to stammer an answer.

"I didn't think so," he continued. "But she used to be *able* to speak. Believe it or not." He burped into his hand, straightened up against the wall. "Couldn't shut her up, actually. And my wife, I don't know how much time you've spent around *her*, but she was a nurse, before."

"I didn't know," Tabitha said.

If Tabitha called for help, the Constable would come running. The man had been watching her all day, keeping an eye on her between barking directions at the town's adults. If she called for the Constable, though, Mr. Trent might demand to see his dead daughter. If he did *that*, if he made a scene and threatened to leave town, he'd be dead before the day was over. Him and his nurse wife.

Tabitha couldn't do that. She couldn't be the cause of more death. Even if she'd only be the indirect cause in this case.

She stepped deeper into the alley, moved so her body was partially obscured by the ladder.

"See this?" Mr. Trent asked, pushing his long black hair out of his face.

There was a break in his hair, like a reverse widow's peak. Mr. Trent stooped so she could follow how the off-center scar wrapped all the way to the back of his head.

"I got this in the real Kettle Springs."

Tabitha shivered. She knew most of the settlers had been there, that they were in hiding, but it was a forbidden subject. The Pastor told them to imagine that they were time travelers. They couldn't remember anything that'd happened in Missouri if they were from a time *before* Missouri was a state. Correct?

"I beat a kid half to death." *Death* came out *deaf*, but otherwise Mr. Trent's language was lucid, sharp. He took another sip from the flask. "Put her on a ventilator. And I didn't know it was a girl, either. I don't hit women. But she'd been wearing a mask, so I guess I hit this one. But before I beat her unconscious she used a broken bottle and got me, almost as bad as I got her."

He let his hair fall back down, hiding the scar.

"It was bad. A real bad cut. Only reason I didn't need to go to a hospital, only reason I'm not in jail, is . . . hey, my wife's a nurse." Mr. Trent slumped back against the wall. If there was anyone inside the general store, they'd be hearing all of this, but she wasn't sure they were open, with everyone out helping with the party.

"We didn't realize Amber was watching me get stitched up until it was too late. Gash was deep enough she could see my skull. Blood all over the kitchen table. Three months living out of a motel after that. Money started to run out, and we were able to get some from Alton—the Pastor," he corrected. "He was collecting donations. Then, when those dried up, he hit us back to repay. We gave what we could, sold my wife's car for cheap. Then we moved here. And, that whole time, Amber didn't speak. Not a peep since she saw me seated at that kitchen table."

"Hannah, Amber, she . . ." What could Tabitha possibly say that wouldn't take this ruined man and beat him even further into the ground?

"She don't have the Father of the Year," Mr. Trent said.

271

"That's why I need to see her. Is she with him? Is she with that sick fuck? Don't be lying to protect him, girl. I know you people from before used to be all love thy neighbor, but I know you have no love for your *new* neighbors."

"She's not with him," Tabitha started. "She was—"

"What's going on back there?" the Constable asked, his voice interrupting, making Tabitha jump.

She leaned around the side of the ladder, trying to put herself between the Constable and the drunken man.

But there was no hiding him.

The Constable craned his neck and cupped his hands over his eyes, trying to cut the midday glare.

"That you, Trent?"

"Yup," Mr. Trent said, sounding drunker than he had when speaking with her. He was pretending. He *was* the town drunk, and he was *really* drinking, but it was also a role he was playing. A story he told the rest of the town. "Sorry, Officer. Girl caught me taking a piss."

The Constable wrinkled his face, then smiled.

"Remind me to chew you out for public urination when this is all over and I'm not as busy."

Wait. The Constable wasn't angry?

"Will do."

Maybe the two men were drinking buddies.

"Now leave this girl be," the Constable said, acknowledging Tabitha for the first time, but still talking to Mr. Trent.

"She's gotta get up on that ladder. Only a couple hours until the special guest arrives."

"Do you know who it is?" Mr. Trent asked. Tabitha looked back at the drunk man. He was looking Tabitha in the face, eyes pleading. He was begging for her to play along, to not let the Constable know he'd been confiding in her, that he'd broken character to speak with her, not as Mr. Trent but as Amber's father.

She nodded that she understood.

"I'm not at liberty to divulge," the Constable said. "But it ain't the Adversary, I will say."

"Interesting," Mr. Trent said. "That was my guess. Means I lost a bet with Samuel."

"Betting. Shame on you. Try to stay sober long enough to see who it is."

"Will do," Mr. Trent said.

"You said that already."

The Constable left and Mr. Trent got close to Tabitha and hissed:

"I don't give a shit who the guest is. While they're all distracted, I'm taking my wife and daughter out of here. Now, please, tell me where she is."

Tabitha made the man promise not to scream.

Then she breathed in deep, exhaled, and told him the truth.

* * *

273

Vivian hated how good it felt to wash her face and apply makeup.

She'd watched a man's torture and murder. She'd done nothing to try to escape from his killers, her *captors*. And for all that impassiveness and cowardice she'd been rewarded with lavender soap, a washbasin, and a gift bag of brand-new products from Sephora.

But it felt *so* good to wash her face and apply makeup.

So good she was doing it twice.

She applied everything but lip gloss and eyeliner, admired her work in the mirror, allowed herself to remember a version of herself from long ago, then washed the slate clean and began again. She relished in the sensation of toweling the water from her upper lip. The tacky tick of a dot of foundation on her forefinger. The gentle plush kiss of the applicator against her cheek.

The greenroom was located in a church, above a set of stairs at the back of the building.

This room could have been a priest's living quarters. Except there was no bed, no furniture at all beyond a floor lamp, a chair, a mirror, and the table they'd set her washbasin on.

The lamp gave off a soft orange-yellow light, it was oil, not electric, and the room smelled of perfume. Too much perfume, as though the wood of the walls and floor had been soaked in it.

Shitty perfume. The kind she would have judged another woman for wearing. Back when she'd been in a position to judge.

It was strange, how she thought of the room as a "greenroom" without having used that term, or even thought about the phrase, in close to a decade.

But that's what the room was. There were even Nutri-Grain bars and half-sized bottles of Dasani water set on one corner of the table.

The room had two doors and no windows. One door led outside, to the stairs—that was how she'd entered—and the other led deeper into the building.

The second door was locked.

But the door to the outside wasn't.

She could leave, if she wanted to.

Or at least *attempt* to leave. The worst that could happen was she would be shepherded back inside by the boys.

No.

She wouldn't try to leave.

The greenroom may have been a holding area, but she wouldn't go so far as to call it a prison. *Actual* prisons didn't have Nutri-Grain bars.

Vivian imagined that, outside this windowless room, they were still in Pennsylvania. But what point of reference did she have for that? Her life with Janet's father had been on the West Coast, then Alec had moved her to Missouri, and that was where her life's eastern progress had stopped.

It was difficult to tell in the dark, dozing in the back seat on the ride here. They'd left the car in a field abutting dense, sloped woods.

The boys covered the vehicle with a camouflage tarp, then ushered her into the woods, telling her that they'd need to go the rest of the way on foot.

It hadn't been an easy hike, in the cold and dark. But it wasn't a death march, either. One of the boys, Colby or Taylor—they weren't identical, but she couldn't tell them apart—had always been there to lend Vivian an elbow or to catch her if she tripped.

Taylor and Colby were her captors, they were sadists, but they were watching out for her.

Vivian hadn't given Janet any siblings, and the boys may have been older than they looked, but they were young enough, treated her with enough maternal reverence, that they could almost be—

The knock at the door stopped her from finishing that thought, which was probably for the best.

Vivian looked at her reflection, saw that one wing of her eyeliner was now longer than the other.

Where the knock had come from was hard to pinpoint until the second rap, with the odd acoustics of the mostly empty room.

Someone was knocking at the outer door.

She didn't answer.

"Mrs. Murray?" one of the boys asked from the other side of the door.

She flinched at being called Mrs. Murray.

There were steps Vivian could have taken to stop hearing that name. She could have tried to have the marriage to Alec annulled, if that were a thing an incarcerated person could do.

But she hadn't. It was a kind of penance. To see that motherfucker's face anytime she heard her own name.

Here, in this instance, she could have requested the boys refer to her by her maiden name. Or even her first husband's name.

But they wouldn't want to do that.

Neither of those names was the name of a *Founder*.

"Mrs. Murray, it's Taylor. You haven't answered so I'm opening the door now."

The boy entered, concern on his face. Once he saw that she was fine, that she wasn't trying to escape, he immediately turned his eyes down to the floor.

Respectful.

A good boy.

He was holding a garment bag, one hand on the hanger, the other arm cradling the middle of the bag.

"We thought you might want to change out of that dress, before you come down for your dinner."

Was Taylor nervous? How was that even possible? She'd just seen him mutilate a man.

It was possible because she'd been bailed out of jail by *admirers*. She was here—wherever here was—to make a public appearance. They'd explained that much to her, that the person who'd paid her bail was doing so to have her appear in front of her . . . what? Supporters? Well-wishers? Fans?

It was all so . . . what would Janet call it?

She'd call it "Super Mondo fucked up."

Or something like that.

There had been correspondence delivered to Vivian in prison. Fan letters. She hadn't responded to any of them, had done nothing to provoke the letters.

But still the letters came.

Maybe it was because there wasn't much to do, maybe it was because reading the letters bolstered Vivian's ego, made her feel more like the pretty, popular young woman she had been, before two marriages. Maybe it was because hearing that she *meant something* to a group of people, even if it was the wrong group of people for the wrong reasons, allowed her to sit up straighter in the cafeteria.

But she'd stopped reading them.

It'd happened about six months ago, and it had happened with a head nod.

She'd been reading a long, handwritten letter from a man in Macon, Georgia. She was nodding along with the man's reasoning, his philosophy, listening to how great she was, how brave. And she agreed with him, on those points. She was starting to believe him, maybe just a bit. And then she'd reached the line "I'm so glad you had the strength to do what you did for the cause. Janet deserved to die."

Vivian didn't open any more of the letters after that.

The letters told her that she was some kind of hero, an American patriot.

When in reality she was a mother who'd allowed her only daughter to be killed. Talked into it by a second husband, a man who wanted to marry her so he could brag that he'd married a beauty queen, an "exotic" one at that.

Vivian couldn't let herself forget what she'd done. Couldn't nod along with their reasoning. Couldn't let herself forget Janet and how she'd failed her.

Taylor unzipped the garment bag.

Vivian was a coward. Vain. Codependent. A weak woman who'd been convinced by a mediocre white man that Janet had to die so they could save the shitty little nothing town she'd never liked to begin with.

But the *dress* Taylor was holding.

The dress was brilliant.

Vivian didn't deserve the garment, but reached for it anyway.

It was white, but with enough color that the effect was less wedding dress and more hippie folk goddess. There were dyed crepe pastel accents sewn across a chest that was modest enough for a business meeting, but with enough bust to ensure a raise during that same meeting.

Upon closer inspection, the colorful accents were small knit flowers of different shapes. Roses, lilies, daisies. So much variety, but nothing about the dress looked "busy" and none of the colors or textures clashed.

"If you, uh, like it," Taylor said, "I'll leave so you can change."

She nodded, then cleared her throat.

What could it hurt? She'd speak to the boy. Show him some of the kindness and respect that he'd shown her.

"Thank you," she said, "it's beautiful."

He left and she stripped off the black dress.

And then the underwear that she'd been wearing since Illinois.

The funeral dress had been in the presence of Janet's body. It was a relic of her old life. A monument to her shame.

The new dress was—

Vivian stood, nude, admiring the dress one more time before the fabric was against her body.

It was white and bright and pure.

Vivian Murray was in the back room of a church, and she was being born again.

Tears came as she stepped into the dress, raising up first one strap, then the next, and then bending her arms around so she could work the buttons in the mirror.

They were happy tears, though. She'd made it. She'd stayed quiet, suffered in silence, and now she was being offered a reward that may have confused her, but was greatly appreciated.

Her fingers trembled, only one of three buttons at the back of the dress clasped.

Wood creaked. Not the floorboards under her or the groaning of an old church. There was someone else in the building. Closer. In the next room.

"Knock-knock," a voice said.

She took her eyes from the buttons and whirled, one strap falling from her shoulder.

The locked door that led deeper into the church stood open.

And not open just a crack, but had somehow been swung wide while she'd been admiring the dress.

The doorframe was a black rectangle, the light of the lamp not reaching inside.

Her flesh, which had been warm and dewy in the over-perfumed air, contracted into goose bumps.

She peered into the darkness.

The faint outline of a figure resolved itself but didn't step into the light.

"I didn't mean to interrupt," the man said. His silhouette was wide, but it wasn't his build. He was dressed strangely.

But she'd seen robes like that before.

Janet's father had been Anglican. *Vivian* had been Anglican, during that period of her life.

Standing in the doorway was this parish's priest.

"I was just getting changed," Vivian said.

She couldn't get the intonation right, was out of practice. What she meant to say with her tone was: *I'm getting changed, close the door and get out. Dickhead.*

But he didn't get out.

"Enjoying your freedom?" the man asked. He didn't step into the light. He was hiding from her, watching from the shadows.

"I'm free?" Vivian asked the priest. Then she tried to get some sarcasm back in her voice. "That's news to me. That I'm free."

"Sure, you're free. But there's a lot of very excited people outside, waiting for you. I hope you won't disappoint them."

She hugged the dress closed, wished she'd had time to do more of the buttons.

"You're a very important person to us."

"A Founder," Vivian said.

"Yes. The people out there, my flock, they've given much, to help set you free. It would be a kindness, if you stayed for the night. Or even just a few hours, for dinner. They would appreciate it. *I* would appreciate it."

"Excuse me for asking, but w-who . . ." Vivian shivered.

She was losing conviction, losing her feistiness, her internal Janet. "Who the hell are you?"

He stepped forward, into the lamplight.

The priest entered the greenroom, and a stench stronger than the perfume entered with him.

The last vestiges of comfort and joy came spilling out of Vivian Murray. The makeup felt cheap on her skin and the beautiful dress began to itch.

She looked into the priest's face.

It was Arthur Hill.

SEVENTEEN

FIFTEEN MILES OUTSIDE SHIPPENSBURG, PENNSYLVANIA

It was only money, Quinn told herself.

But it was the last of the money.

Spending it meant another kind of ending. Because *if* she survived this—looking like a big if—she'd need to find more money.

And that was without considering that she'd trusted the stack of cash to Johnny D Lawson, a boy who, while she'd been sleeping, had used Wite-Out to graffiti the word "bloodfart" on the center console of the RV.

No, she could trust him to follow directions. There was a seriousness and competence to Johnny that he hid under a layer of clown makeup and wallet chains. Besides, doing this final task for Quinn would make him feel better about leaving. It would absolve him of his guilt, before he allowed himself to be left behind.

That and there was no other way. She needed supplies. She needed weapons. Fiercer weapons than what she kept in the duffel.

"You'll need more than what a one-handed shitkicker can carry out of a hardware store," the ghost of Arthur Hill said in her ear.

She didn't look over at him, just turned up the radio, drowning him out with an advertisement for laser eye surgery.

The dead guy wasn't wrong.

Quinn and Johnny had searched the RV before leaving Maryland, Quinn hoping there'd be a gun stashed somewhere. They'd even explored "the basement" that Cheryl Dozer had mentioned. It ended up being a six-foot-long and four-foot-wide cabinet, about three feet deep and accessible by lifting a flap between the wheel wells. It'd been filled with more T-shirts and some Christmas lights, nothing useful like a shotgun or a hunting rifle.

At this point Quinn would have overcome her bad memories and learned how to use a crossbow if she could have gotten her hands on one.

Cheryl and Gabriel Dozer didn't own weapons. And that made sense: What did people built like them need a gun for? Not protection, surely. And they wouldn't be able to hunt enough to cover their protein requirements.

Quinn watched out the side mirror as Johnny rolled the hand truck back toward the RV. The red-and-white True Value Hardware sign behind him illuminated with a series of clicks.

It was almost dark now.

"Oh yes," Arthur Hill snickered. "The cover of darkness. That'll save you from certain death."

Quinn told him to shut up.

"What?" Johnny asked at the RV door, starting to load plastic shopping bags inside using his good hand.

"Nothing."

Quinn stood from behind the wheel, walked past the living corpse in the passenger's seat, and started digging through bags.

"Oatmeal?"

"Trail mix too. But the food stuff's mostly so I didn't look suspicious to the checkout lady," he said. "You have a lot of other, uh . . . camping equipment here."

She sifted through, starting with the most innocuous items. Lighter fluid, weatherproof matches, two flashlights.

"That one strobes. Says it's got a fuck-load of lumens. Whatever those are."

Quinn lifted two pressurized cans labeled "bear spray."

"Those are single use. You break the seal and they spray for nine seconds. Toss it, don't inhale, and stay the hell away from wherever you pop it, because the cloud hangs around."

"How do you know that?"

Johnny smiled, but there wasn't much happiness in it.

"I like to talk shit and lose bets."

Then came the blades. Pocketknives. Utility knives and break-apart razor refills, like the thing that'd almost killed her dad.

Dad. Quinn would need to call him one final time, after she got rid of Johnny.

She shook her head, sniffed, continued going through the blades.

There was also a large, curved machete, complete with sheath. And a hatchet. The hatchet seemed like the winner of the bunch. It was carbon fiber, all one contiguous piece of metal with no wood grip. Quinn took a practice swing in the air. It had a six-inch cutting surface, four-inch spike on the back.

"Fancy," Quinn said, her voice flat.

"Hell yeah," Johnny said. He closed his unwrapped hand into a fist, sticking out the second knuckle of his pointer finger, showing the tiny hatchet tattoo there.

Quinn rolled her eyes, but couldn't stop the small smile. She'd been inducted into the Insane Clown Posse.

She kept looking through the bags. She pulled out a multipack of bandannas, all of them camo patterned, two of them prominently featuring skulls.

"Yeah. I'm sure you didn't look suspicious at all, buying

all this in the same transaction."

"You said you wanted options and you said to spend all the cash," Johnny said, hoisting a large item out of the cart, needing to brace the box against his shoulder to lift with one arm.

Quinn stood in the RV's entryway, looking down at what he placed at her feet.

"Come on."

"What?"

"This isn't like the movies. What am I going to do with that? Look how big it is."

"First of all, half of that's the Styrofoam packing. Also, don't think I didn't consider that. This one's battery powered, so it's not like you're dragging around a compressor. Second of all—"

"Shouldn't this be third?"

"*Third* of all: This isn't like the movies? Please. This is *exactly* like the movies. I've done this a thousand times. Stretch a rubber band against the muzzle guard and you're good to go." He tapped two fingers on the nail gun. "You've just gotta be close, is all."

"How do you— Never mind. I'm not carrying that."

He frowned. Then started to climb the three stairs into the RV.

"I can carry it for you."

Here it goes.

"Look, you did a good job," she said, stepping over the nail gun so she could block his progress. "There's a lot here I can use."

"Let me come with you. These pricks killed my brother. I want to—"

"I'll get them," Quinn said. And she meant it. Not in the way she meant to "get" the clowns on her list, following her rules to leave them with broken bones and no head injuries.

She thought of how badly the bodies—Trevor Dale, the copy store clerk—had been mutilated.

She was going to kill them, the guys who did that.

She wanted to promise Johnny that. That his brother's killers would be dead sometime in the next twenty-four hours. Probably sooner.

And she was about to, but he spoke first:

"Or maybe *don't* get them," Johnny said.

She blinked. That was not what she'd been expecting to hear.

"Look. I don't care how lame it makes me sound, because fuck the cops," he continued. "But please. Please. Give that map to the cops and let them sort it out. You can drive me home. I see how much you like sleeping in a bed." He motioned to the RV's bedroom. She'd made him sleep on the kitchenette's bench. "My house has three beds. One's even on a box spring."

"You want to . . ."

He pursed his lips like he was about to cut her off, but she held up a hand, looked down at all the weapons and supplies he'd just purchased for her.

"You want to play house with me, Johnny D?"

She didn't intend for the words to sound so cold.

But they did.

"Well . . ." Johnny rubbed his nose, looking frustrated. "I didn't think you'd actually go for it, but yeah, you're welcome to—"

"I am not interested in doing that."

"You could—"

"You need to stop, Johnny. Thank you for the supplies, I'll—"

It was his turn to interrupt.

"I see what you're doing," Johnny said. He'd raised his voice, but she could tell he wasn't fully in control of his tone. Tears would be next. "I see it in your eyes that you think you're going to die. You don't *have* to die. You—"

"I don't want to fight with you."

"Then don't. Just—"

"How much money do you have left?"

"What?"

He was perplexed.

"What was left over and how much change did they give you?" she asked, waving down at the hardware store haul.

"Not a lot."

She didn't say anything.

"Shit's expensive, and you *told* me to spend it."

She'd given him six hundred dollars cash.

"A couple hundred bucks," he said.

She paused, wanted him to think she was considering what to do.

But she didn't want it back.

"Keep it. There's a Sheetz a half mile back. You can buy a phone and call a ride. Get that wrist looked at."

She backed into the RV, unblocking his way into the living space.

Johnny D followed her inside, but didn't join her in the cab, instead taking a seat at the kitchenette's table.

She turned the engine over and navigated out of the lot.

She assumed he was sulking back there, defeated, but then she flicked her eyes back and realized he was studying her maps.

"You figured out where it is?" he asked.

"Yes," she said. She watched him in the rearview. He was tracing roads with his finger, comparing the map from the PO box to the road atlas.

She would have been worried about him memorizing the location, or making a copy of the map for himself, then stealing a car and following her.

But he wasn't going to do that.

Once she was out of his sight the spell would be broken.

Johnny D could go back to Alabama, bury his brother, and start to forget about her.

It was a two-hour drive to the location she had circled on the map.

If she drove directly there after dropping him off, she would arrive a little before eleven p.m. But her plan was to walk part of the way. If the topography in the road atlas wasn't too out-of-date, there would be forest to cover her approach.

"There's a line on this printed map that they didn't draw on theirs," Johnny said. "An old road, maybe? Or a road they didn't want to show you?"

"I know."

"Girl knows everything. No use trying . . . ," he mumbled, then some more she couldn't hear.

It took five minutes to get to the Sheetz.

There were two pay phones out front. He wouldn't even have to buy a burner, if he knew how to make change and dial an operator.

Quinn hadn't known how to do that, starting out on this trip. But she'd learned.

"Pull to a pump. I'll top off your gas," Johnny said. She hadn't even heard him creep up into the cab.

"I've got enough."

He leaned over her shoulder and tapped the gauge. This

close, it was less about the smell of him, than the heat of his breath.

"Not enough if they have you driving to a second location, after wherever they've got you going. When the goose chase continues."

He wasn't wrong.

She stood. And he hugged her.

"It's been real," he said.

"Be safe," she said, allowing herself to be hugged.

He smelled musty, but not gross.

He let go.

"I love you," he said. And the words were like a punch, even though she'd been expecting them.

"You don't love me, Johnny D. You have Stockholm syndrome." It was a response she'd thought of while lying awake last night, when she first thought this might happen, alone in that bed.

"Sure," he said, turning. "And you can just call me Johnny. Didn't need the D there." Then he walked out the door of the RV.

She watched him enter the Sheetz, saw through the glass as he paid the clerk, then left, then heard the clack of the gas cap cover and him begin pumping. She didn't lean to watch him once he entered the mirror's blind spot.

If she saw him walking away, she might call him back.

"You did the right thing, Quinn," the imagined voice of Arthur Hill said. "No reason for the boy to die."

Instead of watching Johnny pump gas, she dipped into her cupholder, fishing out quarters, then exited the RV from the driver's seat, not looking back.

She called her dad, left him a voicemail.

When she was finished she looked back at the pumps. The nozzle had been replaced and Johnny D Lawson was gone.

"Time to end this," her traveling partner said, looming over the back of the driver's seat.

"Yeah," she said, Quinn Maybrook and the dead man finally in agreement.

EIGHTEEN

THE SETTLEMENT OF NEW KETTLE SPRINGS

"Once more around the maypole!" the Pastor yelled.

Tabitha listened to the groans.

This wasn't the crowd's response four hours ago, as the Pastor stood on the raised platform and made his announcement, revealed that the special guest was . . . Vivian Murray.

Then, the response had been rapturous.

Townspeople that Tabitha had never heard grunt more than a few syllables were speaking in tongues. Others wept tears of joy. Some pounded so hard at their place settings that one of the four particleboard tables collapsed.

Mrs. Murray said a few words—*very* few—but she spoke so softly, her voice shaking so much, that most of what she said was drowned out by a chorus of ill-timed amens.

But were the townspeople, half-starved and delivered

none of the prosperity they'd been promised, upset that their tithes had been used to bring this woman here?

No. Of course not.

In that moment, four hours ago, they were energized, would probably starve in hardship with their leader for another ten years, if he asked.

But . . .

Why were they still out here in the town square?

Three times now, Tabitha thought the party was coming to an end.

Three times now, it hadn't ended.

The only attendees who still seemed to be having a good time were the Pastor himself and the children overjoyed to be awake past their bedtime.

She looked over at the children, watched little Nate throw a glob of mashed potatoes like a snowball.

Tabitha wasn't seated with her schoolmates at the kids' table.

She'd *tried* to sit with them, would have rather, but Mrs. Hill had shooed her away.

Instead, she was seated between her parents.

Her father's eyes were glazed, his hand on his fork, a hunk of unnaturally orange cheese skewered in the tines, its surface drying in the night air. Her mother was muttering. For a half hour now, the woman had been saying her nightly prayers aloud, stuck in a loop. Tabitha felt sorry for her mother, the poor woman needed rest.

Several table lengths away, the Pastor stood from his seat.

All chatter ceased as the townspeople leaned forward, hopeful that they might be dismissed.

The Pastor cleared his throat and pumped his fist as he said:

"One. More. Dance."

The Pastor shook his head at their disappointment, then leaned over to Mrs. Murray, cupping his hand to whisper something.

The woman looked pained as he brought his face to her ear.

Tabitha knew what Vivian Murray must be smelling: the stink of rot.

The Pastor retook his seat. He and Vivian Murray had been installed behind a squat, oblong table covered in a red silk tablecloth. The table sat on a dais, the wood platform tilted toward the other tables. Below the raised section, the dais was flanked by the Constable on one side and Isaiah Dunne at the other. The two men working security weren't given seats. Each looked exhausted from standing for hours.

The Pastor leaned away from Mrs. Murray and waved to the Constable, gesturing something as he spoke.

It was like the Pastor was expecting something else to happen, but whatever that was kept being delayed and he was running out of ideas to buy time.

Tabitha looked down at the plates in front of them. Flies buzzed around store-bought mince pies and landed to rest on cold ground beef, the fat long ago congealed into white globs.

Only half of the town's adults had listened to the Pastor's instructions to dance the maypole. The remainder stayed in their seats, a few with their heads down in their place settings, snoring.

The dancers had no coordination, no rhythm.

Most of the maypole's ribbons had been completely knotted, draped out of reach after the first few dances. The rest hung down in tatters.

Tabitha turned her attention from the dancers, watched the Pastor open his leather-bound pocket Bible, read something quickly, and then slip the book back into his robes.

Why were they all here? Why had money, supplies, and manpower been spent to bring in a scared-looking woman who'd spoken to the crowd for thirty seconds?

Furthermore, what purpose did Isaiah Dunne's sculpture serve? The wood construction unnerved her, surely, but was that all it was meant to do: menace her, unlighted and hulking, in the space between the Pastor's table and the church steps?

Tabitha searched around them, trying to locate a specific townsperson in the crowd as the dancers returned to their seats. Was Mr. Trent here? His nurse wife? The party was being lit with torches and candles, but the orange of the fire-light threw harsh shadows and made it difficult to tell her neighbors apart, especially the men with their beards.

There weren't exact dividing lines, but generally there were gradations of stupor on the faces she was scanning. The settlers who'd been first to move into town had been taking the host the longest, from the moment that the Pastor had incorporated the practice into his services. Those settlers were the worst off, the most distant in their expressions and most sluggish when acting or reacting. Those were the peo-ple who'd stayed seated during the dance or the ones who'd wandered out to stand under the maypole and remained there long after the song ended.

Tabitha's parents weren't that bad. Not yet. Her father had taken some convincing—a campaign of intimidation and duress—to enter that damned church on Sundays. Her parents had started taking the host later than many of the adults around them, earlier than the newest arrivals, who still seemed fairly clear-eyed and coordinated.

Tabitha finished searching the crowd.

Mr. Trent wasn't here.

She hadn't seen Hannah's father since she'd talked to him in the alley.

When she told the man his daughter was dead, he needed to bite into the meat of his palm to stop from screaming.

When he was finished he asked Tabitha if she knew

where the body was. She described how she'd wrapped Hannah—Amber—in a bed of hay.

Mr. Trent then threw his plastic flask, half-full, onto the ground and ran out the back of the alley, into the woods beside town.

If he'd taken his wife and had the good sense to just leave, they could be in the next state by now.

With everyone here, there would be nobody guarding the roads. They could make it. They could run.

Tabitha hoped they did.

But she didn't think they would.

She leaned back in her seat.

Her body ached. Her calves throbbed from a day spent climbing ladders.

Around her, the banquet seemed to quiet.

She could almost fall asleep here if she . . .

Not even working through the entire thought, Tabitha let her eyes begin to close.

Her head dipped.

Then the church bell rang.

She sat upright, dazed.

The bell chimed again. It seemed louder than usual. But it wasn't, she was just closer to the steeple.

The bell chimed ten more times.

When the twelfth toll finished reverberating out over

the fields and buildings of New Kettle Springs, the Pastor stood, clasped his hands together, and yelled:

"It's midnight!"

Tabitha looked around at her neighbors, who stared at each other, mouths agape.

Was this what they'd been waiting for?

"Which means it's Sunday. And with all you gathered here, under God's sky, near God's house, this feels like midnight mass," the Pastor shouted.

No.

He couldn't have kept them out here just so that he could . . .

"And what do we do during mass?"

This wasn't fair.

This was changing the rules.

Tabitha thought she had one more night to ready herself. One more night as a child. One more sleep to dream and to rehearse what it would be like, walking through the greenish whitewash of those church doors. . . .

The crowd around her roared. But it was a different sound from the one they'd made for the introduction of Vivian Murray and the news that she had decided to stay, to live among them and help them build Kettle Springs to its full potential.

Not news that the woman herself had imparted, of

301

course, but remarks the Pastor had related on her behalf.

The rumble the townspeople were making now was a *hungry* sound.

"Host. Host. Host." The word started low, gained momentum until it became a chant that the Pastor paused with a slice of his hand through the air.

"Amen," the Pastor said.

"Host! Host! Host!"

"Please. Form a line. We'll begin. And if anyone here is taking first communion tonight"—he pointed right at Tabitha, finding her in the crowd without needing to search—"blessings be upon you."

More cheering. Louder.

They were addicts.

They were fanatics.

And Tabitha was about to join them.

Up on the platform, Mrs. Murray looked scared. But the Constable was beneath her. He was waiting below the Founder, ready to catch her if she fell. Or if she tried to flee.

Tabitha's father stood both himself and Tabitha up, her mother following. "No resisting, girl," her father said, his fingers pinching where they met around her arm. "We've enough trouble because of you."

The townspeople rose from their seats, a ragged but orderly line beginning to form. The civility lasted only seconds. The first gentle pushes escalated, turned to jockeying for position, and the crowd was frenzied. Wives clawed at husbands. Platters of half-eaten food were swept to the dirt as the line swelled to overturn tables. The children were left with no supervision as Mrs. Hill ran to join the scrum.

"Don't push. Don't push," the Pastor urged. "The body is eternal and everlasting. There is more than enough for everyone."

He pulled back the red silk tablecloth to reveal the glass casket he and Vivian Murray had been using as a table.

The casket glowed like a white-hot treasure in the night. An almost supernatural brightness that stood out from the orange-and-yellow flames of the banquet.

It was man-made light, electric light, run along the seams where the glass panels of the casket joined together.

Vivian Murray screamed.

The Pastor ignored her, opening the lid to the casket.

The Constable took the screaming woman by the hand and led her, roughly, from the dais. They were done with their guest, apparently.

The Pastor then produced a golden knife and golden serving fork and began to carve at the body in the casket.

"One at a time!" Isaiah Dunne yelled, a muscular arm sweeping three parishioners back as they tried to rush the stage.

The first settler to be allowed up to the space in front of the casket was Margery Queen. The Pastor laid a half-inch square of flesh, about the size of a sugar cube, onto her tongue, and she exited the stage.

The crowd seemed to collectively calm after that, finding more patience now that the ceremony had begun. The winding-snake press of the line evened out and Isaiah Dunne's shoulders slackened, crowd control no longer necessary.

The Pastor continued, beckoning the next townsperson to the stage, either handing them their host or placing the morsel on their tongue, then moved on to the next.

There was no music. No talking. No shouts of amen. Just quiet chewing, from those who'd been granted their gray corpse square, and gentle breathing, salivating, from those still waiting.

Tension among members of the congregation returned only when the Pastor needed to cut more cubes, his two-tined fork and carving knife finished in gold, working as quickly as he could.

No matter what the Pastor told them, Tabitha could tell that the body was not "everlasting." Even from here, a few yards away as Tabitha and her parents approached, the body looked close to picked clean. The left leg was skeletal, the bone bleached from exposure to the air. The right thigh was the same, and the man's chest was pockmarked with a thousand crisscrossed cuts, rib cage exposed in some areas, fat, flesh, and muscle in others.

As they drew closer to the front of the line, Tabitha could

see that the Pastor had begun to cut away at the host's neck meat. The plastic clown mask that covered the corpse's face was cocked to the side, lending the body an inquisitive look.

"Please," Tabitha said. The night was cool, but she was sweating. She tried twisting her arm, to see if it could be wrenched out of her father's grip.

He held firm.

"I'm sorry," was all her father said.

Tabitha found it impossible to conceptualize the mixture of fear, poison, and misplaced faith it would take to get her to turn on her own family.

But she'd soon find out, once that poison was in her.

There were five townspeople in front of them.

Then four.

The Pastor paused the line to cut more host.

She watched a long sliver of organ meat be drawn from inside the body cavity. The offal hung from the fork for a moment, until the Pastor set it flat and sectioned it with the knife.

Three.

The toe of Tabitha's shoe touched the bottom step leading up to the platform.

"No," she said. "No, I won't."

Isaiah Dunne growled at her.

The Pastor shook his head, warning Dunne off. The Pastor then guided the next parishioner off the stage.

"Mother Werther. Father Werther. Your daughter, please," the Pastor said, holding out his hand. His voice *was* beautiful, charismatic.

But at some point during the ceremony he'd lowered his hood.

And no matter how beautiful the Pastor's voice . . . his face was gone, the face he'd greeted the town with a year ago, convinced them down this path of death. That face was covered by the horrible mask that stared back at her.

Tabitha couldn't look away from it. And as she stared she was lifted up from both sides, her mother trembling with the exertion to hold her up by her arm.

Tabitha's parents took the host, neither loosening their hold on her arms, just opening their mouths and being served swallows straight from the fork.

She looked down.

There was something . . . wrong with the host's flesh. It was shingled. Diseased with growths, a fungus that sprouted into shelf mushrooms around the underarms.

"You must both be so proud," the Pastor said.

Tabitha looked up and the Pastor was pushing the fork toward her, meat glistening.

"No," Tabitha said, but as she spoke the first tine was inserted into her mouth. She bit, teeth clinking against metal. She had stopped the flesh, cold and dead, from entering her mouth. She felt the host press against her lips. It was a much bigger portion than he'd given anyone else.

She wriggled, catching another glimpse into the lighted casket, into the eyeholes of the clown mask, the shriveled gray eyeballs beyond. Masks no matter where she looked.

"No . . ." She squealed the word, teeth grinding together.

The oils clinging to the fork were bitter, not rotten or sickly sweet like she'd anticipated. She'd been expecting jerky removed from the smoker too early. This tasted like the fumes of a blacksmith's quenching tank.

"Come now," the Pastor said, turning the fork to pry her jaws apart. "Let him in."

She felt a tooth chip, prepared herself for the sensation of a punctured cheek next.

No.

I won't.

But she didn't have a choice. Metal made contact with a nerve ending on her chipped tooth. Her mouth opened, the fork was tipped up, and the dead flesh was forced first over and then past her tongue.

But before Tabitha was made to chew and swallow, there was a gunshot.

Then another.

Then another.

The Pastor's body twitched and he was thrown forward. He landed across the casket, the glass holding his weight for half a moment, then shattering under him.

There were three smoking entry wounds in the back of the Pastor's robes.

"She's here! The Adversary is here!" someone yelled.

Then there were lights and screams and Tabitha Werther couldn't make sense of any of it, because she was falling backward off the stage.

She was falling into all that chaos and her mouth was full.

Even before her body hit the dirt, she was choking.

NINETEEN

THE WOODS OUTSIDE NEW KETTLE SPRINGS

Taylor looked at Colby.

Colby shrugged.

It was getting late. It was nearly midnight.

And there had been no sign of her.

They'd opened the gates, taken down the "Warning: Road Out" and "Detour" signage, and even moved the fallen tree enough that they'd unblocked the road. Mostly unblocked the road. Enough to drive the mobile home through.

"What do you think?" Colby asked. "Is she dumber than we thought or smarter than we thought?"

"Dumber would be her not finding the key and the map?"

"Correct."

"No way." Unless the cops got there first. But they'd have

heard about that by now. "What do you mean by smarter, then?"

"She does her research and finds the southwest road."

"Could happen, sure, but there are all the cameras and trail cams," Taylor said, holding up his phone. It was silly, sacrilegious, actually, to make them disguise their phones as pocket Bibles when they were inside the borders of NKS.

"Maybe," Colby said. They'd jumped at each push notification from the surveillance equipment, but so far they'd all been false alarms. Three deer and a mother opossum, the eyes of the babies on her back glowing in the camera's night vision.

The boys looked out into the road for a moment, passing the binocs between them.

"Or," Taylor said, "maybe there's a third option. What if she's *way* smarter than we thought?"

It was Colby's turn to look unsure.

Taylor waited for the other boy to shrug again.

"Giving up and going home," Taylor said when the shrug finally came. "She could just pack it in. That'd be the smartest thing to do."

"Smart, maybe. But that's . . ." Colby paused. "Counter to her nature. She can't help it. She'll be here."

Taylor didn't think he agreed. They'd spent time studying Quinn Maybrook. They'd watched her eat alone, sleep in her car, gotten familiar with the different hats she wore when she needed to fill up on gas. Holding on to pay phone handsets, most times never dialing, just listening to the tone for a minute before hanging up. To Taylor, Quinn Maybrook *looked* like somebody about to quit, ready to pack it in and go home.

But Taylor hoped Colby was right.

It would be a disappointment if none of this plan to lure her in worked. Especially when Taylor considered that at any point in the last two weeks, they could have walked up behind her and just grabbed her. Or slid a knife into her heart.

They were being paid, yes, beyond gas and expenses. And they'd been given the sales pitch for the town itself, for what Alton planned to turn it into. Very convincing guy, if you bought into that kind of shit.

But they weren't doing this for the money or because they'd drunk the Flavor Aid. They were sitting in their naturally occurring blind, lying in wait to hunt Quinn Maybrook, because it was the right thing to do.

As they waited in silence, the temperature dropping, the church bell began to ring.

They listened through a few tolls.

"It's plan B, then," Colby said, taking back the binocs. "You go back and get some sleep. I'll take the first shift."

"No, I'll stay a little longer, just in case," Taylor said.

What was the difference between dozing out here, as

backup, on the ground or back in town on a mattress stuffed with horsehair?

Taylor's phone buzzed again. He loaded the app, waited a second for the video to process.

It was another deer, the animal pushing its wet nose right up to the trail cam, fogging the lens.

Listening to the final toll of the bell echoing through the night air, they waited, watching the road.

Plan B.

If the Pastor couldn't deliver the Adversary, if she was slow to arrive for any reason, then he'd keep his doped-up ghouls awake until midnight to offer them a payday advance on their meds.

It wasn't ideal, but it would allow him to save face, if they needed to wait to kill the girl until tomorrow, in the daylight.

Around them, the sound of crickets had been replaced by the excited shouts of the townspeople in the distance, eager to ingest a little of their Lord and Savior.

They listened for a few moments.

"I saw the way you looked at Mrs. Murray back there," Colby said, breaking their companionable quiet. "You like the woman."

Taylor didn't say anything in response. He wasn't sure what to say, there was no question in what Colby said.

"You *really* like her," Colby said. He was trying to goad him.

"I was just being nice," Taylor said.

"*I* was being nice. You were being *nice*."

"She's almost fifty."

"Forty-four," Colby corrected.

But Taylor knew that. And Colby knew that Taylor knew that.

Maybe Colby wasn't looking for a fight, maybe he was about to launch into a sermon about impure thoughts.

Because Taylor was devout, but he wasn't "lecture the guy you were stabbing about his tattoos" devout, like Colby.

He'd even had a coffee or two on this trip. Not that either of the boys was LDS. Not really. But when you dressed the part . . .

The outfits were *great* cover. Taylor and Colby weren't blood related, had met each other in middle school, when they'd been kicked out of the same youth group, so they didn't look much alike. But in their white shirts and black slacks they could have been brothers, twins if you weren't looking hard. The outfits disarmed people and made it so most didn't want to get stuck in a conversation. If they were caught on a security camera, they were nondescript. Nothing about their looks raised a flag, would help on an APB. If the cops bothered to ask around about them in their wake,

Taylor and Colby became: "Two Mormon kids, I think. Can't remember what they looked like."

But Colby was right:

Taylor *did* have impure thoughts about Vivian Murray.

But his attraction and admiration were more than physical. Seeing her in Illinois, lost and bewildered, standing outside the prison . . .

He saw a woman who'd been smeared and spit on by the entire country, yes. But he also saw a woman strong enough to sacrifice her only child for the notion of a better world.

There was something biblical about that.

She was a true martyr.

A martyr with toned legs in a little black dress.

Martyr I'd like to—

"You know, if she refuses to play along," Colby said, interrupting the thought, "then that's going to be a job for us, too, right? If she gets feisty, he can't allow her to leave."

"I know," Taylor said, trying to sound unbothered by the idea.

"I can do it. If you can't . . ." Colby flicked out his knife, played with the handle. "Or if you just want to watch me carve off her—"

"Shut up."

Not something he'd ever said to Colby. And not something he would ever recommend anyone else say to Colby, unless they were curious what their small intestines looked like.

"What did you just say to me?" Colby asked, the cadence of his words slow and even.

A voice that said: *We met as kids, bonded over violence, got so good at it we started charging for it. Li'l entrepreneurs. But one day there will be nobody left for me to kill. On that day, when the supply dries up . . . you're next, pal.*

Taylor needed to de-escalate this. Now.

"I'm sorry, I—"

And then, like a miracle, there was the *pop pop pop* of gunshots in town.

Colby nodded, the blankness gone from his expression, Taylor's friend *looking* human again.

They grabbed their gear and started to run.

And while there was plenty on the line—their pay, their eternal souls—as they moved toward the panic and screaming, Taylor was most worried about Mrs. Murray.

It'd been a risk, swiping the knife off her plate, but in the low light of the festival, neither the priest nor the man dressed like an old-timey police officer had noticed.

Nobody in New Kettle Springs seemed to notice *much.* They didn't strike Vivian as a detail-oriented people, as they opened their mouths to be stuffed with the stinking remains of a dead man.

Magical thinking, dead bodies, clowns: maybe these people really *were* worthy successors to the original Kettle Springs.

But while standing beside the stage, Vivian Murray had lost the grip on the handle of the steak knife she'd pocketed. With one of her captors standing over her, she had no choice but to squeeze the blade itself or risk dropping it. The serrated teeth poked through the fabric, bit into her fingers and palm.

Vivian's initial thought, taking up the knife, was that she was going to need to use it on Arthur Hill.

Or, she should say, the man wearing Arthur Hill's face.

When they'd been alone in the church, he'd lifted his leathery mask up. And he'd done it like it was some kind of reveal. Like he was expecting to be recognized. But he wasn't a *Scooby-Doo* villain. He was just a man in his mid-thirties Vivian had never met before, wearing the skin of a dead millionaire she used to know in passing.

The bastard had bailed her out, forged proof of residency papers for her, and hired a fresh team of lawyers without her knowledge, and he expected her to trade one prison for another.

She could live here, the man told her. She could be a figurehead in his church.

Could.

Jason Alton had phrased it as a choice. But she knew all

316

about choices like that. The real Arthur Hill had pitched his vision as a choice, too. And look at the "decision" that he and Alec had pressured Vivian into making.

Janet's head separated from her shoulders, her body still running.

Sometimes a woman's choices were just a man's plan.

But now, moments after grabbing the knife, she didn't need to worry about the priest.

Someone else had taken care of the man with three quick gunshots to the back. Now she just needed to worry about getting out of here.

"Stay here!" the man who'd pulled her from the stage screamed in her face. He was wearing a badge over his chest, must have been what passed as law enforcement around here. To punctuate his words, he pushed down on her shoulders. Her shoes, modest flats that matched the dress, sank into the mud an inch or two.

The crowd had split into three distinct groups.

One group was screaming, "The Adversary! Murderer! Don't let them get away!" and swarming the area beside the church, skirting behind the large sculpture toward the direction the shots had come from. The fake police officer ran to catch up, screaming orders to "fan out!"

A second group, led by the muscular man in overalls, was storming the stage, rushing to tend to their wounded leader.

And the last group, possibly the largest, was standing

and doing nothing. This group was watching, eyes distant and disinterested, some of them staring at their hands or into the torches, watching the fire dance. This group seemed unaware that anyone had been shot.

"Gkkkkk . . ."

None of the townspeople, even the most alert of them, seemed concerned with the girl who'd fallen off the stage. She lay where she fell, twitching and sputtering, foam bubbling out of her mouth.

That girl was different from the rest. Younger, yes. But Vivian had been watching. Unlike those ahead of her in line, the girl hadn't been eager to eat the tainted meat. She hadn't even been *willing*.

It had been difficult to stand by and watch Alton pry the girl's mouth open.

Vivian had thought about using the knife then, but told herself no. That it wasn't the time. That she didn't understand these people and their customs, and if she used up her one shot trying to save a girl she didn't know, she wouldn't get another chance at escape.

But now Vivian looked at the girl, flopping around in the dirt.

Her parents had stayed on the platform, both of them now being pushed back by the muscular man in overalls.

They'd left their daughter alone while she choked.

What kind of parent? What kind of—?

Vivian Murray pushed away the thought. It was a refrain she'd heard a lot, a mantra she'd used to punish herself on her bad days.

She looked away from the townspeople and out at the trees and fields barely visible in the night. To one side of her lay madness and violence, a press of bodies, and to the other lay freedom.

She'd been left unattended, unnoticed.

She wasn't going to get another opportunity like this.

She remembered the walk she'd taken with the two boys . . . it hadn't been too long. She could be waving down cars on the main road within the hour.

"Not all at once, but help me," the muscular man yelled. He was picking up the slack body of Jason Alton under his arms, jewels of glass embedded in the man's face. But not really, they were embedded in Arthur Hill's face, the mask protecting him as he fell into the casket.

The crowd, fifteen or so people in close proximity, surged forward. If they moved a few more feet to the left, they would trample the choking girl to death. It would happen in an instant, since none of them were looking down. But the crowd didn't care. They had their hands extended up, out. They were reaching toward the bodybuilder so he could hand the priest over to them.

Jason Alton's robed body began to crowd-surf, facedown, arms out, the bullet holes in his back still smoking.

"Wait, don't go," the muscular man said. "Protect the host too, get him inside, return him to the church altar." Then he hoisted the mangled corpse in a Frendo mask out of the shattered casket. Vivian's gorge rose. She'd eaten lamb chops and turnips off that LED-lighted sarcophagus, thinking it was just a regular table.

Frendo's skeletal leg detached, fell onto the stage.

The muscular man was crying, the body propped onto one shoulder, then he kissed two fingers and planted that same kiss on the Frendo mask.

He had such respect for the dead body, such reverence.

Frendo's body flopped into the waiting arms of the crowd.

And then they were carrying it back toward the church. Yes, they were doing what the muscular man instructed, but they were also tearing off hunks of flesh, shoving them into grease-streaked mouths.

Vivian was going to be sick.

"Stop that!" the muscular man yelled, brushing the broken glass off the platform, clearing the area that had been the casket. "Stop that and put him back! Right now!"

Vivian dropped her eyes, and that view wasn't much better. Because watching the girl lying under the stage slowly asphyxiate was agonizing, the worst guilt she'd felt since . . .

"Gkkk . . ."

Beneath all this action, the choking girl gave one final strained convulsion, a snot bubble expanding out of one nostril, then popping. . . .

No.

Vivian Murray wasn't that kind of parent. No matter what the world thought, she was not that kind of mother.

She readjusted the knife so it was held in place by the dress's waistband, hopefully it wouldn't cut her too badly, and began to run.

Three yards from her destination she slid, feet first, arriving beside the girl with her knees gritty.

The crowd, tossing the corpse back onto the stage, was too close. Vivian had to get them both out from under their feet. She grabbed hold of the rough fabric of the girl's pinafore and pulled.

Vivian was petite, but she wasn't weak. A certain level of muscle definition had been important in pageants. And the young woman she dragged through the mud didn't weigh much.

When she was sure they were out of the path of the townspeople, the gore-streaked pallbearers, Vivian began to work.

She pushed the girl's chin up to clear the airway, remembering bits and pieces from a CPR class she'd taken twenty years ago.

She flipped the girl onto her side and slammed a hand

into her back, aiming between the shoulder blades.

She wasn't sure it was the right thing to do, but it was the only thing she could think to try. She slammed again.

It wasn't working.

In the low light, the girl wasn't turning blue or any other identifiable color, but she was going paler by the second.

"Please," Vivian Murray said. "I don't know if you can hear me, but—" She hit the girl again. "Don't die."

She hit the girl one more time, her fingers and palm lingering on the girl's back, and suddenly she was remembering a night with Janet, when her daughter had been fifteen.

Janet crying and swearing to Vivian that she'd never drink again.

Vivian was angry, yes, but also a little amused. She'd remembered what she'd been like at Janet's age. The stupid things she'd done.

Of course, Janet hadn't kept that promise. That hadn't been the last night she'd drunk, wasn't the last night she'd gone to a party. But it was the last night Vivian had been allowed to hold her daughter's hair.

Vivian rubbed at the pilgrim girl's back until she remembered what she was trying to do here, that the girl wasn't drunk but dying. She closed her knuckles into a fist and banged on the girl's spine and the backs of her lungs.

The sound, still distinct among the praying and moaning of the townspeople, was like the pop of a cork.

The girl rolled over onto her back, coughing. Next to her, where her face had been braced in the mud, a glob of meat lay in a gooey puddle of saliva and bile.

It didn't take long for the color to return to the girl's features, then confusion, and finally recognition.

Before she could speak, there was another gunshot. Somewhere in the woods at the edge of town, the mob had caught up with the gunman.

"Can you walk?" Vivian asked, still in that memory of Janet with her chin resting over the toilet seat, her tone maternal, hushed. "What's your name, baby?"

"T-Tabitha," the girl said.

Vivian held her hand out to help the girl up.

"Okay, Tabitha, let's get as far from this place as possible."

But instead of eagerness, instead of a hand gripping on to hers, the girl's eyes shifted over Vivian's shoulder and she said:

"He's behind you."

TWENTY

THE OUTSKIRTS OF NEW KETTLE SPRINGS
There was no right way to do this.

Going to the location on the map was a mistake, no matter how Quinn approached that final destination.

But *this*, what she was doing right now, was the best of the bad options.

At least that was what she told herself.

There was no hiding the abandoned RV. There was barely space to park it where it wouldn't block traffic, with only a few feet of shoulder on the road before she hit guardrail.

Not that there was any traffic to block, at this hour, on this remote road.

It didn't matter. No matter the outcome, live or die, it was unlikely that she'd be coming back for the RV.

She pulled the ring of surgical tape up to her mouth and

bit down. She tore, wrapping the newest length of tape down onto her inner forearm.

"Looks like effective body armor to me," Arthur Hill said.

Fucking dick.

He used to be a scary ghost, a waking nightmare, but in the last few days he'd devolved into shitty jokes.

Finally, a real clown.

Quinn didn't respond, continued what she was doing, checked the tape on her other arm and flexed both elbows, making sure she wasn't limiting her mobility.

Five bodies, four she'd seen, one she'd read about: the copy clerk, the boys in Alabama, and Charles Rome.

All but one of them had been killed with bladed weapons.

She was going to protect her arms.

She unloaded and rechecked her equipment, trading her duffel bag for a backpack she'd scavenged from the Dozers' bedroom.

With that finished, she took one last walk around the RV, saying a silent goodbye to its bed and its shower, and then headed out into the night.

Using the scale of the road atlas, comparing it to the imprecise proportions of the sketch they'd found in the PO box, Quinn was embarking on anywhere between a two- and four-mile hike.

The fresh blacktop of the main road reached a turnoff that would have been completely invisible if not for the break in the guardrail.

The road beyond the turnoff wasn't *blocked*, but its narrow single lane was almost completely obscured from view by an outgrowth of . . . rosebushes? She hadn't known rosebushes could grow that large, their branches and thorns dropped down on the pavement, nearly meeting in the middle. Using one of the flashlights, Quinn could see that the bushes had fresh black mulch at their bases. She was no botanist, but she guessed the plants hadn't been here for more than a season.

The road beyond the wall of roses *was* paved, but hadn't been resurfaced in many years. Tall clumps of weeds pushed up through cracks, old tar drying to dust.

Quinn didn't walk any of this disused road, but instead wound through the woods beside the road, shallow enough in the tree line that she kept the pavement in sight.

She wouldn't have seen the first trail cam if not for a trick of the moonlight against the lens and the downy white tail of a deer. The movement drew her eye, caused her to stop and crouch.

The animal was fleeing from Quinn's approach, but it was also like the deer was pointing to the small device with the tip of its tail. Warning her. The camera was one by one foot square, fixed to the tree trunk three feet off the ground.

Quinn walked as wide as she could to avoid the lens,

then, keeping her eyes on the trees and not the road, after only a few more minutes of walking spotted a second camera.

That was it.

Another ending.

The end of stealth.

She had to assume she'd already missed a camera or two, possibly as far back as the rosebushes.

She had to assume they knew she was here.

The thought didn't discourage her, didn't cause Arthur Hill to pipe up with a "witty" remark. If anything, the realization freed her.

Quinn slipped the plastic sheath off the hatchet, readying her weapon, then broke into a jog.

There was a scenario where, after dropping Johnny off, she'd found another library and used the computers there to log on to Google Maps and get an aerial view of the location.

But there was sensible preparedness and then there was procrastination.

And Quinn didn't need a satellite image to tell her what she was going to find in this remote part of Pennsylvania, the road she'd entered through blocked off from civilization.

There was going to be a barn. Probably. And likely a silo, too.

But the one thing she was *sure* she was going to find, wherever she was being led, was a cornfield.

"The rule of threes," Arthur Hill said, peeking his mask out from behind a tree.

She wanted to throw the hatchet at him, to turn it into a tomahawk. But that would be stupid. He wasn't an intrusion in her reality, he was more like a child's imaginary friend. He spoke because, on some level, she *wanted* him to speak.

The first building Quinn encountered was not a barn or a silo. She wasn't sure what the small rectangular structure was until the wind changed and she smelled it.

It was an outhouse, on the edge of the woods, behind someone's property.

She kept to the trees, but beyond the outdoor toilet was a small single-story house, no lights.

Beyond the abandoned house, *probably* abandoned, it seemed so ramshackle and dark, was a long expanse of nothingness. Not a field and not a moor, just flat unworked dirt.

Quinn kept walking, sticking to the trees, and before long, beyond the dirt: lights.

Firelight, tiny in the distance, maybe a half mile away. Pinpricks of flame that were so small and far away they lowered the skyline, became a continuation of the star field. Between those there were larger orange orbs, either torches or lanterns.

The lights disappeared and reappeared, the flicker irregular, so not the wind displacing them.

There were bodies passing in front of the flames. Many bodies.

Quinn readjusted her grip on the hatchet, realizing for the first time that her palms were sweating.

She reached the edge of the woods and turned north to keep the trees as cover, no longer using the road to guide her, but the firelight her destination.

As she grew closer, she heard the voices.

And then the chant.

It was hard to tell what they were saying.

Hope? That couldn't be right.

There were so many of them.

Quinn hadn't spotted any more trail cams, but still felt exposed. So she jogged northwest, deeper into the woods, passing more houses and two barns. There were no lights in any of the windows. Clouds rolled in, covering the stars and blotting the moonlight to turn the barns into huge dead husks of black on the horizon.

Then she stopped.

The chant and voices had died away.

Which made the gunshots so much louder.

Quinn flinched, the pressurized cans in her backpack clinking together.

Pop pop pop. Three shots, grouped.

Then came the screams and shouts of dismay.

This wasn't some dopes throwing a party and firing their guns into the air.

What the fuck was going on out there?

And how had the shooting started without her?

She jogged, nearly parallel with the firelight now, the movement of the bodies in front of the flames more frantic.

The voices were now pitched louder, but under the panicked screams, closer to Quinn's location, then closer still, was the strained, ragged breath of someone at the end of a sprint.

Quinn ducked behind a dead tree, partially fallen, and waited to see who was approaching.

She'd heard sweaty, terrified breathing like that too many times now.

Teenagers running for their lives.

Out-of-shape men and women in clown masks close behind, also coughing, their lungs burning, mass murder demanding more cardio than they'd anticipated.

But the man who broke from between the growth in front of her was neither a teenager nor an adult in a clown mask.

He was a guy . . . at a Renaissance fair?

No. That wasn't right. The man, his hands on his knees, dry heaving against his exertion, had the beard, dark hair, and dress of a pirate, woven shirt untied below the neck, vest unbuttoned.

But he was carrying a modern handgun and had modern tattoos covering his bare forearms. The gun was a revolver with a velvet silver finish, the glow-in-the-dark dot of a tritium sight over the barrel. Rust had a similar weapon. She couldn't remember the name. Quinn had target shot with it a few times, but Rust had so many guns and the names were always the first thing she tried to forget, since names didn't aid in their operation.

Staying low, Quinn snuck around the tree, trying to do her best to flank the man. It seemed like he was right to stop. He'd eluded his pursuers, for now. There was torchlight in the wooded hill to the north of them, but none circling back in this direction.

As she approached, she smelled him. Or, more precisely, she smelled liquor.

Should she unclip the strobing flashlight from her belt and try to blind him?

No. She didn't need the light to see by, the moon was back now, and this close he might hear the click of the metal snap being undone.

She had to act now if she didn't want him to catch his breath and escape.

"Drop it," Quinn said, turning on him from behind the slumped tree.

But they never "dropped it."

And she knew that, so she'd brought up the hatchet,

reeled back, and was about to place the ax-head into the space between the man's shoulder and neck as he turned to face her, gun rising.

But he'd stopped, the gun at her belly and then pointed away into the dark.

And *she'd* stopped, ax-head juking, pulled up short.

And they both stared at each other.

Quinn didn't know what the man had seen that'd made him stop, but she knew who she was looking at.

This man was not an aggressor, but a victim.

Wild eyes and tears, under the stink of booze the smell of sweat that had dried, then grimed, then been sweated on again. The smell of fear.

This was a hunted man. A scared man.

"It's you," he said.

"He knows you. Kill him," Arthur Hill said.

Quinn ignored the dead man.

"Put the gun down, tell me what's happening here."

But the man acted like he couldn't hear her.

"Oh my Lord. Oh heavenly Father. Oh Christ and all the saints and the Founders."

The man was losing it. And he was one twitchy flick of his wrist away from putting a bullet in her stomach.

"Sir," Quinn said. She could still see the torches behind him, but couldn't move her eyes to focus on if they'd turned to get closer or continued receding up the hill. "Who's after you?"

"You are," the man said, then moved his free hand to slick back his long, greasy hair. He started speaking to himself. "I am a fool. I was being tested. They're dead. And it was all a test and I failed."

"Please talk to me."

But he couldn't hear her.

"He said you'd come. I was too drunk to listen. So they took my family. My wife, she wouldn't stop crying and hitting me, and my daughter . . . they killed my little girl. And that was the last straw because I walked up to that stage and I shot him. I killed him. I killed him and he was telling the truth, he was right. All his prophecies and sermons. He was right. You were on your way here all this time. And now you're here."

"Who did you kill?"

"I betrayed him and now I'm damned for all time."

"I think you're confused." Quinn's head throbbed, trying to decode this gibberish at gunpoint. "I want to help you. Your wife . . . where is your family now?"

"A better place than I'm going," he said.

"What are you talking—"

The man met her gaze, defiance in his eyes.

"Take me to hell, then, Quinn Maybrook."

Before she could move to stop him, he put the gun under his chin and pulled the trigger, the top of his head punching upward, becoming a crimson geyser in the moonlight.

But there wasn't time to think about why.

Not even time to wipe his blood off her face.

There was only time to grab the gun.

The man's pursuers must have heard the shot, and she had to assume they were headed her way.

TWENTY-ONE

Transcript excerpt of the final known video recording of Jason Alton before assuming alias "the Pastor."

Source: a portable thumb drive collected from the NKS compound, behind secret panel in church storeroom. Logged into evidence alongside tripod, camera equipment, and laptop used to broadcast sermon livestreams and create pledge videos and updates.

Note: a truncated version of this sermon appears on the official AM YouTube account. Full versions have been distributed throughout the

Frendo community and similar, sympathetic orga-
nizations.

Recording date: unknown, as tape master is dupli-
cate. Probable May or June 2022.

ALTON: Let's hear it again for Carl. Thank you
for that update, my friend. Every penny that you
all tithe, Carl's got his eye on it and is making
sure that it is used to uplift the ministry with
maximum efficiency.

[Break for applause and shouted amens. The camera
is static and the video never shows the crowd,
but we would estimate no more than twenty or
twenty-five people are in attendance.]

ALTON: Brothers and sisters, during today's sermon I'm going to pose a question. I always ask
questions. I ask that *you* ask questions. But
today you're going to find my question shocking.
A question you might even call out of character,
since we preach nonviolence and tolerance here
in this house.

[Pause for shouted amens.]

ALTON: This country is changing. We all see it.

[Pause for shouted amens.]

ALTON: Try as we might, though, it's not changing for the better.

[Amens pivot to boos.]

ALTON: You can see on the news that there are ministries bigger than ours, better funded than ours, groups all across the country pushing against these changes. There are patriots fighting to keep pornography out of our schools, fighting to keep perverts away from our kids, and fighting to keep our values and way of life American and Christian.

[Transcript will now omit noting shouted amens. They are copious.]

ALTON: Yes. Yes. Amen. Of course, amen to those causes. But—and I hate to say this—but these soldiers in what they like to call the "culture war": they are *losing*.

[Discontent. Shouts of "No!"]

ALTON: I don't enjoy saying it. Believe me. I'm with you. But here's that question I said I was going to pose: What if . . . what if they're right?

MULTIPLE PARISHIONERS: Who?

ALTON: The people of Kettle Springs, Missouri.

[Pause, negligible crowd reaction.]

ALTON: You don't sound shocked. You don't seem provoked. Are we really so few in number these days that I can't get a reaction out of my congregation?

[Shouts of "No!"]

ALTON: Then let me clarify: I'm not talking about the survivors of the Kettle Springs Massacre. I'm talking about the murderers. I think the *murderers* had it right.

[Gasps.]

ALTON: I told you. I told you you'd be shocked.
But judge not, yes? And hear me out, before you
gather the knives and the pitchforks. Before you
cancel me.

[Laughter.]

ALTON: There are people out there who hold them
up as Founding Fathers. As heroes. But let me be
clear: they were murderers. They'll never be any
kind of hero to me, or anyone in this room, yes?

[Affirmative shouts.]

ALTON: Of course. They will never have my admiration. But what if their ideas were *right*, even if
their methods were tragically misguided?

[Silence.]

ALTON: Now. Stop me when you disagree. They wanted
to protect their children. Who here could disagree with wanting to do that?

[Silence.]

ALTON: They wanted to stamp out what had become a prevailing culture of disrespect in their town. We all can agree there, correct? We've all heard what the teens in *that town* had done. Arthur Hill and George Dunne's goal, their *stated* goal, was to preserve life the way it was in the good old days. Now speak up if you think *that's* wrong.

[More silence.]

ALTON: Couldn't we all use a little more good old days?

[Shouts in the affirmative.]

ALTON: Now, indulge me, brothers and sisters of Alton Ministries. What if those good old days they were after weren't *old* enough? I mean, where were they aiming? The 1980s? Reagan in the White House. Great man. But too much wrong with the country. He couldn't save it. The seventies and the sixties? Sex, drugs, and hippies sowing doubt against righteous war. The fifties? Closer. Closer, to be sure. Malt shops, wholesome, yes, but, ever hear of James Dean? The fifties were the start of teen delinquency, the cracks beginning to show. Forties? Men were men, but—and remember this—women started to be men, too, right? Thirties. Dust bowl. Twenties. Flappers. Not old enough. Not American enough. Not a clean enough slate. The men and women of Kettle Springs that took this "turn back time" ideology and added murder, they were putting Band-Aids onto bullet wounds. They weren't rewinding the tape *far* enough. They needed to reach further back. They needed to go where the spirit of America was true and pure and devout and fresh. Cull the rotten crop? No. I say no. I say, raise a generation that has no *concept* of rot. Isolate yourself completely from the sickness that's killing this country. Correct? Am I correct? Can one of you—just one of you—please tell me that I'm correct.

[He breathes heavily. Although this speech builds in intensity and cadence, and although Alton gestures wildly to punctuate his most clipped sentences, there is no applause when he finishes. There are no shouted amens. Alton stands on the stage. He is silent. Although the video quality is poor, he glistens with sweat.]

ALTON: I don't know. Just something I've been thinking about.

[He moves to the lectern and takes up a book.]

ALTON: Grace, a little hymn music, please? Page one oh eight. "Blessed Assurance," everyone. Then we'll go right to "Onward, Christian Soldiers" on the next page.

TWENTY-TWO

THE SETTLEMENT OF NEW KETTLE SPRINGS
The last thing Tabitha saw, as the dimness of asphyxiation blotted out the stars, were her parents. They didn't follow her. They didn't help. Instead they stood at the Pastor's side, the closest parishioners to him, staying with him after he was shot.

They made their choice.

Tabitha tried to cough, the mass in her throat seeming to swell under its own power. Maybe their religion was correct, and this was how Tabitha had her moment of revelation. Their messiah, Arthur Hill, was reaching out and choking Tabitha Werther from the inside.

When she couldn't bring the mass up: blackness.

Then, an indeterminate amount of time later, someone was slamming on her back and the host was in the mud, dislodged.

343

Tabitha's throat burned and her face tingled.

But she was alive.

The woman rubbing Tabitha's back, with her modern makeup and resplendent white dress, seemed like an angel in the haze.

Vivian Murray crouched above her. She was speaking, her words too low for Tabitha to hear well, even though she was inches from her face.

". . . walk . . . let's . . . here as possible."

Tabitha said her name when prompted.

Then she saw him:

If Vivian Murray was an angel, then the form over the woman's shoulder—with its dark robes, its face doubled, skin sloughing off, a dozen pale arms like spider's legs extending to place him gently onto the ground . . .

That was a demon.

But Tabitha had known that for months. Even before the cow had exhumed Ruth Miller and her family. Even before the last glimmer of warmth and love had been wrung out of her father's eyes. Tabitha had always known that the Pastor was a demon.

"The Pastor lives! It's a miracle!" Isaiah Dunne declared from the stage.

"Miracle! Miracle!" the crowd yelled. Tabitha picked her mother's face out of the gathered villagers, saw that she was sobbing, not that her daughter was alive, but that she'd witnessed a different kind of resurrection.

But *did* the Pastor live? Or had the crowd only managed to balance a corpse on its feet?

Vivian Murray turned, watched with Tabitha as they waited to see if the Pastor tipped forward into the dirt.

He did not.

The Pastor's hand rose, unsteady in the firelight, and readjusted the flesh mask that had slipped down to cover his eyes.

"Mrs. Murray," he said, then groaned in pain.

"Stay the fuck away from me."

He shook his head.

"Get away from me!" the woman yelled, grabbing at something under the fabric of her dress. She kicked out in his direction, her dress flying up, mud streaked. "You fucking lunatic!"

There were gasps from the crowd, all of them staying close to their leader, watching and listening to this exchange.

Instead of continuing his conversation with Vivian Murray, the Pastor turned to face the crowd.

"Back up," he said. "Back up, all of you goddamned jackals. Give me room to breathe."

The crowd, the section of it still capable of registering shock, looked hurt and confused to hear their leader blaspheme.

There were bullet holes in the Pastor's back. Three of

them, one high, nearly at his neck, and two lower, on either side of his spine above his ribs.

He was not bleeding.

Which wasn't a miracle, Tabitha was sure, but a trick.

The assassination attempt was either completely faked, another part of his theatrics, or the Pastor had *really* been shot and had been saved by some kind of body armor worn under his robes.

Slow, as if it had taken time to decode what the Pastor had said, the crowd stepped back. There were maybe ten of them, her parents included. They gave the man space, but didn't disperse, didn't join the villagers staggered to the south of them in the town square. The group wandering the town square outnumbered them, twenty or so villagers who seemed completely disinterested in the attempted assassination of their leader. These settlers had their eyes rolled up into their skulls, thralls to the act of flesh eating, riding out the immediate effects of the host.

"Carl!" the Pastor shouted. "Where is Carl?"

Who was Carl? Tabitha wondered.

Tabitha took this moment of confusion as an opportunity to sit up. Vivian Murray stopped rubbing her back and put that same arm across her shoulder. The two of them sat in the mud, listening to these madmen. There was more warmth and comfort in the woman's touch than Tabitha had shared with her own mother in months.

"The *Constable*," Isaiah Dunne replied, descending the stairs, trying to get between his boss and the increasingly agitated and disillusioned crowd. "You mean to say the Constable, Father. He leads the search for your, uh, attacker."

So the Constable's real name was Carl.

"Yes. The Adversary must be found. But"—the Pastor turned to the crowd, his voice resuming the cadence and tone he used on the pulpit—"do not worry, my children. She cannot harm me. I am sheathed in the armor of God."

He held his arms out, turned so they could see where the bullets had torn through the fabric of his robes.

There were sounds of awe and wonderment. He'd snapped at them, blasphemed, used an old name, but still he was winning the crowd back by displaying this "miracle."

The miracle of a bulletproof vest under his robes. A coward protecting himself from assassination.

"It . . . ," Isaiah Dunne said, pulling at his beard, clearly torn over whether he wanted to keep speaking.

"Yes, my son?"

The muscular man in the overalls leaned forward, lowered his voice so the crowd wouldn't hear.

The crowd may not have heard, but Tabitha could.

"It may not *be* the Adversary, Father. I saw your attacker with my own eyes. It . . . it looked like Fredrick Trent."

The Pastor nodded, eyes black and unknowable in the shadows of his mask.

"That's good. That's good, my son." Then he turned back to the crowd, raised his voice. "It may well have been Fredrick Trent who fired the gun. *She* has many agents in her war against us. Go now, Isaiah. Help Carrr—help *the Constable* in the search. Take your axe. Make the Adversary wish she'd never come here to try and disrupt our way of life."

The crowd cheered.

The Pastor turned and stooped.

Mrs. Murray hugged Tabitha tight.

"But first, take these two to the jail. It gives me no pleasure to say this, but I don't think it's a *coincidence* that Mrs. Murray arrived the same night as an attempt on my life. I fear she's made an unholy alliance."

It made no sense. The Pastor had brought the woman here himself, had said that many times tonight. But logic and reason were beyond the gathered townspeople now. They looked at Vivian Murray. Gone was the adulation and respect they'd heaped on the woman mere hours ago. They began to spit and curse.

"Judas."

The crowd yelled, moving to surround them. Vivian Murray hugged Tabitha tighter.

"Apostate whore!" a man said, a scuffing kick to shower dirt clods onto Mrs. Murray's exposed legs.

"Kill her!" Mrs. Hill shouted.

Tabitha wondered who was watching the children.

The Pastor quieted them with a single motion.

"Does the mob tell us what to do?" he asked. "Here, in Kettle Springs? Or do we have a trial process for apostates?" They backed down. "Are you all so *eager* to revisit what brought you here, into hiding, in the first place? Tear the town asunder with your mindless hate?"

The crowd shrank back, Mrs. Hill putting her head in her hands, the teacher now acting like a scolded child.

Tabitha wanted to yell at them, join the Pastor in pointing out their hypocrisy and madness, but Isaiah Dunne's big hands were pinching her behind the neck, lifting her up. She scrambled to her feet, pulling Mrs. Murray with her. She couldn't let the woman resist, Vivian Murray didn't know how little the man had hesitated to pull Lizzie across the ground by her hair.

Dunne pointed them toward the community building and started to march.

Then the Pastor called him to a halt.

"Isaiah?"

"Yes, Father?"

"Cover your face. This is wartime, and you are our anointed combatant."

"Yes, Father," Dunne said, reaching into his overalls and taking out his executioner's mask. He pulled the white fabric down over his face, and Frendo the Clown, not Isaiah Dunne, led Tabitha and the Founder to their jail cell.

TWENTY-THREE

THE SETTLEMENT OF NEW KETTLE SPRINGS
Quinn Maybrook ran through the woods, the man's gun in one hand and hatchet in the other.

She was able to work the cylinder on muscle memory, barely needed to slow to see that the revolver had only two shots remaining.

It was better than nothing.

The blood splatter on her face was beginning to go cold and tacky in the night.

She tried not to think about where the blood had come from, who the guy was, or *why* he'd shot himself.

It wouldn't help her run, to know what he meant by—

"'Take me to hell, then, Quinn Maybrook,' I think were his exact words," Arthur Hill said.

She spit, her saliva coming out long and stringy.

God, she hated Arthur Hill.

Between this current sprint and the hike beforehand, she was winded.

It was too early to be winded.

Her joints burned. This was what living in a car felt like. The accrual of months and months of no exercise, fast food, and no sleep.

Every time she looked back to the woods behind her to check if her pursuers were gaining, the number of torches shrank. There were only four now. It looked like she was losing them, but she didn't think she was. They were extinguishing their torches, either by accident or on purpose, and it was disguising their numbers.

Behind her she could hear footfalls and the crunch of dead leaves. Way more than four people's worth.

It didn't matter. The four torches were still a ways back. She could do this. She could outrun them.

Quinn was so busy looking and listening to what was behind her, she hadn't noticed what was ahead. She was being flushed out into the open, only realizing once the terrain under her feet had changed from firm forest floor to soft, muddy clay.

Quinn froze.

She was in a large open clearing, a semicircle of buildings starting maybe fifty yards from where she stood.

She was in a town.

And she wasn't alone.

The dirty white siding and steeple of the church rose above lower, uglier buildings, no lights in any of the windows, but the exteriors lit by a few firepits or cisterns on ground level, figures moving in front of the flames.

But there were more figures, much closer, only a few paces away.

They weren't easy to see in the darkness, standing as still as they were, but they were all around her.

Quinn was surrounded.

She pushed the gun up, taking aim at the closest of the shadows, hatchet up and ready to swing at the next person after her first shot.

She stepped closer, making a bigger target for herself.

Couldn't be wasting ammunition.

The man in front of her pistol's glowing sight bead was in old-timey dress similar to the gun's previous owner. Without the leather vest the other guy had been wearing, Quinn could see that the costume was intended to be less pirate, more seventeenth- or eighteenth-century farmer.

The man in front of her was unarmed.

And he wasn't attacking her.

But he didn't raise his hands in surrender, either.

So she circled him, moved to try to catch the light with the hatchet, demonstrate to him without speaking that she was a threat.

It took Quinn a moment of posturing to realize that the man wasn't blind, but he wasn't *seeing* her at all. His eyes were open, but mostly white. His mouth hung wide enough that even in the low light she could see he was missing a few teeth, that a few others glinted with metal caps.

From beside the man, a woman shuffled forward out of the darkness. The woman wore a dirty gray bonnet and a dark ankle-length dress with a stained off-white apron over top. Quinn moved the gun to her, and the woman didn't flinch to see it. Instead she nodded politely, then readjusted her stance so she didn't fall over.

And Quinn would know that sudden readjusting of balance anywhere:

These people were high. *So* high they *saw* the girl holding the gun right in front of their faces but didn't care.

There were shouts from the forest's edge.

Quinn looked back, saw the few ragged torches floating there between the trees.

Her pursuers had caught up to her but hadn't spotted her yet.

Quinn crouched, thought for a moment.

Was this really the only way?

Only one she could think of right now.

Staying low, she crept forward, farther into the forest of two dozen wavering, staring bodies.

The men and women in colonial garb weren't a threat.

But still, her skin tingled at their stoned stillness, their subtle muscle twitches, their stink.

As if it were a children's game, Quinn kept away from the sides of the maze, unsure what would happen if she bumped into a body and forced a zombie villager to acknowledge her. They might be roused, start grabbing at her, or they might scream, or any number of things she didn't want.

Quinn ducked under the elbows of a woman pointing her hands up, praying, mouthing gibberish words at the moon, and sniffing back tears.

She then skirted around a man and two women, their hands locked in a circle, swaying in the breeze while the man sung a tune Quinn didn't recognize, with words she did: "A little drop of Baypen . . ."

"Can you believe it, kid?" Arthur Hill asked, sneaking beside her, snaking between the bodies with a grace his real-world frame wouldn't have allowed. "That's my song."

Quinn couldn't shush him, barely heard him. She *wasn't* reliving the Kettle Springs Massacre, there was no corn here, and no choir of screams yet.

No, what she was doing was maneuvering her way through a fallow cornfield of addiction. A row of fun-house mirrors where every face was her mother's, Samantha Maybrook's, slumped over in the stands at regionals, vomit on her chin.

"Where is she?" someone outside the web of bodies yelled.

The figures around Quinn twitched a bit, but none of them turned their eyes to watch her pass.

The torches reached the beginning of the human maze.

"Brother, wake up, she's here!" one of her pursuers said, grabbing the man nearest the forest, trying to shake him awake. He didn't respond, didn't offer up Quinn's location.

"Find her!"

The men and women after her might have been slower in a footrace, but they weren't spaced-out statues, either: she watched the posse fan out, entering the crowd of sleepwalkers at different points.

They were going to find her. She needed to run. She—

A hand fell on Quinn's shoulder, a man with a strange beard and a straw hat, getting close, like a drunk at a party who wanted to tell you something:

"We do this for the children," he said, his breath stinking like moldy bread and gasoline.

He kept his hand on her shoulder, but didn't try to lunge for her weapons, didn't even seem to see them.

If Quinn were able to keep her composure, she probably would have been able to squirm out of his light grasp. But this close, the combination of the smell and the words, she couldn't stop herself: she yelped.

And all the men and women around her, all the *husks* of men and women, they repeated the sound. Her scared yelp, multiplying and rippling out over the crowd.

And when the sound reached the end of the telephone chain, got to the edge of the forest and echoed into the hills, the yelp returned, coming back different, until the men and women around Quinn were all saying, "Amen."

Quinn didn't bother with stealth anymore, she ran. There was no avoiding the limbs that slapped into her, but there wasn't much strength behind any of them, either. She dropped her shoulder, bodychecking all resistance aside.

It was too much. She needed to get free, needed to be out of the press of their strange mannequin bodies.

And eventually she was, emerging on the other side of the crowd, closer to the church now.

Quinn stood in the open air and breathed heavily. The hatchet trembled in her hand.

"There she is," a man said, then he raised not a torch or a gas lamp, but an LED flashlight into Quinn's face.

She squinted, and as she did more shadows joined the man's side.

The gun rose in Quinn's hand, even though she couldn't see who she was aiming at. In the terror and strangeness of the last few minutes, she'd forgotten everything she'd learned about firearms.

Her finger was already tensing.

No trigger discipline.

A picture of the man resolved out of the flash of her temporary blindness.

He was dressed differently than those around him, and even though he carried a modern flashlight, his attire was still from back in time. His police costume was reminiscent of a Civil War uniform, the dark blue of a Northern soldier.

The men and women beside him had weapons. If they could be called that, more like antique farm equipment. Wooden pitchforks, spades, a hand scythe where the blade had turned dark brown with rust.

Quinn spotted the man's makeshift badge: the nose, mouth, and hat of Frendo the Clown stitched onto the breast of his jacket.

Maybe he was their leader.

Maybe she could end this right now, cut the head from the snake.

Quinn squeezed the trigger and shot him in the face.

The man and his flashlight fell backward, the bullet having smacked into the bridge of his nose, killing him instantly.

The reaction of the men and women behind the dead man was muted, for a moment.

Then they screamed as one, not a battle cry, but grief.

He had been the man in charge, then, that was good.

Quinn smiled.

"Get her!"

Quinn had one more shot. Then as many as she could get with the hatchet. Their weapons were dull enough that she could probably parry a few attacks with her wrapped fore-arms before they overwhelmed her.

If this was the end, it could have been worse, but it could have been better. She could have died knowing what the fuck was happening here.

One more shot.

And she used it poorly.

The bullet caught the broadside of an iron cleaver, drawing sparks but no blood.

The gunshot caused her attackers to pause, though, back up a pace or two.

They weren't trained.

Could she bluff her way out of this?

"It's over," she said. "Why am I here?"

They looked at her, all confused by the question. Maybe they weren't as far gone as the meat statuary she'd just run through, but they still had a stoned dreaminess in their eyes, didn't seem capable of answering her.

And then, nearly as one, Quinn's brain breaking at the sight of it, the men and women arrayed around her put their weapons down and went to one knee, hands sinking into the soft earth as they bowed low.

They were bowing. Supplicating themselves at her feet.

One figure didn't bow: the ghost of Arthur Hill stood above them, the stitches of his Y incision looking ready to burst open as he laughed.

"All hail Quinn Maybrook, lord of hell," Arthur Hill said, chuckling. "Or something. This shit is weird."

The men and women kneeling in front of Quinn were streaked with mud. Some had leaves in their hair from where they'd been running through the forest after her. They stole glances up at her, their eyes sunken. They were terrified. Terrified of her. They were cold and scared and possibly even starving, some were so thin.

"Get up," Quinn yelled. She grabbed at one of the men, but he went limp, turning into dead weight to stop her from lifting him up and keep his position on the ground. "I said get up!"

None of them answered.

"Somebody tell me what you're all doing out here! Tell me how we stop this!"

Whatever *this* was.

"You don't stop what's preordained," a voice behind Quinn said.

She whirled, strong hands clamping down on each wrist as she did.

The boys Johnny had described were inches away. Their white shirts made them almost glow in the dark, in a town where everyone was filthy. They'd snuck up behind her, one on each side. It made sense that they'd been able to, with the soft ground and her focus ahead of her.

"Drop them or we break your wrists," the boy on the left

said, already lifting the gun out of her grip.

But the boys weren't the ones who'd first spoken.

They weren't the ones who'd prompted the crowd to kneel.

That was the priest, standing a few feet away, his arms outstretched.

"Stand, my children. Please," the man said.

The man was speaking loud and clear, but his lips weren't moving.

Quinn heard the crowd crawl to their feet.

These last few days, Quinn had convinced herself she was driving the highways and back roads of America in search of an ending. But maybe the ending had already happened. Maybe she was dead, her body decomposing in a field somewhere. And this was the strange, ghastly postscript her mind had fired off in its final functioning moments.

Or maybe the man who'd put the gun under his chin had been on to something.

Maybe this was hell.

"That's better. No need for kneeling."

The priest's lips weren't moving because the mouth she was seeing wasn't his mouth. She was looking at a face that'd been cut away from its skull, leathered, and worn as a mask. Its features were vaguely familiar, those of an older white man, but also made alien by the folds and rips of the mask.

The man standing beside the priest helped to anchor Quinn to reality.

That was more like what she'd expected to see on her way out here:

A huge man in a cloth clown mask, an ax crossed across his muscular chest.

Quinn recognized the physique immediately, she'd been seeing it on promotional eight-by-tens and T-shirts for the last day or so.

And in recognizing Gabriel Dozer, she had a better idea of who the men and women kneeling behind her were.

She'd found the disappeared. Not just one or two, but all of them. And she'd undercounted. There were more than the twenty or thirty or so who'd dropped off her hit list, there were probably double that number if you counted the sleepwalkers.

She'd found them. They'd built a life here, they'd built a world where they could start over.

Witness protection, off the grid.

So far off the grid their grid was twine and tin cans. Their grid was woven cotton shirts and a town square without paving stones or proper irrigation.

And they were being led by a priest.

"Jason Alton," she said. Taking an educated guess.

"If she speaks that name again," the masked priest said to the boys, "gag her."

"Gabriel Dozer," she said, nodding over at the wrestler. The clown readjusted his grip on the ax, and the hands at

Quinn's wrists grew tighter, warning her. They didn't look it, but the boys were very strong. They'd have to be, to leave the carnage they'd left. "And is there a Benjamin Koontz out there?" she continued, raising her voice. "Or his sister, I want to say . . . Maggie Koontz? It's over. The cops are on their way here. Time to come back to reality."

"Don't listen to her," the priest snapped. "The Adversary knows much, but she doesn't know your hearts, she doesn't know the changes we've all been through together. Your old names hold no power over you. You've been reborn in the blood and flesh of the Founder, Arthur Hill."

"And there's no way she called the cops," the boy on her right said, sadistic smile on his face. He had both hands on her, twisting. His fingernails were digging in, cutting her, feeling only a couple of pounds of pressure away from a spiral fracture. But she wouldn't let the pain show in her face. She would stay defiant.

She didn't *want* it to be the end, not anymore, but if this was the end, she'd face it baring her teeth at the bastards.

Face.

The Founder.

Arthur Hill.

Of course.

That was the face Alton was wearing over his own. It was all connected. And it hadn't been a prank: these people had been to Missouri. They'd been to the real Kettle Springs.

They were the ones who'd robbed the funeral home.

Her imaginary friend didn't materialize. The imagined ghost of Arthur Hill didn't stand beside Alton to make a pithy comment about how bad he looked, that he needed a new skin-care routine. Quinn doubted she'd be hearing from him anymore, now that the mystery of his body's whereabouts had been put to rest.

The ghost was free of her and she was free of him.

"Arthur Hill died crying like a baby," Quinn said.

The disappeared behind her gasped.

"His last act was to whine about how his fan club didn't recognize him," Quinn continued. They needed to hear this and she needed to say it. "I was there with his son. We saw it all. I think he pissed himself as he died. We were both laughing. So. Hard."

"I think it's time for that gag now," the priest, Alton, said from behind his mask.

The pressure on her left wrist eased as the boy there was handed a handkerchief and a length of torn cheesecloth.

Quinn didn't bite or resist, just opened her mouth. No reason to have him force the gag in and end up suffocating her.

"Put her with the others," Jason Alton said, yelling to be heard through the dead face of Arthur Hill. He turned to Dozer. "Brother Dunne, prepare the kindling. We begin the ceremony at dawn."

TWENTY-FOUR

THE SETTLEMENT OF NEW KETTLE SPRINGS
Tabitha gasped to see the Adversary up close.

No.

She reminded herself that the Adversary was just a person—and that her name was Quinn Maybrook.

The boys in white shirts, the ones Tabitha had glimpsed but never known the names of, closed the cell door behind the girl. Vivian Murray had called them Colby and Taylor. They told Quinn Maybrook to step to the bars. One of them reached through and untied the fabric knot from the back of her head that held a twisted wad of handkerchief in place in her mouth. Quinn coughed out the wet handkerchief like a dead snake.

The boys left, but not before one of them took a meaningful, longing look in Mrs. Murray's direction.

She didn't meet his gaze.

The first thing Quinn said, upon regaining her voice, was a long string of profanity—all directed at Mrs. Murray.

"It's nice to see you too, Quinn," was all Vivian Murray said in response.

Quinn rolled her eyes, opening and closing her fists.

Tabitha decided that if Quinn lunged at Vivian, she would put herself in the middle. She would try to protect the woman who'd saved her life, even if Tabitha knew there was little she'd be able to do to stop the bigger girl.

The four of them in the jail cell were all close, knees nearly touching. The cell had been built for one person for an overnight stay, back when the town hadn't even had a sheriff, just a volunteer neighborhood watch that traded the keys to the community building as needed.

Tabitha had her legs curled beneath her. She'd taken a seat on the floor, leaving the bench for Lizzie, since she was with child, and Vivian Murray. It would take effort if she needed to spring to her feet.

"Yeah. I'm not going to attack her," Quinn Maybrook finally said to Tabitha. "You can relax."

Was Tabitha's body language that easily read? Or did the Adversary have knowledge, sight beyond sight?

No. She had to actively stop herself from remembering the rumors and impossibilities she'd heard townspeople whisper about the Adversary.

There *was* a God. And God was great. But God hadn't chosen a teenage girl as his nemesis.

The older girl's arms were misshapen, swollen, and criss-crossed with lines from where Colby and Taylor had peeled away whatever she'd wrapped there.

"You're local," Quinn Maybrook said, pointing at Tabitha, then moved her finger over to Lizzie. "And you're not."

Tabitha nodded. Lizzie did, too.

"Can—" Quinn Maybrook started to ask something, then shook her head. "Jesus, it sounds so stupid to put it like this, but can you two tell me what you're in for?"

Lizzie didn't answer.

Tabitha wanted to answer, but found herself . . . hating the girl? Which wasn't right. A year ago, she could say, truly, that she'd never hated anyone. But that number had grown quickly once the floodgates were open.

"May I ask you a favor first?" Tabitha said.

Quinn Maybrook nodded.

"Can you please not do that?"

"What?"

"The profanity is fine, but, please, don't say the Lord's name like that, like it's just another curse word. He's not a curse."

Quinn Maybrook looked around them at the cell, condensation weeping from the stone walls, and then to the bucket in the corner that Lizzie had already needed to use twice.

"Sure . . . ," Quinn said, all the smugness of the secular world in her voice.

Yes. Tabitha hated the girl, the same way that Quinn Maybrook seemed to hate herself.

Then Quinn Maybrook did something Tabitha wasn't expecting. She coughed, changed her loose fists into open hands, and said: "I apologize. I meant no disrespect."

Tabitha accepted her apology and introduced herself.

"Your parents brought you here?" Quinn asked.

"I've lived here my whole life, even before . . ."

Tabitha wasn't quite sure how to explain, but Quinn made a face like she somehow understood.

"That makes sense. There was a town here and then . . . cuckoos."

Tabitha knew enough to know what Quinn meant. She even knew the term, from one of her old books. Brood parasites. Birds that laid their eggs in the nests of others. She smiled, happy to understand.

"One of the townspeople I met, they mentioned a child." Quinn pointed at Tabitha. "How many other kids are here?"

Tabitha didn't like being called a child, but she understood.

Lizzie made a noise, a whimper, crossed her hands over her stomach.

"There's fifteen. All of them younger than me. But I'm the only one from before, who was already living here. My family is all that's left of the original town."

"Meaning?"

"They'll kill you," Lizzie said, speaking before Tabitha could think of a satisfactory way to answer. "The children are killers. They killed my boyfrie—" The woman stopped, corrected herself. "Fiancé. They aren't *kids* here. They're monsters."

Quinn nodded again. There was not only intelligence behind Quinn's eyes, but an efficiency, like she was working through a mental checklist. Tabitha watched as those eyes made a decision, Quinn moving the possible rescue of children off her checklist, no longer a priority.

"And you," Quinn said, turning to Vivian Murray. "You're here because they loved you. But now you're in *here*"—she indicated the jail cell—"because you didn't love them back."

"More or less," Vivian said with a shrug. Vivian's makeup was streaked, but only on one side of her face where she'd been rubbing at it.

"But how are you out of prison?"

"They bailed me out. He must have more money than he lets on, I think."

"Alton?" Quinn said the Pastor's name like a question, then when Vivian Murray didn't immediately respond:

"It's him, under that mask?"

"Yes."

Quinn stood from where she'd squatted against the bars.

"Okay. We—*I* have until dawn. How do we get out of here?"

The other occupants stared back at her, Tabitha included.

Outside there was the fall of hammers and the *shunk-shunk* of saws. The Pastor wasn't letting the townspeople rest, they were already preparing for . . . something else.

Quinn looked to the door, then the window of their cell. She estimated about ten feet between the shelves on the far wall and the bars of the cell.

"If we can fashion something with our clothes," Quinn said, "maybe I can fish my backpack off that hook. There's all kinds of stuff in there we can use."

"How are you going to do that? Are you, like, a master fisherman now?" Vivian said.

"My aim was good enough for your husband," Quinn said.

And for a moment, it seemed like Tabitha might need to intervene.

"The fishing thing's not going to work, our clothes are cotton. Too soft." Vivian pointed to herself, then Tabitha.

"I have a belt," Lizzie said. They all turned to her, saw that she was looking down at her waist, a slight bulge that

369

was maybe there, maybe Tabitha was imagining because she knew the woman was expecting. "Oh. No, I don't. I guess they took it."

Quinn gave a frustrated grunt.

"Look. I'm just trying to be proactive here."

"Did you bring a phone?" Vivian Murray asked. "Does anyone know you're here? Did you even think to call the cops before storming in? Because *that* would have been proactive."

"Look," Quinn said, "I'm getting real tired of your attitude—"

"I have a knife," Vivian Murray said.

It wasn't a threat; it was an epiphany.

Quinn put her hands back into fists.

"What?"

"They searched you coming in, but no one searched the rest of us." Vivian Murray looked over to Tabitha.

"Let's see it."

The woman then worked the steak knife out from the waist of her dress. She held it in two hands so they all could see.

Quinn moved to grab it, but Mrs. Murray pulled it back.

"Don't trust me?" Quinn asked.

Vivian Murray considered this.

"Do *you* trust *me*?" Mrs. Murray asked.

"No. Of course not."

"Good, at least we're being honest," Vivian Murray said, and handed the blade over.

They were all silent for a moment, Quinn looking at the blade, hope in the girl's eyes.

"Thank you," Quinn said finally.

"Do it for Janet," Vivian Murray said.

Quinn's expression darkened.

"I barely knew her," Quinn said. "But I knew her long enough to say: Don't you fucking use her name."

And Vivian Murray, who had seemed to come alive in these last few minutes, stopped talking for the rest of their time together in the cell.

TWENTY-FIVE

THE SETTLEMENT OF NEW KETTLE SPRINGS
The ceremony was about to begin.

Dozer collected Quinn from the jail, saying nothing to the other women in the cell beyond telling them to step back against the wall. Dozer growled at Quinn that his name was Dunne when she called him Dozer, then he gave Quinn some instructions that boiled down to: Don't ruin the show or I'll lop off your head.

Outside, there was a horse cart and a very skinny horse. The horse wore a white hood, and a pom-pom nose made of red yarn had been attached to his bridle. Dozer helped Quinn step up into the cart, one wagon wheel groaning like it was about to fall off.

Loaded into the cart, Quinn turned back to the building and saw that the missionary boys were waiting on either side of the door. They didn't look up at her as the cart began its procession, stepping away inside the jailhouse instead.

Quinn thought of that one guy in Alabama, Johnny's friend, his skull they scalped clean, and the man with the copier on his head, and she worried for her fellow prisoners.

But she didn't worry *too* much. She had her own problems.

The town was still lit by braziers and torches, but there was a faint blue-orange glow over the buildings to the east.

As she moved closer to the church, the attendees of the ceremony began to sing and cheer.

There was no uniformity to the clown faces.

They leered up at Quinn as she rolled by, each of the masks done in a different style, out of different construction materials. Only a few of the handmade masks included Frendo's signature porkpie hat.

The face of Frendo the Clown also peered down at her from above: large paper, wood, and canvas builds hoisted up on poles, some with straggly arms like Muppets and others with large, articulated mouths like Chinese lion dance costumes.

The town square had been given a makeover in the few hours she'd been in the jail cell: the villagers had decided to throw Mardi Gras.

Behind her in the cart, Gabriel Dozer grunted. He had the head of his ax down at his feet, handle held between his knees so he could keep his arms out for balance.

It was pageantry, it was old-world charm, but—and Quinn was no historian—it all seemed wrong. None of the decorations held up to scrutiny. None looked like they were quite right, once you looked closely at the materials and spotted a cardboard toilet paper roll or a wax-coated Dixie cup.

Even the *number* of townspeople watching the parade was bolstered by fakery. About half the gathered crowd was asleep on their feet. Quinn could tell from their sideways lean and the tilt of their heads. The rowdier townspeople were chanting "Ad-ver-sar-ee" and "Ab-so-lution" as she passed— while the strung-out men and women were no more alert or spry than they'd been when Quinn had crawled through a crowd of them earlier.

Quinn didn't know why she took comfort in that, but she did. There weren't *that* many people out there who could put up a fight. It wasn't like she was going to be able to escape from her perch, then personally deliver an ass beating to every single inhabitant of this town, but, hey, she could fantasize.

So close, but so far: everyone missing from her list had gathered in one place. She could end it all right here, right now, finish up and go home, if they weren't about to kill her.

No, she had to be realistic, accept that there wouldn't be beatings for all.

But there still *could* be beatings for one or two of them.

374

Or.

She felt the knife against her. She'd tucked the blade into her jeans, handle covered with her shirt.

It wasn't a beating she had in mind.

But it wasn't much of a knife, either.

So *maybe* she could get one of them, if she was lucky.

The question was: Which one? She'd have preferred Alton, but was she ever going to be close enough? She should choose some alternate targets, in case she wasn't.

Dozer was right behind her, a foot or two away and unaware she was armed.

Killing either of them would bring her total in the last few hours to two bodies.

A slow day as far as these things, her biannual survival of mass murders, went. Quinn didn't know how many people she'd killed, total. She didn't know her lifetime score. How fucked up was that? Any time she tried to count, after she reached the fourth or fifth death, she would feel on the verge of a panic attack and need to stop.

A rod-puppet clown waved out over the cart, colliding with her. A crepe-paper streamer tore free, sticking to the blood and grime on her face.

"Back up!" Gabriel Dozer yelled, pointing at the man working the puppet. Dozer used two fingers, turning them back toward the eyeholes of his mask in an *I'm watching you* motion.

Quinn wondered if Jacksaw Dozer had ever had a grander ring entrance than this during his wrestling days.

She also wondered if he would care that his wife was dead.

It was something she could use to throw him off guard. She could lean over to him and whisper: *Cheryl's dead*.

But that felt like a betrayal to the woman. Cheryl Dozer hadn't done much wrong . . . well, except for flipping over their car and trying to kill them.

The hoofbeats slowed, then stopped. The woman who'd been leading the horse stroked the animal's neck, soothing him still, wagon wheels rocking into place.

Quinn looked back toward the jailhouse.

They were only a few dozen yards from where the ride had started.

Quinn was disappointed that the girl, Tabitha, Lizzie, and Vivian Fucking Murray weren't let out of their cell to attend this "ceremony."

They could have helped Quinn by causing a distraction.

Or something.

"Brothers and sisters," Jason Alton's voice boomed.

It was close enough to dawn to begin, apparently.

Alton stood on a raised wooden platform, the stage bare except for a sprinkling of broken glass at his feet. He'd undergone a costume change. His new outfit was a simple black tunic with a Roman collar.

He'd ditched the mask.

The man looked more like he had in the cardboard cut-out, maybe a little thinner and less groomed.

"We have had setbacks, tonight," he said.

And he wasn't just projecting his voice, speaking from his diaphragm. He was wearing a wireless microphone and there were speakers, hidden somewhere in the town square, amplifying his voice out over the crowd.

That felt like more than an anachronism. It felt like cheating.

"We've had delays. I've been shot. But not injured, of course."

The crowd cheered, yelled words of praise and support and hallelujahs.

Alton stuck out his finger, stopping them.

"It's not *all* cause for celebration. The sacred host was despoiled. *His* leg, his holy leg, has been torn off. It was only for a moment, and maybe it was because the Adversary had drawn so near, but tonight *greed* overtook your friends and neighbors."

The crowd booed, and when the sound had begun to fade out, one woman screamed, "Forgive me!"

Quinn was slightly lost.

Beside her on the cart, Dozer must have interpreted her confusion as impatience, because he'd raised his ax, got the head pointed in the right direction.

"It's been a long time, since you've seen me like this," Alton said, hand waving over his face, free at last of Arthur Hill's skin. A clean hand. A clean face. So somewhere in town there was a bar of soap.

"Believe me, brothers and sisters, I do not say anything I'm about to say lightly. Arthur Hill has taught us all so much. And I do not give up the visage of that great man because I'm through learning. I do so because I believe the host should be whole—as whole as possible—because we are closing a chapter here. This blessed Sunday morning we are ending persecution that you all, every one of you, have faced down and *survived*."

Alton looked to Quinn for the first time, then beyond her to Dozer, giving the man a slight wave of his hand.

"As prophesized, the Adversary has arrived. She's found our sanctuary and she's tried to kill me. Well, she failed, so what do you say to that?"

The townspeople screamed at her, called her horrible names. Someone threw a head of cabbage, the ragged leaves exploding against one of the cart's posts.

Dozer helped her down off the cart, hand on her shoulder, then pushed her to her knees once she was standing on mud.

It was calculated, a wrestling move, force applied only when she had cushioning to fall forward on.

But the crowd loved it.

"Up," Dozer said, ax in one hand.

"This young woman has hunted your friends and family," Alton said. "And the law and order of the old world, those in power, have done nothing about it. You are less than human to them. You are the faceless, homogeneous drones of the country outside those gates." He pointed to the back of the crowd, to the paved road that ended in dirt. "It is a country that started with such promise, but it lost its way. The people in power there hate you. Because of the clothes you wore. Because of the jobs you worked. Because of your car radio presets. But, most of all, because of how you spent your Sundays. *They* think you are stupid. *They* think you believe in fairy tales. *They* don't think you are worth saving. But *they* couldn't be more wrong."

"Amen. Amen. Amen," the chant began.

Nothing like a little persecution complex to get the crowd revved up, Quinn thought.

A large hand on her shoulder, Quinn was marched toward the dark structure on the horizon, the first rays of dawn beginning to reveal the texture of wood grain and rough bark.

None of what Alton was saying was true. "Law and order" had never caught up to Quinn, because Quinn had been smart. She hadn't been *targeting* people based on their faith. Or their socioeconomic status. That was deranged. She was meting out justice to the people who tried to hurt her, had hurt her family and friends. . . .

But then she thought of where Johnny D had lived. Where she'd found Cheryl Dozer. How many crosses and church placards she'd seen on the back roads between those locations. The broken streetlamps and antifreeze spills in a hundred different parking lots and rest stops. Of motel balconies and the kids who played there, their parents locking them out for the afternoon.

Of all the people sleeping in their cars.

Shit.

Was Quinn menacing vulnerable people? Was she—the daughter of a doctor—hunting the poor for sport, confident that if things ever got too serious, she could just go home?

Fuck.

God.

She looked around at the masks, the eyes behind the masks, some sharp, some dull, all angry.

And then she looked up to the stage.

Through the torch smoke against the glowing horizon, Vivian Murray's words came back to Quinn:

He must have more money than he lets on.

Yes. And whose money was it? Every bank account drained. Websites calling for donations to "resettle Kettle Springs." Credit cards maxed and no further transactions once the disappeared had gone into hiding.

About one thing, Jason Alton had been telling the truth:

he *had* learned a lot from Arthur Hill.

And Quinn knew where the knife was going if she got the chance.

"Light the fires," Alton said. "Let us sing a hymn."

Two masked townspeople, a man and a woman, walked out of the crowd, holding their torches aloft.

The torchbearers crossed ahead of where Dozer had pulled Quinn to a stop.

Then, in perfect sync, they dropped the ends of their torches to the base of the large black structure in the shadow of the church. Though the singing had started, Quinn could hear the flames lick at kindling, straw, sticks, pine cones, all lighting.

"A little drop of Baypen," the townspeople sang, "makes everything better."

And the shape of the sculpture revealed itself.

Flames ran around the base, becoming the jawline and teeth.

Pale smoke rose from the small kindling fires inside, smoke hitting the hollow dome of the head, the eye sockets becoming chimneys.

"Open up and let him in. Let him in," the song continued around her. Alton and his followers had added verses to the ten-second song. They'd turned Arthur Hill's shitty radio jingle into a hymn.

The fire at the base grew hotter, bark beginning to ignite,

the glow of orange embers making the nose stand out.

Whoever had designed the effigy hadn't forgotten the porkpie hat.

Oh God.

They weren't going to hang her or shoot her or chop her head off.

They were going to burn Quinn Maybrook alive.

"Let him in and make it all better," the crowd sang.

Vivian sat in her cell and read the note twice before making the connection that "T." stood for Taylor, one of the two boys who'd entered the room after Quinn Maybrook had been escorted out.

DO NOT read note out loud. Trust me. I Can Protect You. He has a gun. —T.

The small block letters had been written in thick graphite, as if from a very dull pencil, the lines gone over several times to help legibility.

The note had been thrown in the window wrapped around a small stone. Lizzie had read the note first, after the stone landed on her lap, then quietly passed it to Tabitha, who then, finally, showed Vivian.

Vivian looked up at the two boys.

She wouldn't have been able to tell Colby from Taylor, if one of them hadn't been looking at her, eyes pleading, while the other practiced flicking open his knife.

The singing had just begun.

"A little drop of Baypen . . ."

That fucking song. Vivian hadn't heard the jingle in so long. She'd been relieved when the Baypen factory burned down. Secretly relieved, of course. That relief wasn't something she could voice to Alec, who'd lost his job over it.

But secretly she was happy about that, too.

"I need to use the bathroom," Lizzie said.

Colby folded his knife back into its handle.

"You have to wait," he said. "It won't be much longer."

"Until what?" the girl asked. Her face wasn't streaked with tears, just wet all over, sweat and tears in one uniform sheen. If Vivian had her makeup, she could have helped.

"Until I say you can stop holding it. How's that?"

"Look, I'm pregnant. I've got a baby pressing on my bladder. I need to go to the bathroom. We've got a bucket and I'll do it with you watching if I have to."

"There's no reason to be . . . anatomical about it," Colby said. "In a few minutes we're taking your roommates out of here and then you and the baby can take as many number ones as you'd like—"

Lizzie stood, not breaking eye contact with the boy as she slid the bucket from against the wall with her foot. She kept eye contact as she undid the top button of her jeans and grabbed the zipper pull.

"I'm warning you," Colby said.

Tabitha turned her eyes away.

So did Taylor, who spoke for the first time since entering:

"Just let her go. Close your eyes and let her go."

Vivian didn't turn away. There'd been only a few days in lockup where she *hadn't* watched another woman go to the bathroom.

"No," Colby replied, then stood. The knife's blade had returned, a motion so smooth Vivian hadn't even noticed.

She remembered Taylor's note. That Colby had a gun. But where? In his pocket? Vivian searched for an outline in his slacks.

"Hey! Stop it. I said stop it."

Colby poked the knife through the bars.

He traced an X in the air over the pregnant girl's stomach.

But he couldn't reach her with the knife, and Lizzie persisted, starting to unzip her fly.

"Don't," Colby said, a vein over his temple throbbing now.

Good girl, Vivian thought, admiring Lizzie's bravery.

It was two decades ago now, but Vivian could still remember how sick she'd been for the first and second trimesters carrying Janet. It had been one of the reasons, one of many, Janet had been an only child.

Behind Colby, Taylor stood from his seat.

The knife tip hovered. Lizzie leaned back, still squatting,

Colby's shoulder as pressed against the bars at it could go.

"God put me on earth for one thing," Colby raged.

Taylor moved behind his friend, silent.

"And I will open this door and *show you* what it is if you drop those jeans and—"

Taylor punched Colby in the back of the head with enough force that the boy's forehead bounced off the bars.

There was a stunned second, all of them quiet, Taylor staring down at his half-curled fist.

But Colby didn't fall, didn't even drop the knife or take his arm out from between the bars.

He turned his head to his friend and calmly asked: "What?"

Taylor didn't answer. Just punched him again. The boy hit the bars a second time, his hand slipping down but not dropping the knife.

Vivian Murray had spent the first forty-two years of her life without ever seeing a fistfight.

And then the last two years witnessing *many* fistfights.

The thing that fascinated her—other than how much blood there was when someone lost a tooth or got a cut on their forehead where the skin was thin—was how difficult it was to knock someone unconscious from a blow to the head.

Vivian had seen women, their faces pulp from being slammed into concrete floors, still lucid enough to scream insults as the COs dragged the other fighter off.

"Get the knife!" Taylor yelled.

Vivian, Tabitha, and Lizzie watched Taylor, his forearm on Colby's neck, keeping the other boy pushed against the bars.

"Now!" he added.

Tabitha was the first of them to shake off her bewilderment and jump into action.

Vivian *wanted* to move to help. She did *want* to. But it wasn't how she had been living her life. Since her last days in Kettle Springs, she'd been a spectator. She'd seen violence, condoned violence, she'd even cosigned violence.

But she hadn't *done* violence.

The girl in the apron, both the youngest and smallest of the three women in the cell, put her full weight against Colby's upper arm, trying to keep him from whirling on Taylor with his weapon.

"Help me!" Tabitha said, the end of the knife whipping around, the boy's forearm spasming like an unmanned fire hose.

Vivian . . . her knees trembled, muscles in her legs tight, ready to spring, but she . . . she couldn't get close.

Instead, Lizzie roared, jeans still unbuttoned, waistband slack, face still sweaty, and rushed at the waving arm.

Vivian winced, sure she was about to see the knife bury itself into Lizzie's stomach, into the baby.

It didn't, but Lizzie wasn't fast enough.

The blade ran across the back of the girl's arm as she yelped and jumped back out of range.

Watching this struggle, Vivian remembered how strong the boys were. She remembered how easily, working together, Colby and Taylor had overwhelmed the copy shop clerk, a man almost twice their size.

Tabitha was never going to be able to hold him by herself.

And there was still the gun, somewhere, in his left pocket, she thought.

Dropping to his knee, Colby wrenched his arm out from under Tabitha and the girl fell to the floor.

"Whipped," Colby said to Taylor, standing. "He sees an upper thigh and he's ready to risk it all." Taylor threw another punch. But as he did the other boy spit, a pink glob exploding on his face as Colby sidestepped.

Faking with his knife hand, Colby sucker punched his friend in the stomach, fist leaving a dirty gray smudge on the boy's fresh white shirt.

"I knew you'd try something like this," Colby said. "To tell you the truth, I was hoping you would."

Colby had his back to the bars while he spoke.

Now. Now Vivian could move.

If the fucker wanted to talk about her upper thigh.

Vivian put two arms through the bars and wrapped them around Colby's neck, pulling him back against the iron.

If she could get the leverage and keep her arms locked,

she'd be able press his windpipe shut.

She groaned, and so did the boy under her embrace.

His arms.

Nobody was holding on to his arms anymore.

Colby reached up, the knife entering the back of Vivian's right hand. It was a shallow cut, but maybe that was worse, the sharp blade bumping over the tendons just under the skin, cutting a flap from her wrist to her knuckles.

The wound wasn't painful, not immediately, but the entire back of Vivian's hand felt cold. It was like she'd taken off one glove on a bitter winter's day.

She didn't let go, kept her arms wrapped around the boy's neck as he reared back to stab again.

Taylor launched himself off the shelves at the back of the room, coming up with a knee in Colby's stomach.

The blast in the small wood-and-stone room was like a sudden change in pressure. Vivian's eardrums weren't "ringing," she was just deaf, sure that they'd burst.

In Colby's other hand, the gun had revealed itself.

If Taylor had been shot, it hadn't incapacitated him. He was still on his feet, still swinging.

Vivian, arms locked, blood feeling slick against her skin, kept the boy up so Taylor could deliver an elbow to Colby's face.

Then, finally, the knife dropped, landing on its handle,

bouncing into the cell.

The gun didn't go off again, or maybe it did and Vivian couldn't hear it and didn't see the muzzle flash.

Colby's jaw slumped against Vivian's forearms.

She breathed.

The back of her hand was done being "cold": it hurt now.

Immense, perspective-altering pain as the air of the room licked against her nerve endings.

Vivian unlocked her arms and Colby's body dropped forward.

She wasn't deaf. She could hear the sound of him hitting dirt and the song continuing outside.

Taylor kicked the other boy in the side of the head, then kicked again, viciousness in his eyes. A look on his face like when he'd been cutting that man's fingers off in the copy shop.

Were the kicks meant as a killing blow? Or only to ensure Colby wasn't playing possum?

Apparently satisfied, Taylor crouched, collected the gun, and put it in his own pocket.

"Stop moving, I can't see," Tabitha said.

Vivian turned to check on the two girls. Tabitha had begun ministering to Lizzie.

The pregnant woman waved the other girl away. "I won't even need stitches, help her."

Vivian would certainly need stitches. She might need a whole new hand.

She looked down, wanting to take only a quick glance but unable to pull her eyes away.

The blood had begun to pool on the back of the hand. The pool overflowed as Tabitha took hold of the pinkie and gently turned Vivian's hand toward the lamplight.

Vivian lowered to her knees, good hand searching, trying to grab on to something to squeeze against the pain.

Closing her eyes, she felt Tabitha smooth the skin flap over and begin to wrap her injured hand with a strip of torn apron.

Alec used to kiss Vivian's hands. He would start at her wrists, then work down her knuckles to the tips of her fingers. He used to tell her that her hands were his favorite of her features. Then smirk and say something like:

Who'm I kidding? But they're in the top three.

He'd said her hands were made of porcelain.

That she was his little doll.

In addition to everything else, Alec was a racist piece of shit.

They'd been a year or two married. She'd been moved in, she and her daughter inextricably Missourian, before Vivian had realized.

She wasn't a wife, but a fetish object.

Someone was rubbing her back. Had to be Lizzie, as

Tabitha was still wrapping.

Vivian flinched, the pressure on the back of her mutilated hand was too much.

"Sorry," Tabitha said. "It needs to be tight."

"That's good enough," Taylor said.

Vivian opened her eyes.

She'd forgotten about the boy, in the pain, surrounded by these young women.

The boy had the keys in the lock, had opened the cell door. But not all the way, he was standing inside the jamb, blocking their exit.

"Mrs. Murray," he said, holding out his hand, "we've got to go."

She stared at the hand.

"All of us," she said. "Right?"

Taylor looked to the door. The sounds of singing outside were winding down, but apparently nobody had heard the gunshot or cared enough to investigate.

Alton must have been putting on a good show.

"No. I can protect *you*, Mrs. Murray. I can get *you* out."

She rose to her feet and he reached in, pulled her by the shoulder of her dress.

"Come on," he said.

"Why not all of us?"

"There's too many. Every extra person's another chance to get caught," he said, softening his voice. "They'll be okay.

That girl's one of the natives." He pointed to Tabitha, then Lizzie. "And she's got the baby to protect her. Don't worry, these people . . . they're very pro-life." He didn't seem to understand how insane that statement sounded. "We'll have a much better chance if it's just the two of us. They know me and you're small."

You're small. Vivian heard the boy's words in Alec's voice.

Boyish hand touching but not grabbing, Taylor guided Vivian out of the cell.

Then he closed the door and turned the lock.

"At least leave us the key!" Lizzie pleaded.

"Come on," Taylor said, ignoring the girl. The boy's hand, warm and overjoyed to be on a woman, dropped to Vivian's waist. "Let's get you out of here."

My little doll, Alec's voice added.

Vivian didn't hesitate.

Didn't even think about it, not really.

The knife. While she'd been bandaged she'd found Colby's knife, as something to grip.

Vivian put the tip of the blade up to the space that connected Taylor's chin to his neck. Then she pushed up, angling the grip back toward his brain. She planted her feet, kept pushing as hard as she could until she heard a crack.

Then, to make sure the gun didn't come up in Taylor's hand, she pulled the blade out, moved the tip an inch or two to the side, and stabbed upward again.

Tabitha and Lizzie, shocked, both looked green, ready to vomit.

What? Vivian thought.

It was the way you were supposed to kill a lobster, before putting it in the boiling water.

It was humane.

Taylor fell to the floor beside his friend, fingertips and feet convulsing slightly.

Had Vivian really picked up Colby's knife "just to have something to hold," or did she know this was where it would end?

It didn't matter.

She unlocked the cell door.

They *all* could leave now.

Outside, the singing was over. The screaming had begun.

The wood was wet.

Too wet.

Quinn's father was far from an outdoorsman, but when Quinn was little Glenn and Samantha Maybrook had taken her to the Poconos and they'd built fires then. And she'd seen pros do it at the overnight camps she'd tried out as a tween, before deciding she'd rather stay home in Philly, attend day camp for volleyball.

Point was that Quinn knew you couldn't build an effective fire with wood that hadn't properly cured. Or wood that had sat outside, uncovered, while it rained.

The smoke she was seeing wasn't smoke, it was smoke *and* steam.

"Quickly! We need more kindling!" Alton said from the stage. "And one more time, join us in song."

There were small fires covering the oversized Frendo head, but it wasn't burning hot or evenly enough to be called a pyre.

They seemed to think it wasn't enough.

If they stuck her in that thing right now, Quinn would surely die of smoke inhalation. She'd die horribly, every inch of exposed skin scalded with steam.

But she wasn't going to be the one to point that out to them.

The torchbearers were back, now each carrying armfuls of hay. A conga line of volunteers had begun to jog out to nearer the forest, collecting up freshly fallen branches, breaking them into twigs.

"No, you're going to wreck it," Dozer yelled from behind Quinn as he pushed her to the knees again. "Stay there," he said, passing over her, waving to two men who were trying to adjust a log near the bottom of the structure.

Was this really happening?

The front few rows of the crowd had thinned, the spectators who were still alert enough helping to stoke the flames.

Quinn looked up toward the stage. It was maybe

twenty-five feet to run, then three stairs, and she'd be within stabbing distance of Jason Alton.

Fucking idiots.

If she'd been waiting for a chance—or divine providence—this was it.

Quinn lifted her shirt, took out the steak knife, and began to run.

"No," she heard Dozer yell. Probably realizing how big a mistake he'd made leaving her unattended.

". . . makes everything better. Open up and—"

Alton was singing along, but stopped as she approached the base of the stage.

"Stay back!" Alton said, not yelling, but his amplified voice booming out over the crowd.

The singing continued, lyrics garbled. The drugged-up villagers were only humming the words, the rest of the town helping build the fire.

Jason Alton wasn't ready to stand and fight Quinn. And he wasn't ready to sermonize, try to talk his way out of this.

He was terrified.

He was going to run for it.

He knew who Quinn was. And maybe what he'd been telling these people was right. Maybe Quinn was the devil. Because he *should* be terrified.

She caught up with him as he turned, ready to dive off the back of the stage but not having a long enough stride to outpace Quinn's momentum. She slashed at the back of his slacks, the dull but still serrated knife blade connecting with his hamstring.

There was a pleasant tug to the follow-through that indicated to Quinn that she'd caught more than sock.

He screamed into his microphone and any villagers who'd still been singing stopped.

"Let go of him," Dozer yelled. The man was big but had that top-heavy jog of a bodybuilder. He couldn't sprint, not even if his savior's life depended on it.

That said, Quinn knew there would be no negotiating with the wrestler, no putting the blade of the knife up to Jason Alton's throat and telling him to drop his ax.

No. This was an ending. And a good ending.

Quinn was going to stab this bastard until she was either pulled off his corpse or killed.

This man had poisoned these people's already damaged brains, taken what little they'd had left in the world.

Quinn was going to die. She hadn't walked into town thinking that, intending on that, but now she knew it was true.

But she was going to take Jason Alton with her.

She adjusted her hold on the knife, switching from a saber to reverse grip, keeping all her fingers wrapped around the hilt like Rust had taught her. She needed that power if she was going to punch the blade through the man's skull.

"No!" masked villagers implored from the crowd, the bravest of them beginning to rush the stage, crawling on each other's backs to try to reach Quinn in time.

At her feet, Jason Alton began to pray quietly, the words picked up by his hidden microphone and broadcast out.

"Oh Lord," he said. "Save me."

No one's saving you, Quinn thought.

And then, as if the man's prayers had been answered, Quinn spotted the halogen headlights appearing over the rear of the crowd.

TWENTY-SIX

FOURTEEN MILES OUTSIDE SHIPPENSBURG, PENNSYLVANIA

RVs have basements?

Johnny D remembered asking Quinn.

Turns out they don't. Not really. The space under the RV was more like a trunk.

He wondered, too late to do anything about it, if he was going to be able to open the hatch from the inside.

Or, worse, if the "basement" was airtight.

No biggie. If he needed to cut his way out—or drill air holes—he probably had the tools to do it stashed in the pockets of his cargo shorts.

Not that it mattered: in a few moments Quinn was probably going to open the hatch and find him here, a failure at being a stowaway like he'd failed at everything else.

But she didn't.

Instead, he listened as the RV's engine turned over and heard the click of the blinker as Quinn merged into traffic.

Wow. He couldn't believe that worked, offering to top up her gas and then jumping inside the basement hatch.

It *wasn't* airtight in here. As they hit the highway, he could hear the whiz of air and see dots of light through cracks in the trunk's construction. To promote airflow to his pits, Johnny slid one of the boxes of T-shirts over so he could lie on his side, his broken wrist throbbing under him.

So no, the basement wasn't airtight, but it sure was hot, hotter as the engine worked, warming the metal and fiberglass around him.

Johnny tried to remove his shirt, but it was tough to do with one hand and he didn't have enough room to maneuver the sleeves over his shoulders. Instead, he did the only thing he could do—lie there, sweating.

Johnny stayed awake for the first hour or so of the drive. He fell asleep once there were no more streaks of daylight and the night air had begun to cool the chassis around him.

He woke when, a few inches above his head, the RV stopped moving and its aluminum storm door clattered shut. A loud sound, yes, but it was still so warm all around him, he shut his eyes.

It was hard to tell if his eyes were closed for minutes

or hours, but sometime during this hazy period, he flipped onto his back. When he woke with a second start, the nap-time drool snaking down his cheek, into his ear, was chilly to the touch.

How long had they been parked with the engine off?

Johnny was cold, but Quinn might still be up there. He waited and listened. He didn't even risk pulling his shirt down.

After a few more moments of stillness in the RV above, he pawed for the door handle.

But there was no handle, just a vinyl strap, a hand pull to help ease the trunk open on its hydraulic struts.

There was no way to open the basement door from the inside.

Johnny shook his head. This was a clear safety hazard. What if a little kid had gotten stuck playing in here?

It took him a considerable amount of time to take the basement door off its hinges, only his one hand good for anything. He worked in complete darkness. In the rush to stow away, and because he was so used to having one on his phone, he'd forgotten to grab a flashlight when he was sneaking tools out of Quinn's duffel.

Once Johnny was free, his neck and back sore, his first order of business was checking the fridge.

He drank a carton of orange juice, using it to wash down five acetaminophen tablets while inspecting the tools that

Quinn hadn't taken with her.

She'd left all the best stuff behind!

But it was cool, more for him.

Less cool: she'd taken the keys.

Which made sense, but he hadn't factored that into his plan, either. He'd have to get the RV rolling without them.

There wasn't an onboard computer system or anything modern like that, so that was good.

But after a few tries to hot-wire the mobile home, he realized there must have been an ignition immobilizer somewhere along the line.

"Fuck!"

Starting to feel the time crunch, he quickly untwisted and patched back together all the wires he'd stripped.

Ultimately, it was the tried-and-true "screwdriver jammed into the ignition after whaling on it with a hammer" trick that did it. Which only took five minutes, so he should have started there.

Getting the engine going took about an hour. Or longer. The clock on the RV microwave was blinking midnight the whole time.

"You stupid asshole," Johnny said to himself.

Thirsty and exhausted, he was beginning to get depressed. Whatever dramatic rescue he'd been imagining, he'd totally missed his window.

He had to have missed it.

Right? All that time locked in the fucking wheel well, what was he thinking?

No.

That wasn't the attitude Quinn would take. She would keep fucking going.

Time to commit.

Even with the road atlas stretched out on the steering wheel, Quinn's annotations in highlighter, Johnny missed the turn the first time. And U-turns weren't easy out here, in the dark, driving an RV with one hand.

The second time he saw it, though, and coming in from two lanes over gave him a better approach, to roll through the overgrown entrance to the road.

He was a half mile down the narrow road before he realized those might have been rosebushes he'd driven through.

The tire pressure light was blinking.

By the time he reached the town, orange dawn bleeding over the treetops, church steeple hazed in smoke . . . the RV was leaned over to the right, close to riding on rims.

The air coming through the vents smelled like a cookout.

He came to the end of the road, old cracked asphalt turning to hardpack, and saw the fire glow of the town square.

There was a lot to see, a lot of strangeness, but slightly above it all, standing over a kneeling man, was Quinn.

He let out a yelp of relief.

For once in his shitty little life, Johnny D Lawson wasn't too late.

Quinn was there, alive, and armed. But she was surrounded by a whole hell of a lot of angry people in clown masks.

"Oh Lord," an amplified voice whispered, "save me."

The lights and sound of the RV caused most of the crowd to turn back toward Johnny. Tilted mouths and uneven eyes, the clown masks looking like they were products of the arts and crafts hour at an institute for the criminally insane.

Johnny eased off the accelerator, but didn't stop. He tried nosing into the base of the crowd, where the people were more spread out. He honked, but the people nearest the front bumper acted like they didn't hear.

"What are you waiting for?" the amplified voice shouted, and Johnny finally placed the voice as the guy kneeling below Quinn.

It was Fake Tony Robbins.

"Don't just stand there. Save me and kill her!" the man screamed.

No way. Fuck that. Not on my watch, Johnny thought.

"Hang on, baby-girl!"

Johnny D Lawson jammed the gas pedal all the way down to the floor.

The first bodies rolled under the wheels of the RV with a thud. Or a loud, wet splat. Some of the bodies screamed as they were twisted beyond their breaking points, churned up, some were so far gone that they weren't even aware they were being run over.

The next wave of bodies was hit in closer to slow motion. By the time the RV had reached the middle of the crowd, the villagers were aware enough they were in danger that they began trying to get out of the way. It was a stampede. Which meant most of the bodies going under the camper's tires were already on the ground when the pressure reached their legs and spines and skulls.

Eventually, there were so many bodies that the six-ton mobile home lost traction, spun out, and finally pitched forward into a pool of mud and gore, stopping completely.

Quinn watched all of this, knowing she only had moments if she wanted to kill Alton before Gabriel Dozer could cut her down, but also powerless to look away.

Dozer was similarly rapt. He'd stopped running toward her, stood on the steps to the stage, turning his body out to watch.

The Winnebago sat, nose down on an angle, one of its turn signals clacking, headlights stained red with blood and pulp.

Quinn looked over at Dozer, Alton squirming in her grip.

"Cheryl?" Dozer said, blinking. Then he yelled, running best he could out into the crowd of dazed, dead, and dying villagers, "Cheryl, hon? Get the doors open! Don't hurt her!"

Alton breathed feedback into his microphone, stunned that he'd been abandoned.

But, no, Quinn knew that when the wrestler reached the RV, he wouldn't find his wife.

Johnny.

Johnny *D*.

That tricky goddamn Juggalo would be behind the wheel.

Quinn pushed Alton to the footboards, the glass crunching under the man's hands. He whimpered as she menaced him with the knife. "Don't be going anywhere," she said, giving him a slash on his other leg, this one higher, under the kneecap.

He screamed so loud there was a whistling audio distortion over the sound system.

It felt good to be cruel to the cruel.

Not all the villagers had abandoned their leader, some were still climbing up the side of the stage to fight her.

Quinn stabbed a man twice in the ribs, tipped him back over the edge. He landed in a space with no people, falling into the mud with a squelch, not moving.

It didn't scare the rest of them off.

The next clown mask to pull its face over the lip of the stage, Quinn hit with a straight kick, the flat of her heel to

Frendo's cardboard nose. A gout of blood squirted through the mask's mouth hole.

Some of these villagers had been the same people chasing her with torches, some of them still brandished them now, like large extinguished matchsticks. But some had better weapons. Antique farm equipment.

She chose one, a guy with a curved sickle, red with rust but edge of the blade silvery, recently sharpened, and jumped onto him, stabbing. While the man under her reached up to grab at his injured neck, she traded weapons with him. With their hands up, trying to attack her and protect themselves at the same time, she was able to crowd-surf between a few targets before she fell to the dirt.

The remaining clowns in front of the stage were either stumbling over themselves in retreat or were the walking dead, watching Quinn rise to her feet, their eyes red and rheumy behind their masks.

It was harder to see here on ground level, not only because of the smoke and confusion, but because the rising sun was working to warm the mud now, a thin mist hanging at chest height all around them.

Quinn had lost track of Dozer. That was a mistake, made her feel uneasy. The big man could be hiding anywhere, ready to jump out.

Through the bodies, she could see one headlight and the right side of the RV.

The clowns weren't inside the vehicle yet, but a group of them were banging on the storm door.

They couldn't get the door open, there were so many of them pushing the wrong way on it.

As she watched, they kicked in the glass portion of the door and peeled the aluminum portion free from its hinges and out of the frame.

They still needed to break down the wooden interior door.

More clowns were scaling the side of the RV, ready to pull open the sunroof.

Somewhere to the side of her, toward the jail, there were gunshots and more screams.

Quinn couldn't be bothered with that, if that was Vivian Murray and the girls: she wished them luck, but she had to help Johnny.

A man screamed a war cry, streaming out of the smoke and mud, headed straight for her, a shovel arcing over his head in an overhead swing.

Quinn sidestepped.

This deluded chump. An anonymous man in a clown mask was not going to be the one to . . .

Quinn hadn't dodged the shovel. Not completely.

The villager in the clown mask looked down.

Quinn looked down.

The shovel was dug into the ground, the sharpened tip of

the spade had torn through canvas, but not the rubber sole of her shoe.

Her foot.

He'd cut off her fucking foot.

Or at least cut it in half. She felt herself tip, then leaned back, steadying so she wasn't putting weight on the missing toes.

The man in the mask seemed just as surprised about it as Quinn was.

Locked together as they were by the shovel embedded in the ground, man still gripping the handle, Quinn was able to thread the sickle between the man's arms.

The blade cut into the crook of the man's elbow.

She yanked the sickle upward.

The man's left arm separated at the joint, as simple as if she were clearing tall grass.

An arm for a few toes, seemed more than fair.

The man collapsed, screaming and crying, dropping the shovel to grab at his stump.

She sliced down, silencing the cries before stumbling back in the direction of the RV.

Quinn's missing toes . . . the injury wasn't stopping her.

What was she? What was this? How was she doing this? Adrenaline? How had she become what she'd become?

Had it happened over months and years, or was it all at once, becoming the *thing* she needed to be tonight?

It wasn't grit. It wasn't survival instinct. Whatever it was, it wasn't good and enviable. It was the reason she couldn't remember her dreams anymore, but still woke up sweating, throwing punches, her knuckles squeaking against automotive glass.

Quinn had built a callus over her soul.

She limped onward into the haze, favoring the heel of her partially amputated foot.

No one else bothered her. They turned their eyes away the closer she got to the RV. Like if they didn't look up at her, she'd leave them alone to tend to their injured, weep over the bodies.

The area in front of the church was a war zone.

The villagers who still had any fight in them were trying to break into the camper.

She was fifteen feet away, the distance seeming to double as she half limped, half hopped toward the mobile home.

Quinn watched as the sunroof hatch was worked open and a woman gripping a pair of scissors dropped inside, screaming and leading with the blades.

A second later, the crowd outside had pried the main door open, began pouring inside.

If Johnny D had wanted to die a hero, he hadn't. He'd died plowing into a bizarre roadside revival, the parishioners all high out of their minds and itching to tear someone apart.

Quinn frowned.

But she kept on her approach trajectory, stumbling as the nerve endings of her foot began to sop up mud and blood.

She wished she knew a prayer.

She'd say it for Johnny.

Then, screams from inside the RV. A woman's screams and a man's shouts, punctuated by a battery of pressurized cracks, not quite gunshots but—

"Get back! Gun!" one of the villagers yelled.

pfft- pfft- pfft-

The noise of the nail gun continued from inside the RV, the clowns who'd been inside scrambling to get out, bleeding from their torsos, arms, and faces.

The final man out the door had his hand nailed to the side of his head, the cardboard of his mask stuck in between his hand and his face, blinding him.

Johnny D stood in the doorway, machete glistening in its sheath at his belt, red plastic exterior shell of the nail gun resting against his shoulder. The beads in his braids and the grime streaked to his chin made him look like a video game character or the hero of some postapocalyptic tale of adventure.

He met Quinn's eyes from across the mist.

Five or six strides separated them.

Less than ten hopping steps until she would kiss him.

"We're doing it!" Johnny yelled, smiling. "We're winning!"

And then his expression changed, hardened, the smile

evaporating, and he was running.

Quinn didn't run, just followed his gaze with a tilt of her head.

There was an ax on its way to her, flying end over end, thrown by impossibly strong arms and putting curls in the mist.

No. Johnny was wrong.

This thing, there was no winning.

TWENTY-SEVEN

THE SETTLEMENT OF NEW KETTLE SPRINGS

"What are you doing?" Vivian asked.

"We have to help them!" the girl said, pulling at her dress.

"Help who? Quinn Maybrook?"

Tabitha pointed toward the mass of broken bodies and pained cries. "My *parents* are in there!"

Tabitha started running, and Vivian knew she had to stop the girl or she'd have saved her from choking for nothing.

So she slapped her across the face.

Tabitha stopped, jaw working in a click, stunned.

But the slap felt wrong, so before the girl could stop her, Vivian held her close, wrapping her arms around the girl's shoulders, grabbing her wrists around the backpack Tabitha wore. The bag they'd taken from outside their cell.

"Don't struggle. My hand still hurts. Just listen to me,"

Vivian said. "What have your parents done to deserve your help?" She spoke into the girl's ear as calmly as she could.

"I . . ."

Vivian unlocked the grasp she had on her own hands but kept hold of the conservatively dressed girl.

Vivian could not pass any kind of judgment on how the girl and her parents had chosen to live before. Their beliefs were drastically different from her own, but they probably lived a simple life, one Vivian would have envied, when times got their darkest, when her unruly daughter wouldn't talk to her and she hated her husband.

But the world the girl had been raised in was gone. Alton had erased it and there was no going back, not in this town, with these parents, at least.

"You can get free. You can run," Vivian said. "You can get out of this place, away from them, and you can live. There are people out there who can help you. Good people."

"But—"

"Listen to me, Tabitha."

It was like Vivian was talking to the girl, but not. It was like she was talking back in time to a girl who'd drunk too much and was crying about it, letting her tears drip into the toilet water.

Tabitha didn't seem to be listening.

Vivian pointed back at Lizzie. The pregnant girl had her back pressed against the wall of the building they'd just left, ready to run through the alley, get as far away as she could. "Look, you saved that girl and her baby once, yes? *Keep* them alive. She doesn't know where she's going. She'll get lost in the woods. She needs you to guide her out of here."

"Then where will you be?" Tabitha said, not seeming convinced but asking questions in the right direction, at least.

It was a *good* question, one Vivian didn't quite have an answer to.

Vivian had taken Colby's gun, given the girls the bag, with the weapons and tools inside, and the knife she'd used to kill Taylor.

"I'll stay here," Vivian said. "To see if I can help the injured, help your parents."

She knew it was a lie. But did Tabitha?

And how could Vivian begin to explain that she was staying because she'd helped make this place? That she hadn't meant to, but she'd also helped make that scarred, violent girl who'd shared the jail cell with them?

She looked out across what was left of the town. The foundations of the buildings were built up, the town square and thoroughfare sunken a bit.

She remembered looking out on the real Kettle Springs, sending beauty queen waves to people on Main Street, seated on a parade float for Founder's Day.

Different state. Different century. Different clowns. The same stink of rot.

414

Vivian Murray was as much of a mother to this mess as she was to Janet, maybe even more so.

Her plan, such as it was, was to run out there and try to protect Quinn Maybrook. Her alternate plan was to let Quinn kill her, if that's what the girl decided she wanted to do. Vivian deserved it. Deserved worse.

"Go," Vivian said to Tabitha and Lizzie. And to her surprise, they did.

The girl in the long dress took the mother-to-be by the arm, both of them disappearing down the alley, headed away from New Kettle Springs.

Vivian looked back to the killing ground, searching for "the Adversary."

There she was.

Quinn had jumped down off the stage and was running toward a stalled RV.

Vivian ran into the crowd, her own path ready to intersect with the girl's.

She was expecting all the masked townspeople to fall on her at once. But it was the strangest thing: it was as if they'd forgotten that they'd hated her. Every mask that turned Vivian's way froze, awed once again to be in the presence of a Founder.

But eventually the spell was broken, and the villagers started to approach. Curious at first, but then with violence in their eyes and on their tongues. "Traitor!" "Harlot!"

There'd been worse insults in Vivian's past, and many of the masked villagers seemed incapable of words beyond slurred growls.

She'd made it halfway to the RV, but there were enough angry, alert clowns in front of her that the crowd contracted. It was a curtain of masks and blades closing, cutting her off from making any more progress, from even seeing what was happening over there where Quinn had run.

So, she shot one.

Vivian was no markswoman, but they were standing so close together that as long as she kept the barrel at her midsection she would hit something.

After the first clown gripped his chest and fell, there was trepidation. A momentary détente.

Then they began to step forward, not all together, but one step here, another there. Taking their progress in little bites until they began to surround her, a slight bend slowly becoming a half circle.

It was a children's game. Something Janet had played, giggling every time Vivian turned her back, then whipped her head around, trying to catch the girl creeping up.

Red light, green light, one, two—

Vivian turned to her left, shot another one.

And then the right, got the next as they pushed their luck, trying for two steps' worth of progress.

She felled two more in quick succession, wondering when she'd run out of bullets.

Her next shot hit a clown in the shoulder, sent the female form spinning.

Vivian watched as the woman's mask repositioned itself to the side of her head so she was wearing it like a bow or fascinator.

The woman's face looked so . . . familiar.

She wasn't screaming religious invectives or gritting her teeth at the pain in her shot arm. The woman was smiling. It was an expression Vivian recognized. It was the look of a woman who had no choice but to be here, one who knew she was on display so she smiled through it. Put on her makeup and her finery and smiled through her husband's life.

The woman stepped forward, and several more bodies stepped with her.

But Vivian didn't shoot.

These weren't clowns. These weren't masked anonymous killers. They were husbands who'd decided to follow someone else's plan. These were the wives that had followed, too, because what other choice was there?

She hated that, pitied it, but she understood it, empathized with it enough that she couldn't shoot.

The residents of New Kettle Springs fell upon Vivian Murray, tearing her apart with their blades, pummeling her with their bricks, and never knowing why she'd stopped firing.

Was there a reason to believe?

To continue to carry hope and faith in her heart?

Tabitha Werther didn't know what to think.

The wind pushed plumes of smoke off the tall fire, wafting the smell of a charnel house over her and Lizzie as they ran.

Flames, death, chaos: they were fleeing hell.

Which meant, from one way of looking at it, the Pastor had been speaking the truth.

Quinn Maybrook *had* brought hell to their town.

But with every step they took that smell abated, the sounds of screams and gunshots became less jarring.

If it was hell, it was a hell they could escape.

Tabitha and Lizzie were taking the most direct route out of the town. They could have bent their path to the south, so Tabitha could pass her parents' farmhouse, but there was nothing for her there.

Poor Nellie would need milking.

But they could send help back for the animal.

Once they found help for themselves.

They were running through the trees, an uphill climb until they crested the next ridge. Eventually, if they kept this heading, they'd reach a chain-link fence. Tabitha had never been beyond the fence, but she knew there was a break, a gate at the main road.

The sun was climbing higher in the east, and the canopy above was thick and the forest around them still dark. The light turned the shadows a toneless brown.

Tabitha ran, urged forward by the knowledge that . . . they weren't alone in these woods.

It was just a feeling at first. The same paranoia Tabitha had felt as a little girl, on her own and tasked with a chore that would bring her outside after dark.

Tabitha tried to shake the feeling away.

But then Lizzie gasped and pointed to a tree.

"They're here," Lizzie said. The woman had drifted away from Tabitha but now was back by her side, clinging to her. "There's someone over there."

Tabitha didn't see anything. But also didn't speak. If there *was* someone else in the forest, they were likely injured, fleeing the town just like they were.

The pair continued, pace quickening, and then, at the edges of her vision, Tabitha saw it, too.

She pulled them to a stop. There was a slight clearing around them, a few paces from the nearest tree in all directions.

There was someone out there in the dimness. More than one someone.

While they stood still, waiting and watching around

them, a face peeked out at them from behind a tree. Then another.

The children were wearing masks, had been following after Tabitha and Lizzie, and now seemed unsure what to do.

"Oh God. Oh God," Lizzie said.

Tabitha shushed her.

Then Lizzie began pulling at the shoulder strap to the backpack, trying to get Tabitha to take the bag off.

"The bear spray. We can gas them," Lizzie whispered.

Tabitha nodded, unzipping the backpack as quietly and slowly as she could, keeping her eyes on the trees. There was a foot. There was a small pale hand, using a branch as a handhold. It was the reasoning of a child on display: *if I can't see them, they can't see me.*

Tabitha removed the can and slipped her finger into the ring of the pull cord.

She'd never worked a mechanism like this. Never held a pressurized can. But the operation was self-explanatory. She hoped.

Her grip tightened.

Around them, the children began to step out from behind their trees.

Their clothes were filthy. Their hands and forearms were caked in dark splotches, designs drawn onto their skin.

"Ohgodohgodohgod," Lizzie said.

Tabitha repeated similar words, silently, and she *meant* them.

She was praying.

She didn't want to die here, not after they'd come so far. She didn't want to be killed by her schoolmates.

When she pulled the cord, would there be a delay? Would the gas spray from the top or the sides of the can's plastic cap?

The nearest child stepped closer, then tipped his mask up.

It was Noah Blevins.

Or, Noah Blevins was the name Tabitha knew. He had another name, a real name.

The boy, tiny, small for his age, was crying.

"We want to go home," he said.

The rest of the children followed Noah's example, removing their masks, stepping toward them.

Tabitha took her finger out from the loop of the pull cord.

"What are you doing?" Lizzie asked, trying to grab the canister away from her. "I'm not going to let them kill my baby."

"No," Tabitha said, shaking free of the woman's hold. Lizzie would come to her senses, she just needed to . . . "Look at them."

More masks were peeled away, more frightened children entered the clearing, until the whole schoolhouse was standing with them.

All except Amber, of course.

The children weren't holding weapons.

The streaks on their arms weren't blood, they were . . .

Before their parents had been killed, before their parents had even been forced to dance the maypole too many times, the children had been tasked with painting signs and constructing masks.

They were streaked with finger paints.

They were just children.

They were normal, frightened children.

Not hellions. Innocents.

Tabitha opened her arms and let them encircle her, letting her apron soak up their tears as they hugged and she hugged back.

Together, they prayed.

TWENTY-EIGHT

THE SETTLEMENT OF NEW KETTLE SPRINGS
Gabriel Dozer stood, chest heaving.

He'd thrown the ax and missed Quinn.

Missed Quinn but hit—

No. Don't think about it. This is your opening.

He'd thrown away his weapon. And now he was standing there, like he was waiting for applause. Like this wasn't a mud pit filled with the dead and dying. Like the people around him were spectators at a wrestling show.

Quinn made him pay for that, creeping low through the haze. Even hobbled she was faster than he'd ever be.

She passed the wooden handle of the sickle from her left to her right as she took a limping jog forward, her half-footed lope seeming to destabilize him.

The wrestler was squat in his promotional pictures, but

it was an effect of his wide shoulders. In real life, he was tall enough that Quinn needed to jump to connect the curve of the sickle to the side of his head.

His attempt to duck came far too late.

There was nothing satisfying about the sound the tool made as the blade embedded itself into the wrestler's brain, his left eye drifting crossed behind his mask.

Quinn crashed down to the ground, nothing to support herself with, knowing that she was too late.

The big man's thrown ax had landed a direct hit on Johnny D.

Quinn crawled to Johnny's side. She scooped the boy into her arms the best she could, with him being heavier, weighted down by the ax-head.

The ring of nearing gunshots had scattered whatever clowns hadn't fled from the nail gun.

Quinn tilted her head down.

The effects of blood loss made the world ripple. Or maybe it was tears.

"Whoop-whoop," Johnny D said weakly, then his chest made a sucking sound.

"Don't talk," Quinn said. She knew what that sound meant.

"Don't tell me what to do." Hiss. Hitching breath. "Did you get them?"

Quinn was confused by the question, then remembered what she'd promised.

She hadn't seen the missionary boys since she'd been standing in the cart.

She looked around, but there were no clean white shirts on the battlefield surrounding them.

The boys might have run out of the jail to help build the fire. They might have been flattened by the RV. But Quinn doubted it.

Janet's mom, Tabitha, and Lizzie might have escaped, might have even overpowered the two boys, but she *highly* doubted that.

It was Quinn Maybrook's belief that a person was only dead once she'd seen the body.

And, now, with all Arthur Hill had accomplished as a moldering corpse, not even then.

"Yes," she said finally. "I got them. I got them both."

"That's good," Johnny said, allowing his eyes to close halfway.

Hiss.

"But you don't have to be this anymore."

Suck.

"You can stop and go home."

Each word Johnny D said was weaker than the last, every inhale and exhale accompanied by more of the hissing gurgle.

"You can stop," he repeated, and then spoke no more.

It was a nice sentiment, but she couldn't.

Not just yet.

Quinn leaned down and kissed the boy with the braids and cargo shorts and bad tattoos, and when she pulled her head back he was dead.

Around them, there were no more gunshots and no more screams.

She waited beside the body for a moment, to see if a villager was feeling brave, like the shovel guy had been, and wanted to attempt to put her down.

But none approached.

"Please, Lord," Alton prayed, voice low like he was hiding, searching for shelter, but seeming to come from every direction. "I have kept my mind clear, abstained from the host, will you not show me a way out now?"

"Host!" one of the villagers yelled.

In the jail cell the girl had told Quinn about "the host." It was almost too much to believe, too stupid. But she'd seen dumber, she'd seen more violent irrationality than anyone could believe.

Quinn leaned back on her knees, looked out over the square. The remaining townspeople were shadows in the smoke and mist. Even the closest villagers, no more than ten feet away, looked like ghosts. She watched as they, maybe fifteen in all, began to stumble toward the church, climbing up the stairs chanting, "Host! Host!"

Time for another fix, she guessed.

And with them gone, retreated inside the church, Quinn was able to listen.

Through the microphone there was a scratchy bump against the wind guard, then a strained grunt and a moan.

Then a thud against wood. And between and under all these sounds, the approaching crackle of a large fire.

She knew where Alton was.

Quinn stood, taking the machete from Johnny's belt but not the nail gun.

Her foot was bad. Four of her toes were gone, the one that remained stubbornly clinging to the ball of her foot by a superficial band of skin.

The heel of her shoe was heavy with blood, liquid squelching out the hole in the toe as she walked.

If she didn't get a tourniquet around her ankle soon, she'd pass out and die.

It could wait.

Just this one more thing.

Yes. She would be finished with her list. She would be done.

After she crossed off one final name.

Arthur Hill's body was being picked apart right now. Mystery solved. No ghosts, just psychosis. The people *eating* that body . . . they'd suffered enough, they were officially off the list.

There were no more loose ends, except . . .

When she caught up with Jason Alton he was in an army man crawl, dragging his injured legs behind him.

He hadn't made it far from where she'd left him, off the stage. There was a thin snail trail of blood in his wake as he crawled toward the giant Frendo effigy.

The clown sculpture was burning brighter now, the orange flames finally having taken hold, dark, ash-tipped char on the outer logs.

"You're a murderer," Alton said, his words doubling through the speakers. He lifted himself in a push-up, pointed to the town square. "Look what you've done to these people!"

She reached for his face, felt along his sideburns, and ripped the mic away from where it had been affixed to his cheek. There was a patch of hair on the tape.

There, now she could talk with him, if that was what he'd wanted.

"You called me and I came," Quinn said.

"Like a plague unto us, like—"

"Now I have a question for you," Quinn said, ignoring the act. "Why all this? Why wear another person's face? Why build . . ."

She didn't feel like she had to finish the questions for him to understand, just wave her hand.

"I am filled with the light of—"

She poked the wound on the back of his leg with the end

of the machete, touching bone. He squealed and she waited for him to be able to listen again.

"I *just* heard you say you weren't taking the host. The girl explained it to me, what you've been feeding them. He was *embalmed*, you monster. Have you seen them? You poisoned all these people. Why? Speak to me."

He slumped against the ground. His expression seemed to change, like he was going to let her try talking to the old Jason Alton, or the new Alton. Or whatever.

"I tried a lot of methods to find my ministry," he said, no longer speaking in biblical hellfire aphorism. "I changed my approach for years. Kept pivoting. Nothing worked. Then, after something I said at my lowest point, a musing I made because I was frustrated, that maybe the murderers in your town were right: *they* found me."

"They?"

"My ministry. Then the rest, it . . ." Alton tried readjusting so he could look at her, but it must have taken too much effort, so he flopped over onto his side.

"It got out of hand," Quinn said, understanding, not wanting to hear any more.

"Look, I don't *believe* any of it. You got me. You can leave now. Send the police and an ambulance!"

Quinn's skin was hot and dry from standing so near the fire. But she paused, tried to make her expression look like she was considering his suggestion.

"That's a stupid reason for all these people to have died," she finally said.

He wiggled, started to fight her, and she nicked him on the side of the neck with the machete. Deeper than she'd meant to, more than enough to get her point across.

Then she bent, grabbed Alton by the seat of his pants, ready to hoist him into the clown's mouth.

It almost worked, too, then a shot of pain rolled up from her foot, into her spine and neck, and she dropped him down onto his face.

No. Maybe at the beginning of the day she could have lifted him. But not now.

"Fine, we'll go together," Quinn said. She tossed the machete in ahead of her and pulled her shirt up over her mouth. Then grabbed Alton by his wrists.

She dragged the man into the mouth of the clown, the bottom row of burning teeth scraping his belly as she did.

The interior of the sculpture was roomier than the jail cell had been.

Alton screamed as she swung him into one of the flaming mini-pyres, where the clown's left ear was on the outside.

She watched for a brief moment as Alton's polyester robes began to catch, smoke billowing from under his collar.

This wasn't something she would have done a few weeks ago.

And it troubled her, who she'd become.

But maybe it was the natural evolution. What happened when you kept practicing violence . . . eventually you perfected it.

She'd meant to step out once the man was all the way inside.

She really had.

You can stop and go home.

She really did intend to honor Johnny D's wishes. To try to go back to the real Kettle Springs. Once there she would hug her dad, then face the consequences.

Her eyes stung with smoke. It was like a kiln. She needed to leave.

But then the beam supporting the clown's upper row of teeth cracked, she watched as it broke, and it collapsed and barred her exit.

The clown had swallowed her up.

No, Quinn Maybrook thought, *not here, not now, not like this*. She took up the machete, plastic handle already soft. She punched and slashed against her cage.

No. This wasn't the ending she'd chosen.

She burned with the unfairness of it, kicked so that the wound on her foot cauterized with the heat.

She bashed the handle of the machete against the wood, would have clawed with her fingers if it wouldn't have melted her skin.

From inside looking out, she could see that there was

now a blue sky, the sun fighting through the smoke.

Was the sky outside real or wishful thinking? Was the kiss of the cool air hallucination or the music of crumbling ash? Was she standing in heaven or hell?

There was no answer inside the cage.

So Quinn Maybrook broke free.

TWENTY-NINE

KETTLE SPRINGS, MISSOURI

Glenn Maybrook woke at nine fifteen a.m. from the best sleep he'd had in years.

Nearly twelve hours of uninterrupted unconsciousness.

Had he even stumbled into the bathroom for a pee? If he had, he didn't remember.

It made him feel guilty.

Not the pee thing, but sleeping for so long and so soundly.

Like he'd dropped his guard. Even if he wasn't guarding against anything tangible.

Rubbing the muscles on his neck, kneading sense and function back into his nerves, he looked down at his phone on the nightstand, poked it with one finger to wake, and saw what was there.

A missed call and a voicemail.

A number in Pennsylvania, but none of the Philly area codes he knew.

Maybe he was right to feel guilty.

Maybe he was psychic.

Maybe . . .

Maybe it was spam. He shouldn't beat himself—

In the quiet of the room, he could hear the click and gulp of his swallow as he pressed to start the message.

There were three or four seconds of white noise before Quinn's voice began:

"Hey, Dad. I don't call enough. I know. And when I do, I don't answer your questions, I'm sorry. And I'm calling now, and . . . I'm still not going to tell you where I am and where I'm going, just in case. But I . . ."

She lowered her voice.

"I just want you to know that it's almost over. And that when it is, I plan on coming home. I don't know what I'm walking into, but I met a friend and he . . . He's really great. He convinced me to try to make it out. To try and come back to you. So I'm saying it now, to make it true: I'm going to come back."

The handset must have been pulled away from Quinn's mouth, because Glenn lost a few words, heard the sound of a passing car.

"—that I love you. And I'm going to try and survive this."

It sounded like she was crying. Glenn certainly was.

"I love you."

They both said it, and the message ended.

EPILOGUE

KETTLE SPRINGS, MISSOURI

"It's the American madness," Rust said.

Which, Rust was a man of few words, but more and more often, he was saying crap like this.

Montana had turned him into a Prairie poet. Which was a thing Cole liked to tease him with but was also true.

Their time in Montana hadn't been without pain and loss, but overall, it had been good for them, made their relationship stronger.

But now the ranch was closed for some renovation work. Cole waited.

Was a definition of "the American madness" forthcoming? Was Rust going to say anything else profound?

Rust looked meaningfully toward the edge of town.

Guess not.

"Yeah. Uhhh . . . care to elaborate?" Cole asked.

"I think it started way before your dad," Rust said, looking not at Cole but down the street. "Way before Frendo the Clown. I bet they all caught it on the *Mayflower* and it's just been . . . crazy ever since. It's been there festering and changing and infecting new generations."

Cole put his hand on Rust's back. "Sure. I get it. And I love you. Just please try not to say any of that shit around the movie people."

There had been movies made about what had happened in Kettle Springs, of course. The *real* Kettle Springs. But they'd been *bad* movies. TV movies and quickie cash-ins. Add to those subpar movies countless documentaries and enough true crime podcast hours logged that you'd never be able to listen to them all in one lifetime.

But movies were what Cole cared about. Theatrical movies. Movies were legitimate. And none of the movies had gotten it right. And a big part of that, in his opinion, was because none had been granted approval to shoot here, where it had really happened.

That and none of them had netted Cole a producer credit and an IMDb page.

The time was right for a *real* movie.

And Kettle Springs High School needed new tech and a library refurbishment, so it hadn't been much of a battle to get the town government on board.

"When do they get in?" Rust asked.

They were standing on Main Street, across from the Eureka. There wasn't enough shade over here.

"Soon," Cole said. Too soon. Because they were expecting *another* busload before the first of the preproduction crew arrived to set up offices. "I just hope our Pennsylvania friends are on time."

Rust tapped Cole on the arm, pointed in that sly way he did, the way a hunter tells you to check your six or whatever.

Mayor Maybrook had left the municipal building, was headed toward them. Jerri followed behind, the girl in a navy-blue blazer, notepad out, looking like she was ready to tackle the West Wing next.

It made sense they'd join Cole and Rust.

The four of them were the welcome committee.

It made Cole sad to see Glenn Maybrook. The man wasn't himself these days. He was in mourning, yes, but it was more complicated than that.

It always was, when there was no body recovered.

If good old Glenn continued like this, the town would need a new mayor soon. And Cole would probably have a hand in selecting and campaigning for whoever wanted the job.

Ugh. It never ended.

The bus approaching from the south wasn't a full-size bus, not even a short bus. It was more like a big van.

That pissed Cole off.

He thought he'd paid for a *bus* bus, like one of those nice charter buses with WiFi and TVs in the headrest of the seat in front of you.

But now, if he complained about it, Rust would shake his head, tell him how hard life must be with all these rich-kid problems.

So Cole didn't complain, just smiled and waved as the not-a-bus parked at the curb.

"Don't be sarcastic with them," Rust reminded him. "Little kids don't understand sarcasm."

"Don't start teaching them how to build an IED," Cole said back. "Little kids aren't supposed to play with explosives."

Rust narrowed his eyes and the bus's side door rolled open.

There were six children inside. These weren't all of the ones who'd been pulled out of that compound in Pennsylvania, but they were all the ones that didn't have extended family members to take them in. All the ones that would have gone into the system, if the *real* Kettle Springs hadn't intervened by starting a program.

It'd been the mayor's idea. And Cole's checkbook.

"Welcome to your new home," Cole said, shaking the first little boy's hand. He was tiny, and shaking his hand felt weird. But Cole wasn't tousling anyone's hair.

The children kept stepping down from the not-a-bus.

"Welcome."

"Welcome. We've got Mexican food, do you like Mexican food?"

"Welcome. Yes. Yup, it's me. I don't know what your parents told you about me, but please don't shoot."

Rust jammed a finger in Cole's side.

Right, no sarcasm.

"Welcome. Love your dress."

Then the last of them stepped out of the van. The oldest.

"You must be Tabitha, we talked on the phone," Cole said. "Welcome. We'd show you around, but we have a meeting at noon. There's a crew coming to town to film a movie, isn't that cool?"

The girl in the knee-high skirt hid her smile behind her hands, like an old-timey blush. Then she said: "I've never even *seen* a movie before, but that does sound exciting."

ACKNOWLEDGMENTS

A few months ago, I was standing in Kettle Springs, watching the Founder's Day parade roll by.

And then someone spoke into a walkie-talkie, and all the trucks and floats—including a giant Frendo the Clown hitched to a trailer—came to a stop, dropped into reverse, and reset to their starting positions at the end of the block. Then the marching band began to play and they did the whole parade again.

After that I was sitting on bleachers, cheering for Arthur Hill as he delivered a rousing speech.

Then we had to do another take where the crowd of extras mimed cheering—harder to do than it sounds—so they could roll sound on the lead actors.

No, this wasn't something I dreamed. But it sure was a surreal day.

Not to mention that this Kettle Springs, Missouri, was in Manitoba, Canada. But the Kettle Springs from Eli Craig's film adaptation of *Clown in a Cornfield* still felt like Kettle Springs, as I was standing there. So spoiler alert for *The Church of Frendo*, if you're the kind of person who flips to the acknowledgments before reading the book . . . but:

There isn't a whole lot of Kettle Springs in this sequel you just read, is there? Not even ten pages of it take place in Missouri. Not a lot of Rust and Cole, either. And zero cornfields. But I hope that, like that not–Kettle Springs in Canada still felt like Kettle Springs to me, that this Clown in a Cornfield book with no cornfields, far from the series' typical setting, still felt like a Clown in a Cornfield book.

It's probably my favorite of the three, possibly because I got to spend so much of the time going on a road trip adventure with Quinn. A trip across America where both of us had to say goodbye.

But just because Quinn's journey is at an end, doesn't mean I'm going to stop writing about Kettle Springs. Or, I don't want to, so please keep hyping up the books, reviewing them online (Amazon and Goodreads reviews are such a help), telling your friends and librarians about them, etc.

Eternal gratitude to David Linker at HarperCollins and Pete Harris at Temple Hill, who both sometimes raise their eyebrows when I say something like "I know a Juggalo love interest sounds crazy, but it'll work!" They have enhanced these books with their insights and wisdom at countless junctures.

Also at Temple Hill, big thanks to John Fischer, Alli Dyer, Marty Bowen, and Wyck Godfrey. Also to Eli Craig, for being so gracious while I was on set, and to screenwriter Carter Blanchard, who was able to have his own adventure in Kettle Springs.

Thanks to Alec Shane and the rest of the folks at Writers House.

Jessica Berg, Jenna Stempel-Lobell, and every editor, designer, publicist, marketing manager, and salesperson at HarperCollins who helps with these books: thank you.

I think this is my favorite book in the series (so far)—that's my opinion—but it's pretty much an objective fact that Matt Ryan Tobin has outdone himself with this cover art. I mean, we have to keep going to Part 4 to see what he'll illustrate next, right?

Additional professional thanks to Adam Goldworm at Aperture Entertainment.

Personal life thanks to . . . everyone in my personal life who can read this (and the one who's not old enough to, yet).

And, as always, final and most sincere thanks to you: the

reader. Books can be released, books can be promoted, I can talk myself hoarse making TikToks, but they never really come to life until they are read, enjoyed, and discussed.

Thanks for all you've done for me. . . .

With love and appreciation,

Adam